CHAPTER 1

CHAPTER 1:
"ENTER THE MAELSTROM."

SCRIPT BY RILEY DASHIELL BIEHL
ART BY KOI CARREON

COLORS BY BORG SINABAN
LETTERING BY TAYLOR ESPOSITO
SCRIPT EDITING BY BRITTANY MATTER
COVER BY KOI CARREON

BRYAN SEATON: PUBLISHER / CEO
SHAWN GABBORIN: EDITOR IN CHIEF
JASON MARTIN: PUBLISHER-DANGER ZONE
NICOLE D'ANDRIA: MARKETING DIRECTOR/EDITOR
DANIELLE DAVISON: EXECUTIVE ADMINISTRATOR
CHAD CICCONI: CHIEF PORTAL INSPECTOR
SHAWN PRYOR: PRESIDENT OF CREATOR RELATIONS

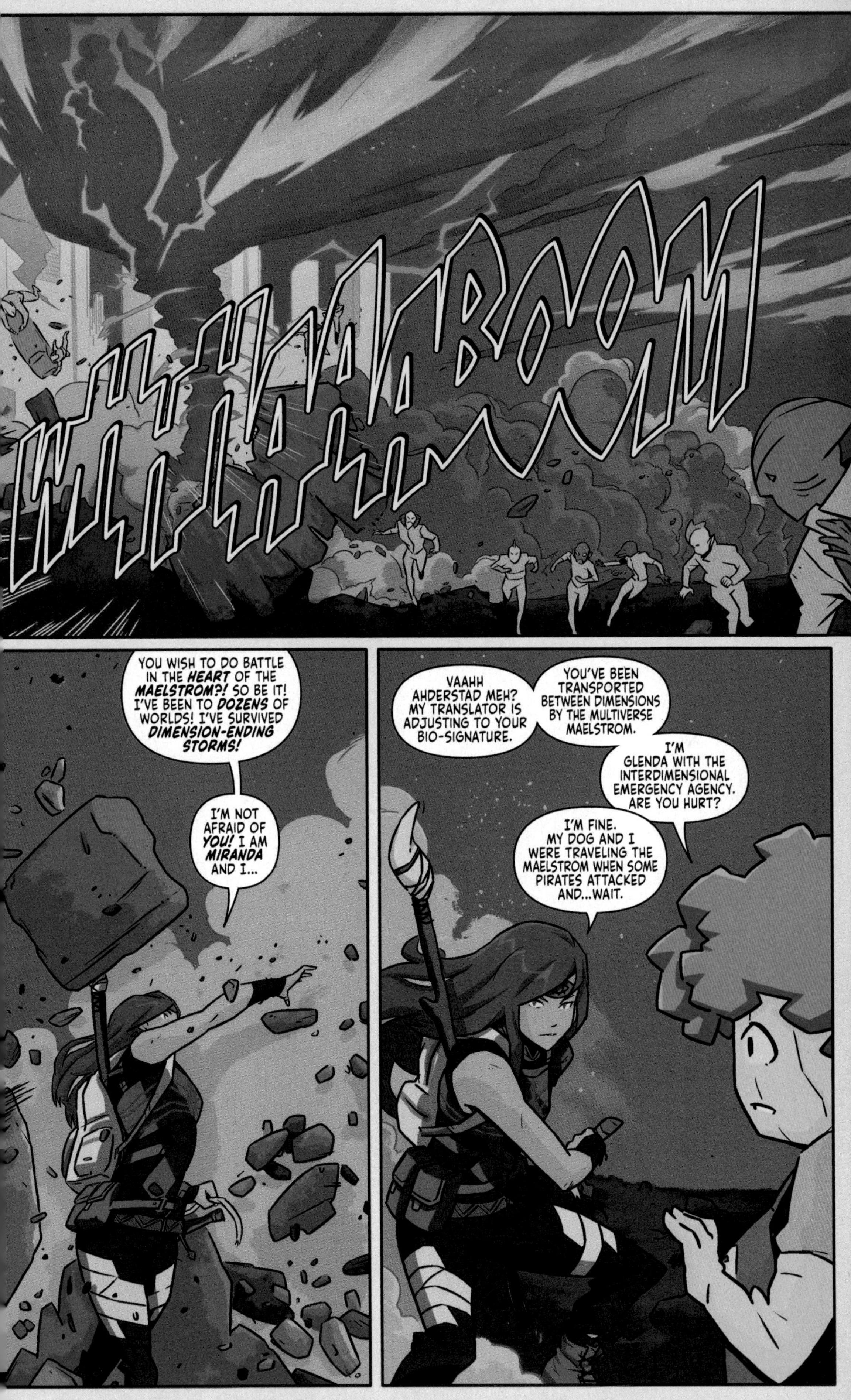
WHHHAAABOOOM
YOU WISH TO DO BATTLE IN THE HEART OF THE MAELSTROM?! SO BE IT! I'VE BEEN TO DOZENS OF WORLDS! I'VE SURVIVED DIMENSION-ENDING STORMS!
I'M NOT AFRAID OF YOU! I AM MIRANDA AND I...
VAAHH AHDERSTAD MEH? MY TRANSLATOR IS ADJUSTING TO YOUR BIO-SIGNATURE.
YOU'VE BEEN TRANSPORTED BETWEEN DIMENSIONS BY THE MULTIVERSE MAELSTROM.
I'M GLENDA WITH THE INTERDIMENSIONAL EMERGENCY AGENCY. ARE YOU HURT?
I'M FINE. MY DOG AND I WERE TRAVELING THE MAELSTROM WHEN SOME PIRATES ATTACKED AND...WAIT.

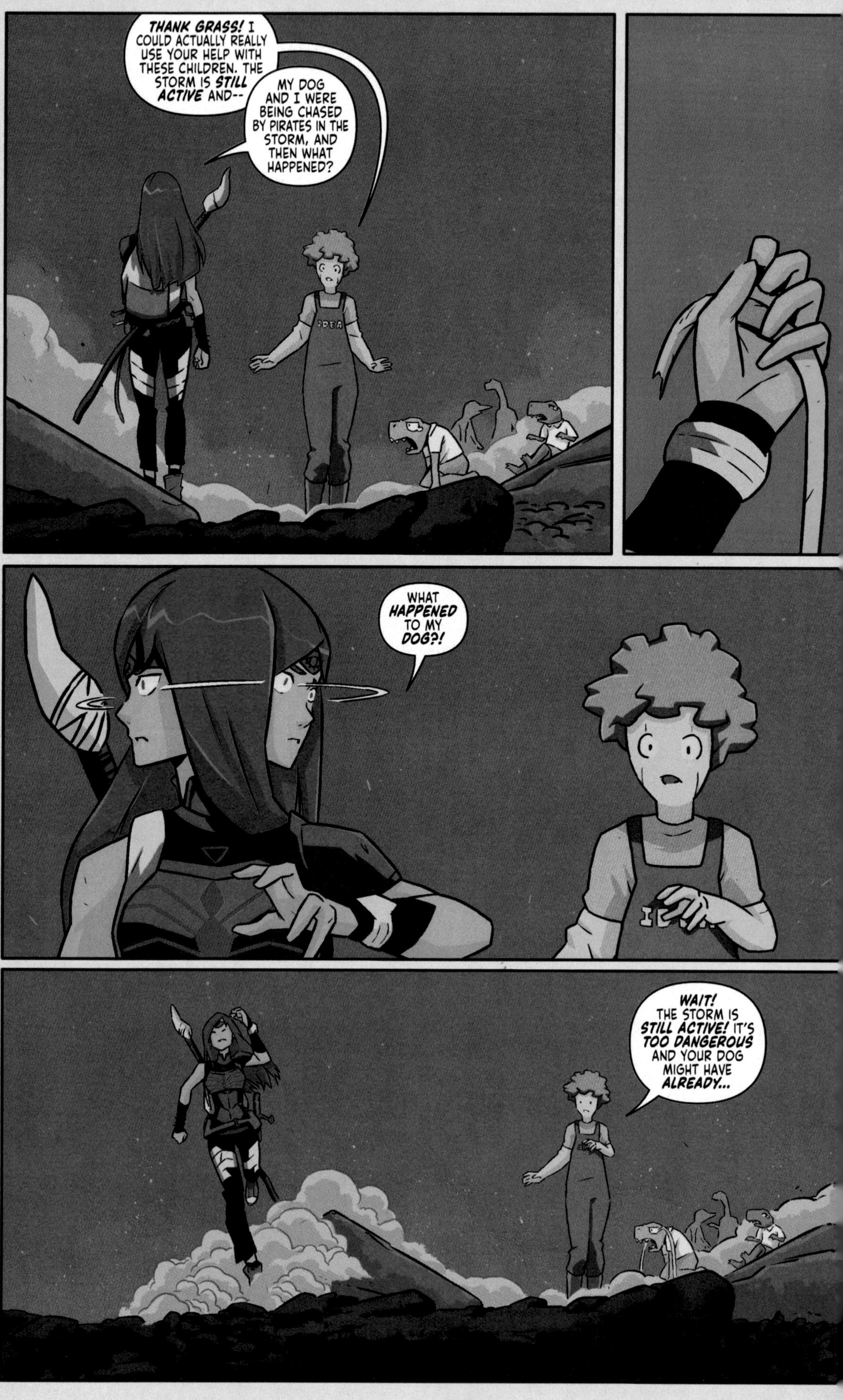
THANK GRASS! I COULD ACTUALLY REALLY USE YOUR HELP WITH THESE CHILDREN. THE STORM IS STILL ACTIVE AND--
MY DOG AND I WERE BEING CHASED BY PIRATES IN THE STORM, AND THEN WHAT HAPPENED?
IDEA
WHAT HAPPENED TO MY DOG?!
WAIT! THE STORM IS STILL ACTIVE! IT'S TOO DANGEROUS AND YOUR DOG MIGHT HAVE ALREADY...

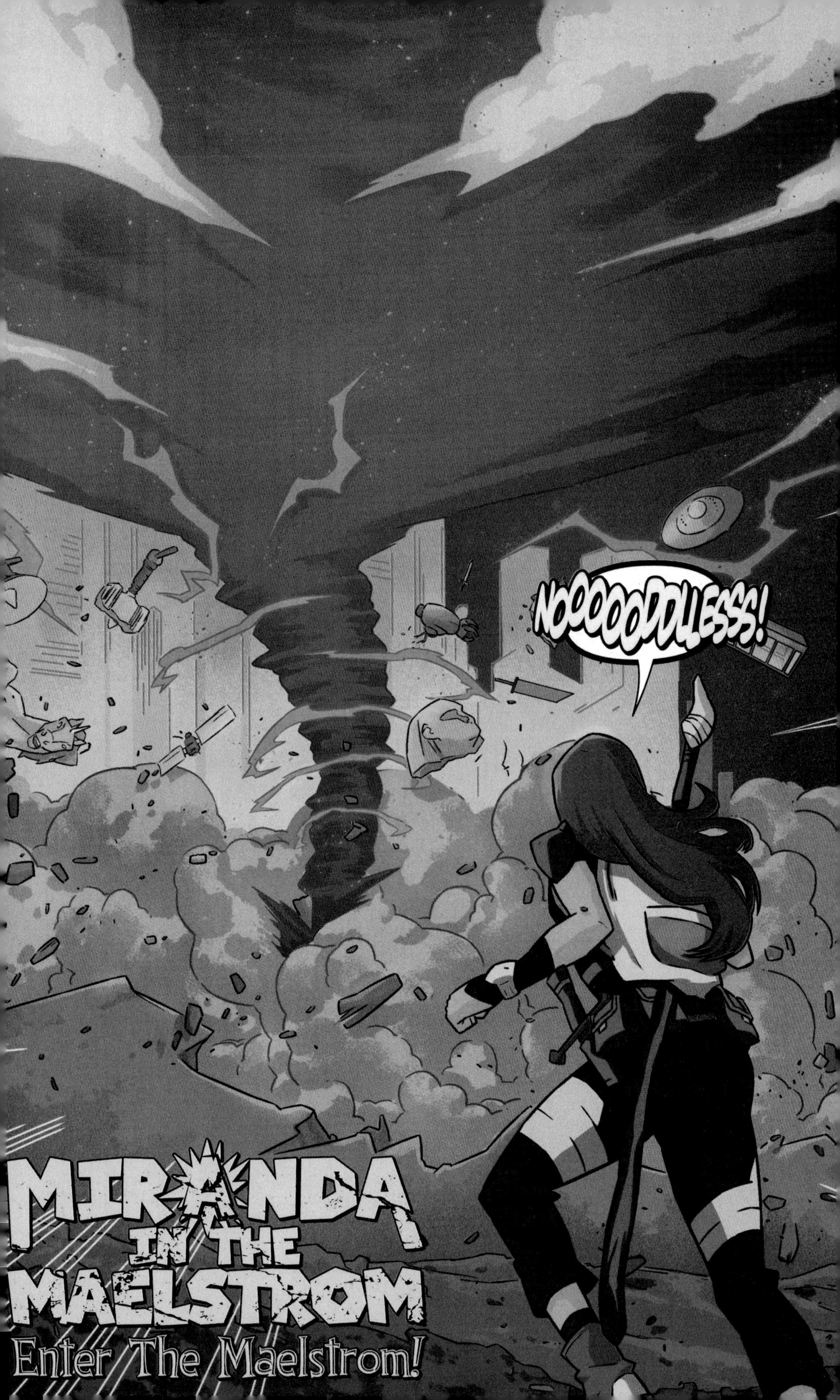
NOOOOOODDLESSS!
MIRANDA IN THE MAELSTROM
Enter The Maelstrom!

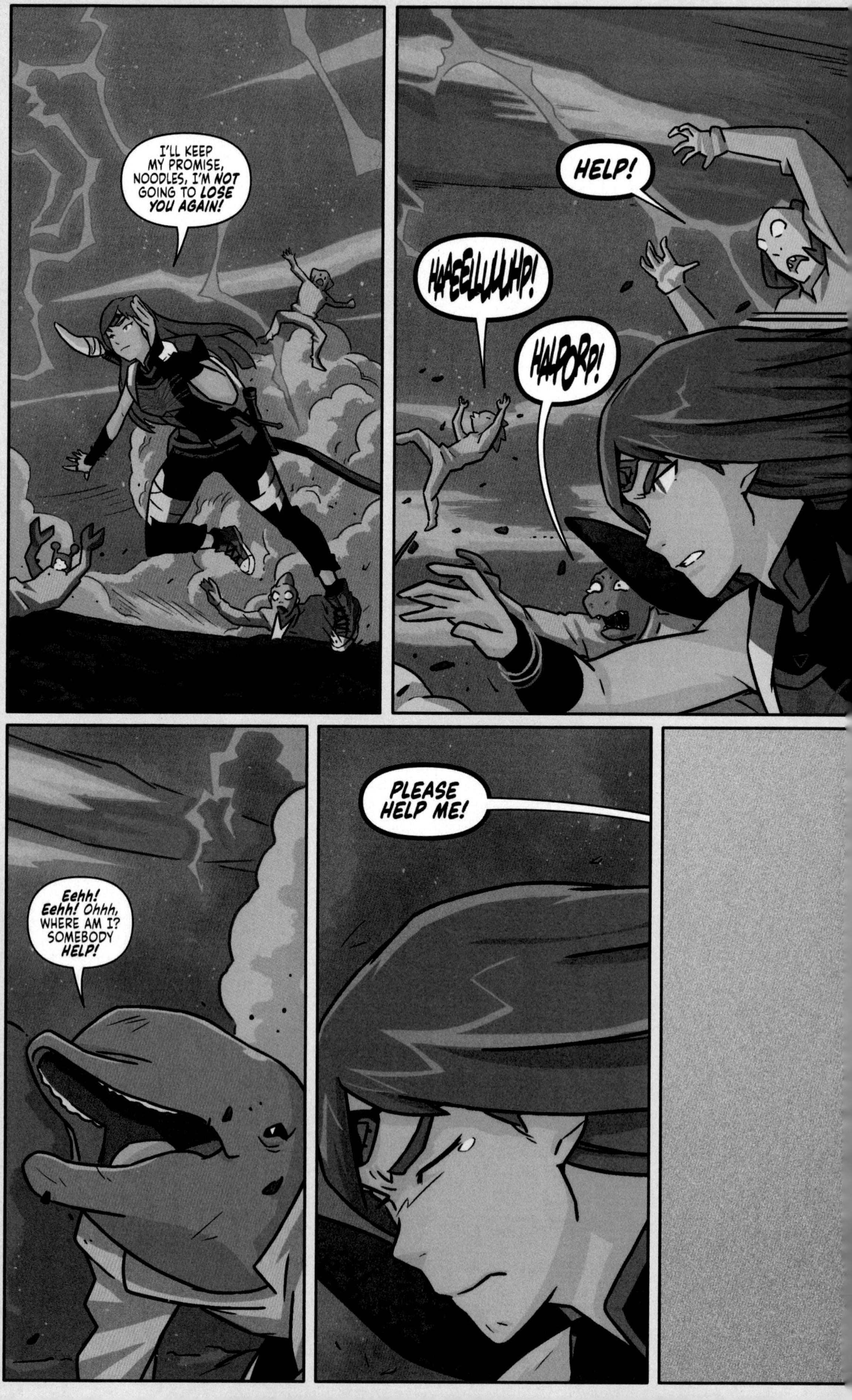
I'LL KEEP MY PROMISE, NOODLES, I'M NOT GOING TO LOSE YOU AGAIN!
HELP!
HAAEELLLUUHP!
HALPORP!
Eehh! Eehh! Ohhh, WHERE AM I? SOMEBODY HELP!
PLEASE HELP ME!

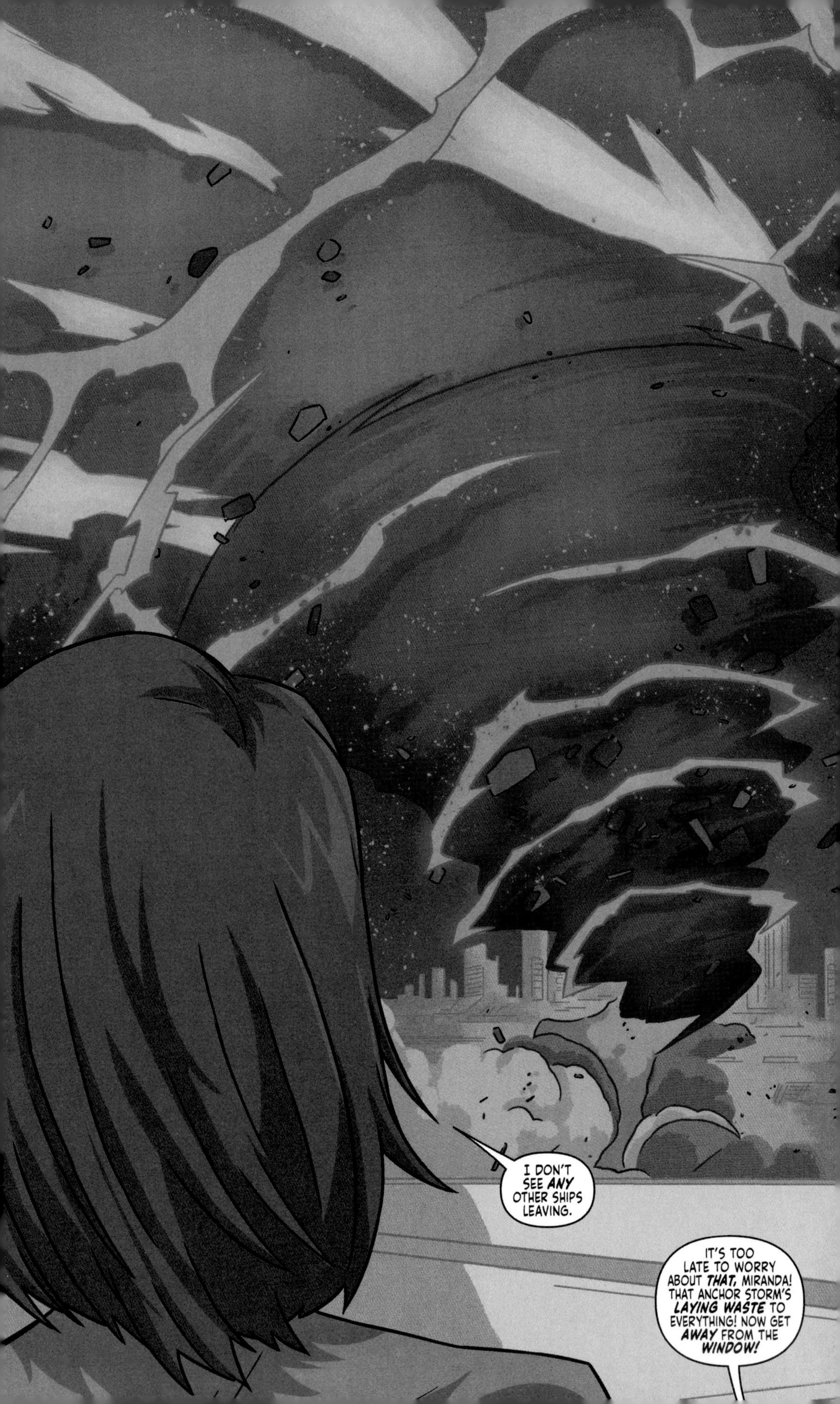
I DON'T SEE *ANY* OTHER SHIPS LEAVING.
IT'S TOO LATE TO WORRY ABOUT *THAT,* MIRANDA! THAT ANCHOR STORM'S *LAYING WASTE* TO EVERYTHING! NOW GET *AWAY* FROM THE *WINDOW!*

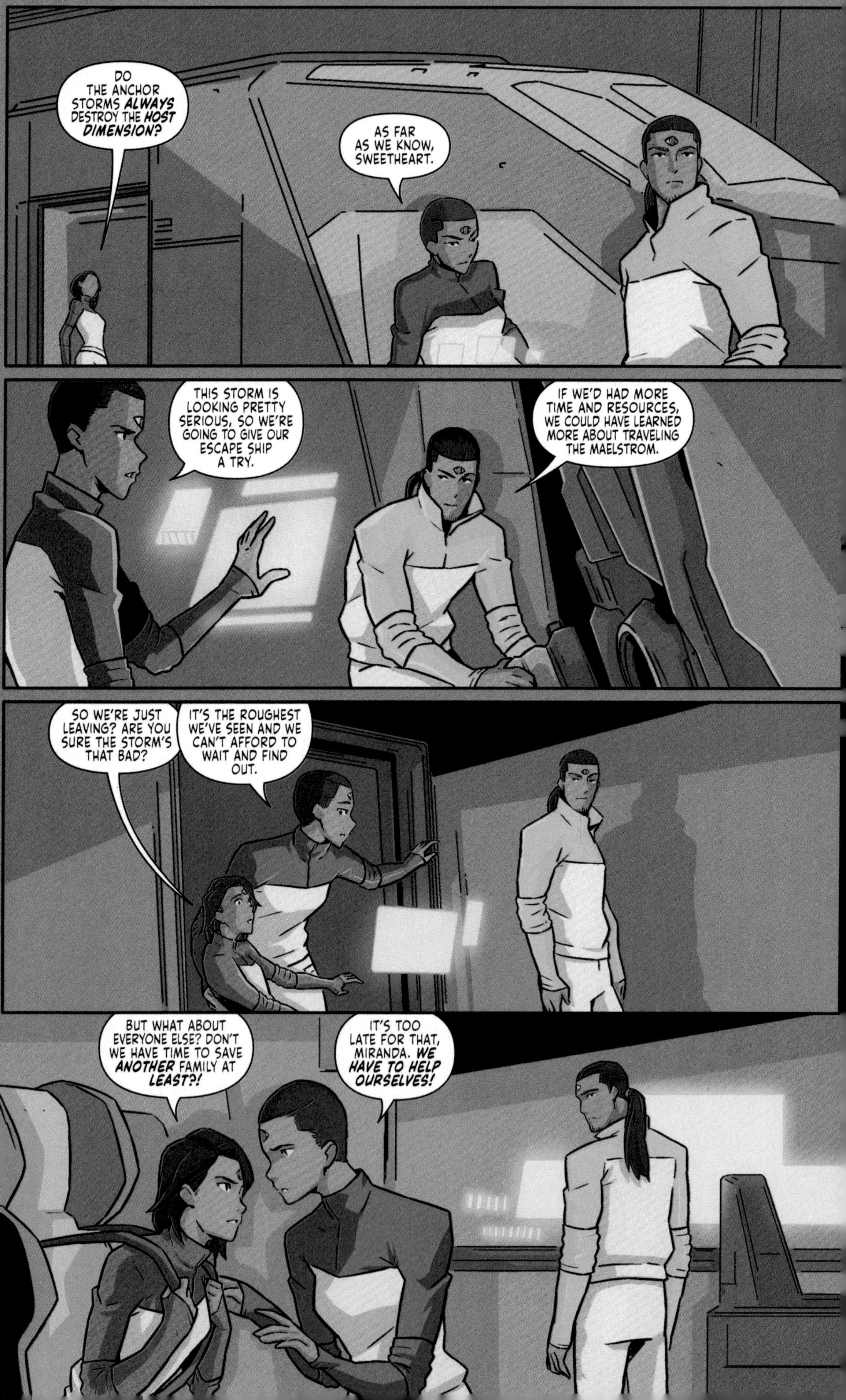
DO THE ANCHOR STORMS *ALWAYS* DESTROY THE *HOST DIMENSION?*
AS FAR AS WE KNOW, SWEETHEART.
THIS STORM IS LOOKING PRETTY SERIOUS, SO WE'RE GOING TO GIVE OUR ESCAPE SHIP A TRY.
IF WE'D HAD MORE TIME AND RESOURCES, WE COULD HAVE LEARNED MORE ABOUT TRAVELING THE MAELSTROM.
SO WE'RE JUST LEAVING? ARE YOU SURE THE STORM'S THAT BAD?
IT'S THE ROUGHEST WE'VE SEEN AND WE CAN'T AFFORD TO WAIT AND FIND OUT.
BUT WHAT ABOUT EVERYONE ELSE? DON'T WE HAVE TIME TO SAVE *ANOTHER* FAMILY AT *LEAST?!*
IT'S TOO LATE FOR THAT, MIRANDA. *WE HAVE TO HELP OURSELVES!*

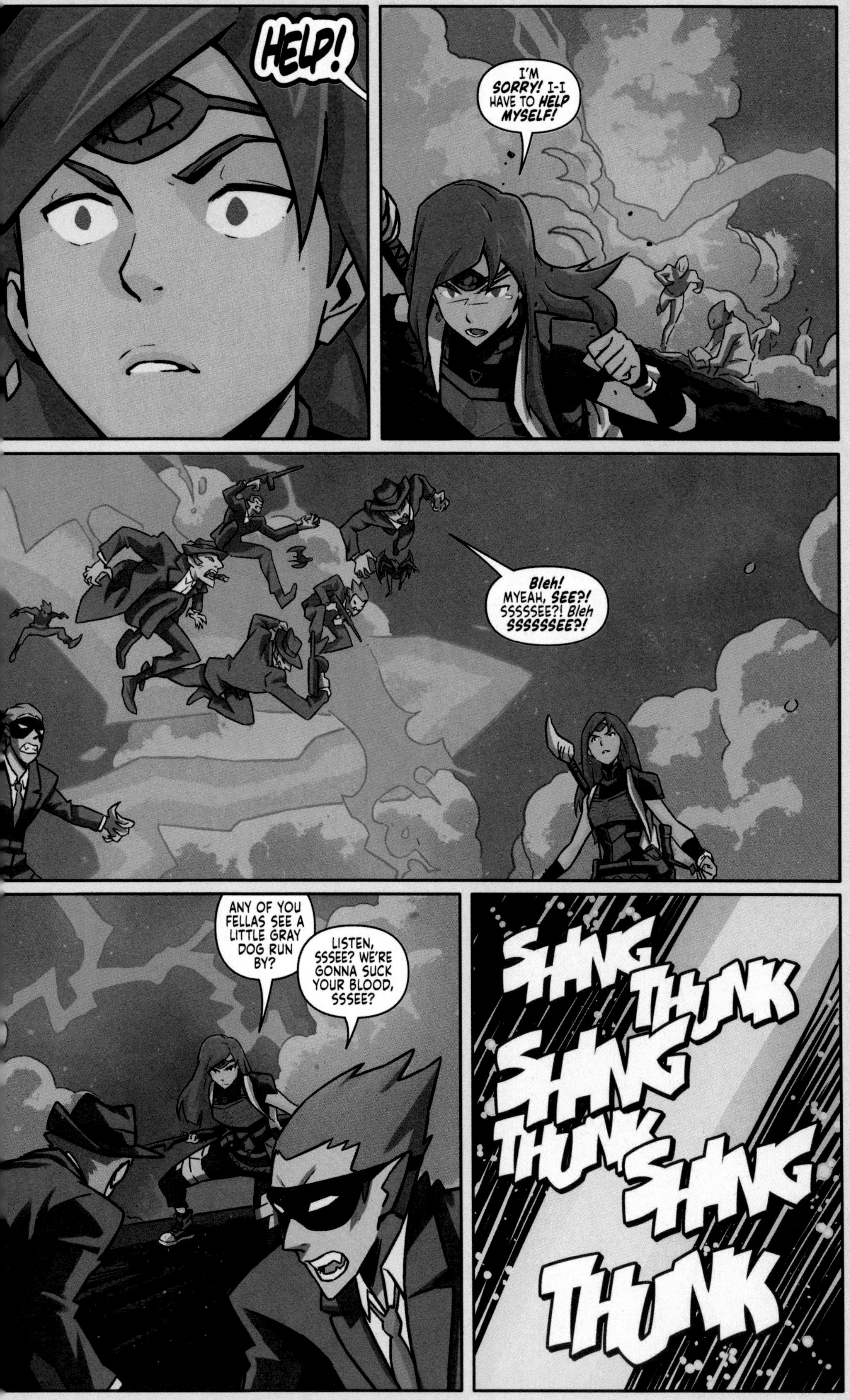
HELP!
I'M SORRY! I-I HAVE TO HELP MYSELF!
Bleh! MYEAH, SEE?! SSSSSEE?! Bleh SSSSSSEE?!
ANY OF YOU FELLAS SEE A LITTLE GRAY DOG RUN BY?
LISTEN, SSSEE? WE'RE GONNA SUCK YOUR BLOOD, SSSEE?
SHANG THUNK SHANG THUNK SHANG THUNK

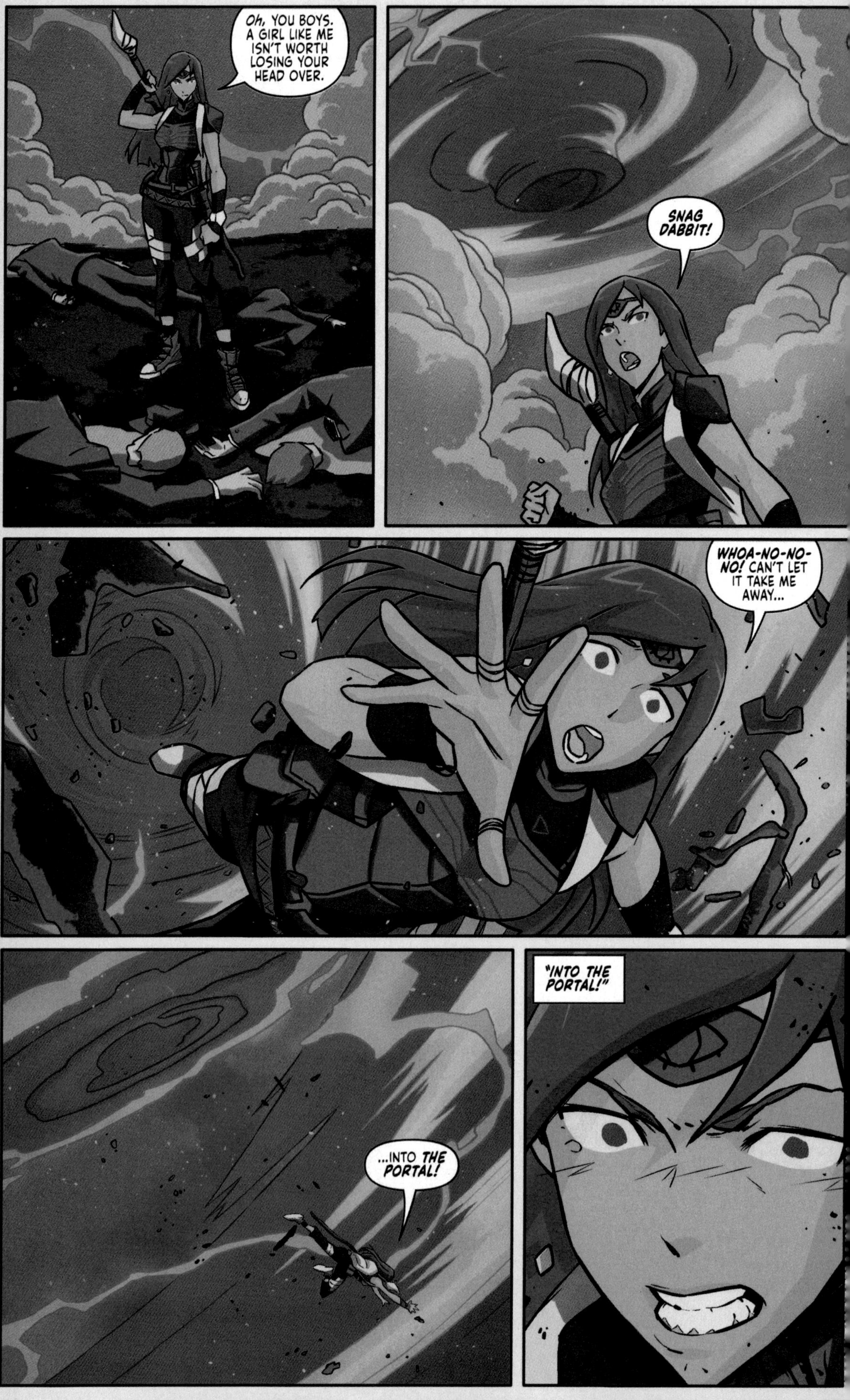
Oh, YOU BOYS. A GIRL LIKE ME ISN'T WORTH LOSING YOUR HEAD OVER.
SNAG DABBIT!
WHOA-NO-NO-NO! CAN'T LET IT TAKE ME AWAY...
...INTO THE PORTAL!
"INTO THE PORTAL!"

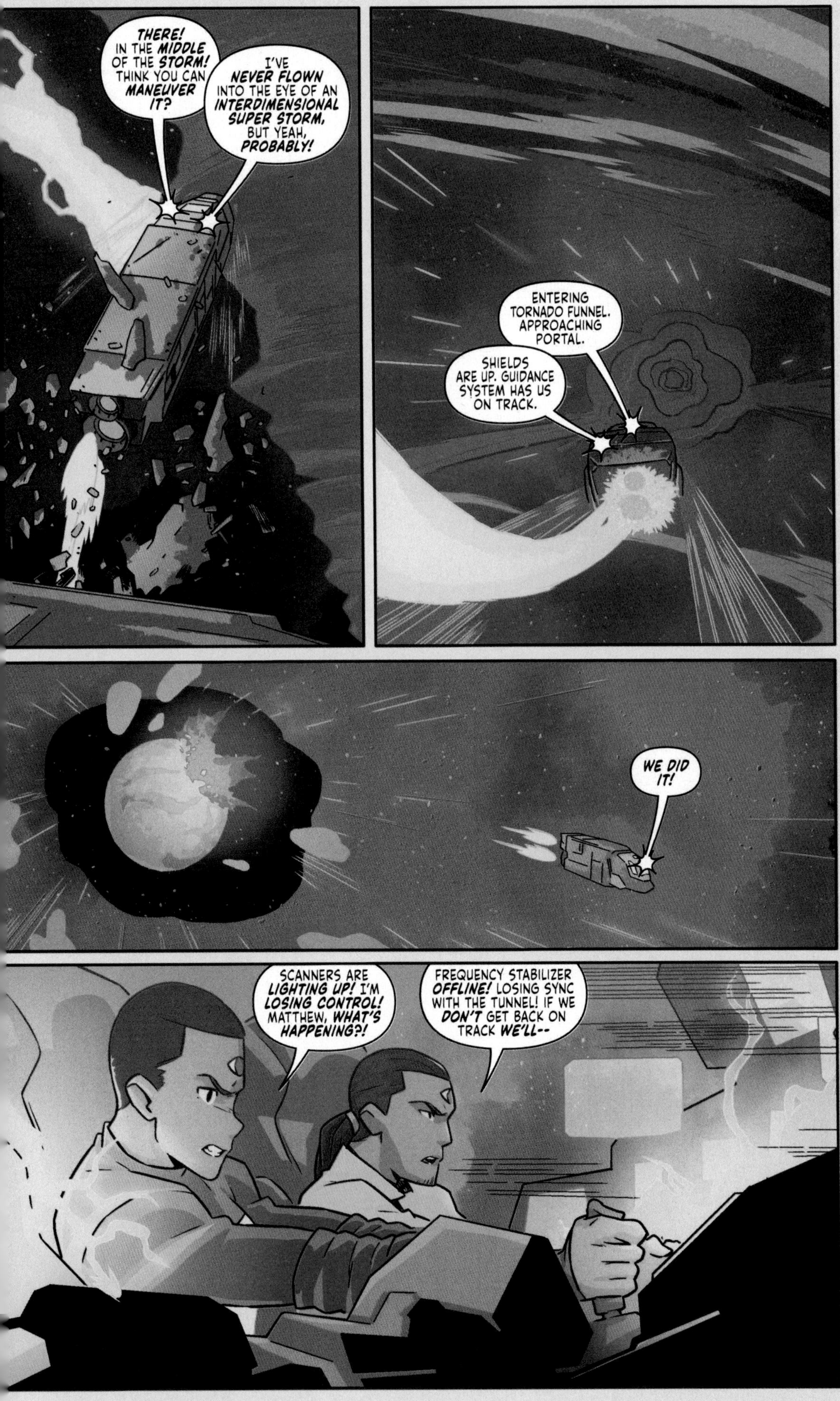

THERE! IN THE MIDDLE OF THE STORM! THINK YOU CAN MANEUVER IT?
I'VE NEVER FLOWN INTO THE EYE OF AN INTERDIMENSIONAL SUPER STORM, BUT YEAH, PROBABLY!
ENTERING TORNADO FUNNEL. APPROACHING PORTAL.
SHIELDS ARE UP. GUIDANCE SYSTEM HAS US ON TRACK.
WE DID IT!
SCANNERS ARE LIGHTING UP! I'M LOSING CONTROL! MATTHEW, WHAT'S HAPPENING?!
FREQUENCY STABILIZER OFFLINE! LOSING SYNC WITH THE TUNNEL! IF WE DON'T GET BACK ON TRACK WE'LL--

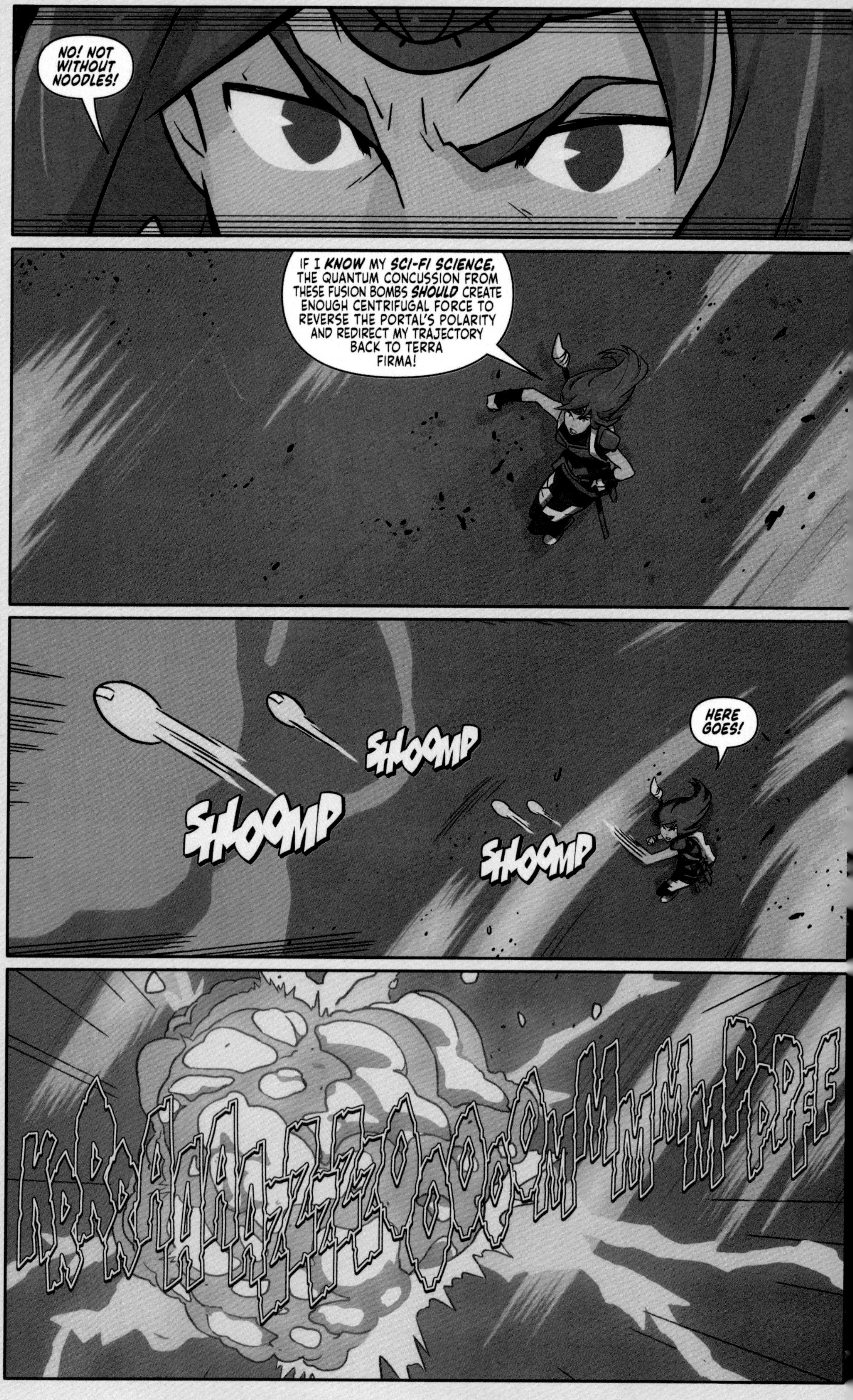
NO! NOT WITHOUT NOODLES!
IF I KNOW MY SCI-FI SCIENCE, THE QUANTUM CONCUSSION FROM THESE FUSION BOMBS SHOULD CREATE ENOUGH CENTRIFUGAL FORCE TO REVERSE THE PORTAL'S POLARITY AND REDIRECT MY TRAJECTORY BACK TO TERRA FIRMA!
SHOOMP
SHOOMP
SHOOMP
HERE GOES!

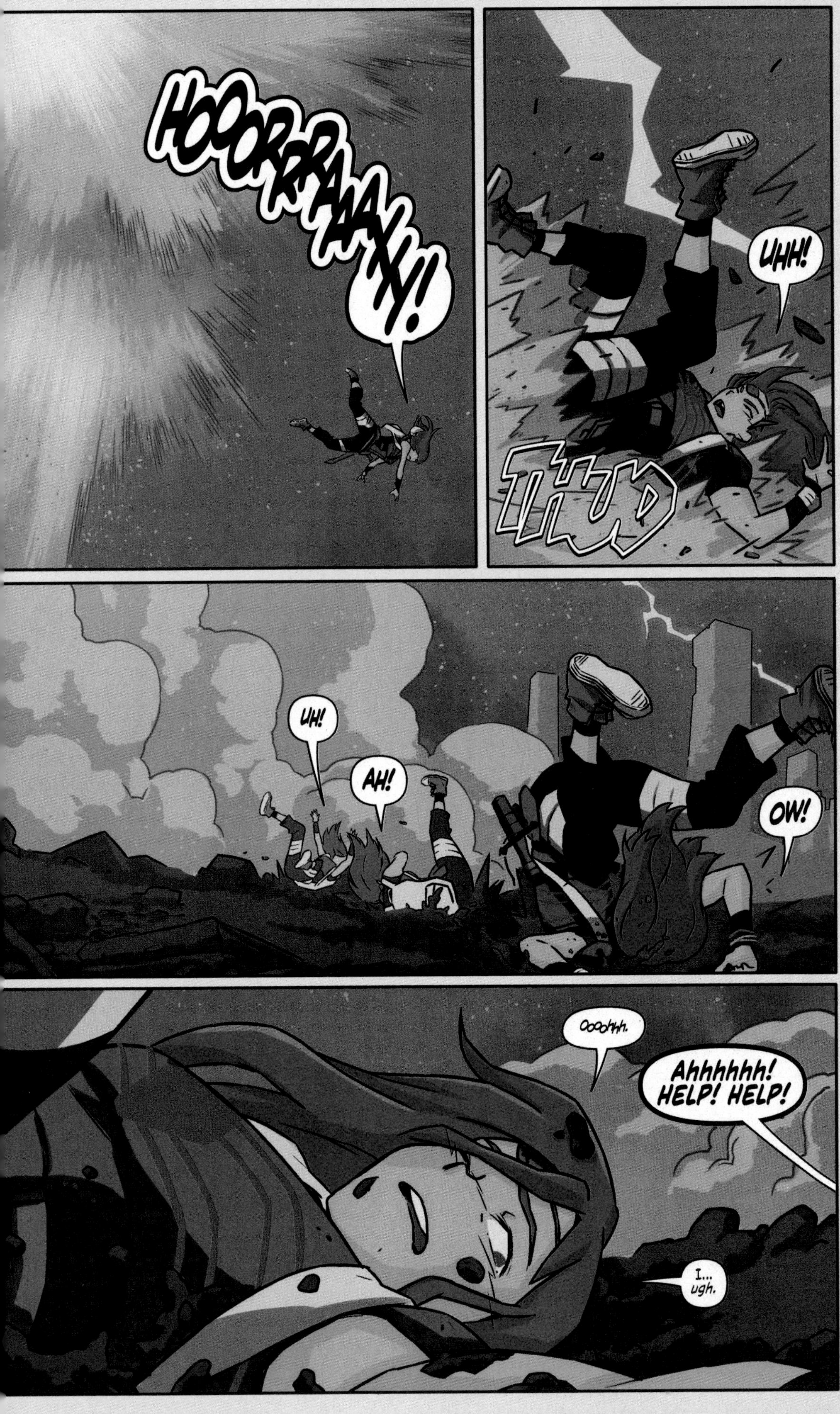
HOOORRRAAAXXHH!
UHH!
THUD
UH!
AH!
OW!
Oooohhh.
Ahhhhhh! HELP! HELP!
I... ugh.

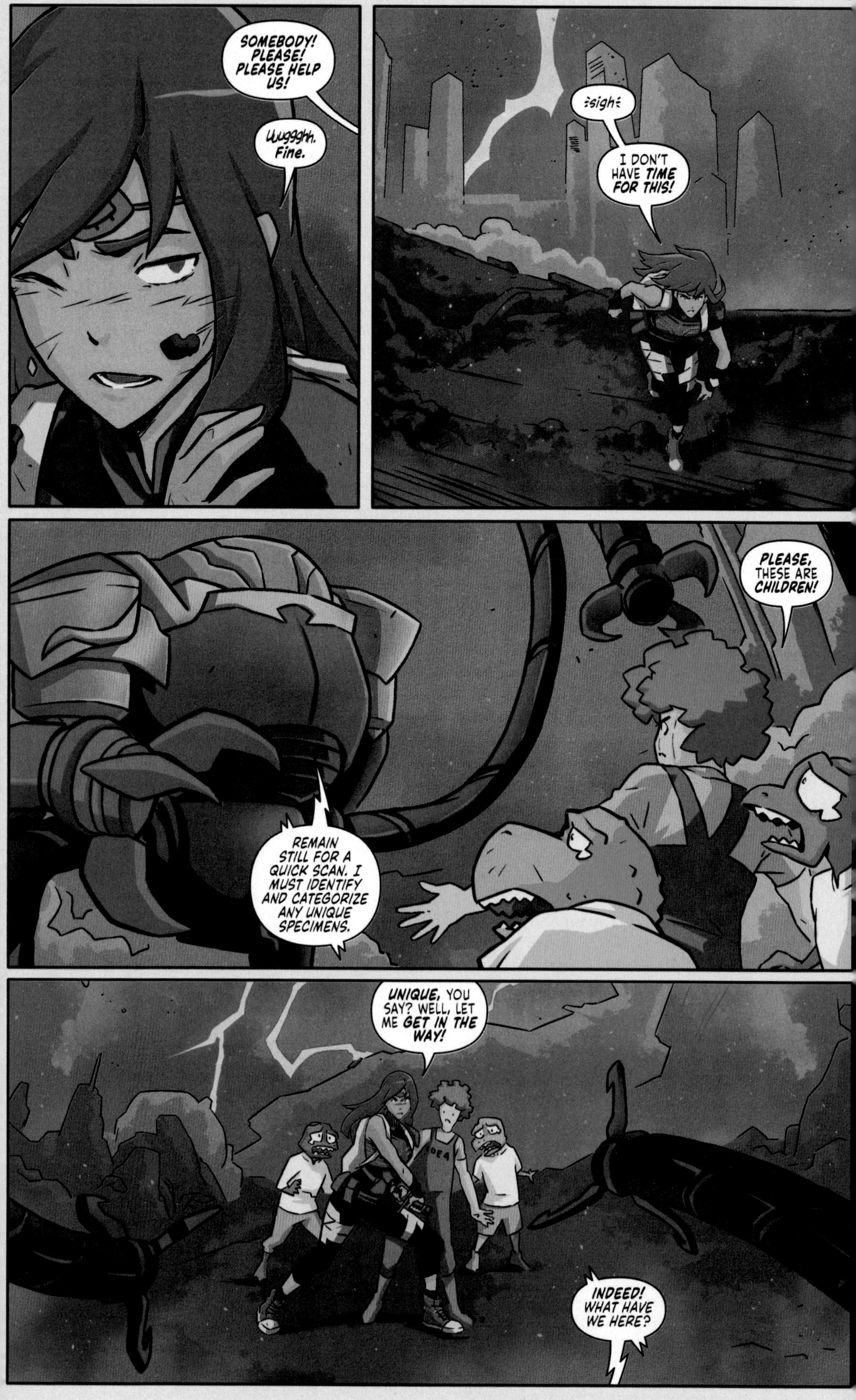

SOMEBODY! PLEASE! PLEASE HELP US!
Uuuggghh. Fine.
-sigh-
I DON'T HAVE TIME FOR THIS!
PLEASE, THESE ARE CHILDREN!
REMAIN STILL FOR A QUICK SCAN. I MUST IDENTIFY AND CATEGORIZE ANY UNIQUE SPECIMENS.
UNIQUE, YOU SAY? WELL, LET ME GET IN THE WAY!
INDEED! WHAT HAVE WE HERE?

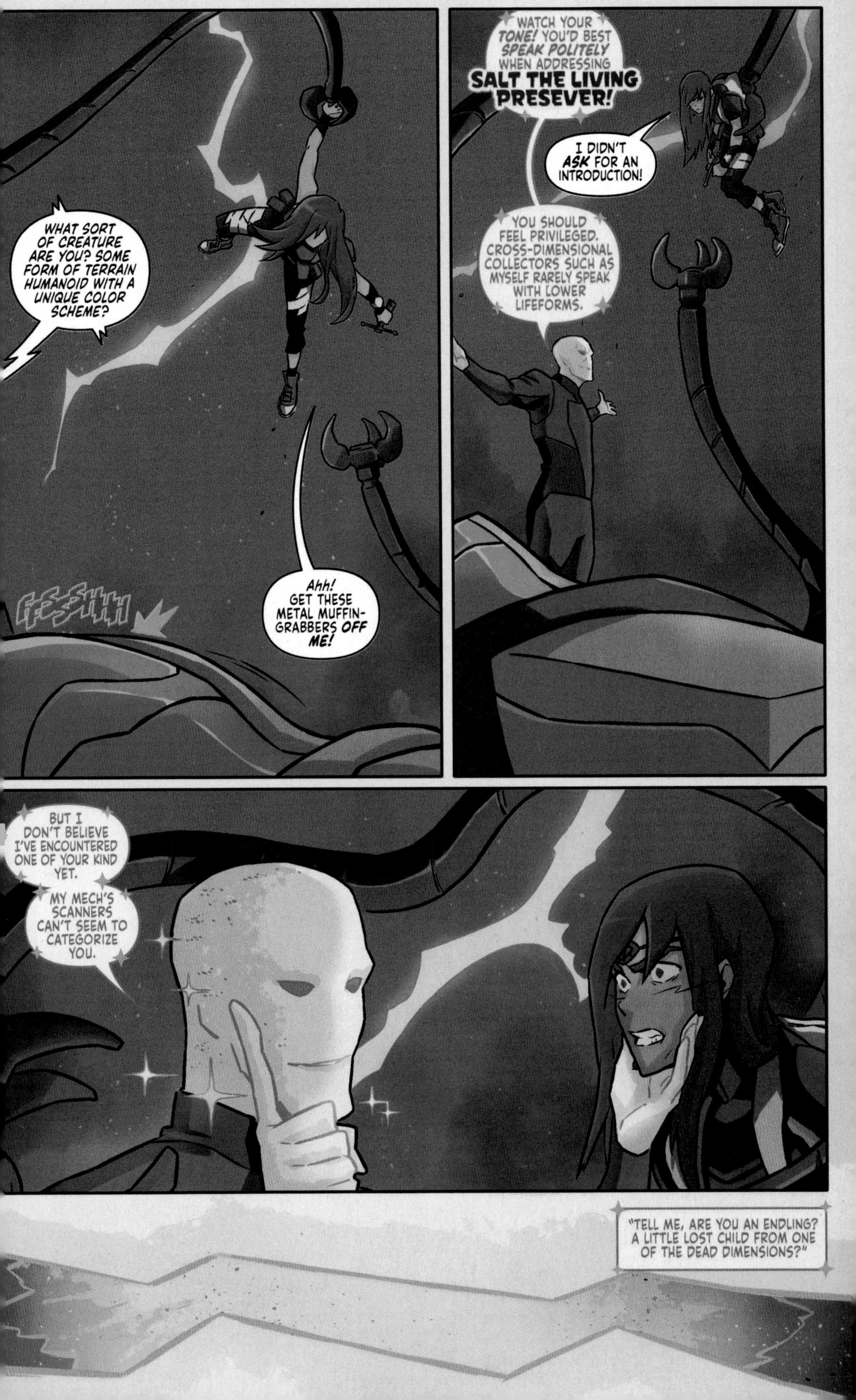

WHAT SORT OF CREATURE ARE YOU? SOME FORM OF TERRAIN HUMANOID WITH A UNIQUE COLOR SCHEME?
Ahh! GET THESE METAL MUFFIN-GRABBERS OFF ME!
FSSHHH
WATCH YOUR TONE! YOU'D BEST SPEAK POLITELY WHEN ADDRESSING SALT THE LIVING PRESEVER!
I DIDN'T ASK FOR AN INTRODUCTION!
YOU SHOULD FEEL PRIVILEGED. CROSS-DIMENSIONAL COLLECTORS SUCH AS MYSELF RARELY SPEAK WITH LOWER LIFEFORMS.
BUT I DON'T BELIEVE I'VE ENCOUNTERED ONE OF YOUR KIND YET.
MY MECH'S SCANNERS CAN'T SEEM TO CATEGORIZE YOU.
"TELL ME, ARE YOU AN ENDLING? A LITTLE LOST CHILD FROM ONE OF THE DEAD DIMENSIONS?"

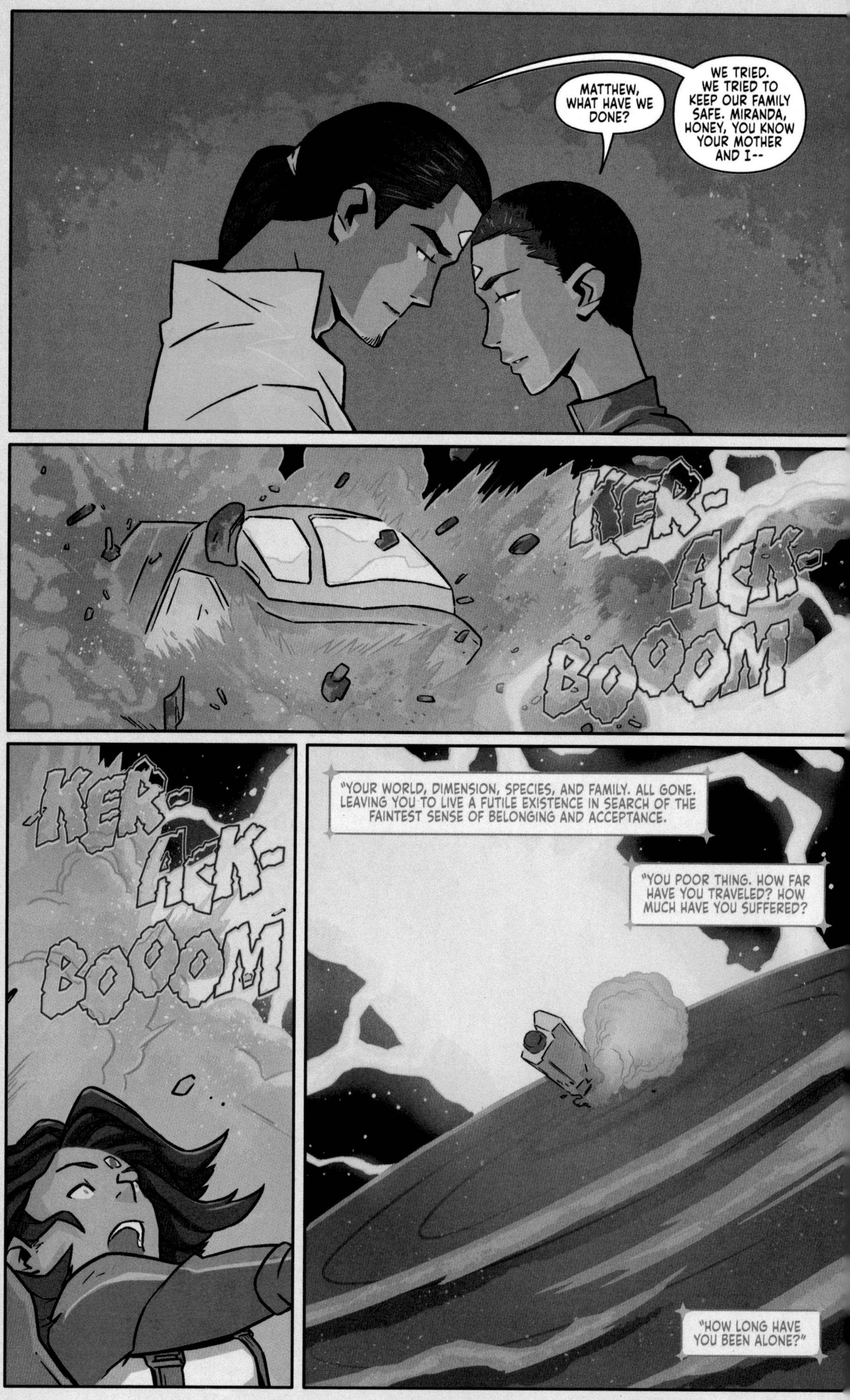

MATTHEW, WHAT HAVE WE DONE?
WE TRIED. WE TRIED TO KEEP OUR FAMILY SAFE. MIRANDA, HONEY, YOU KNOW YOUR MOTHER AND I--
KER-ACK-BOOOM
KER-ACK-BOOOM
"YOUR WORLD, DIMENSION, SPECIES, AND FAMILY. ALL GONE. LEAVING YOU TO LIVE A FUTILE EXISTENCE IN SEARCH OF THE FAINTEST SENSE OF BELONGING AND ACCEPTANCE.
"YOU POOR THING. HOW FAR HAVE YOU TRAVELED? HOW MUCH HAVE YOU SUFFERED?
"HOW LONG HAVE YOU BEEN ALONE?"

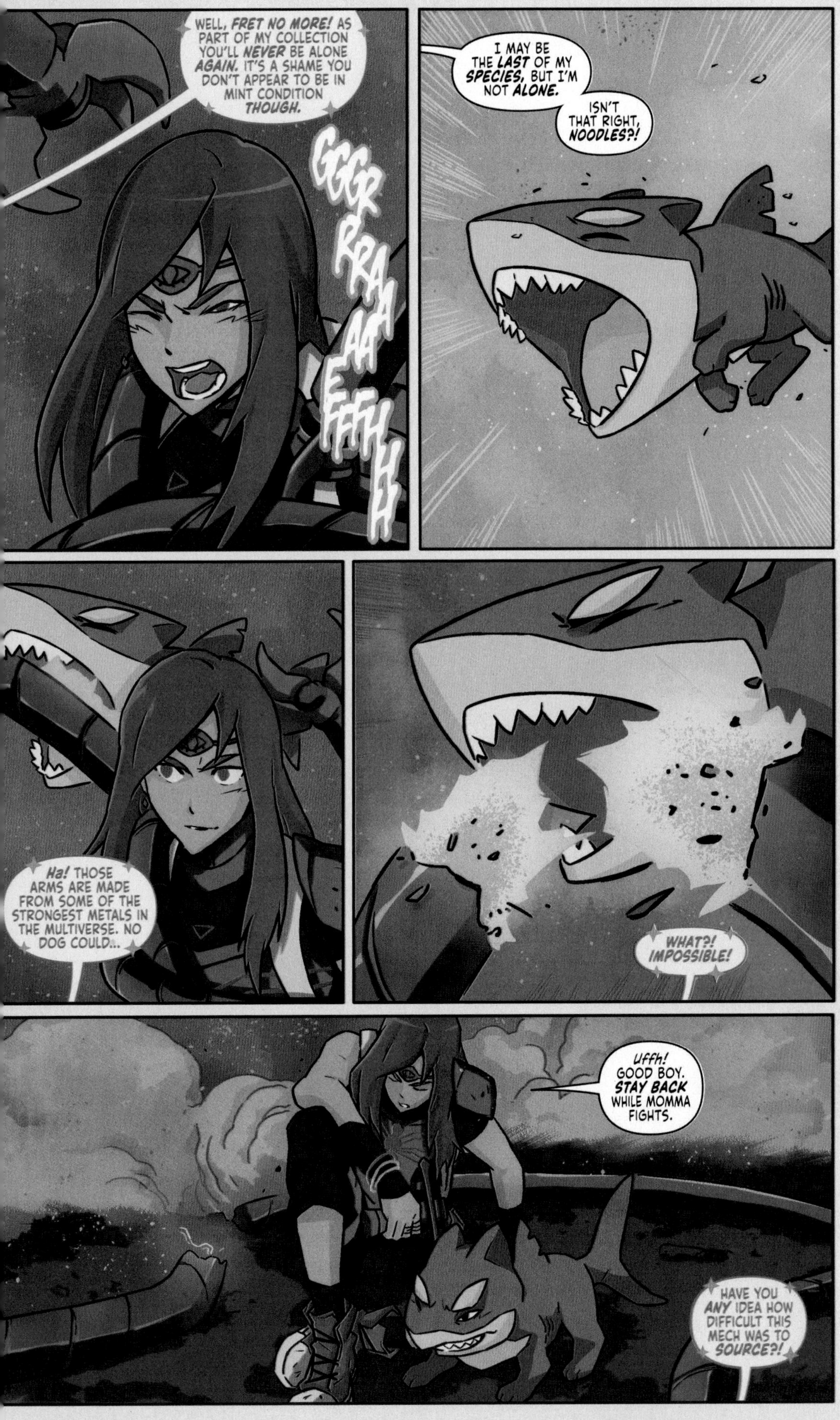
WELL, FRET NO MORE! AS PART OF MY COLLECTION YOU'LL NEVER BE ALONE AGAIN. IT'S A SHAME YOU DON'T APPEAR TO BE IN MINT CONDITION THOUGH.
GGGRRRAAAAEFFHHH
I MAY BE THE LAST OF MY SPECIES, BUT I'M NOT ALONE.
ISN'T THAT RIGHT, NOODLES?!
Ha! THOSE ARMS ARE MADE FROM SOME OF THE STRONGEST METALS IN THE MULTIVERSE. NO DOG COULD...
WHAT?! IMPOSSIBLE!
Uffh! GOOD BOY. STAY BACK WHILE MOMMA FIGHTS.
HAVE YOU ANY IDEA HOW DIFFICULT THIS MECH WAS TO SOURCE?!

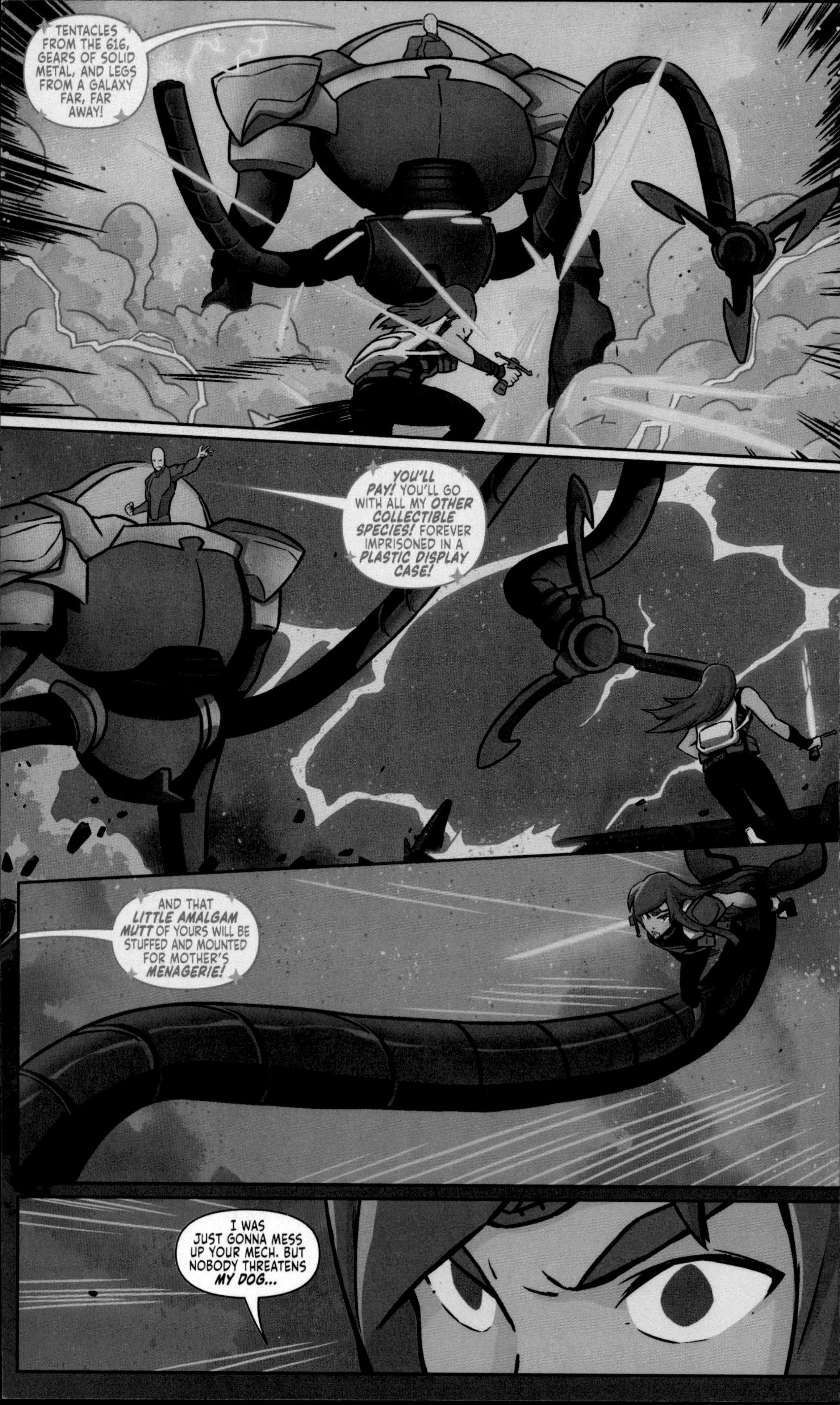

TENTACLES FROM THE 616, GEARS OF SOLID METAL, AND LEGS FROM A GALAXY FAR, FAR AWAY!
YOU'LL PAY! YOU'LL GO WITH ALL MY OTHER COLLECTIBLE SPECIES! FOREVER IMPRISONED IN A PLASTIC DISPLAY CASE!
AND THAT LITTLE AMALGAM MUTT OF YOURS WILL BE STUFFED AND MOUNTED FOR MOTHER'S MENAGERIE!
I WAS JUST GONNA MESS UP YOUR MECH. BUT NOBODY THREATENS MY DOG...

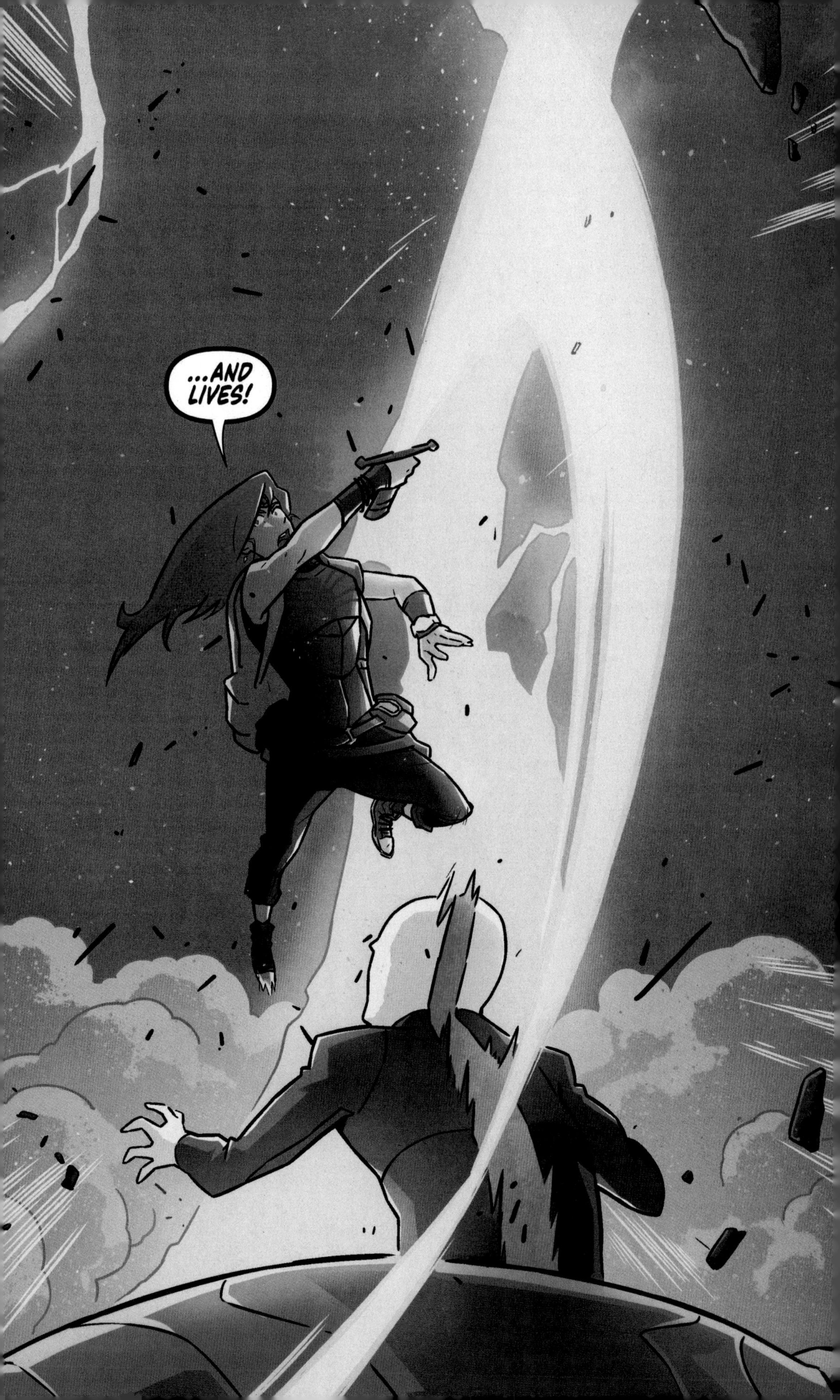
...AND LIVES!

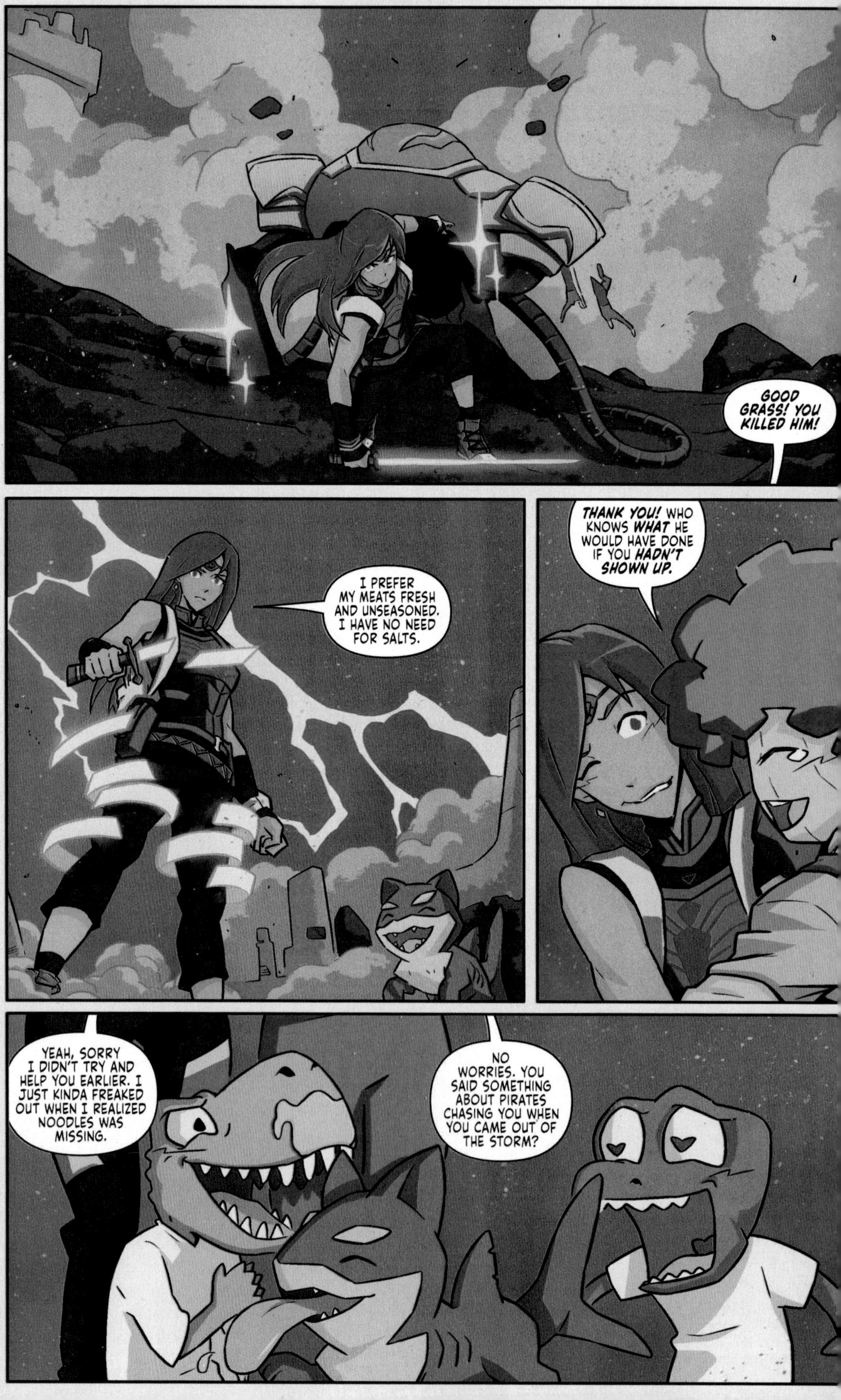
GOOD GRASS! YOU KILLED HIM!
I PREFER MY MEATS FRESH AND UNSEASONED. I HAVE NO NEED FOR SALTS.
THANK YOU! WHO KNOWS WHAT HE WOULD HAVE DONE IF YOU HADN'T SHOWN UP.
YEAH, SORRY I DIDN'T TRY AND HELP YOU EARLIER. I JUST KINDA FREAKED OUT WHEN I REALIZED NOODLES WAS MISSING.
NO WORRIES. YOU SAID SOMETHING ABOUT PIRATES CHASING YOU WHEN YOU CAME OUT OF THE STORM?

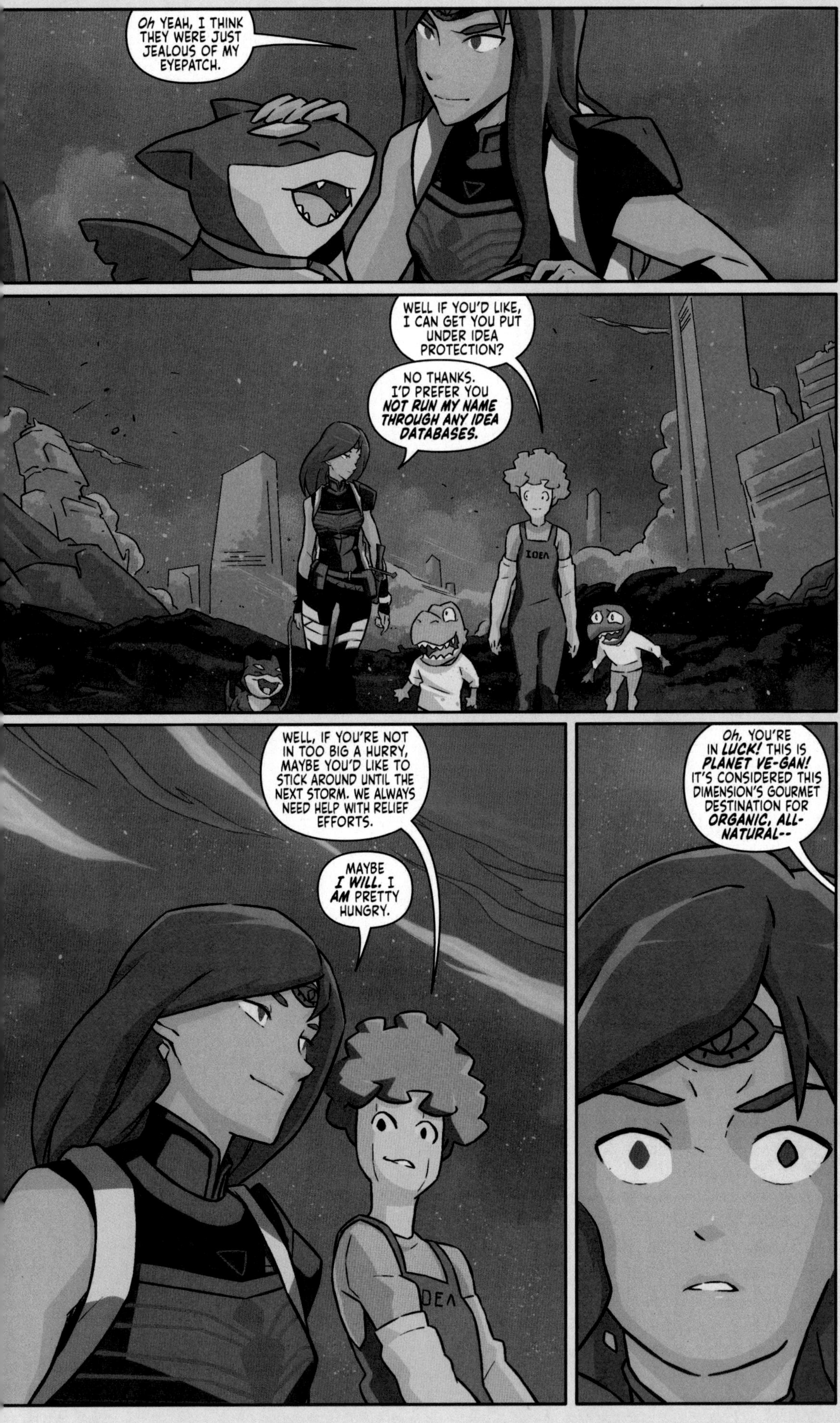
Oh YEAH, I THINK THEY WERE JUST JEALOUS OF MY EYEPATCH.
WELL IF YOU'D LIKE, I CAN GET YOU PUT UNDER IDEA PROTECTION?
NO THANKS. I'D PREFER YOU NOT RUN MY NAME THROUGH ANY IDEA DATABASES.
IDEA
WELL, IF YOU'RE NOT IN TOO BIG A HURRY, MAYBE YOU'D LIKE TO STICK AROUND UNTIL THE NEXT STORM. WE ALWAYS NEED HELP WITH RELIEF EFFORTS.
MAYBE I WILL. I AM PRETTY HUNGRY.
Oh, YOU'RE IN LUCK! THIS IS PLANET VE-GAN! IT'S CONSIDERED THIS DIMENSION'S GOURMET DESTINATION FOR ORGANIC, ALL-NATURAL--

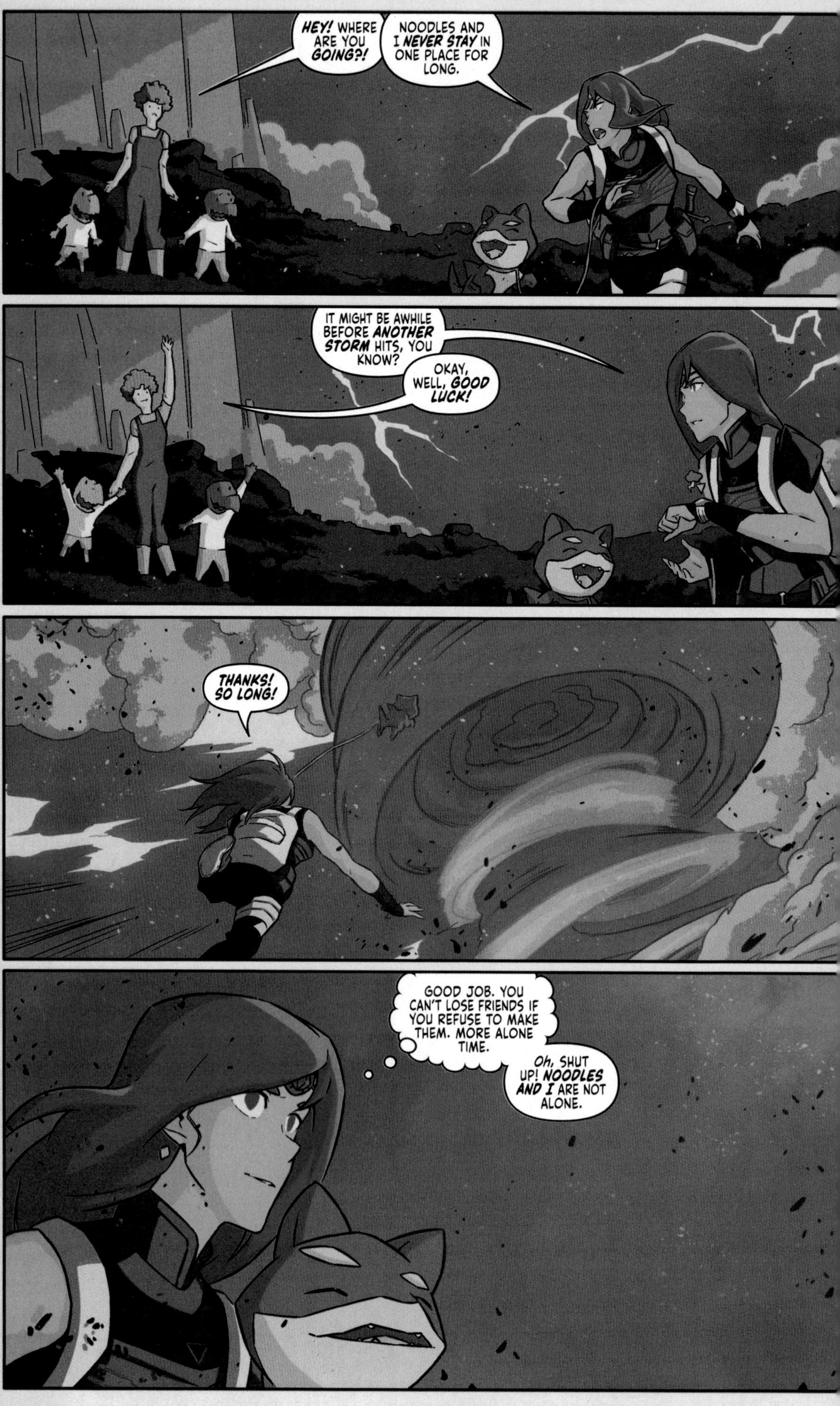
HEY! WHERE ARE YOU GOING?!
NOODLES AND I NEVER STAY IN ONE PLACE FOR LONG.
IT MIGHT BE AWHILE BEFORE ANOTHER STORM HITS, YOU KNOW?
OKAY, WELL, GOOD LUCK!
THANKS! SO LONG!
GOOD JOB. YOU CAN'T LOSE FRIENDS IF YOU REFUSE TO MAKE THEM. MORE ALONE TIME.
Oh, SHUT UP! NOODLES AND I ARE NOT ALONE.

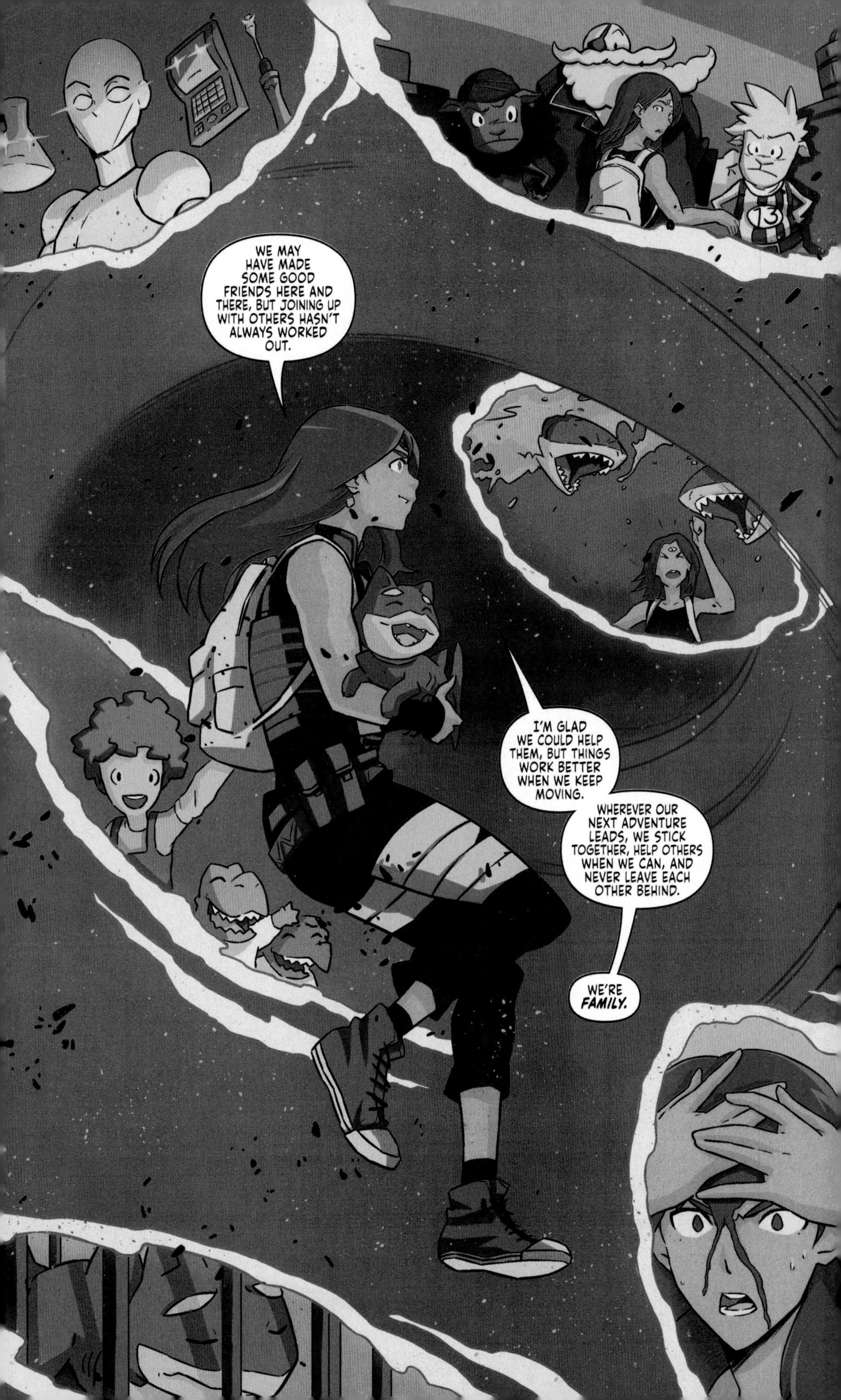
WE MAY HAVE MADE SOME GOOD FRIENDS HERE AND THERE, BUT JOINING UP WITH OTHERS HASN'T ALWAYS WORKED OUT.
I'M GLAD WE COULD HELP THEM, BUT THINGS WORK BETTER WHEN WE KEEP MOVING.
WHEREVER OUR NEXT ADVENTURE LEADS, WE STICK TOGETHER, HELP OTHERS WHEN WE CAN, AND NEVER LEAVE EACH OTHER BEHIND.
WE'RE *FAMILY.*
13

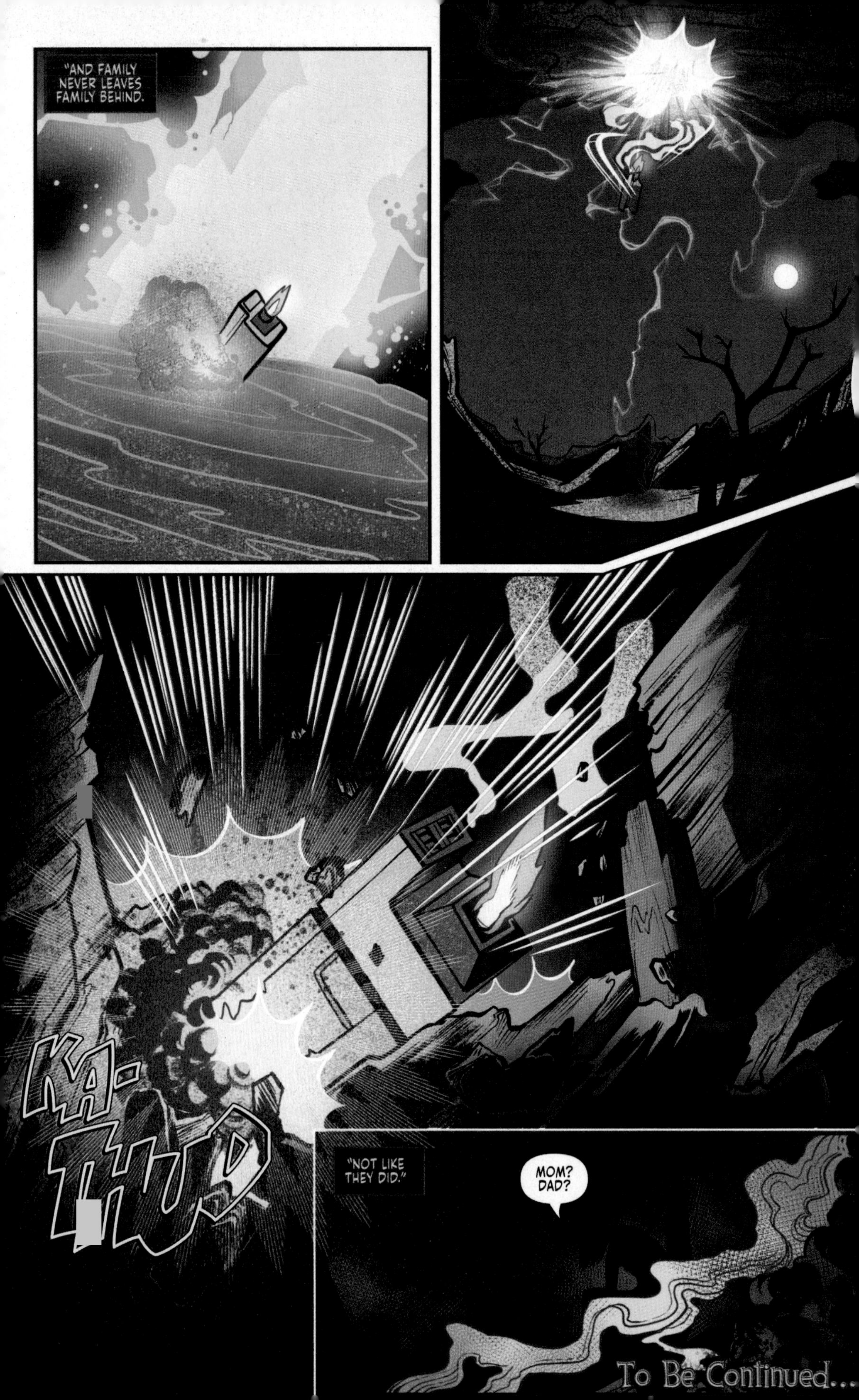
"AND FAMILY NEVER LEAVES FAMILY BEHIND.
KA-THUD
"NOT LIKE THEY DID."
MOM? DAD?
To Be Continued...

CHAPTER 2

PREVIOUSLY:

After their dimension was destroyed, Miranda and her parents attempted to flee into the multiverse. But when their ship failed and broke apart mid-dimension, Miranda was separated and crash landed in a foreign wasteland.

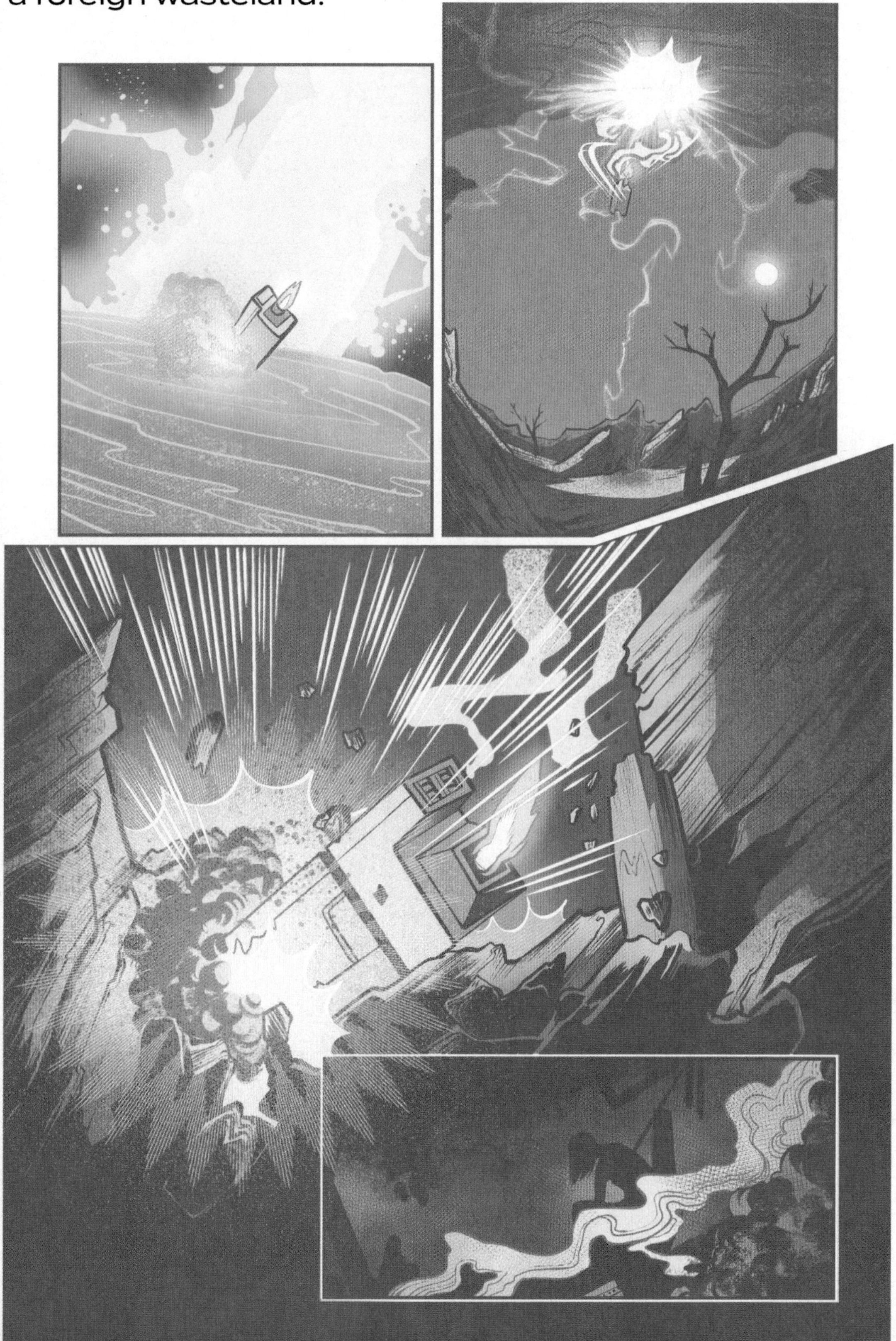

MIRANDA IN THE MAELSTROM

CHAPTER 2:
"A WOLF IN THE WASTELAND."

SCRIPT BY RILEY DASHIELL BIEHL
ART & COLORS BY DAILEN OGDEN

FLATS BY DREW WILLS
LETTERING BY TAYLOR ESPOSITO
SCRIPT EDITING BY BRITTANY MATTER
COVER BY DAILEN OGDEN

BRYAN SEATON: PUBLISHER / CEO
SHAWN GABBORIN: EDITOR IN CHIEF
JASON MARTIN: PUBLISHER-DANGER ZONE
NICOLE D'ANDRIA: MARKETING DIRECTOR/EDITOR
DANIELLE DAVISON: EXECUTIVE ADMINISTRATOR
CHAD CICCONI: CHIEF PORTAL INSPECTOR
SHAWN PRYOR: PRESIDENT OF CREATOR RELATIONS

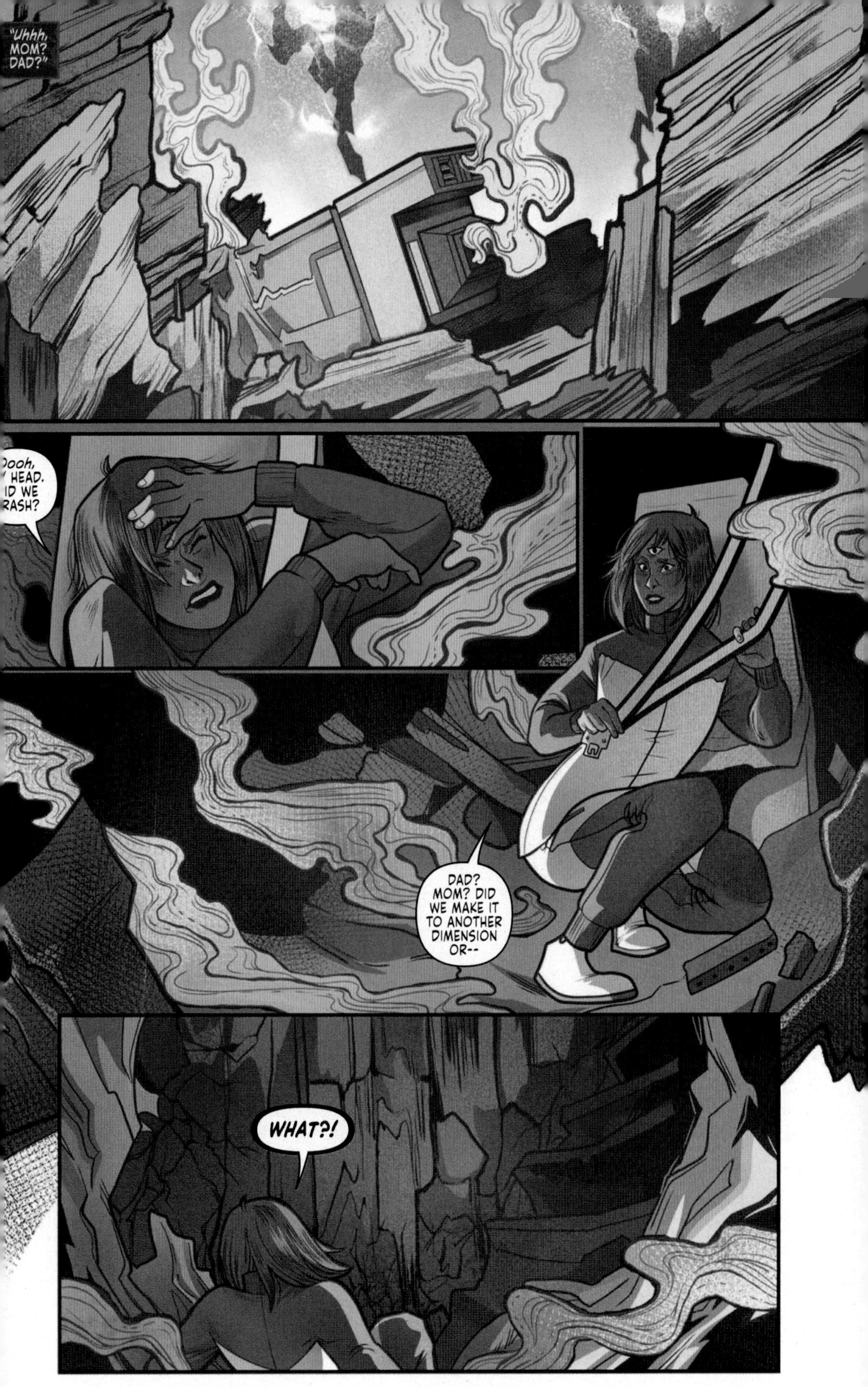
"Uhhh, MOM? DAD?"
Oooh, Y HEAD. ID WE RASH?
DAD? MOM? DID WE MAKE IT TO ANOTHER DIMENSION OR--
WHAT?!

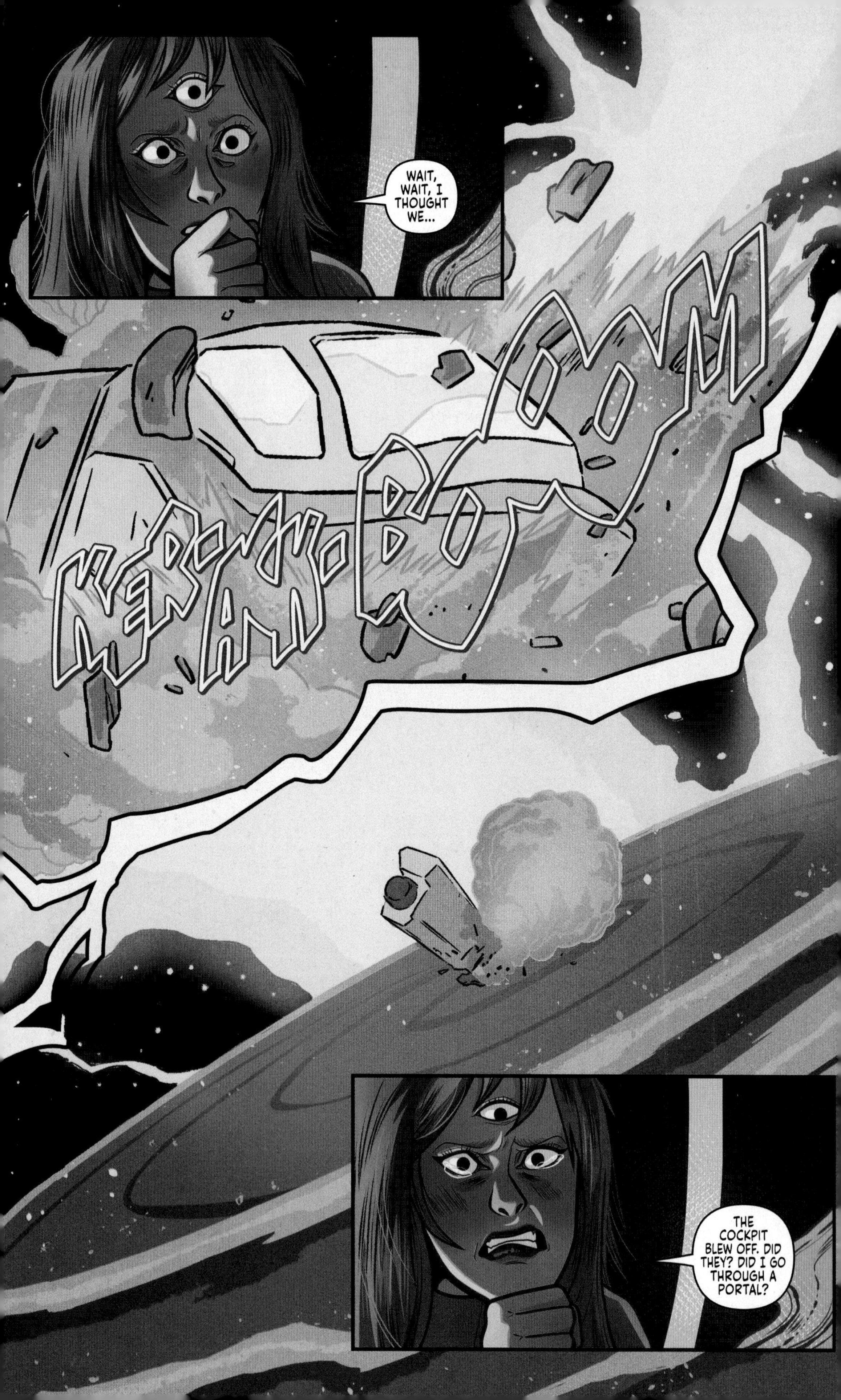
WAIT, WAIT, I THOUGHT WE...
THE COCKPIT BLEW OFF. DID THEY? DID I GO THROUGH A PORTAL?

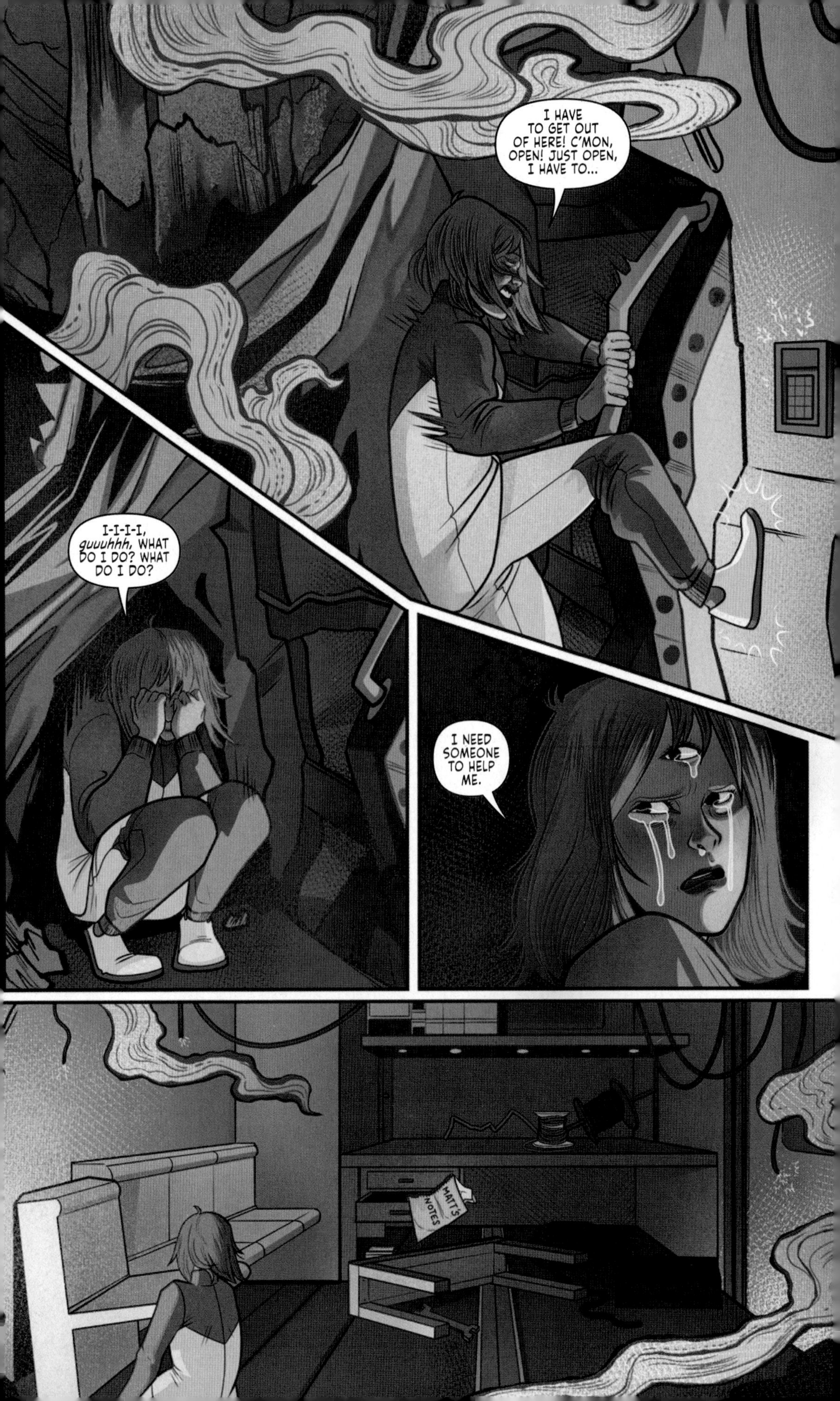
I HAVE TO GET OUT OF HERE! C'MON, OPEN! JUST OPEN, I HAVE TO...
I-I-I-I, *guuuhhh,* WHAT DO I DO? WHAT DO I DO?
I NEED SOMEONE TO HELP ME.
MATT'S NOTES

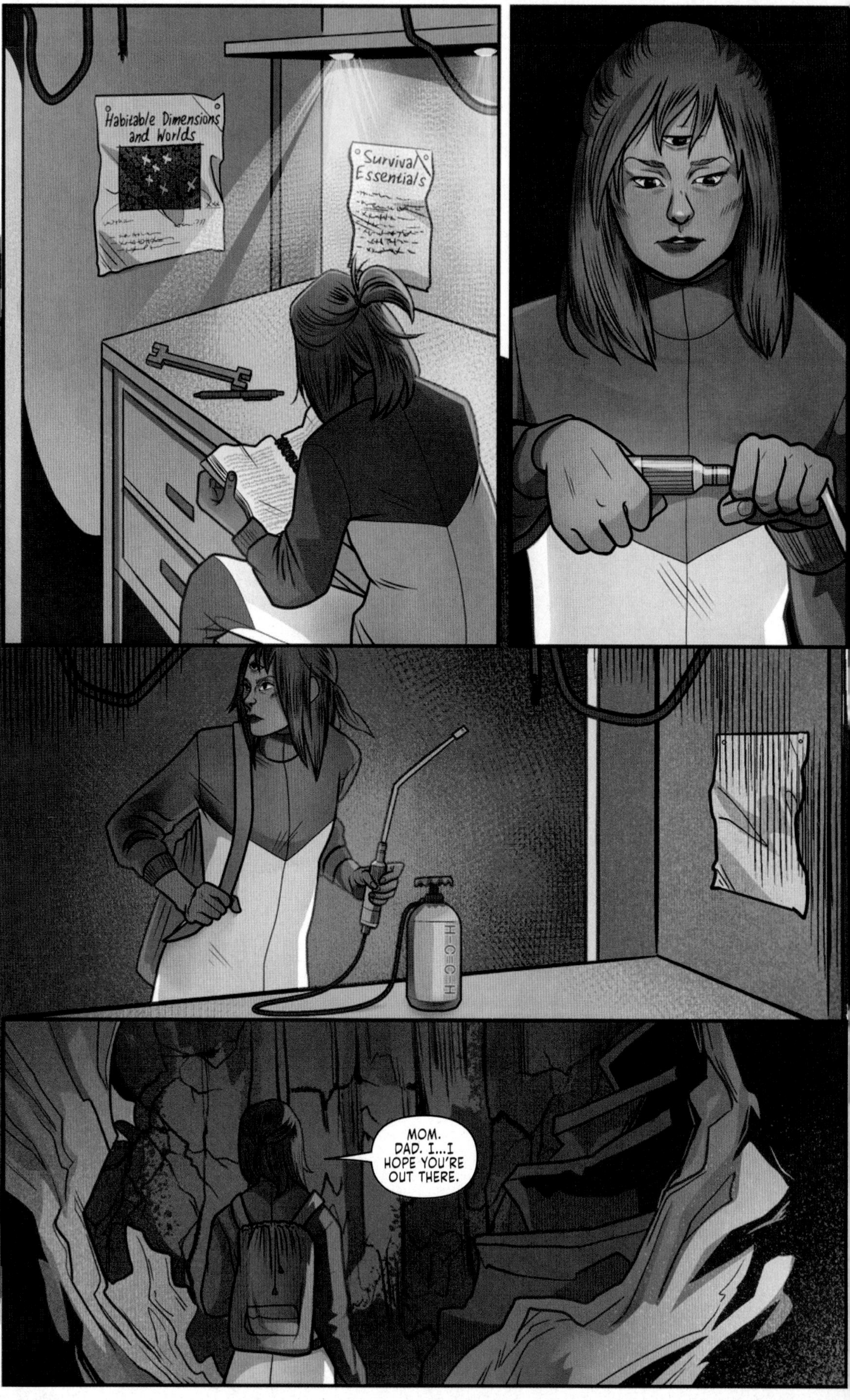
Habitable Dimensions and Worlds
Survival Essentials
MOM. DAD. I...I HOPE YOU'RE OUT THERE.

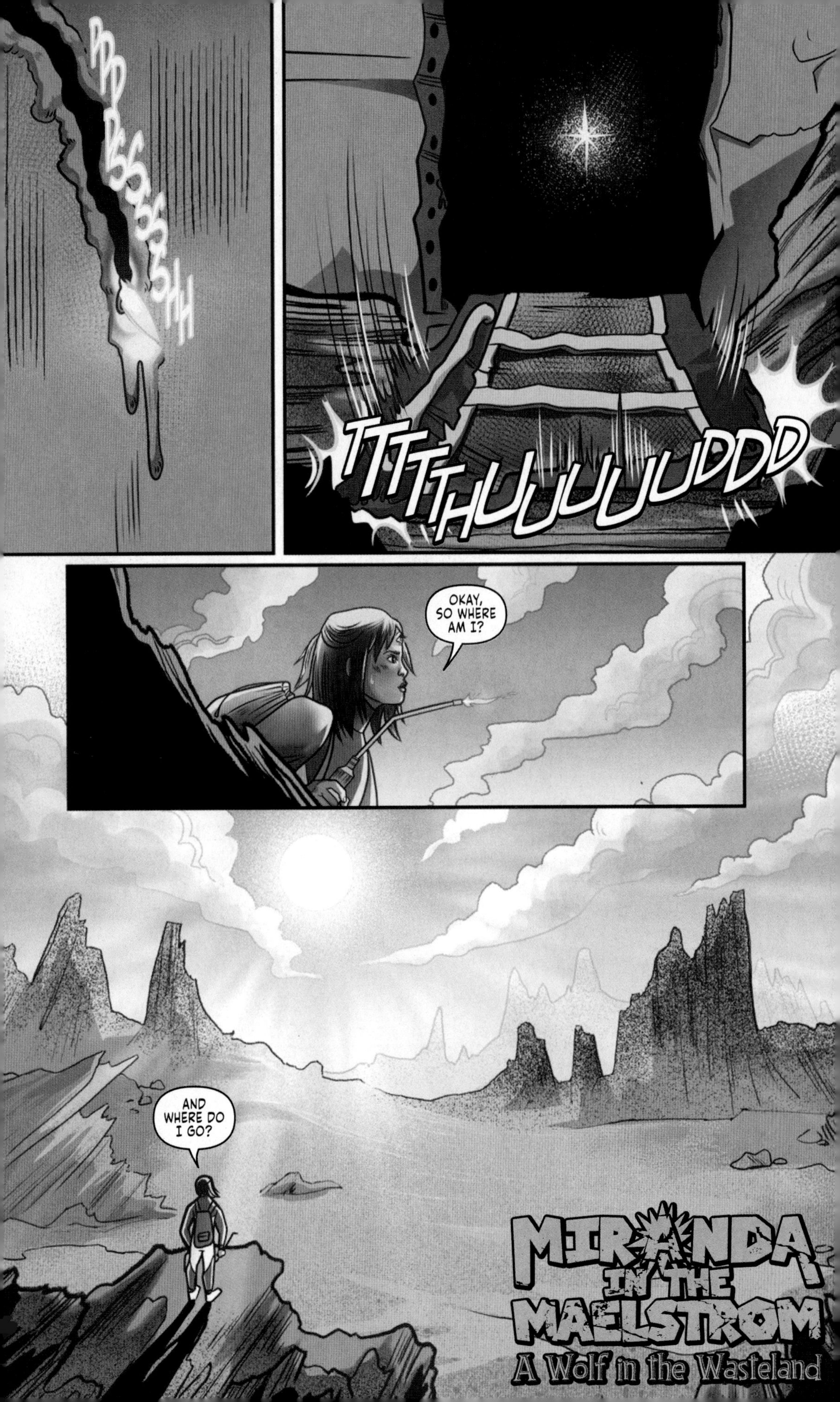
PPPPSSSSSSSHH
TTTTHUUUUUDDD
OKAY, SO WHERE AM I?
AND WHERE DO I GO?
MIRANDA IN THE MAELSTROM
A Wolf in the Wasteland

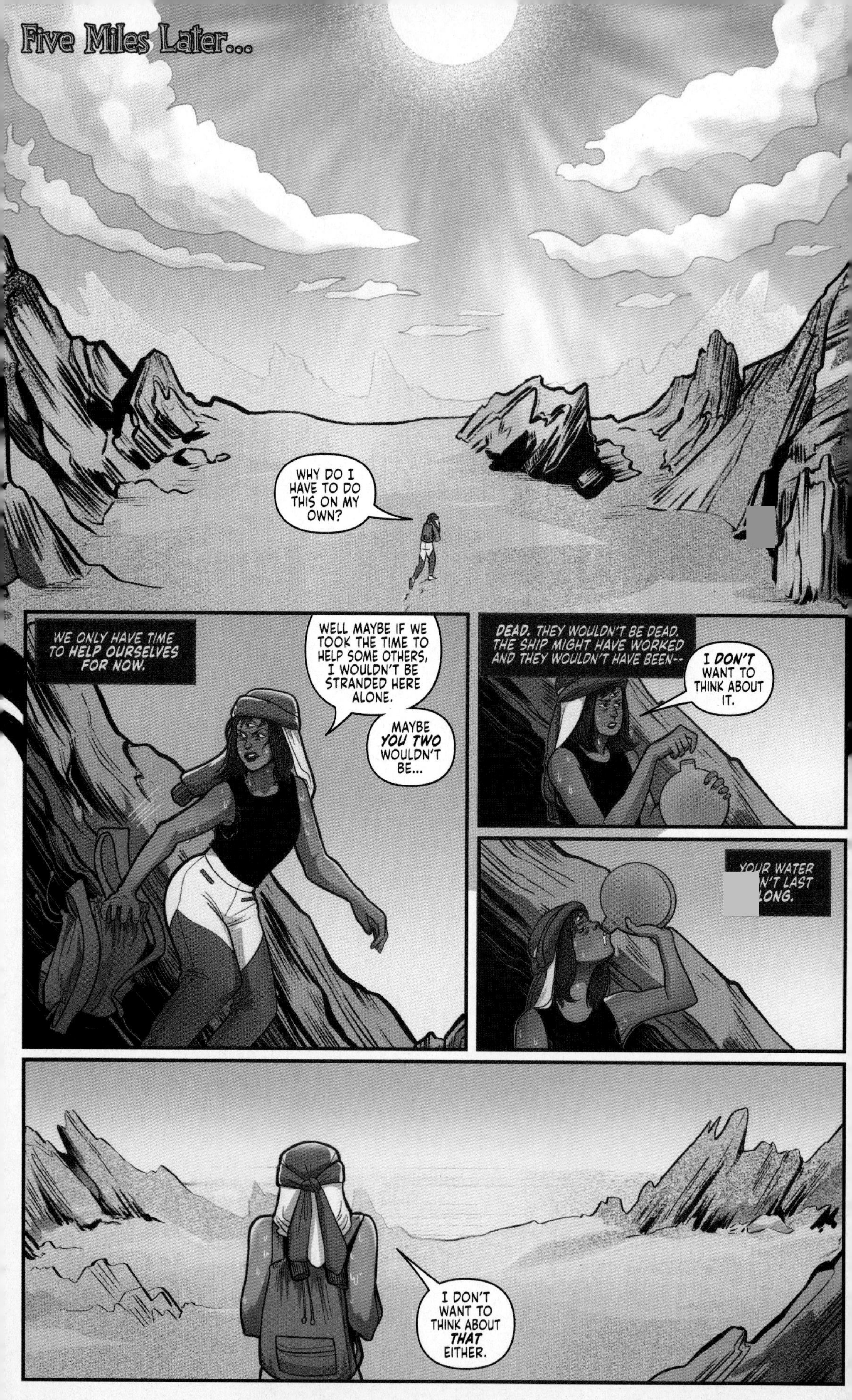

Five Miles Later...
WHY DO I HAVE TO DO THIS ON MY OWN?
WE ONLY HAVE TIME TO HELP OURSELVES FOR NOW.
WELL MAYBE IF WE TOOK THE TIME TO HELP SOME OTHERS, I WOULDN'T BE STRANDED HERE ALONE.
MAYBE YOU TWO WOULDN'T BE...
DEAD. THEY WOULDN'T BE DEAD. THE SHIP MIGHT HAVE WORKED AND THEY WOULDN'T HAVE BEEN--
I DON'T WANT TO THINK ABOUT IT.
YOUR WATER N'T LAST ONG.
I DON'T WANT TO THINK ABOUT THAT EITHER.

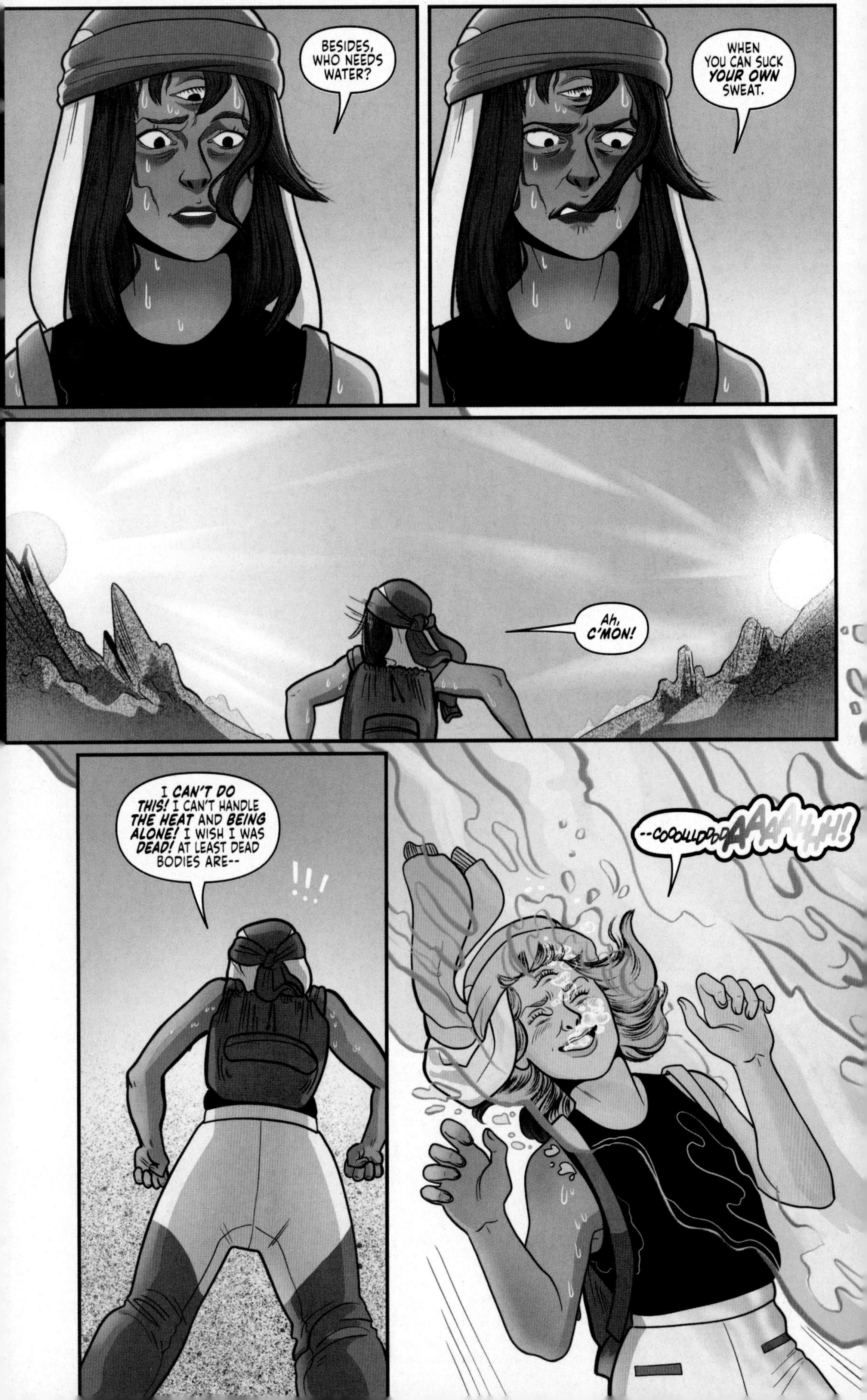

BESIDES, WHO NEEDS WATER?
WHEN YOU CAN SUCK YOUR OWN SWEAT.
Ah, C'MON!
I CAN'T DO THIS! I CAN'T HANDLE THE HEAT AND BEING ALONE! I WISH I WAS DEAD! AT LEAST DEAD BODIES ARE--
!!!
--COOOLLLDDDDAAAAHHH!

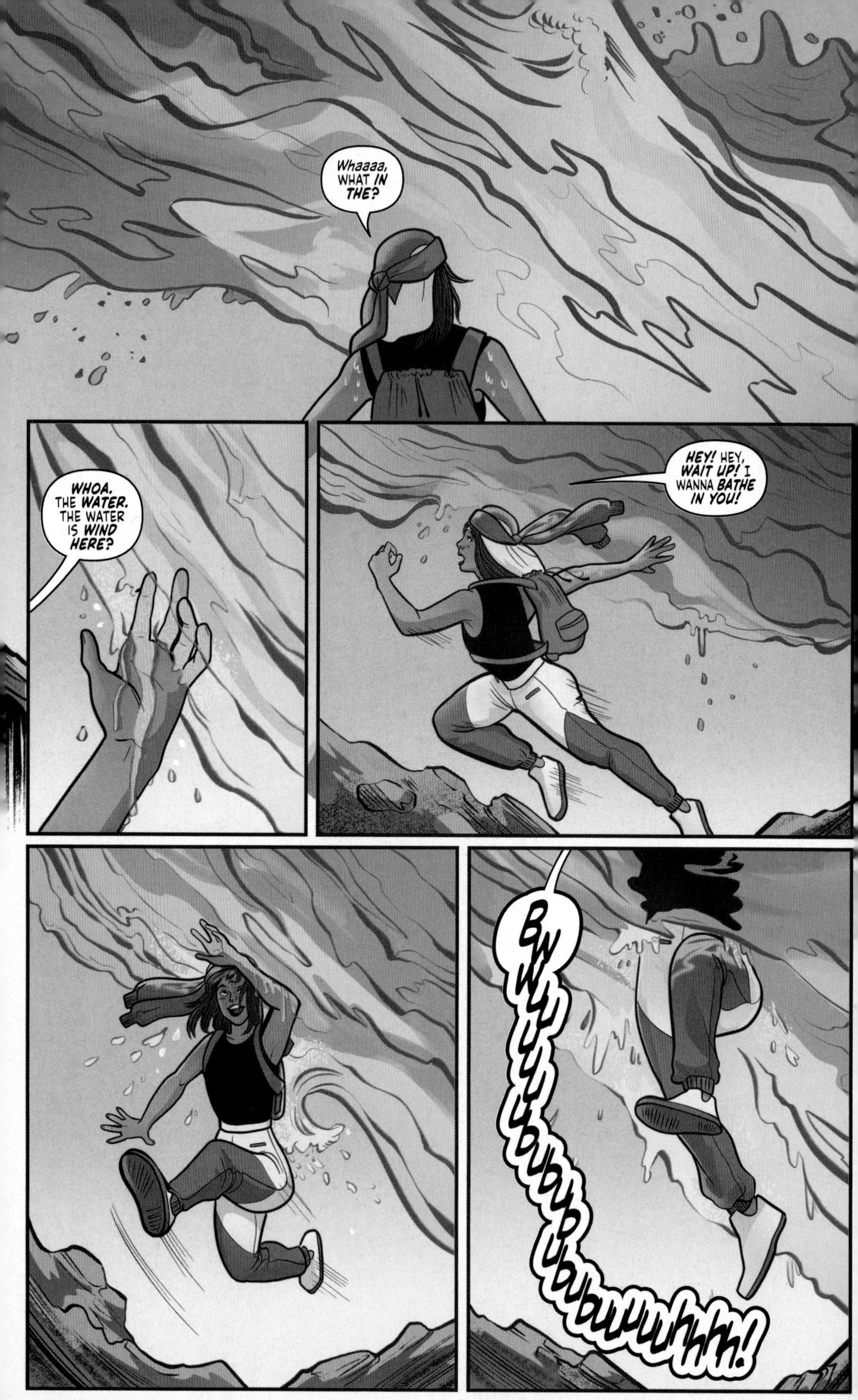
Whaaaa, WHAT IN THE?
WHOA. THE WATER. THE WATER IS WIND HERE?
HEY! HEY, WAIT UP! I WANNA BATHE IN YOU!
BWUUUUUUUBUBUBUUUUHHHH!

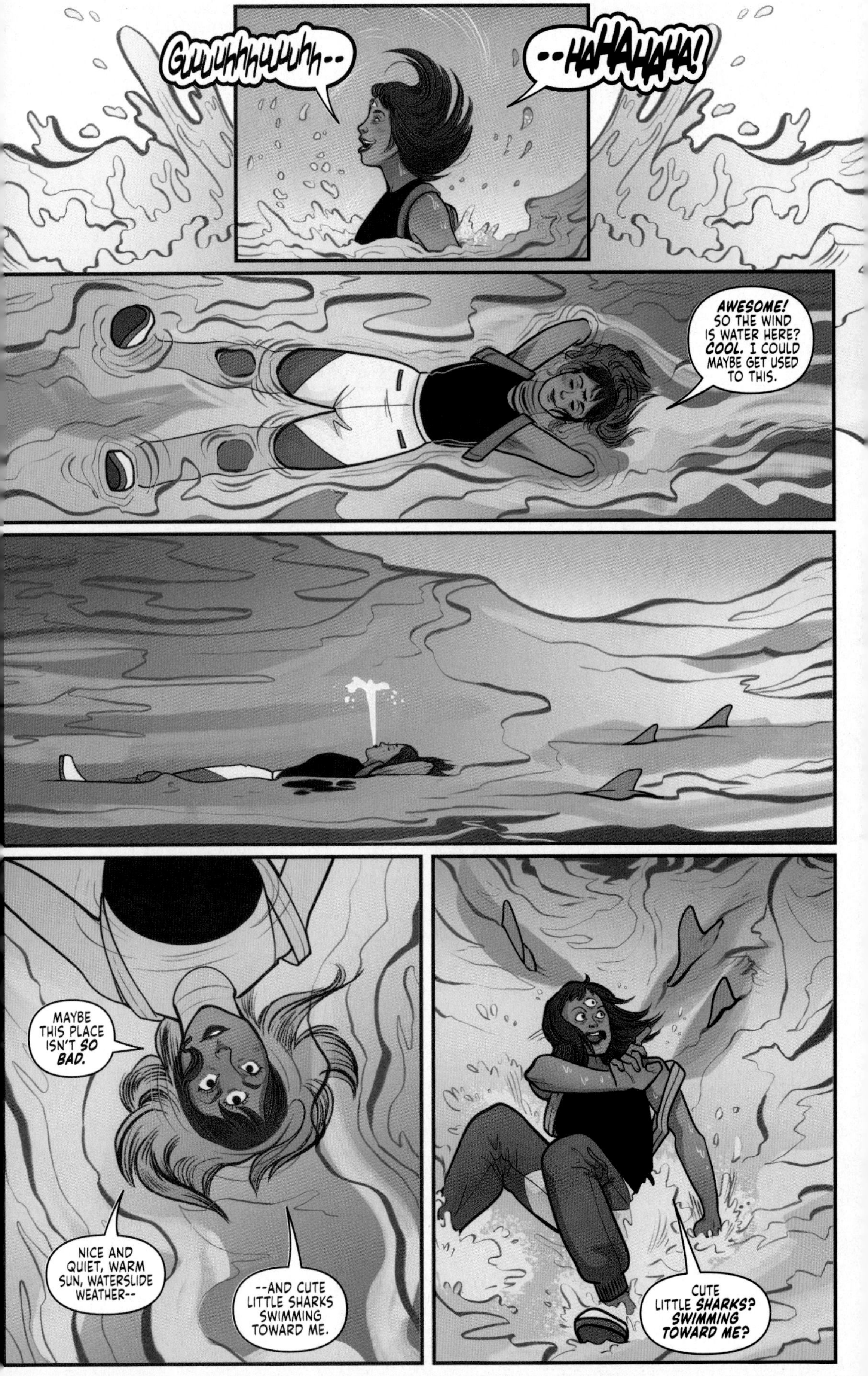
GUUUUHHUUUHH--
--HAHAHAHA!
AWESOME! SO THE WIND IS WATER HERE? COOL. I COULD MAYBE GET USED TO THIS.
MAYBE THIS PLACE ISN'T SO BAD.
NICE AND QUIET, WARM SUN, WATERSLIDE WEATHER--
--AND CUTE LITTLE SHARKS SWIMMING TOWARD ME.
CUTE LITTLE SHARKS? SWIMMING TOWARD ME?

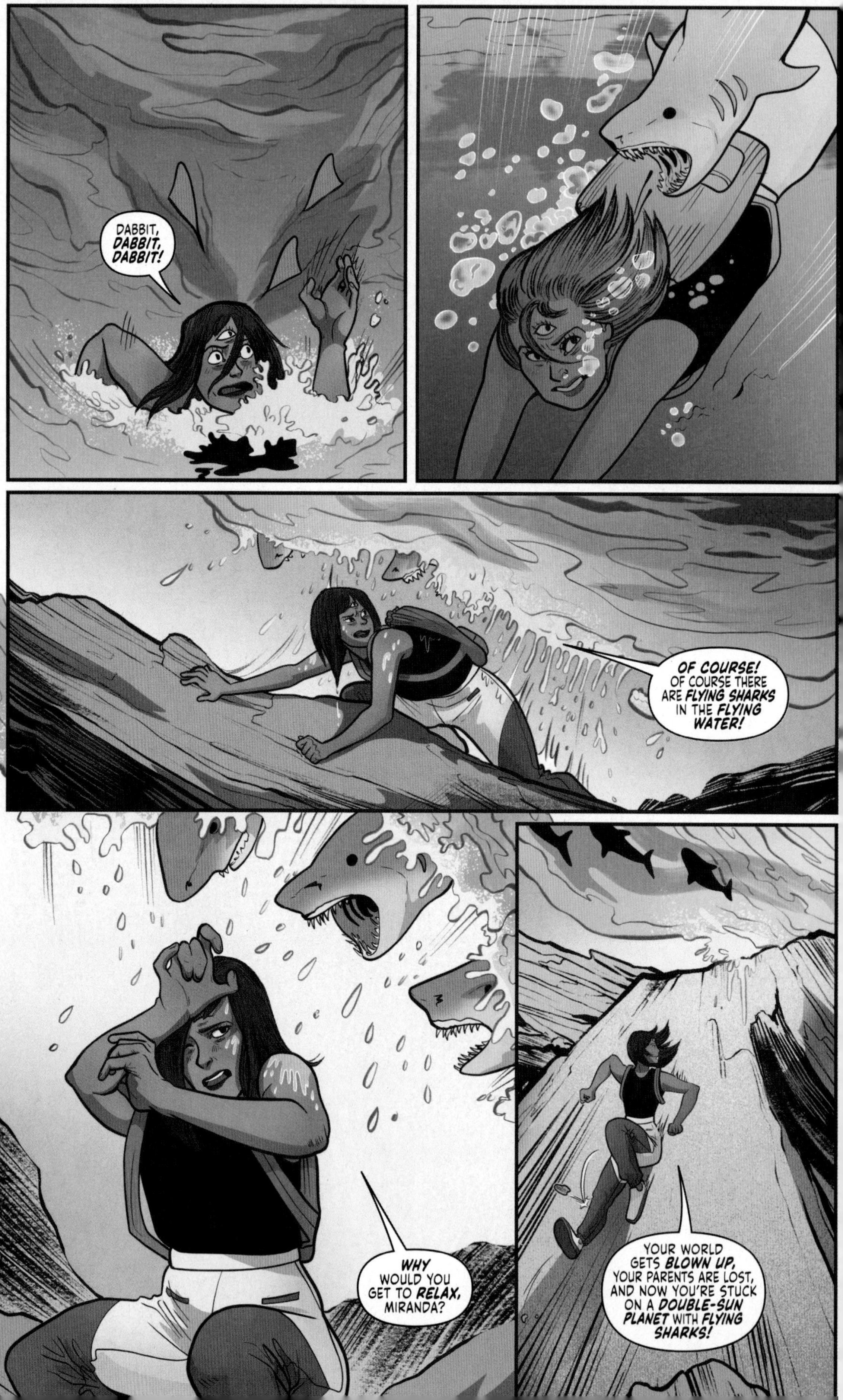
DABBIT, DABBIT, DABBIT!
OF COURSE! OF COURSE THERE ARE FLYING SHARKS IN THE FLYING WATER!
WHY WOULD YOU GET TO RELAX, MIRANDA?
YOUR WORLD GETS BLOWN UP, YOUR PARENTS ARE LOST, AND NOW YOU'RE STUCK ON A DOUBLE-SUN PLANET WITH FLYING SHARKS!

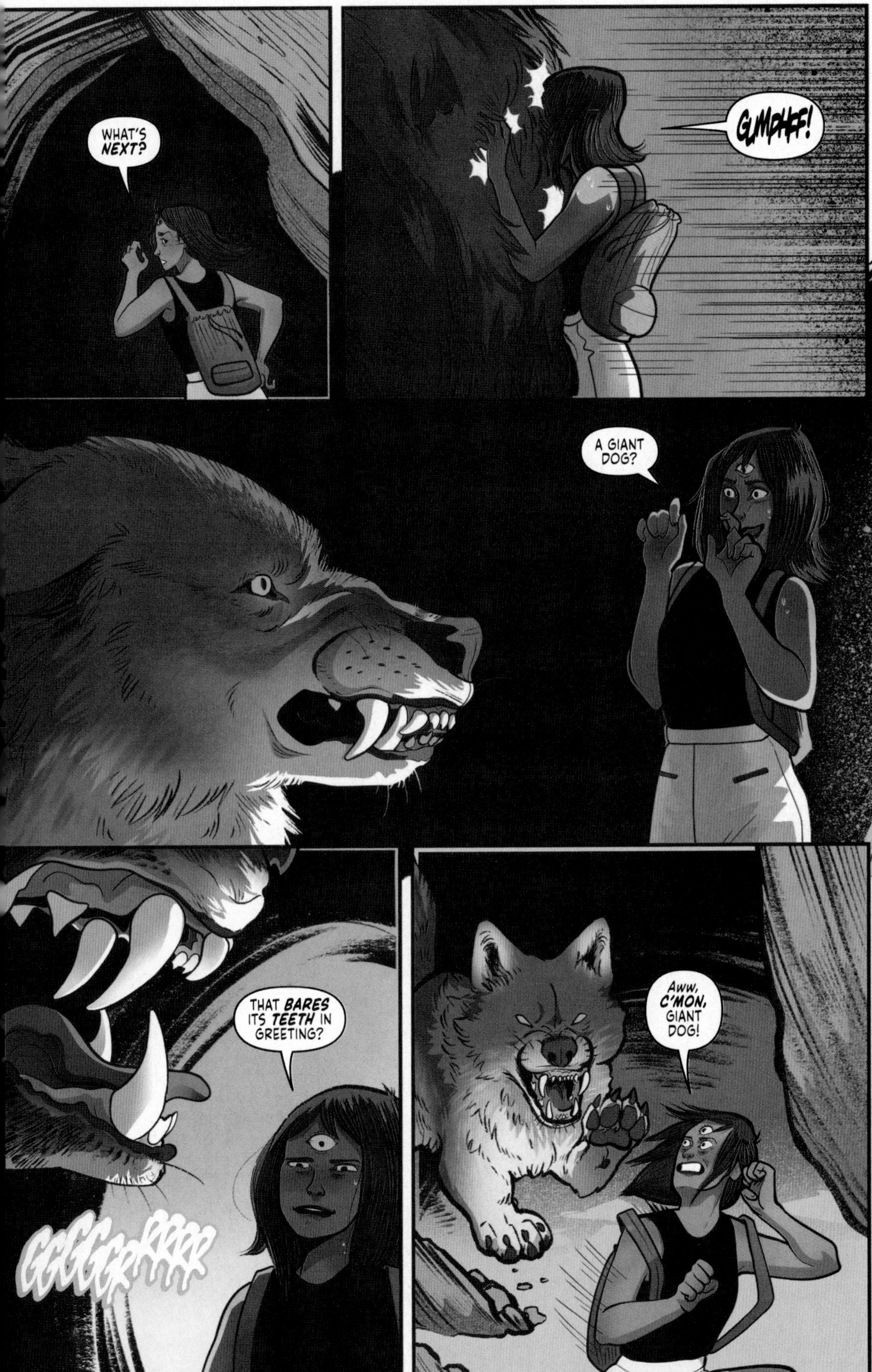
WHAT'S NEXT?
GUMPHFF!
A GIANT DOG?
THAT BARES ITS TEETH IN GREETING?
GGGGRRRRR
Aww, C'MON, GIANT DOG!

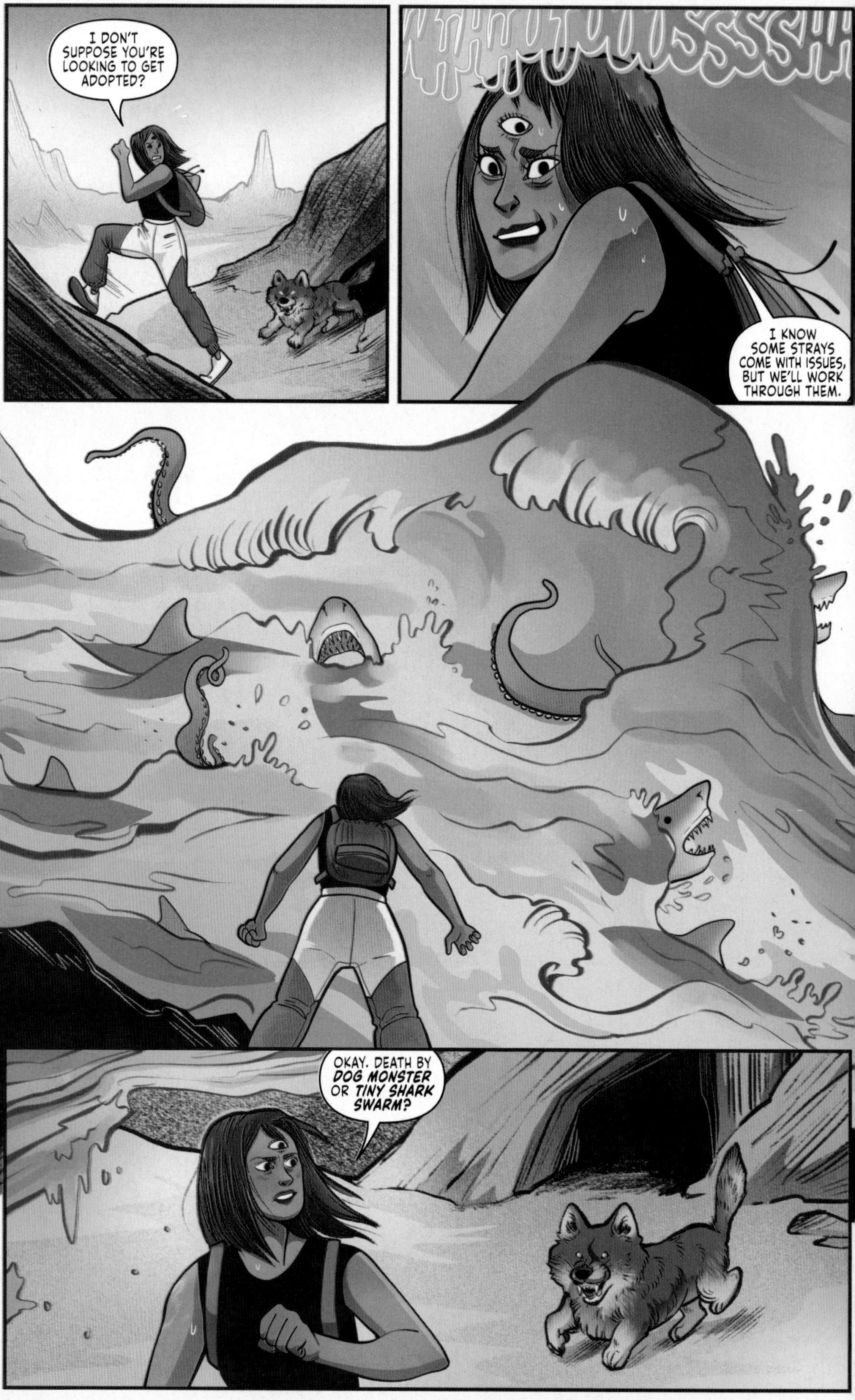
I DON'T SUPPOSE YOU'RE LOOKING TO GET ADOPTED?
I KNOW SOME STRAYS COME WITH ISSUES, BUT WE'LL WORK THROUGH THEM.
OKAY. DEATH BY *DOG MONSTER* OR *TINY SHARK SWARM?*

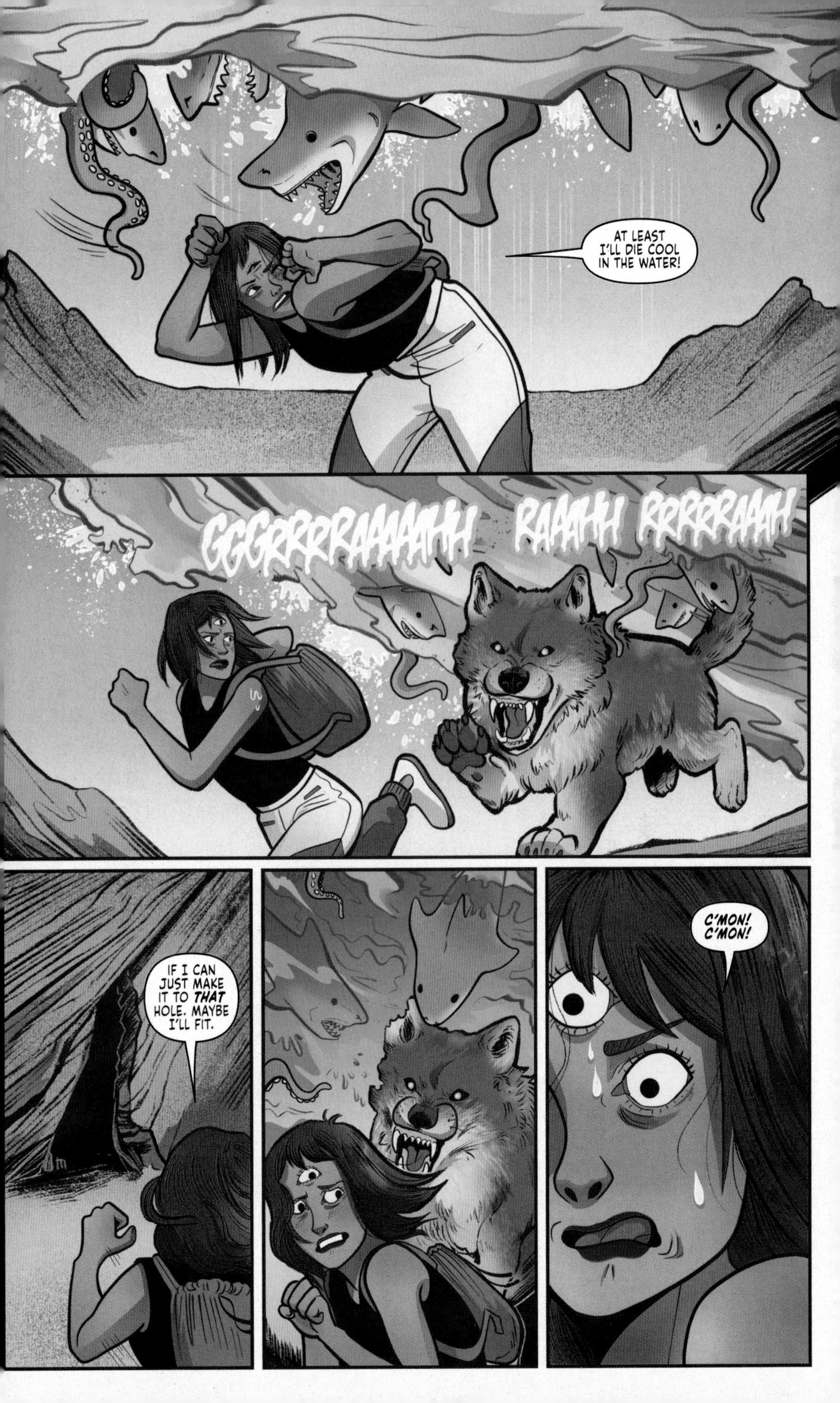
AT LEAST I'LL DIE COOL IN THE WATER!
GGGRRRRAAAAAHH
RAAAHH RRRRRAAAH
IF I CAN JUST MAKE IT TO *THAT* HOLE. MAYBE I'LL FIT.
C'MON! C'MON!

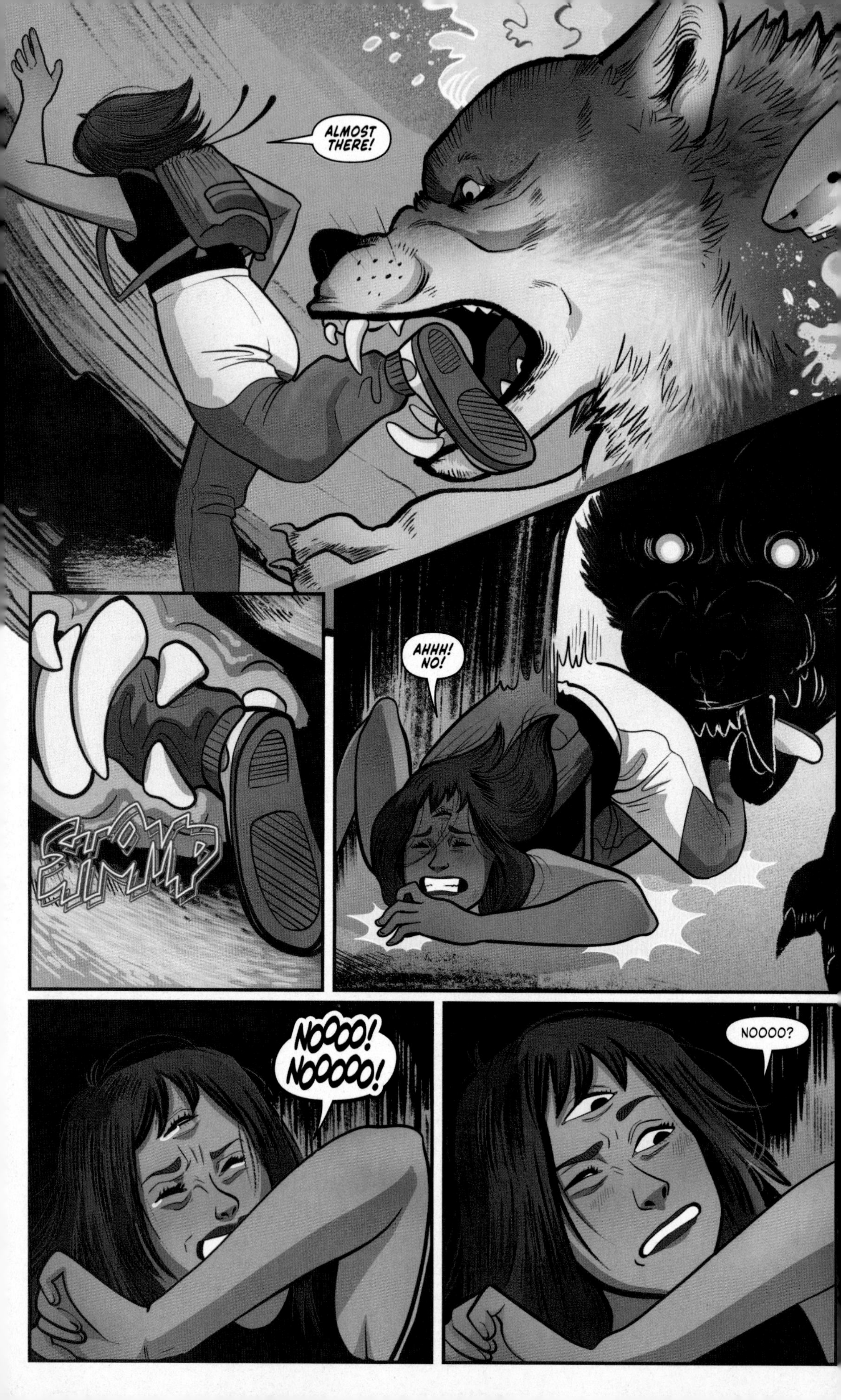
ALMOST THERE!
STOMP
AHHH! NO!
NOOOO! NOOOOO!
NOOOO?

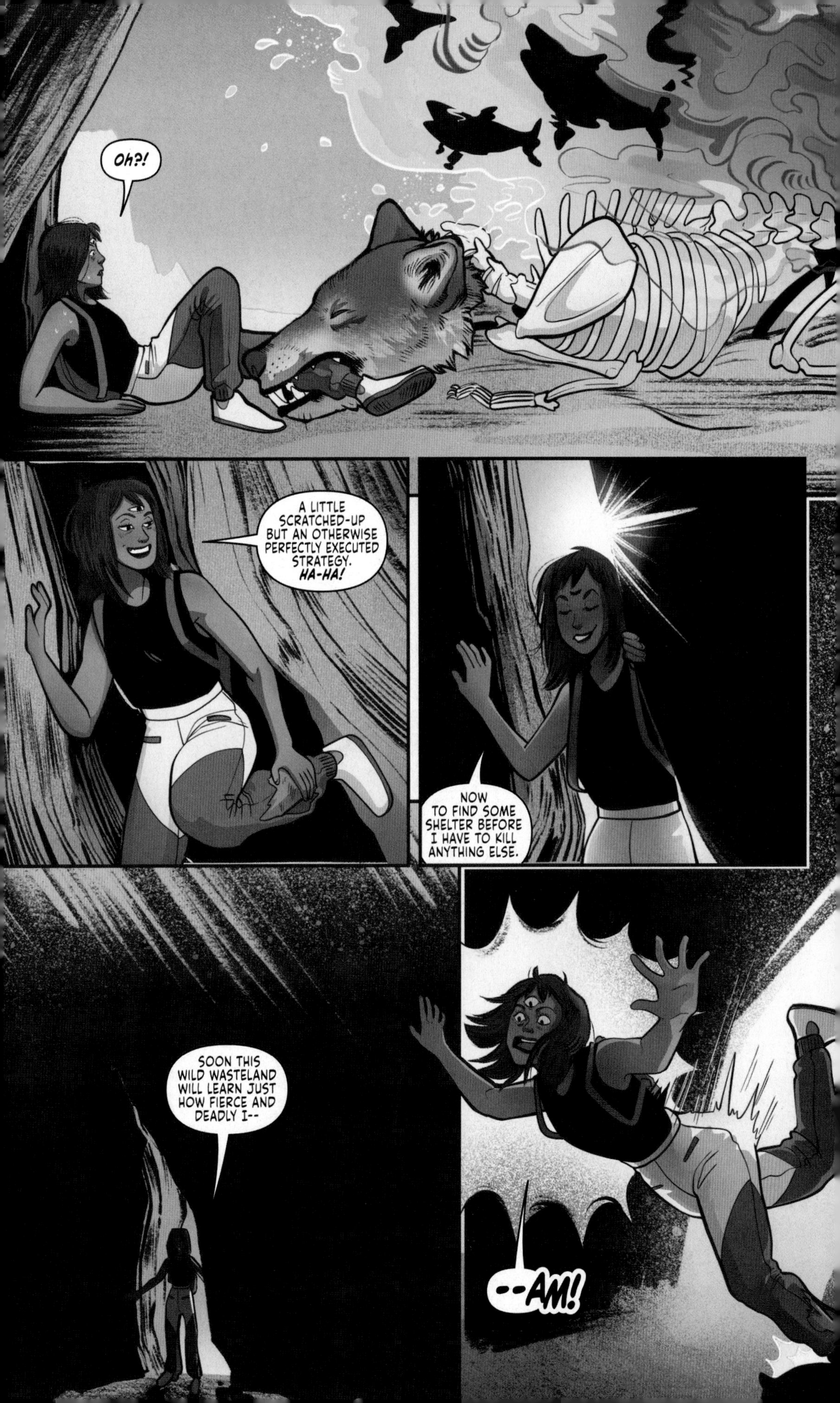
Oh?!
A LITTLE SCRATCHED-UP BUT AN OTHERWISE PERFECTLY EXECUTED STRATEGY. HA-HA!
NOW TO FIND SOME SHELTER BEFORE I HAVE TO KILL ANYTHING ELSE.
SOON THIS WILD WASTELAND WILL LEARN JUST HOW FIERCE AND DEADLY I--
--AM!

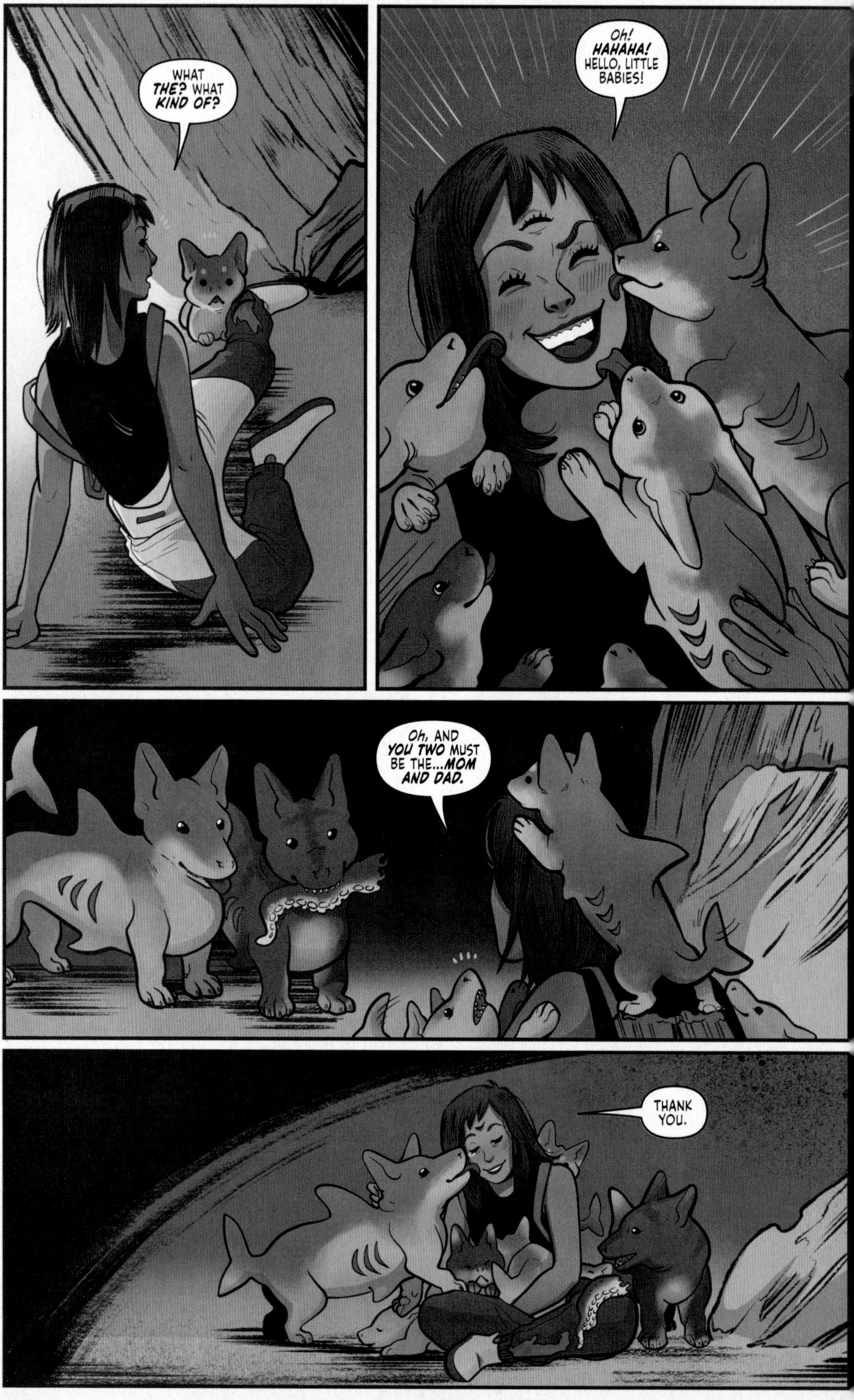
WHAT THE? WHAT KIND OF?
Oh! HAHAHA! HELLO, LITTLE BABIES!
Oh, AND YOU TWO MUST BE THE...MOM AND DAD.
THANK YOU.

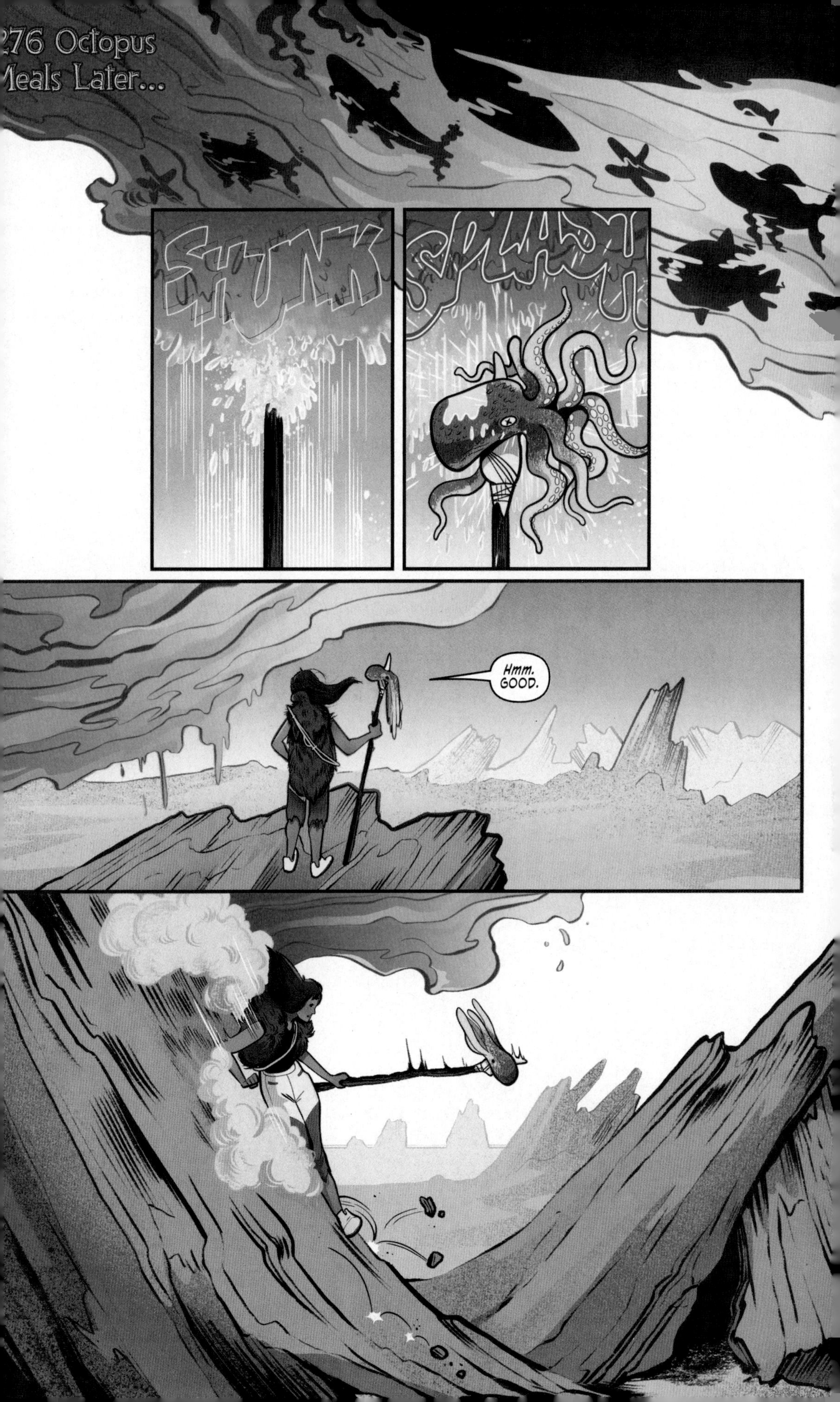
276 Octopus Meals Later...
SHUNK
SPLASH
HMM. GOOD.

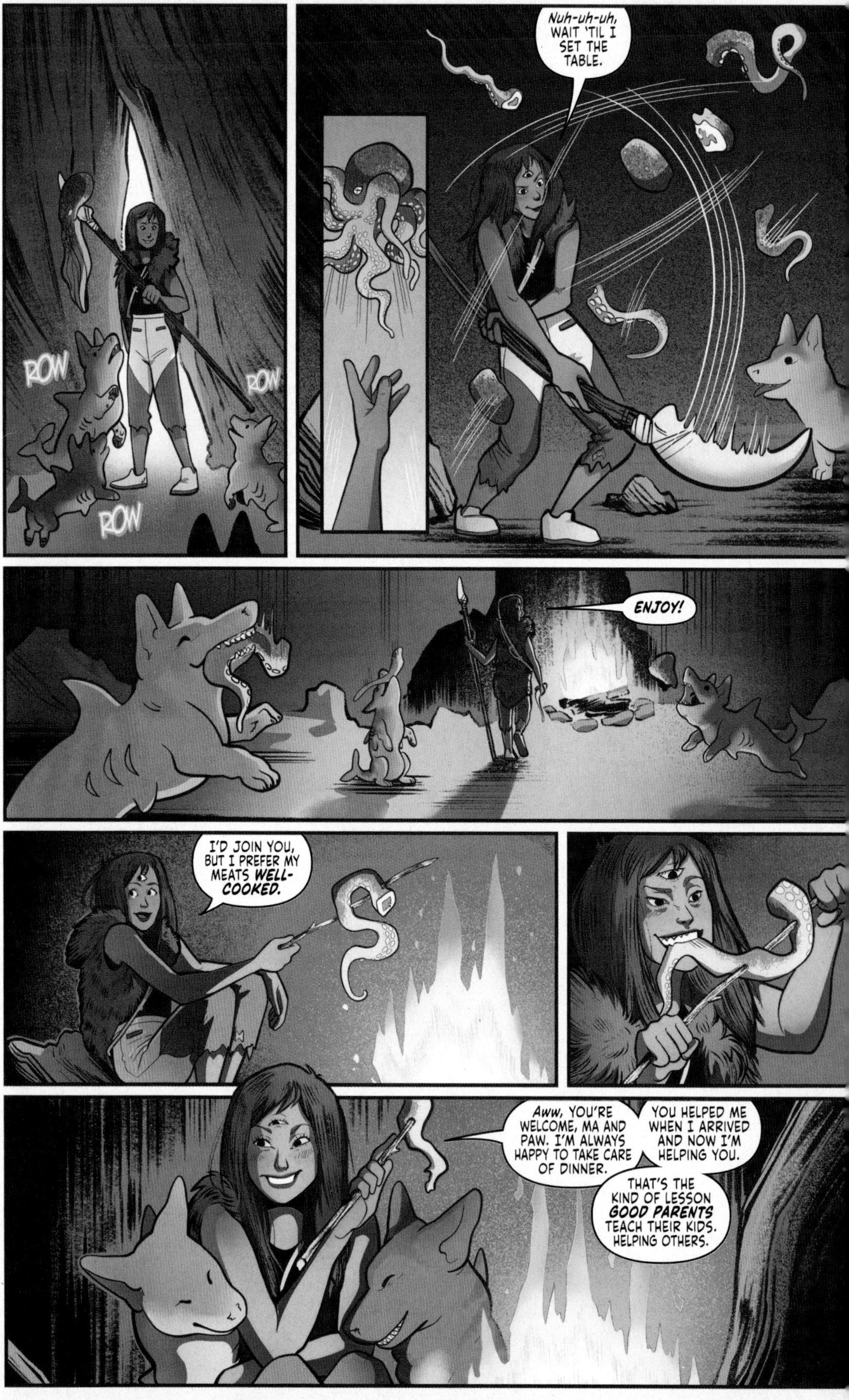

ROW
ROW
ROW
Nuh-uh-uh, WAIT 'TIL I SET THE TABLE.
ENJOY!
I'D JOIN YOU, BUT I PREFER MY MEATS WELL-COOKED.
Aww, YOU'RE WELCOME, MA AND PAW. I'M ALWAYS HAPPY TO TAKE CARE OF DINNER.
YOU HELPED ME WHEN I ARRIVED AND NOW I'M HELPING YOU.
THAT'S THE KIND OF LESSON GOOD PARENTS TEACH THEIR KIDS. HELPING OTHERS.

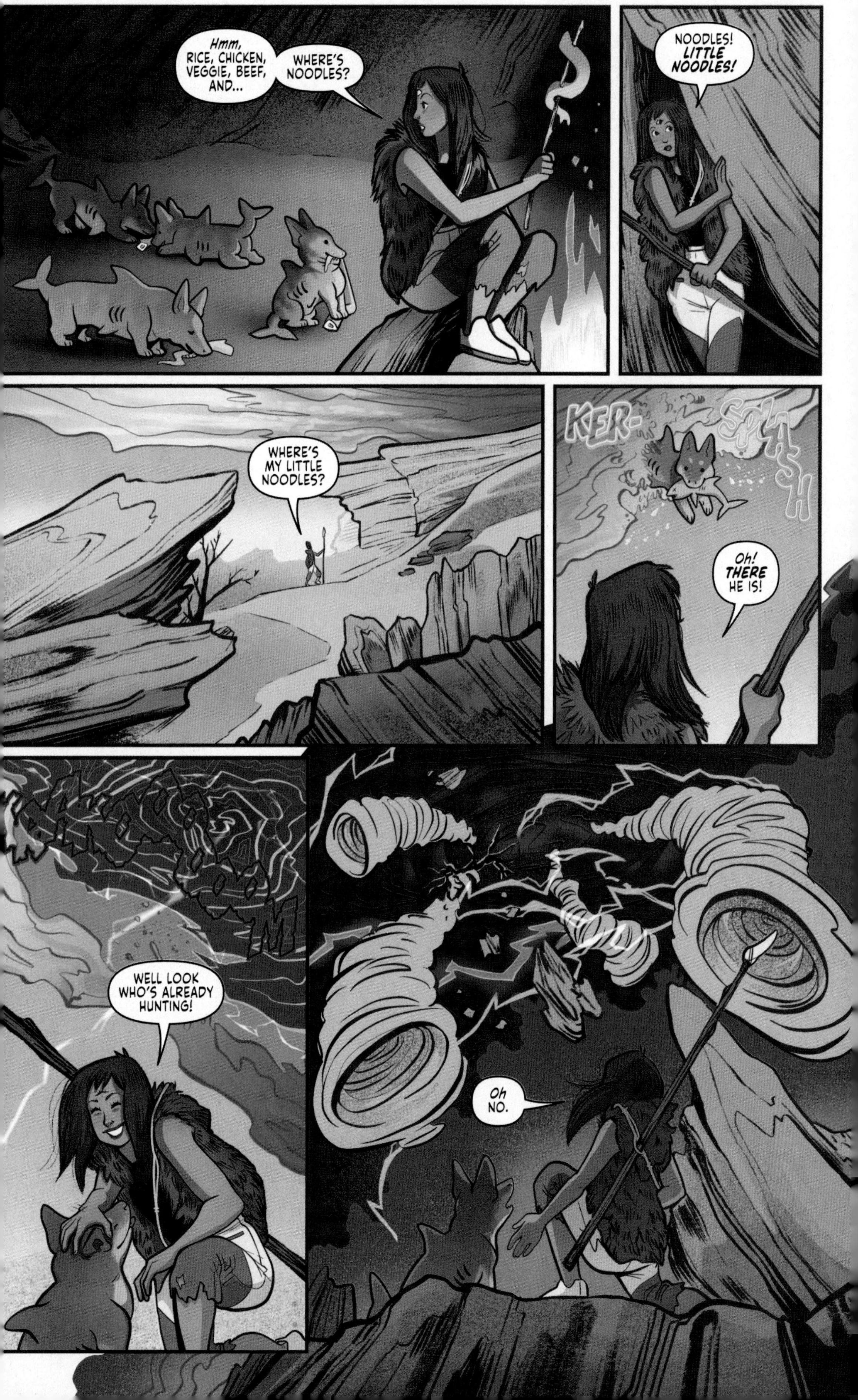
Hmm, RICE, CHICKEN, VEGGIE, BEEF, AND...
WHERE'S NOODLES?
NOODLES! LITTLE NOODLES!
WHERE'S MY LITTLE NOODLES?
KER-SPLASH
Oh! THERE HE IS!
WELL LOOK WHO'S ALREADY HUNTING!
Oh NO.

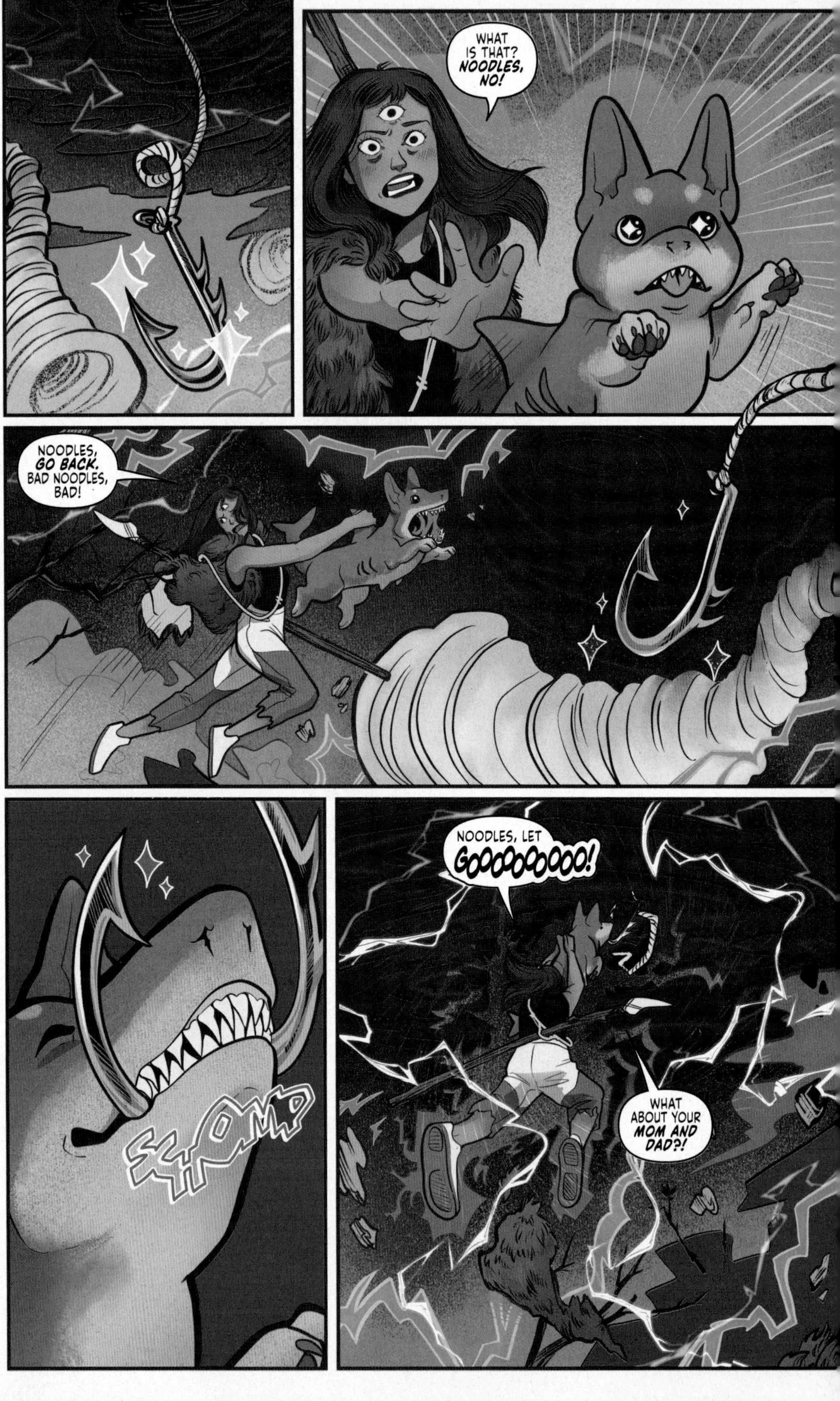

WHAT IS THAT? NOODLES, NO!
NOODLES, GO BACK. BAD NOODLES, BAD!
SCHOMP
NOODLES, LET GOOOOOOOOOO!
WHAT ABOUT YOUR MOM AND DAD?!

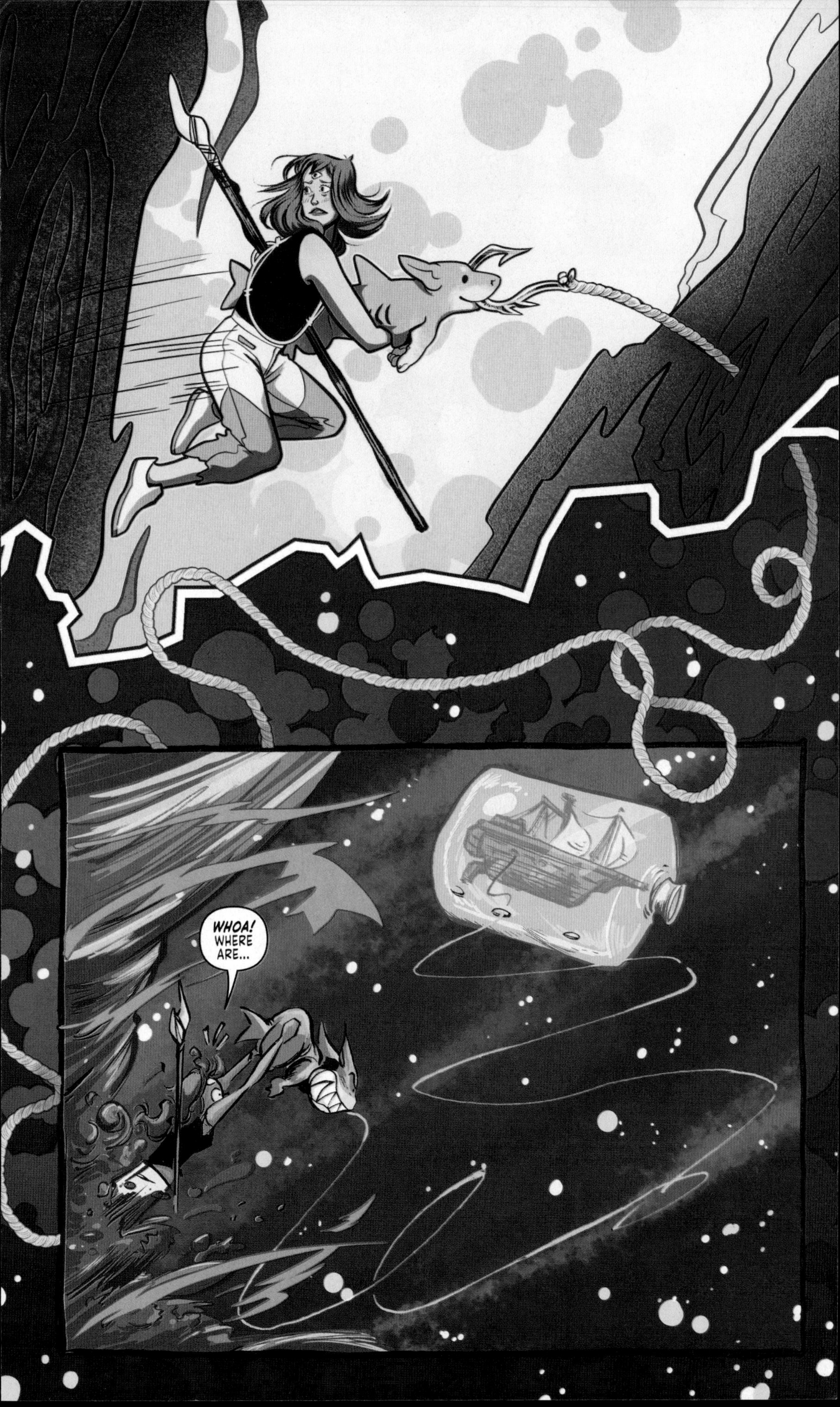
WHOA! WHERE ARE...

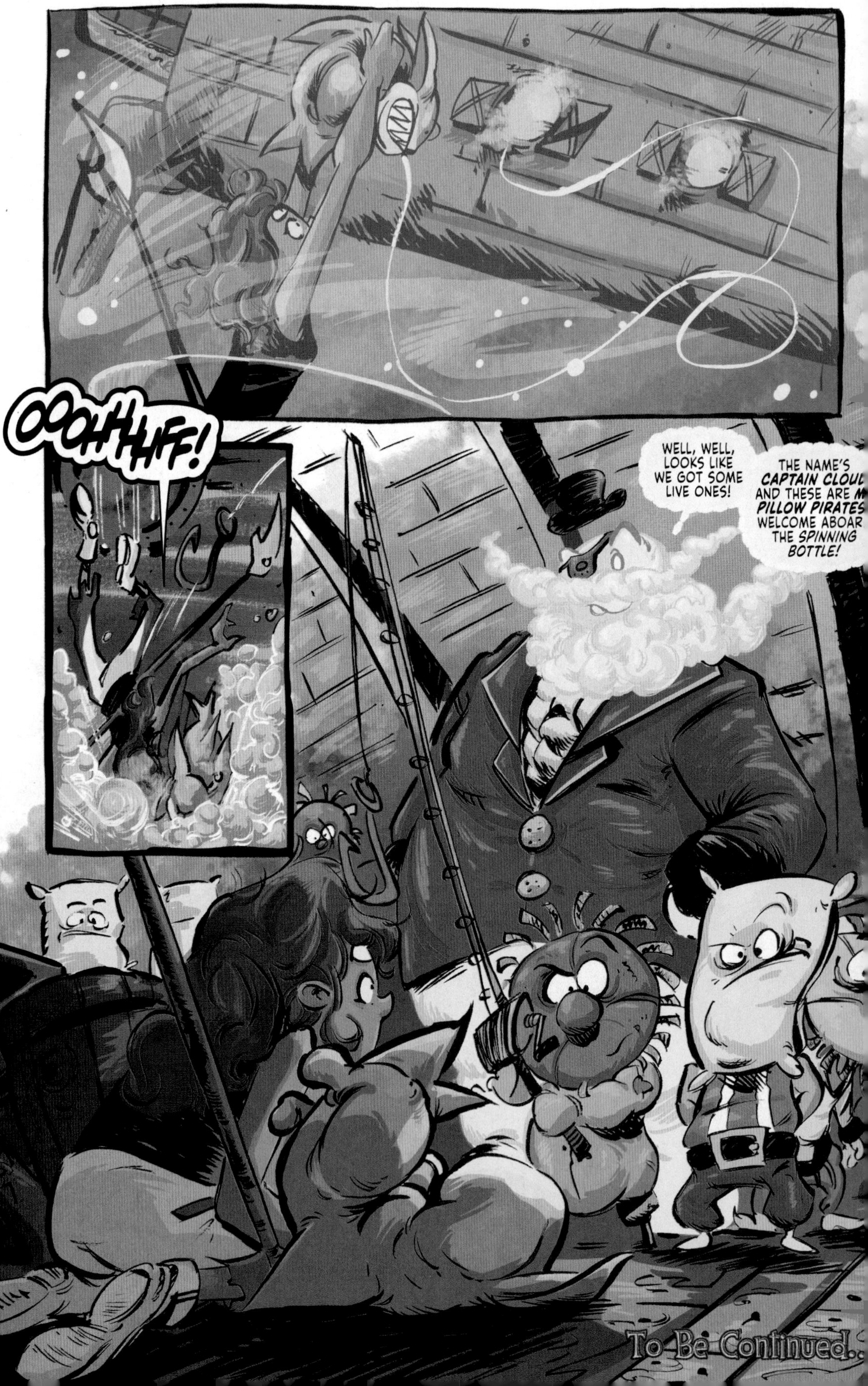

OOOHHHFF!
WELL, WELL, LOOKS LIKE WE GOT SOME LIVE ONES!
THE NAME'S CAPTAIN CLOUL AND THESE ARE M PILLOW PIRATES WELCOME ABOAR THE SPINNING BOTTLE!
To Be Continued..

MIRANDA IN THE MAELSTROM

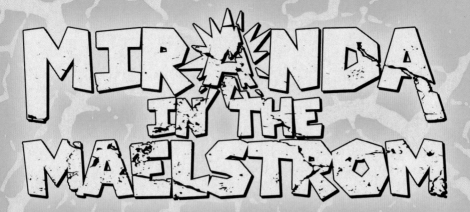

CHAPTER 3: "SAIL THE SPINNING BOTTLE."

SCRIPT BY RILEY DASHIELL BIEHL
ART & COLORS BY JAMIE JONES

LETTERING BY TAYLOR ESPOSITO
SCRIPT EDITING BY BRITTANY MATTER
COVER BY JAMIE JONES

BRYAN SEATON: PUBLISHER / CEO
VITO DELSANTE: EDITOR IN CHIEF
JASON MARTIN: PUBLISHER - DANGER ZONE
CHAD CICCONI: CHIEF PORTAL INSPECTOR

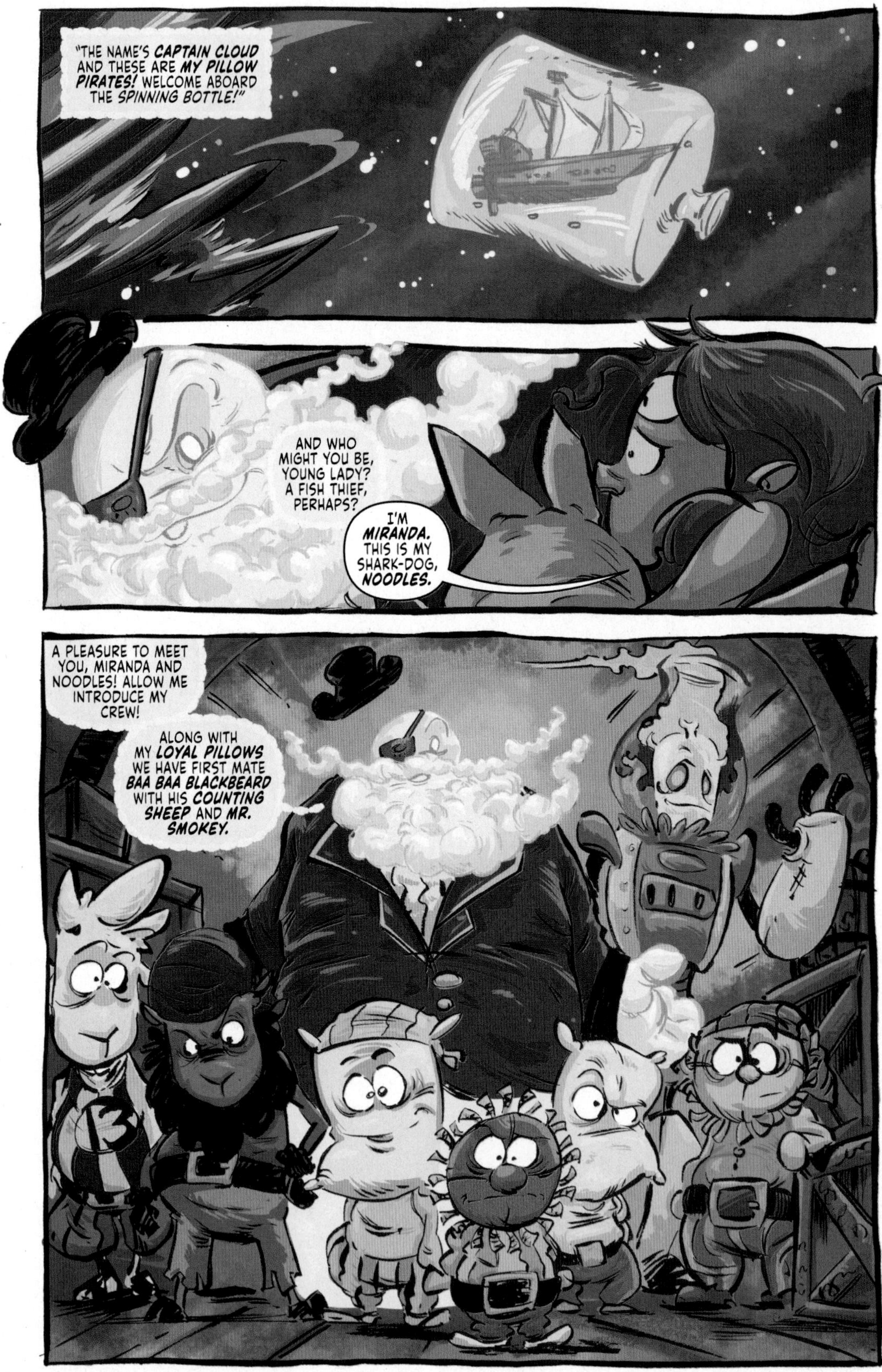
"THE NAME'S CAPTAIN CLOUD AND THESE ARE MY PILLOW PIRATES! WELCOME ABOARD THE SPINNING BOTTLE!"
AND WHO MIGHT YOU BE, YOUNG LADY? A FISH THIEF, PERHAPS?
I'M MIRANDA. THIS IS MY SHARK-DOG, NOODLES.
A PLEASURE TO MEET YOU, MIRANDA AND NOODLES! ALLOW ME INTRODUCE MY CREW!
ALONG WITH MY LOYAL PILLOWS WE HAVE FIRST MATE BAA BAA BLACKBEARD WITH HIS COUNTING SHEEP AND MR. SMOKEY.

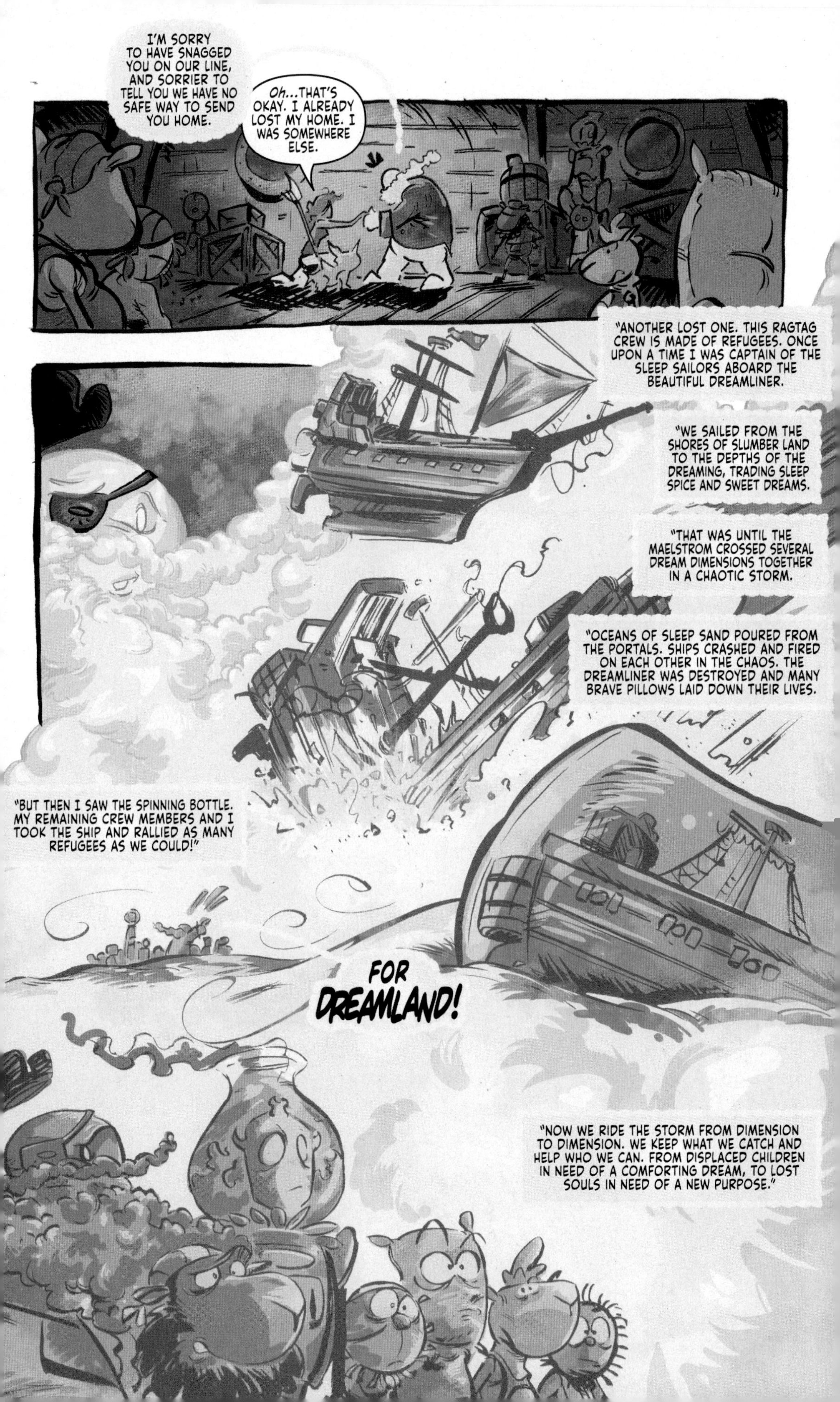
I'M SORRY TO HAVE SNAGGED YOU ON OUR LINE, AND SORRIER TO TELL YOU WE HAVE NO SAFE WAY TO SEND YOU HOME.
Oh...THAT'S OKAY. I ALREADY LOST MY HOME. I WAS SOMEWHERE ELSE.
"ANOTHER LOST ONE. THIS RAGTAG CREW IS MADE OF REFUGEES. ONCE UPON A TIME I WAS CAPTAIN OF THE SLEEP SAILORS ABOARD THE BEAUTIFUL DREAMLINER.
"WE SAILED FROM THE SHORES OF SLUMBER LAND TO THE DEPTHS OF THE DREAMING, TRADING SLEEP SPICE AND SWEET DREAMS.
"THAT WAS UNTIL THE MAELSTROM CROSSED SEVERAL DREAM DIMENSIONS TOGETHER IN A CHAOTIC STORM.
"OCEANS OF SLEEP SAND POURED FROM THE PORTALS. SHIPS CRASHED AND FIRED ON EACH OTHER IN THE CHAOS. THE DREAMLINER WAS DESTROYED AND MANY BRAVE PILLOWS LAID DOWN THEIR LIVES.
"BUT THEN I SAW THE SPINNING BOTTLE. MY REMAINING CREW MEMBERS AND I TOOK THE SHIP AND RALLIED AS MANY REFUGEES AS WE COULD!"
FOR DREAMLAND!
"NOW WE RIDE THE STORM FROM DIMENSION TO DIMENSION. WE KEEP WHAT WE CATCH AND HELP WHO WE CAN. FROM DISPLACED CHILDREN IN NEED OF A COMFORTING DREAM, TO LOST SOULS IN NEED OF A NEW PURPOSE."

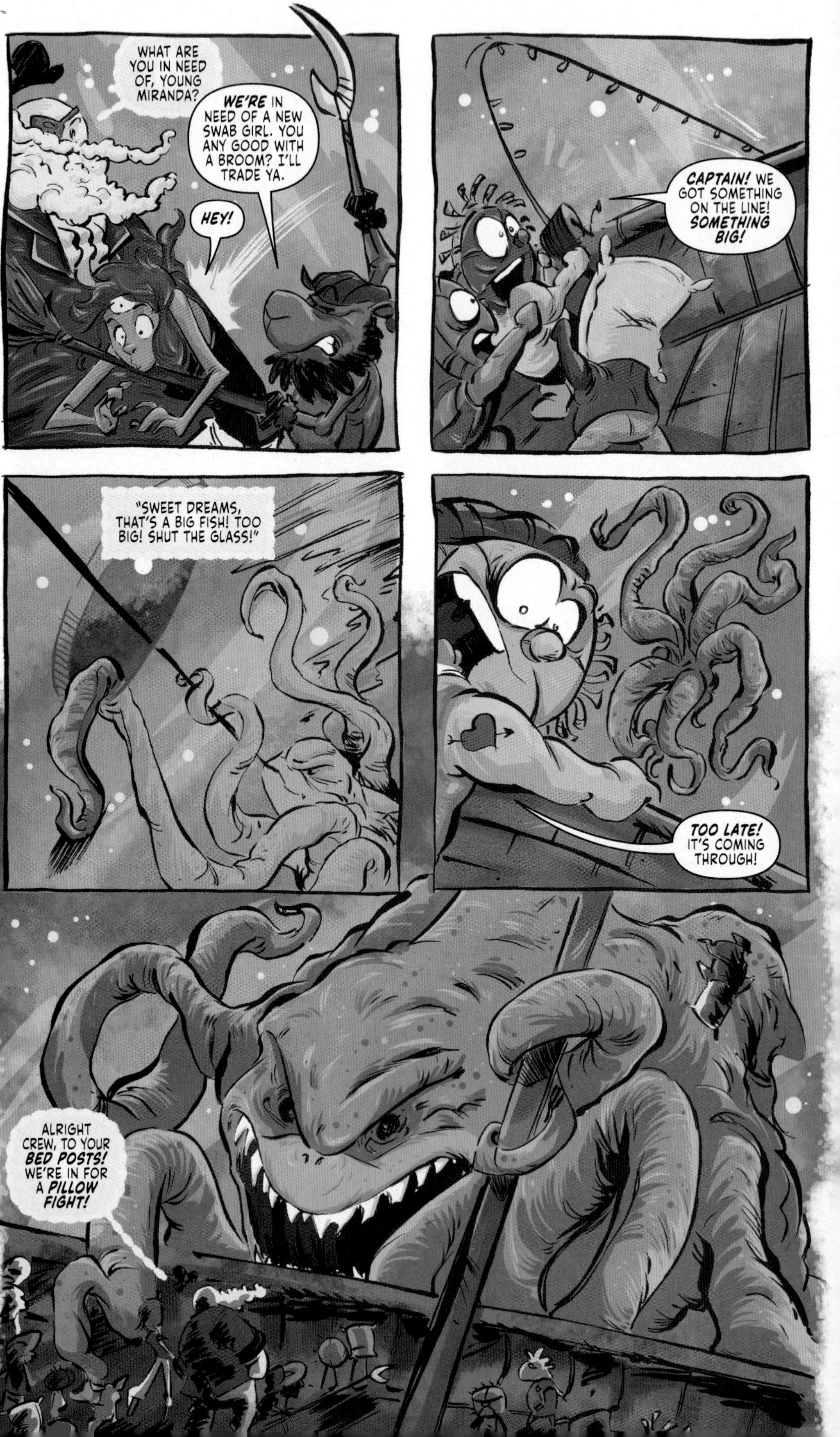
WHAT ARE YOU IN NEED OF, YOUNG MIRANDA?
WE'RE IN NEED OF A NEW SWAB GIRL. YOU ANY GOOD WITH A BROOM? I'LL TRADE YA.
HEY!
CAPTAIN! WE GOT SOMETHING ON THE LINE! SOMETHING BIG!
"SWEET DREAMS, THAT'S A BIG FISH! TOO BIG! SHUT THE GLASS!"
TOO LATE! IT'S COMING THROUGH!
ALRIGHT CREW, TO YOUR BED POSTS! WE'RE IN FOR A PILLOW FIGHT!

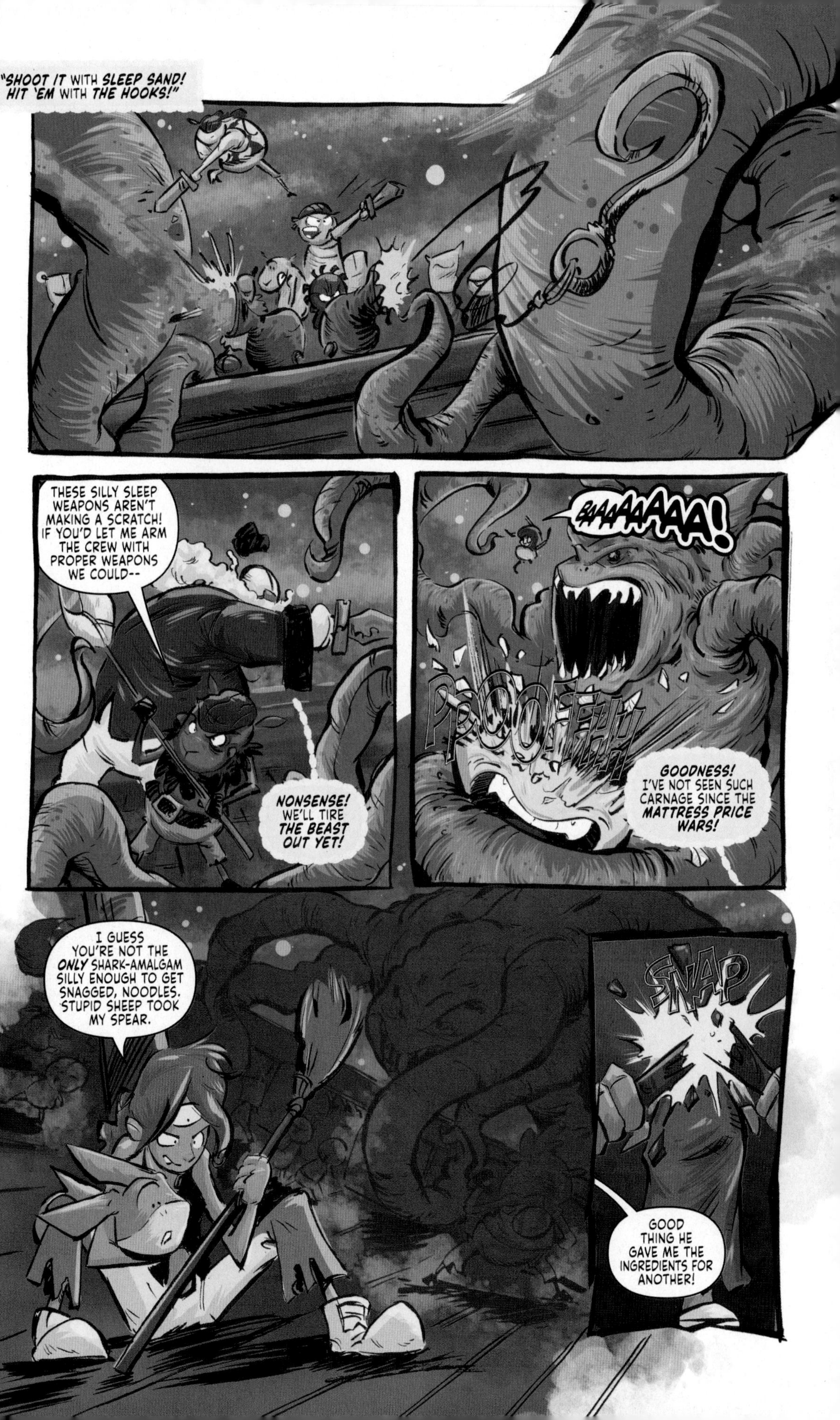
"SHOOT IT WITH SLEEP SAND! HIT 'EM WITH THE HOOKS!"
THESE SILLY SLEEP WEAPONS AREN'T MAKING A SCRATCH! IF YOU'D LET ME ARM THE CREW WITH PROPER WEAPONS WE COULD--
NONSENSE! WE'LL TIRE THE BEAST OUT YET!
BAAAAAAAA!
PPOOFFHH
GOODNESS! I'VE NOT SEEN SUCH CARNAGE SINCE THE MATTRESS PRICE WARS!
I GUESS YOU'RE NOT THE ONLY SHARK-AMALGAM SILLY ENOUGH TO GET SNAGGED, NOODLES. STUPID SHEEP TOOK MY SPEAR.
SNAP
GOOD THING HE GAVE ME THE INGREDIENTS FOR ANOTHER!

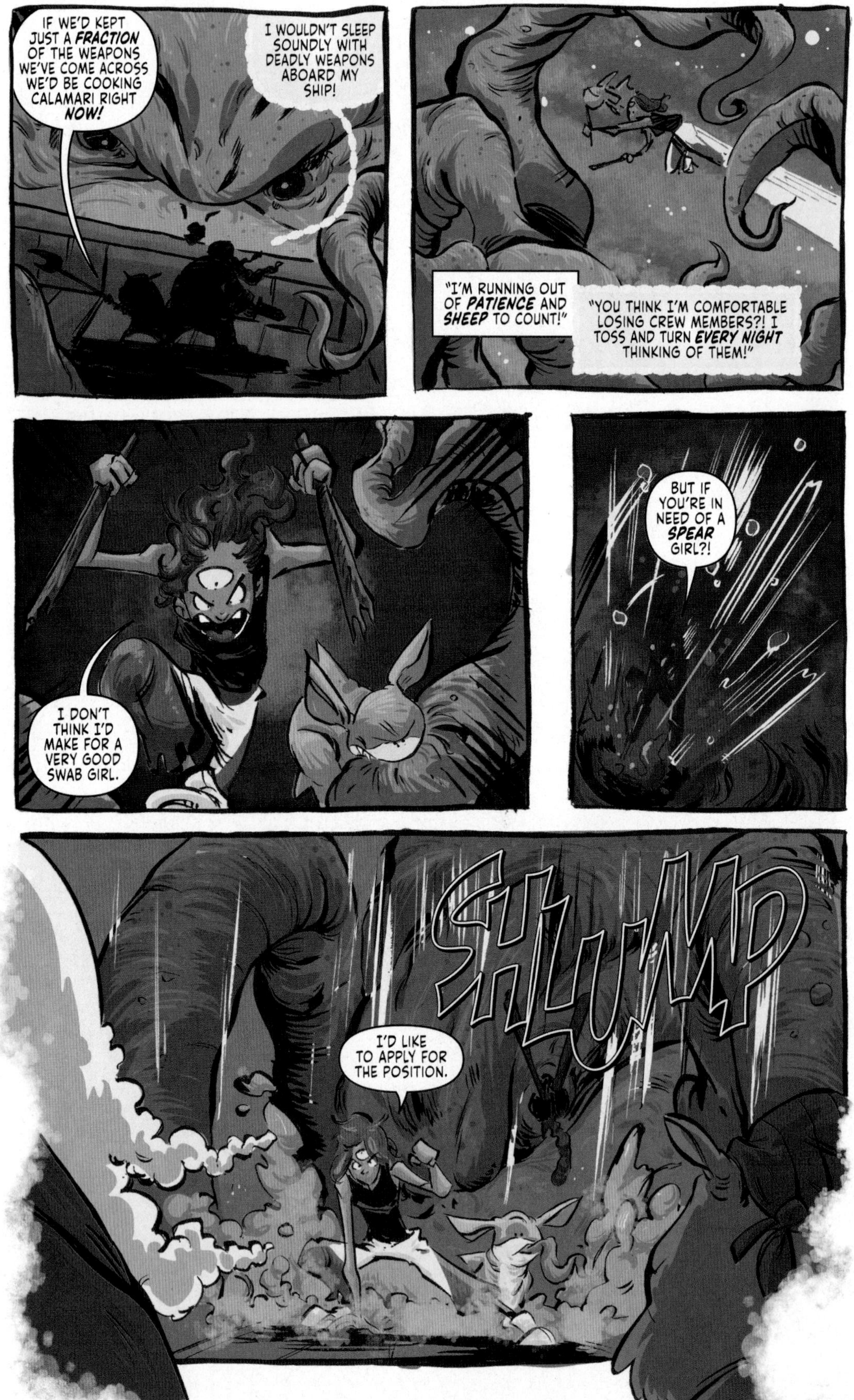
IF WE'D KEPT JUST A FRACTION OF THE WEAPONS WE'VE COME ACROSS WE'D BE COOKING CALAMARI RIGHT NOW!
I WOULDN'T SLEEP SOUNDLY WITH DEADLY WEAPONS ABOARD MY SHIP!
"I'M RUNNING OUT OF PATIENCE AND SHEEP TO COUNT!"
"YOU THINK I'M COMFORTABLE LOSING CREW MEMBERS?! I TOSS AND TURN EVERY NIGHT THINKING OF THEM!"
I DON'T THINK I'D MAKE FOR A VERY GOOD SWAB GIRL.
BUT IF YOU'RE IN NEED OF A SPEAR GIRL?!
SHLUMP
I'D LIKE TO APPLY FOR THE POSITION.

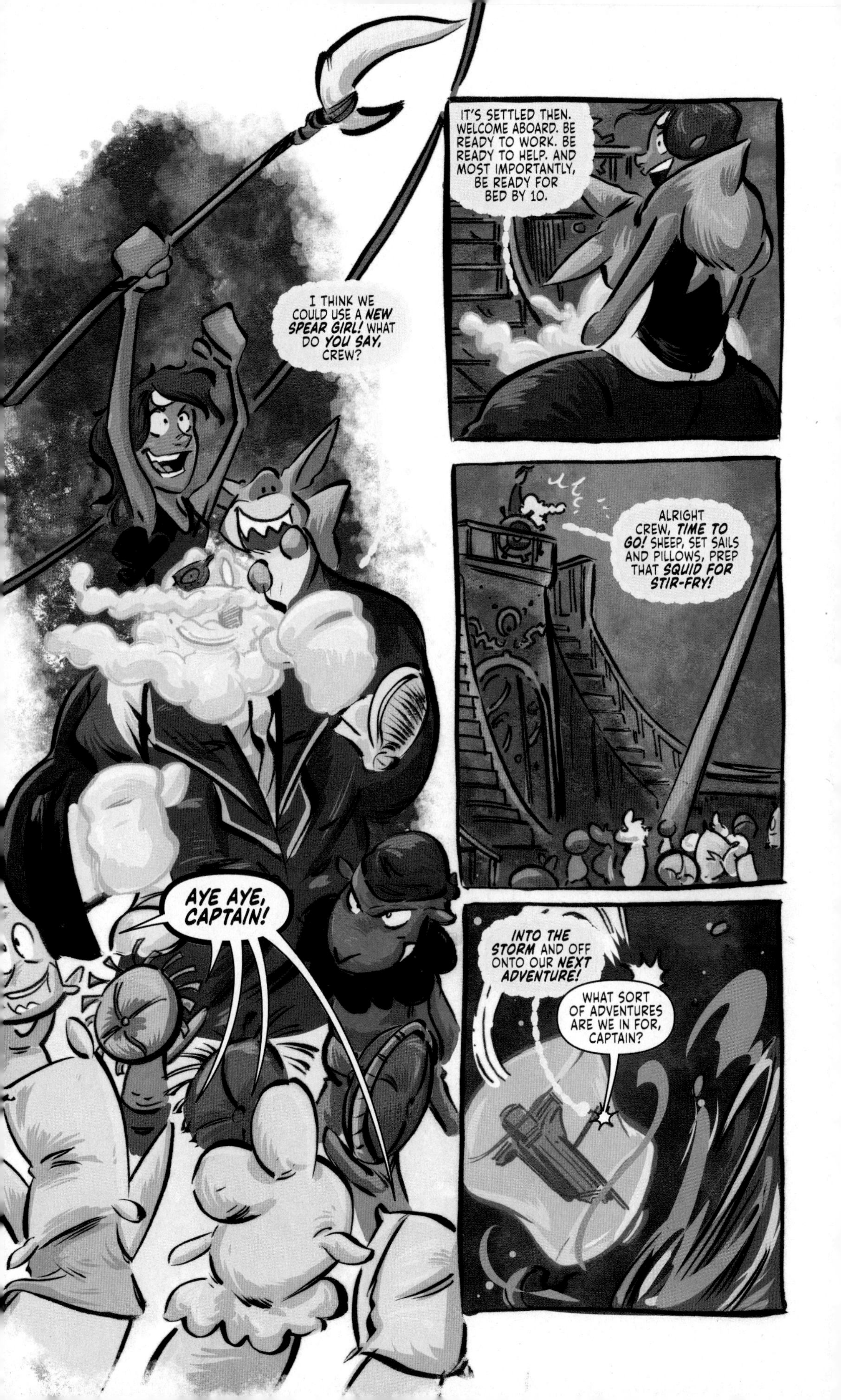
I THINK WE COULD USE A NEW SPEAR GIRL! WHAT DO YOU SAY, CREW?
AYE AYE, CAPTAIN!
IT'S SETTLED THEN. WELCOME ABOARD. BE READY TO WORK. BE READY TO HELP. AND MOST IMPORTANTLY, BE READY FOR BED BY 10.
ALRIGHT CREW, TIME TO GO! SHEEP, SET SAILS AND PILLOWS, PREP THAT SQUID FOR STIR-FRY!
INTO THE STORM AND OFF ONTO OUR NEXT ADVENTURE!
WHAT SORT OF ADVENTURES ARE WE IN FOR, CAPTAIN?

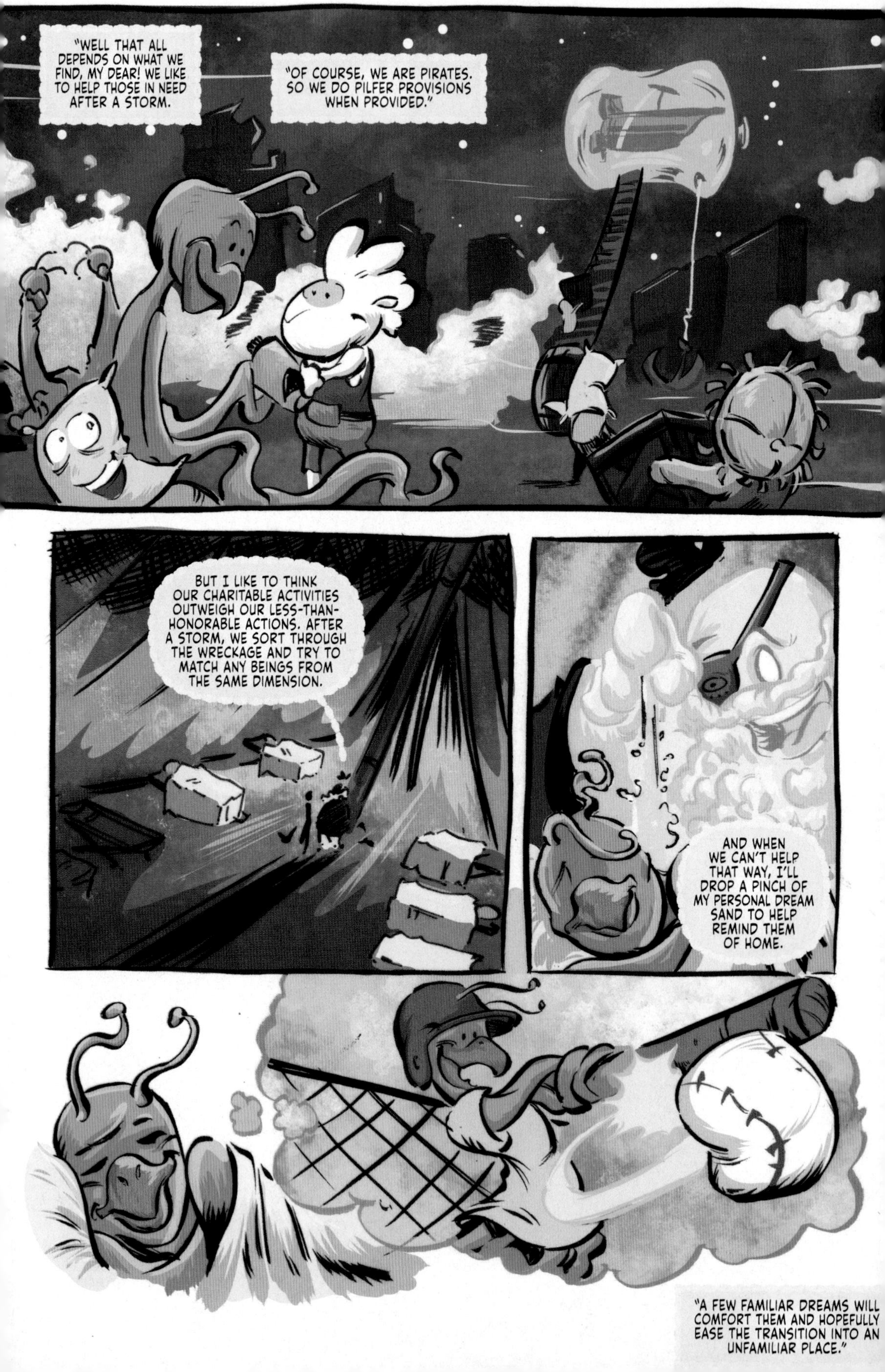
"WELL THAT ALL DEPENDS ON WHAT WE FIND, MY DEAR! WE LIKE TO HELP THOSE IN NEED AFTER A STORM.
"OF COURSE, WE ARE PIRATES. SO WE DO PILFER PROVISIONS WHEN PROVIDED."
BUT I LIKE TO THINK OUR CHARITABLE ACTIVITIES OUTWEIGH OUR LESS-THAN-HONORABLE ACTIONS. AFTER A STORM, WE SORT THROUGH THE WRECKAGE AND TRY TO MATCH ANY BEINGS FROM THE SAME DIMENSION.
AND WHEN WE CAN'T HELP THAT WAY, I'LL DROP A PINCH OF MY PERSONAL DREAM SAND TO HELP REMIND THEM OF HOME.
"A FEW FAMILIAR DREAMS WILL COMFORT THEM AND HOPEFULLY EASE THE TRANSITION INTO AN UNFAMILIAR PLACE."

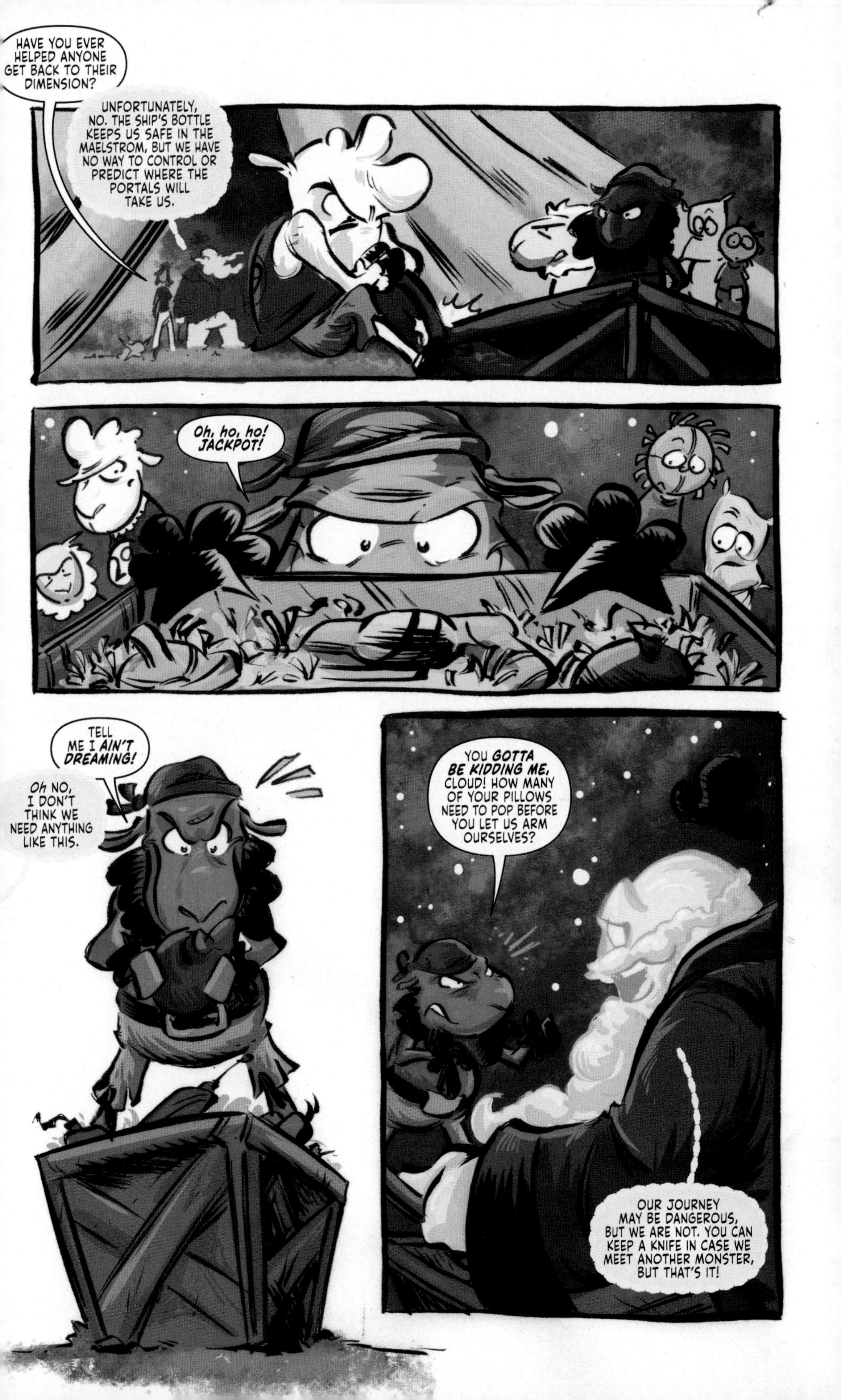
HAVE YOU EVER HELPED ANYONE GET BACK TO THEIR DIMENSION?
UNFORTUNATELY, NO. THE SHIP'S BOTTLE KEEPS US SAFE IN THE MAELSTROM, BUT WE HAVE NO WAY TO CONTROL OR PREDICT WHERE THE PORTALS WILL TAKE US.
Oh, ho, ho! JACKPOT!
TELL ME I AIN'T DREAMING!
Oh NO, I DON'T THINK WE NEED ANYTHING LIKE THIS.
YOU GOTTA BE KIDDING ME, CLOUD! HOW MANY OF YOUR PILLOWS NEED TO POP BEFORE YOU LET US ARM OURSELVES?
OUR JOURNEY MAY BE DANGEROUS, BUT WE ARE NOT. YOU CAN KEEP A KNIFE IN CASE WE MEET ANOTHER MONSTER, BUT THAT'S IT!

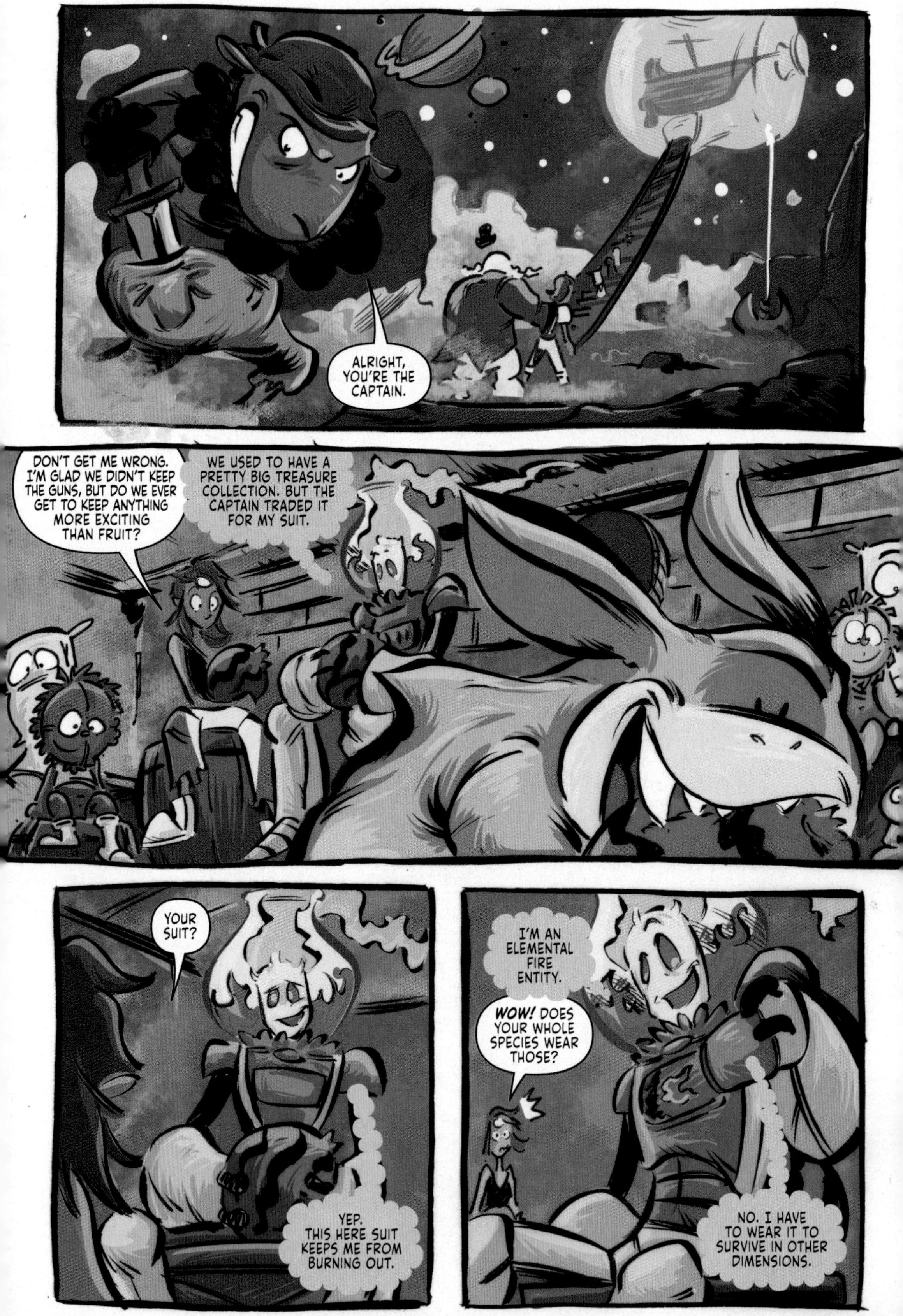
ALRIGHT, YOU'RE THE CAPTAIN.
DON'T GET ME WRONG. I'M GLAD WE DIDN'T KEEP THE GUNS, BUT DO WE EVER GET TO KEEP ANYTHING MORE EXCITING THAN FRUIT?
WE USED TO HAVE A PRETTY BIG TREASURE COLLECTION. BUT THE CAPTAIN TRADED IT FOR MY SUIT.
YOUR SUIT?
YEP. THIS HERE SUIT KEEPS ME FROM BURNING OUT.
I'M AN ELEMENTAL FIRE ENTITY.
WOW! DOES YOUR WHOLE SPECIES WEAR THOSE?
NO. I HAVE TO WEAR IT TO SURVIVE IN OTHER DIMENSIONS.

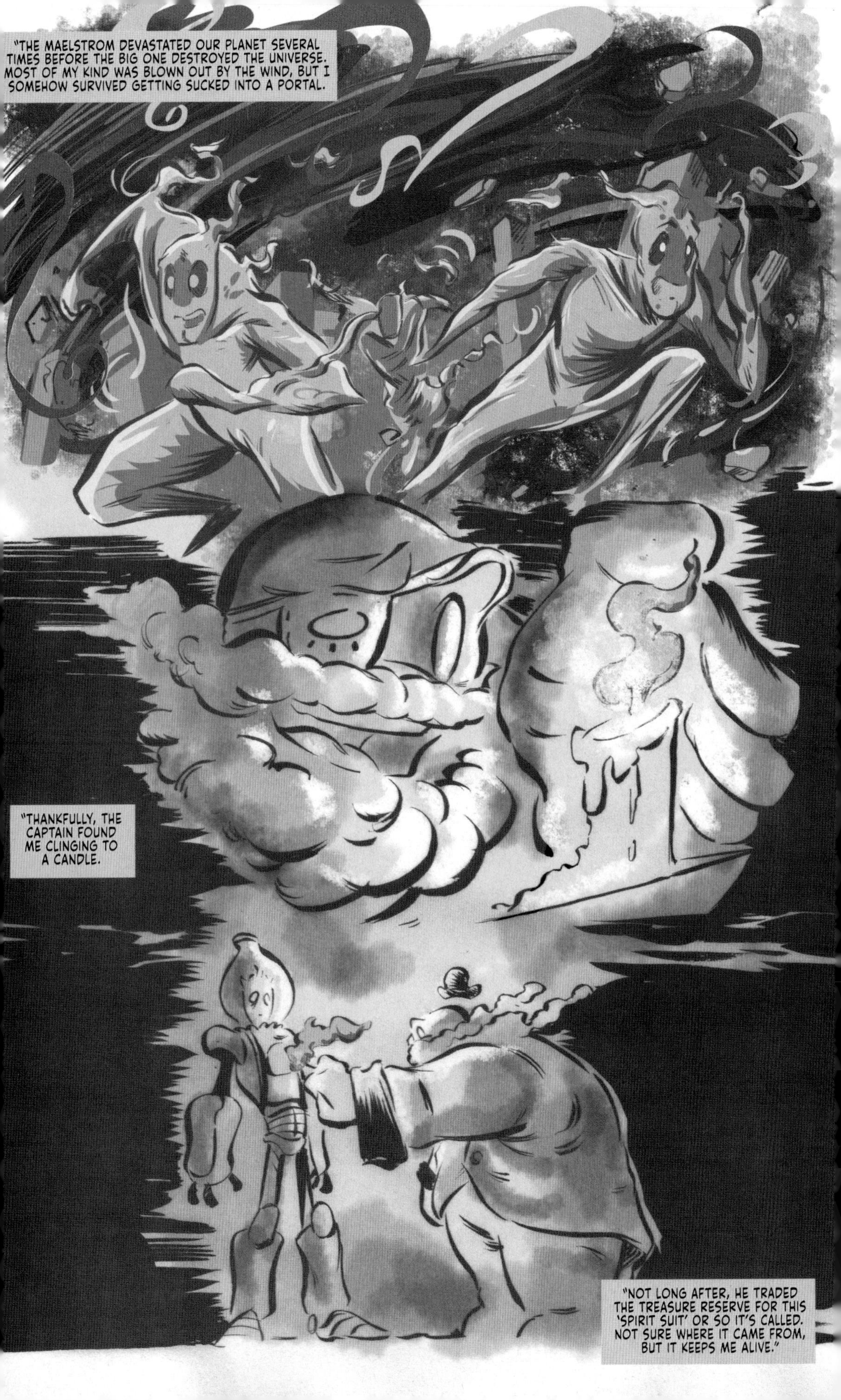
"THE MAELSTROM DEVASTATED OUR PLANET SEVERAL TIMES BEFORE THE BIG ONE DESTROYED THE UNIVERSE. MOST OF MY KIND WAS BLOWN OUT BY THE WIND, BUT I SOMEHOW SURVIVED GETTING SUCKED INTO A PORTAL.
"THANKFULLY, THE CAPTAIN FOUND ME CLINGING TO A CANDLE.
"NOT LONG AFTER, HE TRADED THE TREASURE RESERVE FOR THIS 'SPIRIT SUIT' OR SO IT'S CALLED. NOT SURE WHERE IT CAME FROM, BUT IT KEEPS ME ALIVE."

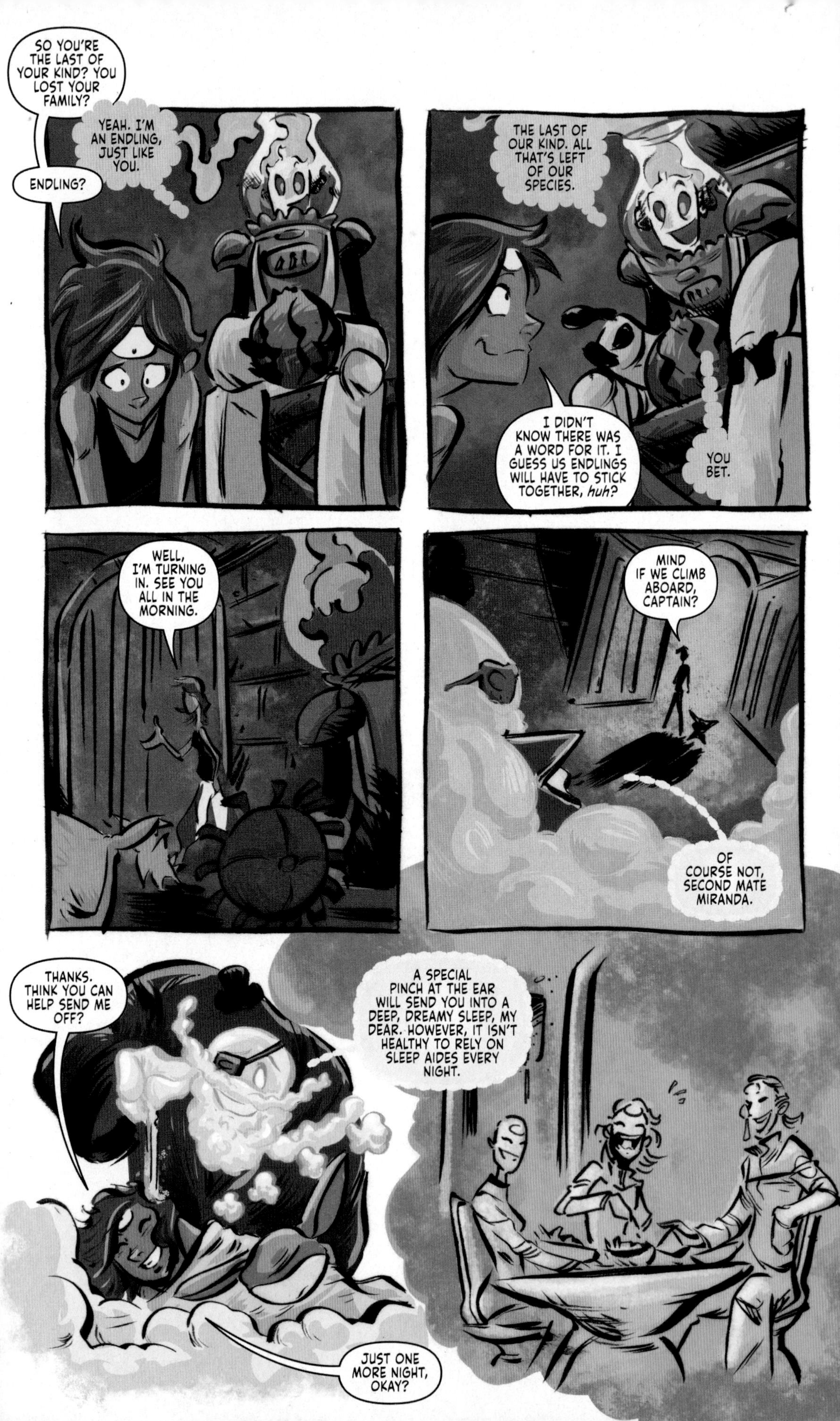
SO YOU'RE THE LAST OF YOUR KIND? YOU LOST YOUR FAMILY?
YEAH. I'M AN ENDLING, JUST LIKE YOU.
ENDLING?
THE LAST OF OUR KIND. ALL THAT'S LEFT OF OUR SPECIES.
I DIDN'T KNOW THERE WAS A WORD FOR IT. I GUESS US ENDLINGS WILL HAVE TO STICK TOGETHER, *huh*?
YOU BET.
WELL, I'M TURNING IN. SEE YOU ALL IN THE MORNING.
MIND IF WE CLIMB ABOARD, CAPTAIN?
OF COURSE NOT, SECOND MATE MIRANDA.
THANKS. THINK YOU CAN HELP SEND ME OFF?
A SPECIAL PINCH AT THE EAR WILL SEND YOU INTO A DEEP, DREAMY SLEEP, MY DEAR. HOWEVER, IT ISN'T HEALTHY TO RELY ON SLEEP AIDES EVERY NIGHT.
JUST ONE MORE NIGHT, OKAY?

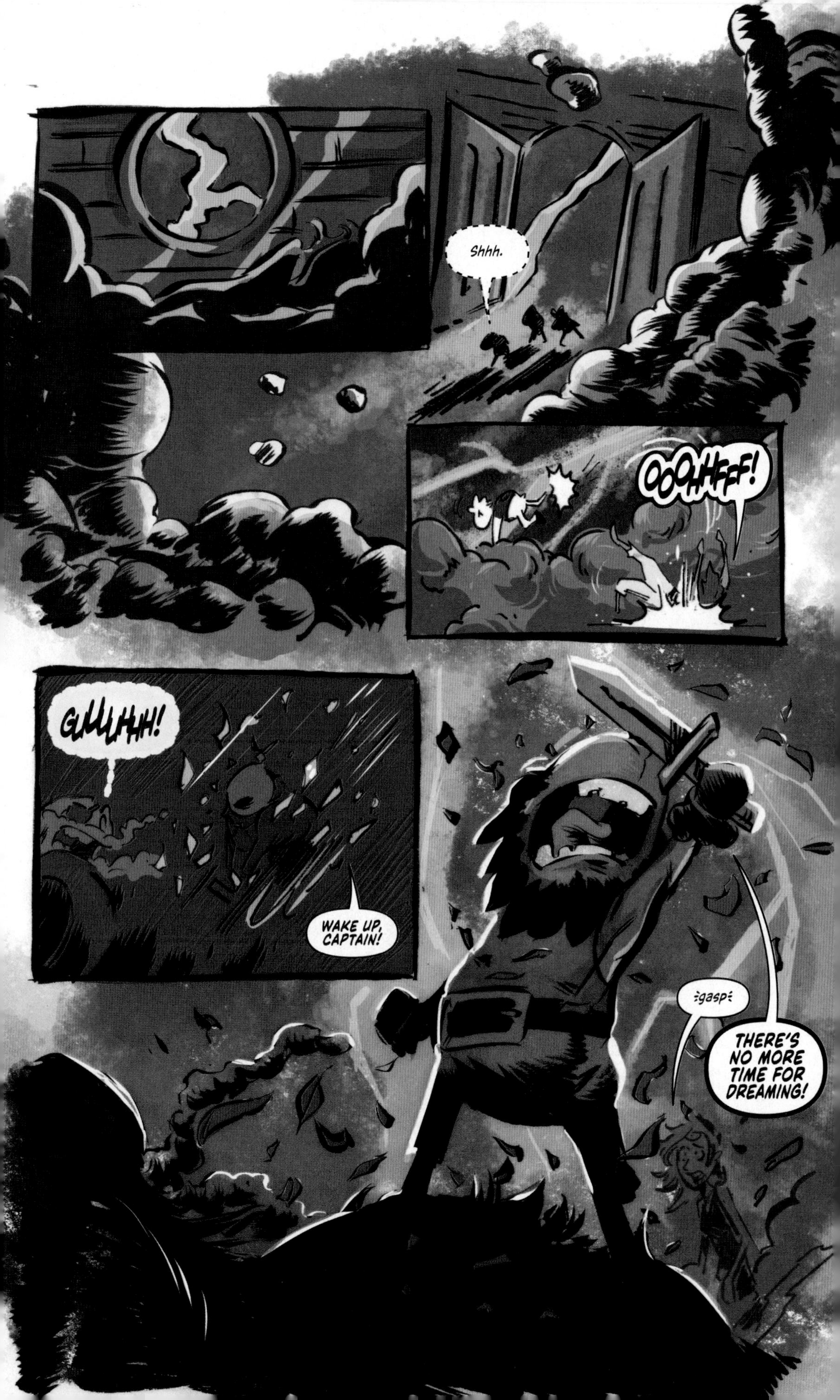

Shhh.
OOOHHFFF!
GUUUHHH!
WAKE UP, CAPTAIN!
gasp
THERE'S NO MORE TIME FOR DREAMING!

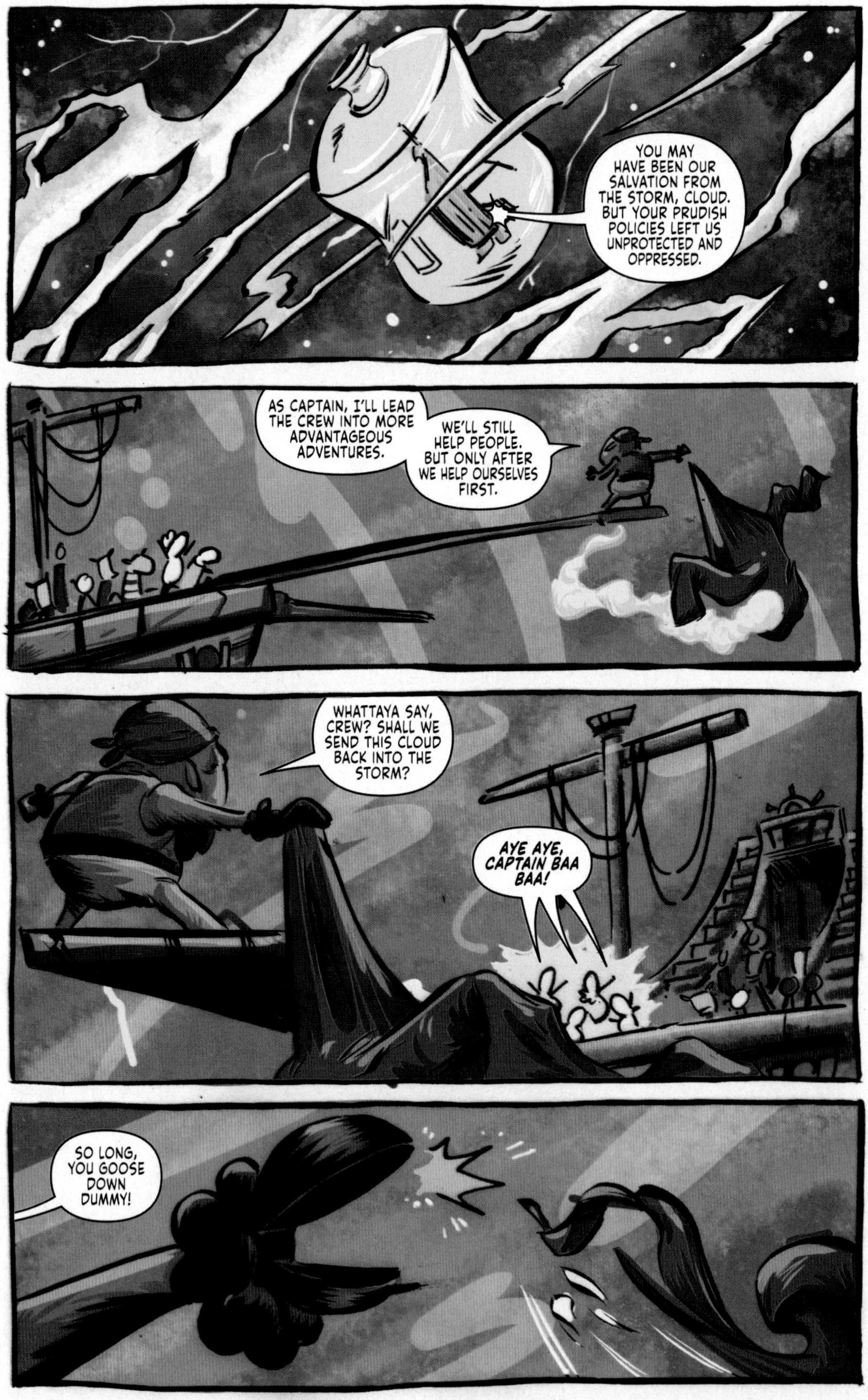
YOU MAY HAVE BEEN OUR SALVATION FROM THE STORM, CLOUD. BUT YOUR PRUDISH POLICIES LEFT US UNPROTECTED AND OPPRESSED.
AS CAPTAIN, I'LL LEAD THE CREW INTO MORE ADVANTAGEOUS ADVENTURES.
WE'LL STILL HELP PEOPLE. BUT ONLY AFTER WE HELP OURSELVES FIRST.
WHATTAYA SAY, CREW? SHALL WE SEND THIS CLOUD BACK INTO THE STORM?
AYE AYE, CAPTAIN BAA BAA!
SO LONG, YOU GOOSE DOWN DUMMY!

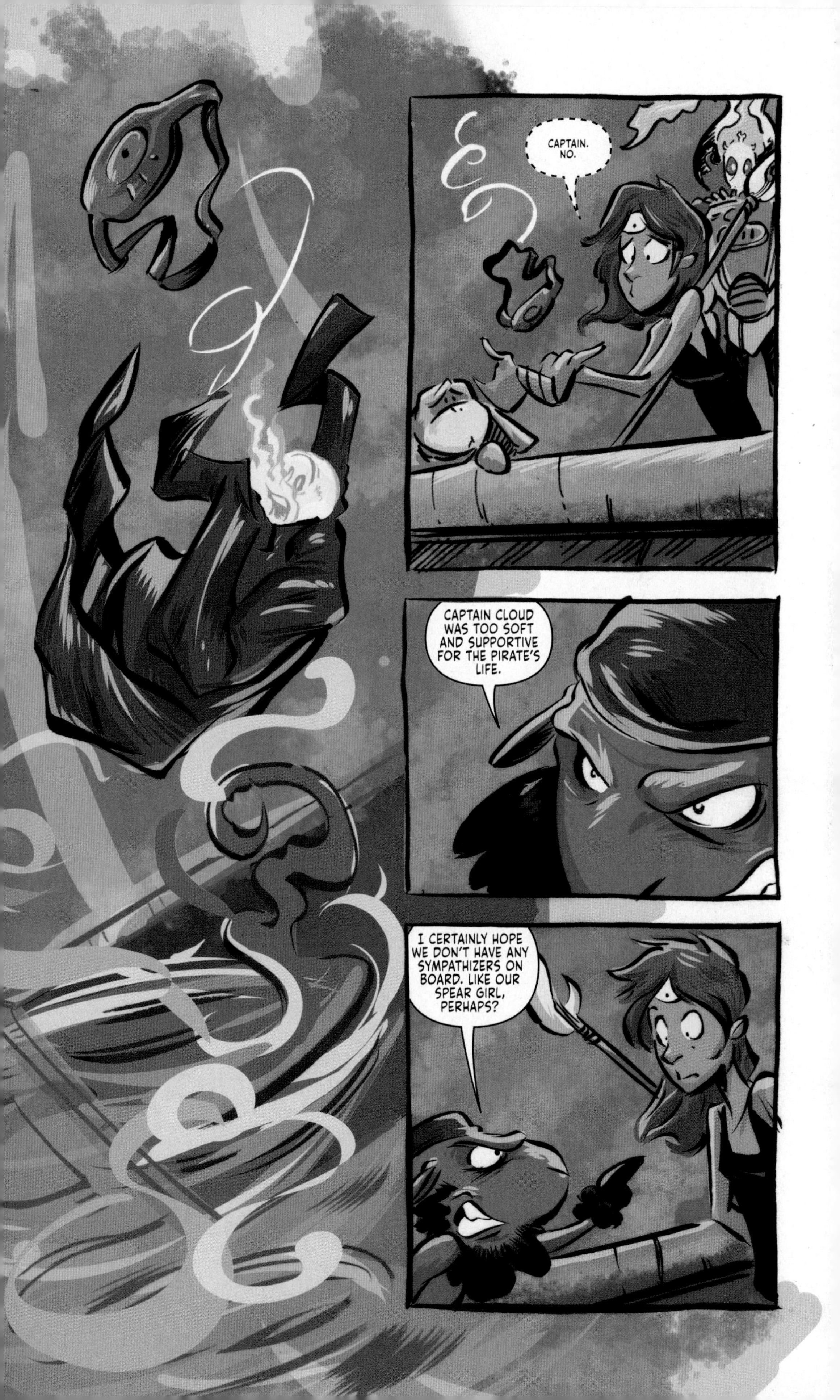
CAPTAIN. NO.
CAPTAIN CLOUD WAS TOO SOFT AND SUPPORTIVE FOR THE PIRATE'S LIFE.
I CERTAINLY HOPE WE DON'T HAVE ANY SYMPATHIZERS ON BOARD. LIKE OUR SPEAR GIRL, PERHAPS?

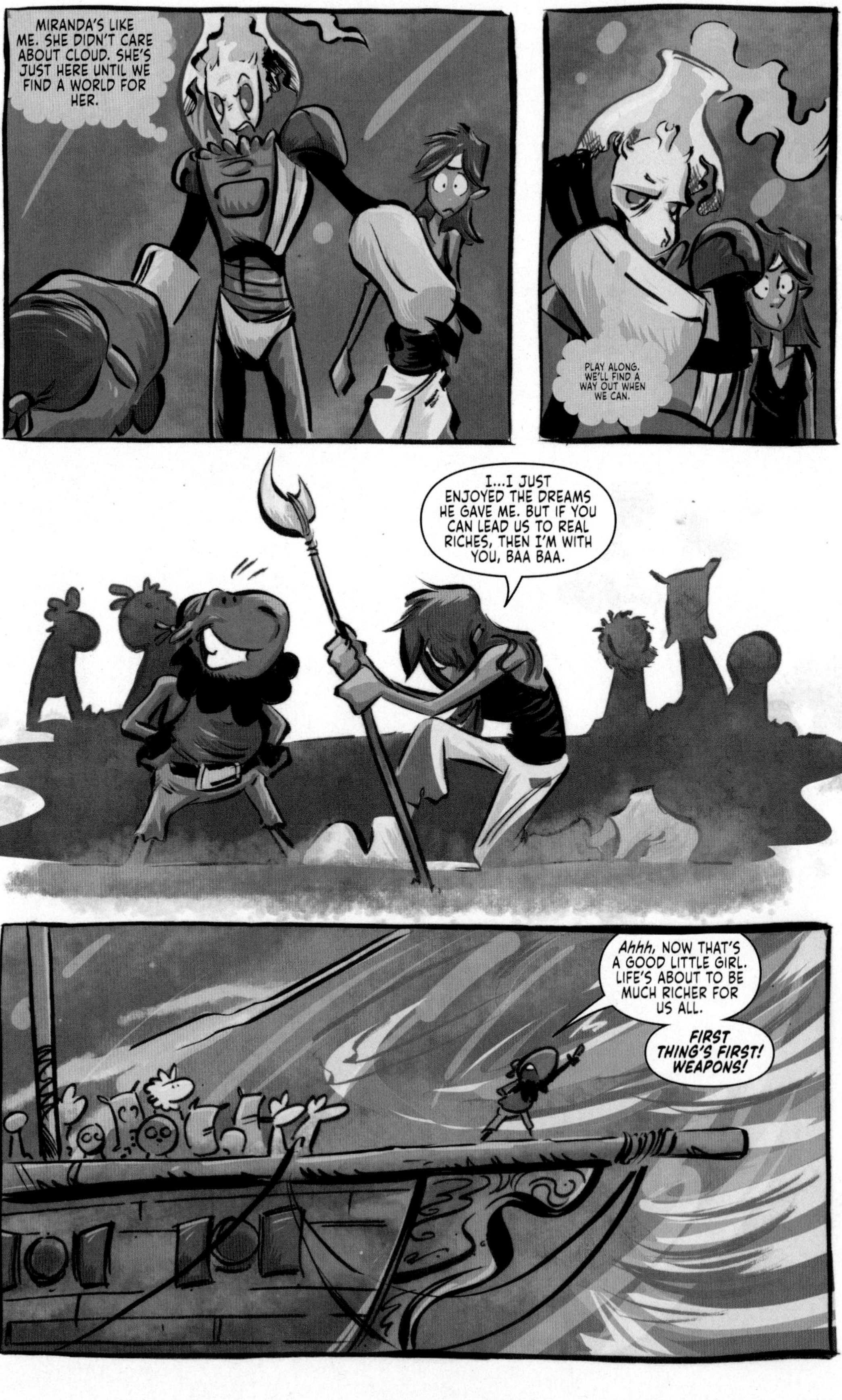
MIRANDA'S LIKE ME. SHE DIDN'T CARE ABOUT CLOUD. SHE'S JUST HERE UNTIL WE FIND A WORLD FOR HER.
PLAY ALONG. WE'LL FIND A WAY OUT WHEN WE CAN.
I...I JUST ENJOYED THE DREAMS HE GAVE ME. BUT IF YOU CAN LEAD US TO REAL RICHES, THEN I'M WITH YOU, BAA BAA.
Ahhh, NOW THAT'S A GOOD LITTLE GIRL. LIFE'S ABOUT TO BE MUCH RICHER FOR US ALL.
FIRST THING'S FIRST! WEAPONS!

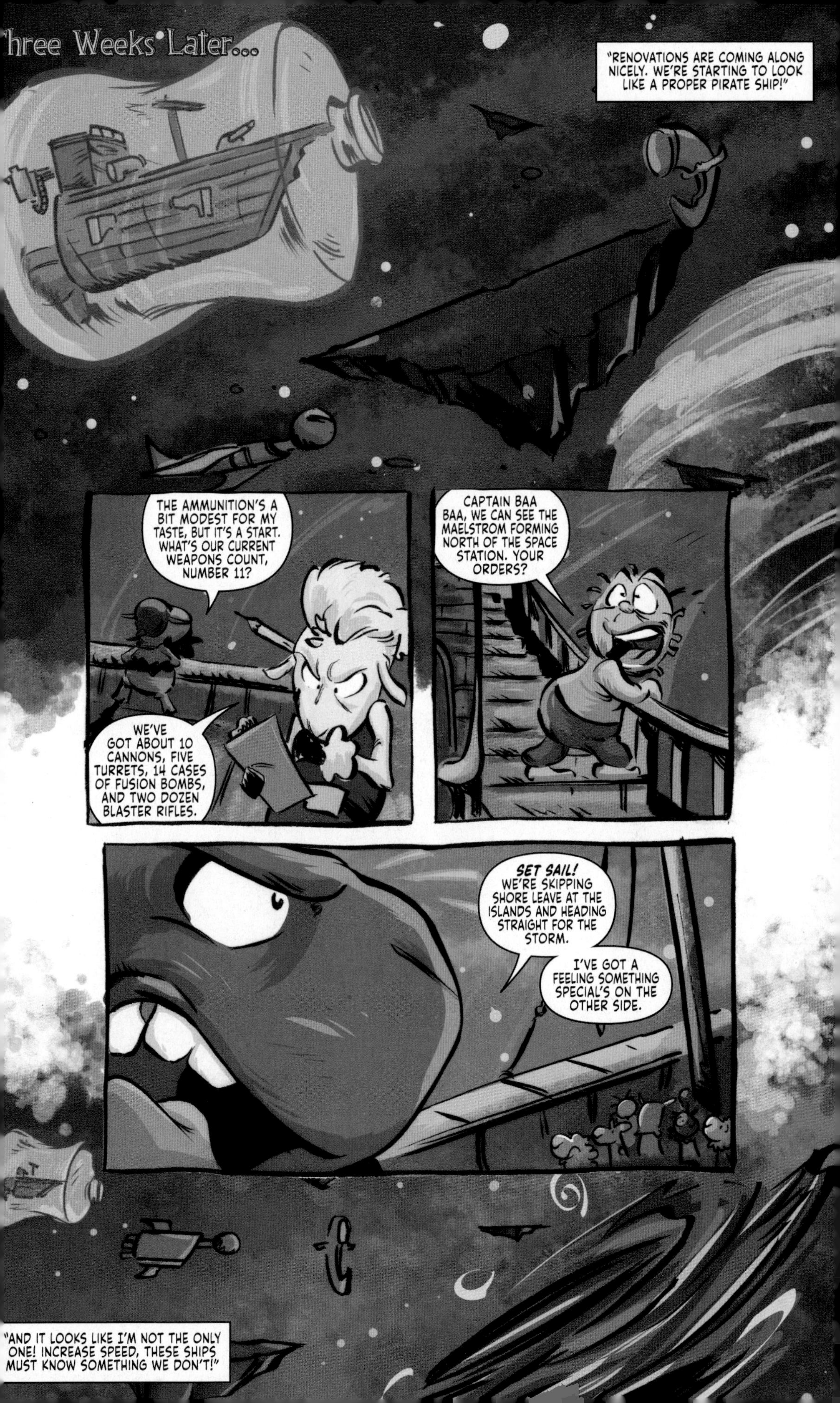
Three Weeks Later...
"RENOVATIONS ARE COMING ALONG NICELY. WE'RE STARTING TO LOOK LIKE A PROPER PIRATE SHIP!"
THE AMMUNITION'S A BIT MODEST FOR MY TASTE, BUT IT'S A START. WHAT'S OUR CURRENT WEAPONS COUNT, NUMBER 11?
WE'VE GOT ABOUT 10 CANNONS, FIVE TURRETS, 14 CASES OF FUSION BOMBS, AND TWO DOZEN BLASTER RIFLES.
CAPTAIN BAA BAA, WE CAN SEE THE MAELSTROM FORMING NORTH OF THE SPACE STATION. YOUR ORDERS?
SET SAIL! WE'RE SKIPPING SHORE LEAVE AT THE ISLANDS AND HEADING STRAIGHT FOR THE STORM.
I'VE GOT A FEELING SOMETHING SPECIAL'S ON THE OTHER SIDE.
"AND IT LOOKS LIKE I'M NOT THE ONLY ONE! INCREASE SPEED, THESE SHIPS MUST KNOW SOMETHING WE DON'T!"

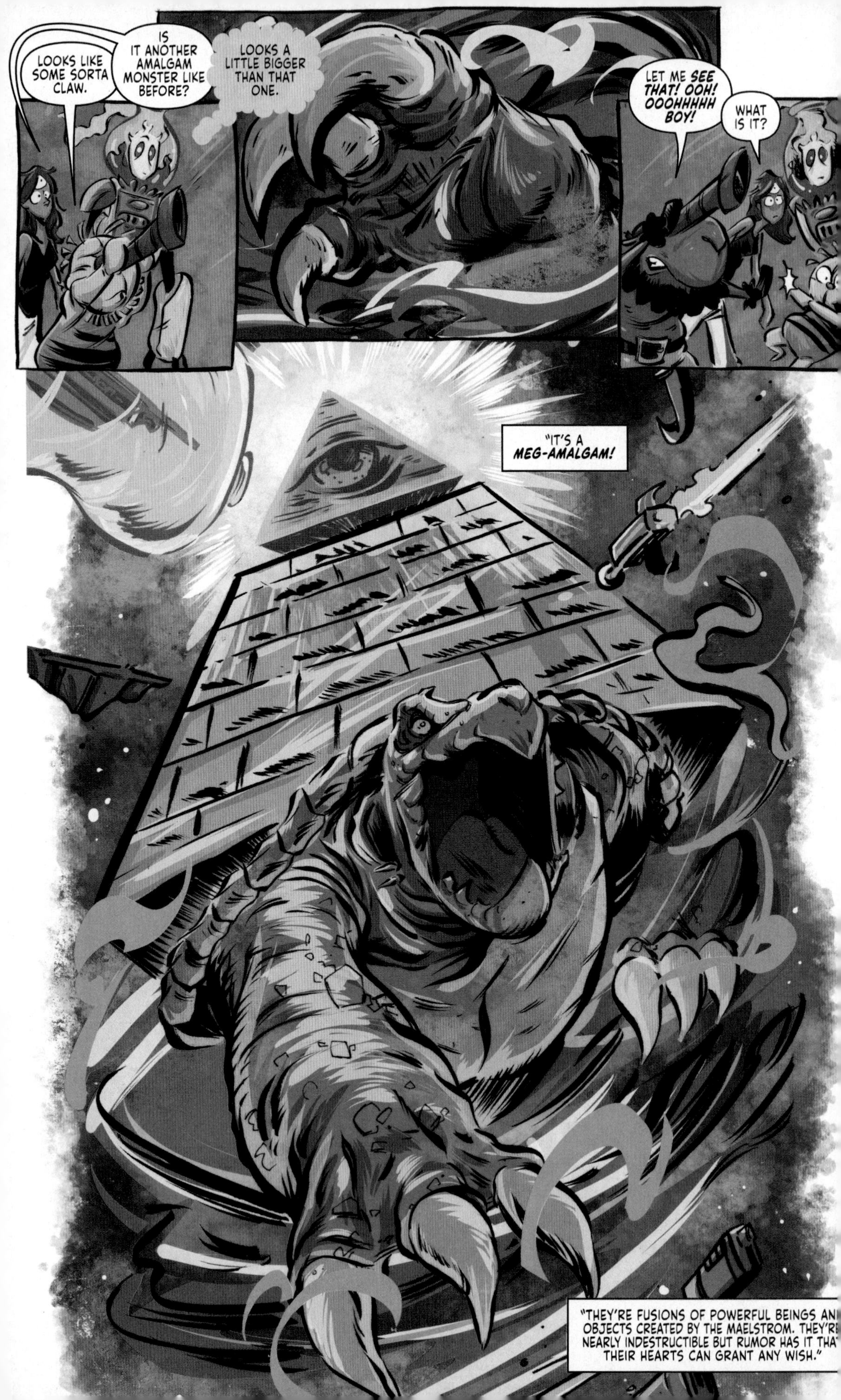

LOOKS LIKE SOME SORTA CLAW.
IS IT ANOTHER AMALGAM MONSTER LIKE BEFORE?
LOOKS A LITTLE BIGGER THAN THAT ONE.
LET ME SEE THAT! OOH! OOOHHHHH BOY!
WHAT IS IT?
"IT'S A MEG-AMALGAM!
"THEY'RE FUSIONS OF POWERFUL BEINGS AN OBJECTS CREATED BY THE MAELSTROM. THEY'R NEARLY INDESTRUCTIBLE BUT RUMOR HAS IT THA THEIR HEARTS CAN GRANT ANY WISH."

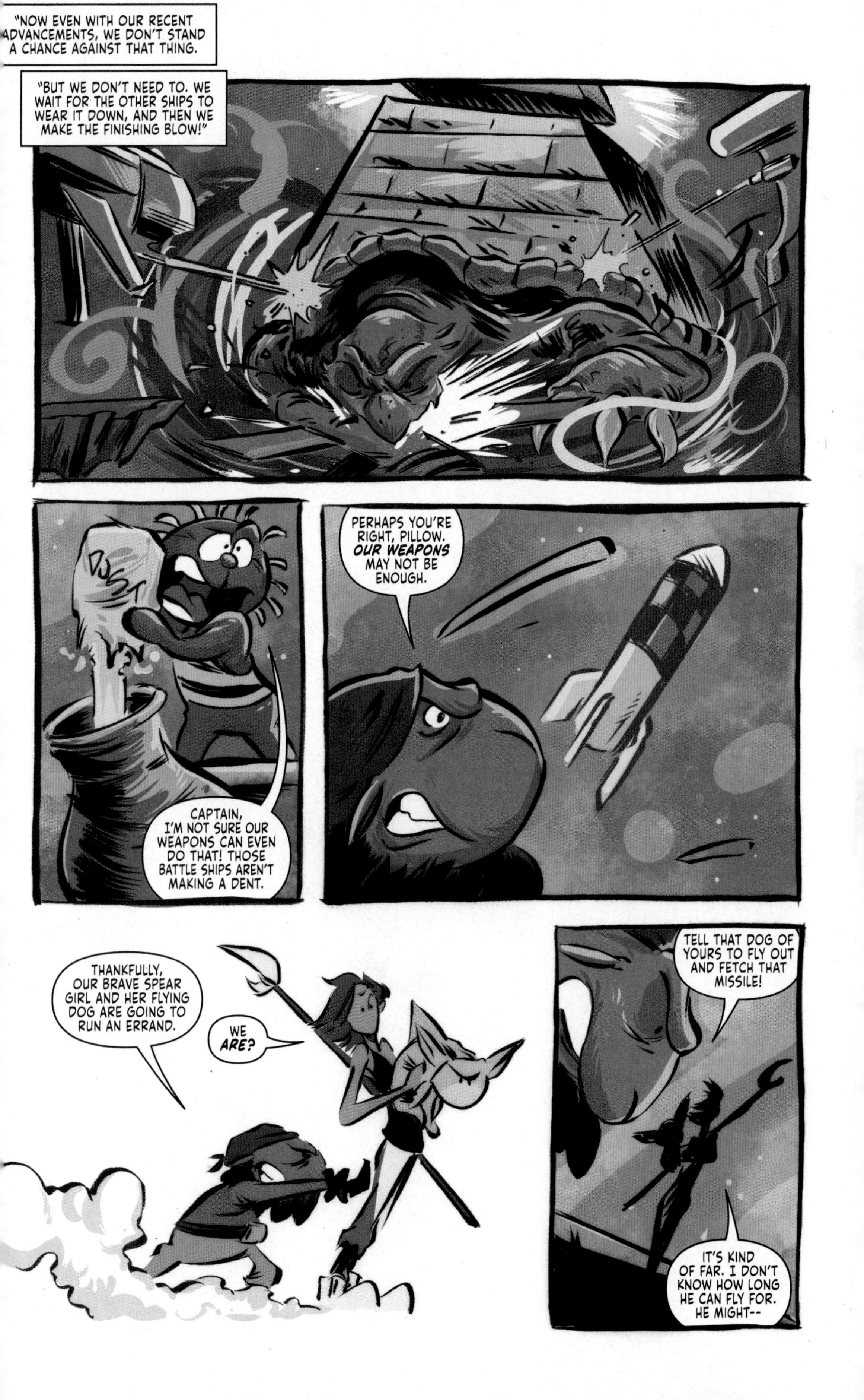
"NOW EVEN WITH OUR RECENT ADVANCEMENTS, WE DON'T STAND A CHANCE AGAINST THAT THING.
"BUT WE DON'T NEED TO. WE WAIT FOR THE OTHER SHIPS TO WEAR IT DOWN, AND THEN WE MAKE THE FINISHING BLOW!"
CAPTAIN, I'M NOT SURE OUR WEAPONS CAN EVEN DO THAT! THOSE BATTLE SHIPS AREN'T MAKING A DENT.
PERHAPS YOU'RE RIGHT, PILLOW. OUR WEAPONS MAY NOT BE ENOUGH.
THANKFULLY, OUR BRAVE SPEAR GIRL AND HER FLYING DOG ARE GOING TO RUN AN ERRAND.
WE ARE?
TELL THAT DOG OF YOURS TO FLY OUT AND FETCH THAT MISSILE!
IT'S KIND OF FAR. I DON'T KNOW HOW LONG HE CAN FLY FOR. HE MIGHT--

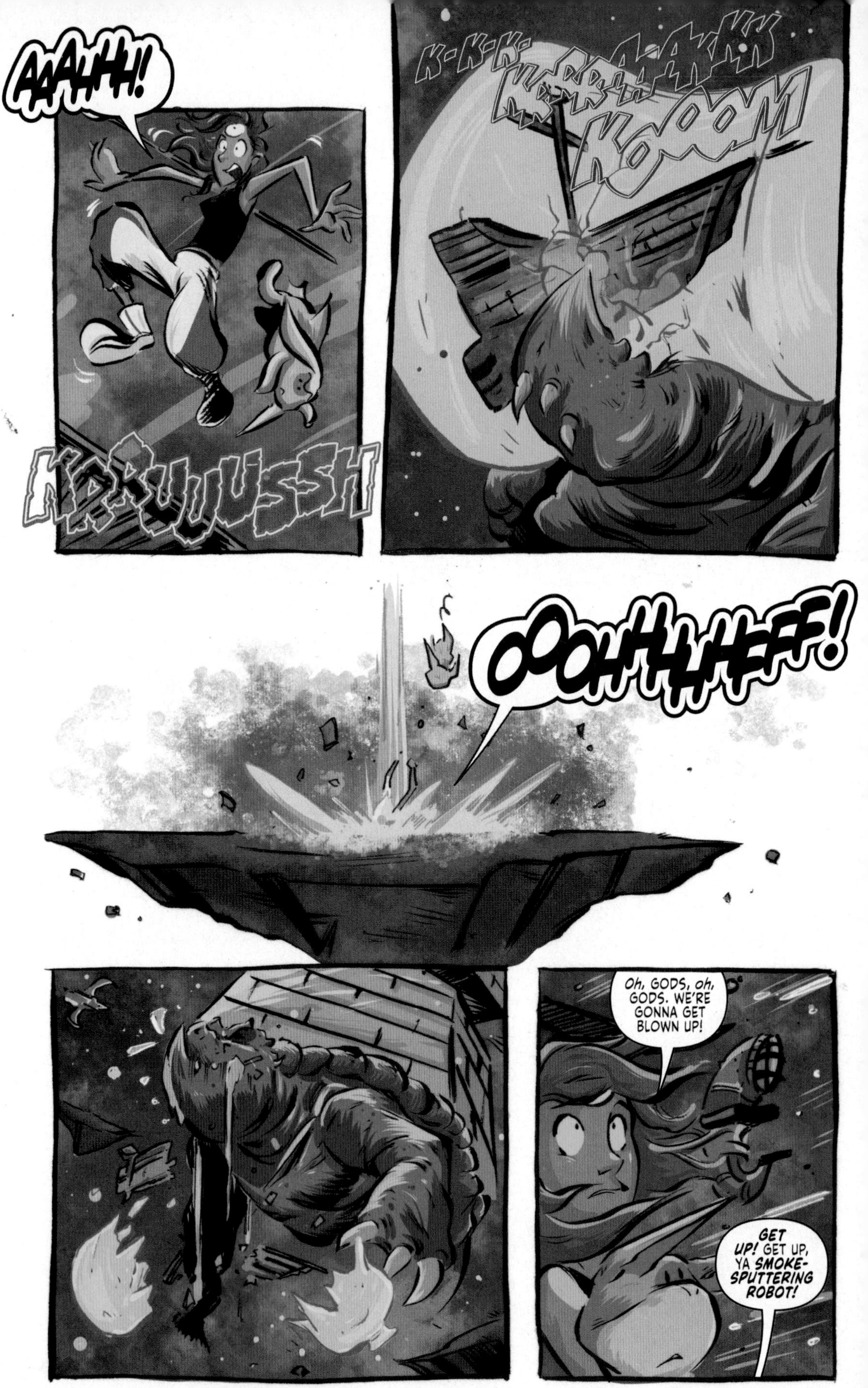
AAAHHH!
K-K-K-
KOOOOM
Oh, GODS, oh, GODS. WE'RE GONNA GET BLOWN UP!
GET UP! GET UP, YA SMOKE-SPUTTERING ROBOT!

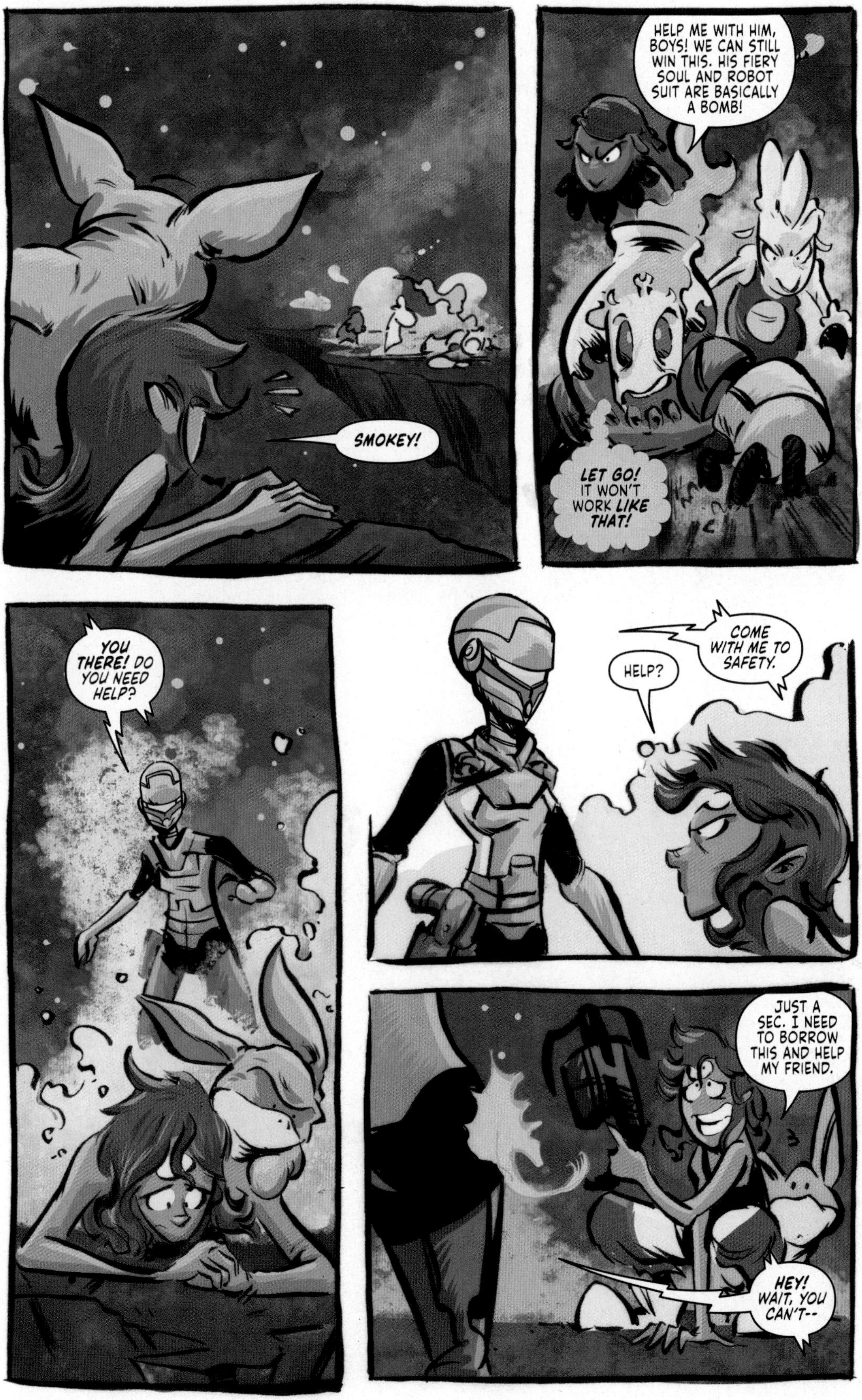
SMOKEY!
HELP ME WITH HIM, BOYS! WE CAN STILL WIN THIS. HIS FIERY SOUL AND ROBOT SUIT ARE BASICALLY A BOMB!
LET GO! IT WON'T WORK LIKE THAT!
YOU THERE! DO YOU NEED HELP?
HELP?
COME WITH ME TO SAFETY.
JUST A SEC. I NEED TO BORROW THIS AND HELP MY FRIEND.
HEY! WAIT, YOU CAN'T--

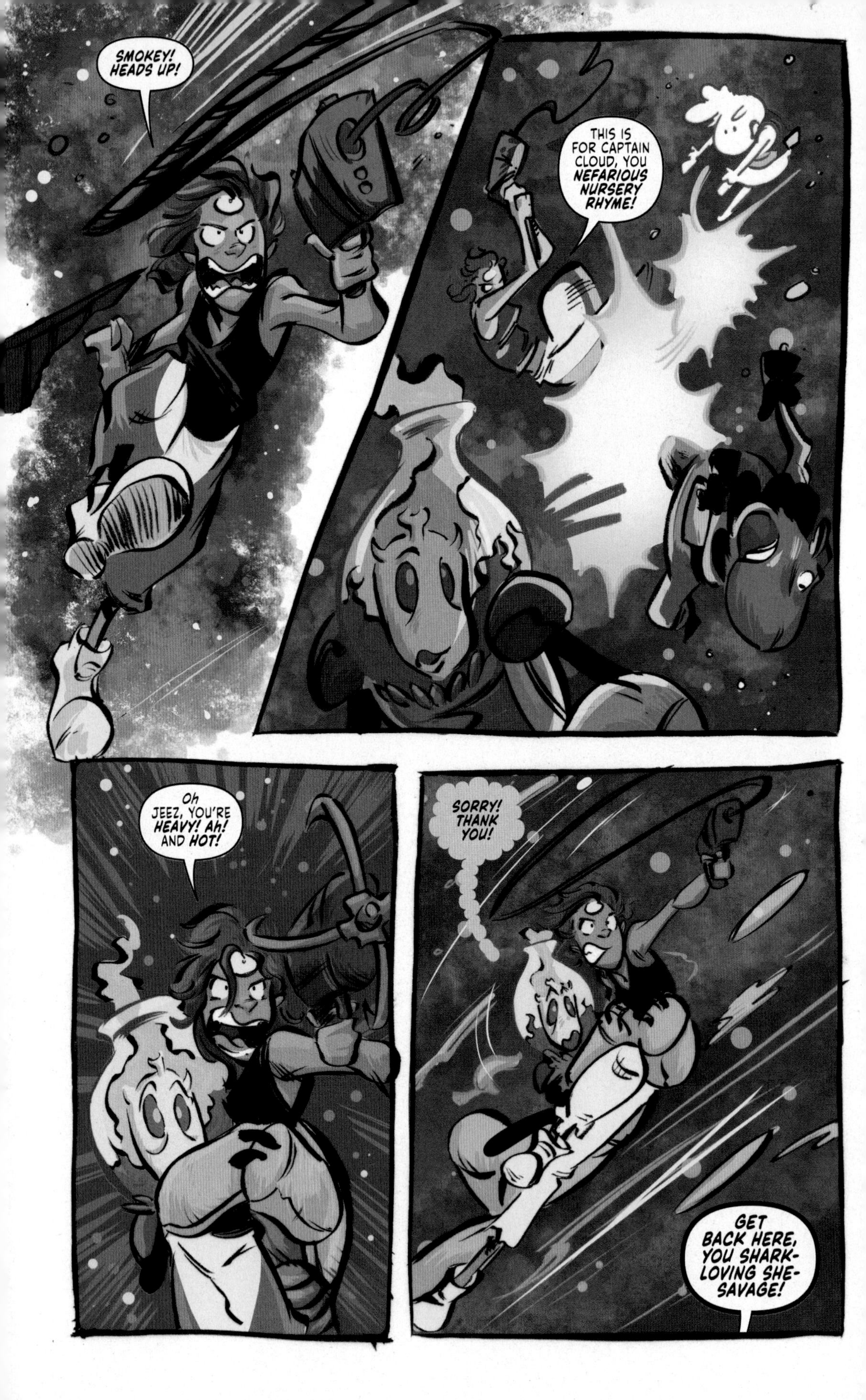
SMOKEY! HEADS UP!
THIS IS FOR CAPTAIN CLOUD, YOU NEFARIOUS NURSERY RHYME!
Oh JEEZ, YOU'RE HEAVY! Ah! AND HOT!
SORRY! THANK YOU!
GET BACK HERE, YOU SHARK-LOVING SHE-SAVAGE!

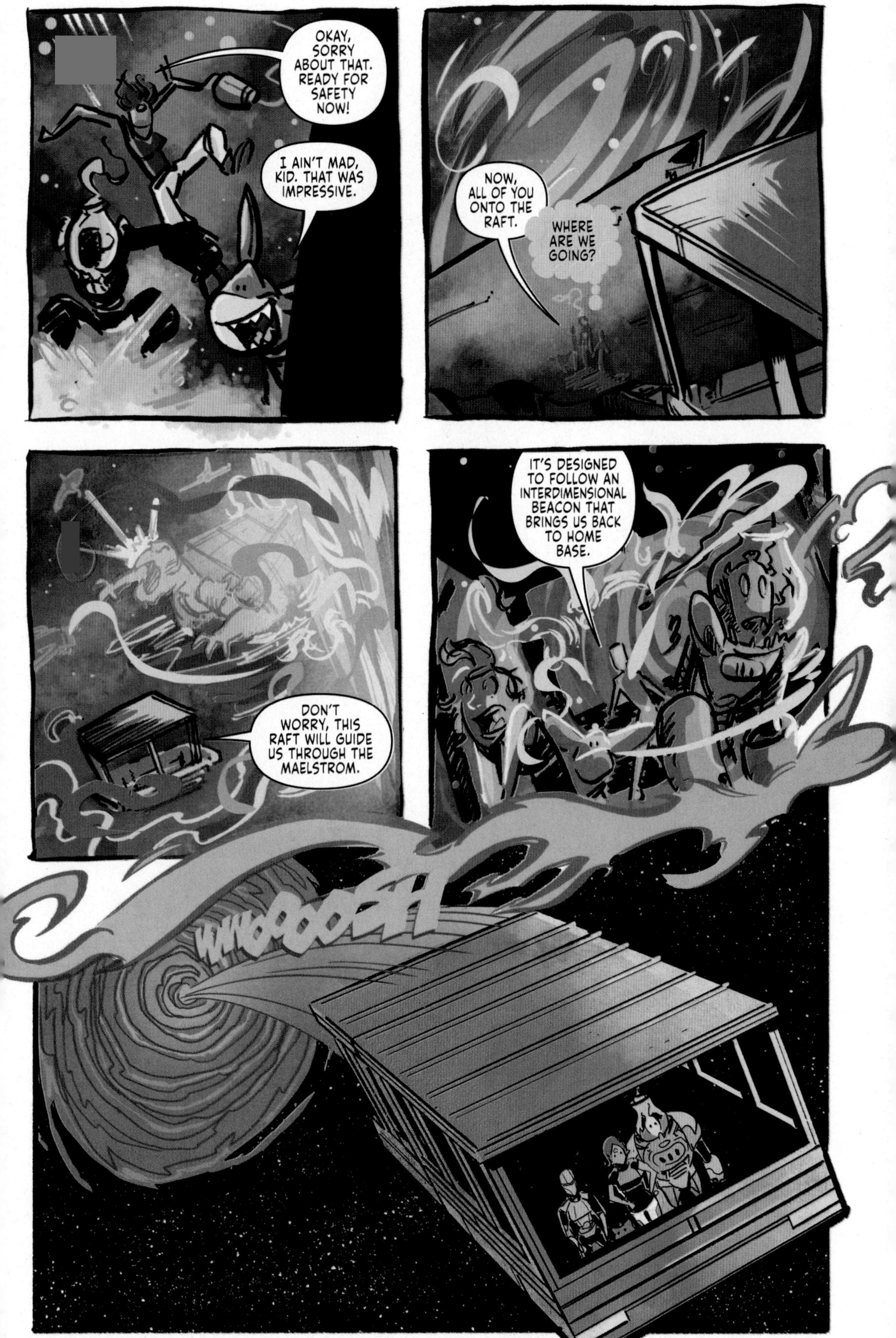
OKAY, SORRY ABOUT THAT. READY FOR SAFETY NOW!
I AIN'T MAD, KID. THAT WAS IMPRESSIVE.
NOW, ALL OF YOU ONTO THE RAFT.
WHERE ARE WE GOING?
DON'T WORRY, THIS RAFT WILL GUIDE US THROUGH THE MAELSTROM.
IT'S DESIGNED TO FOLLOW AN INTERDIMENSIONAL BEACON THAT BRINGS US BACK TO HOME BASE.
WHOOOOSH

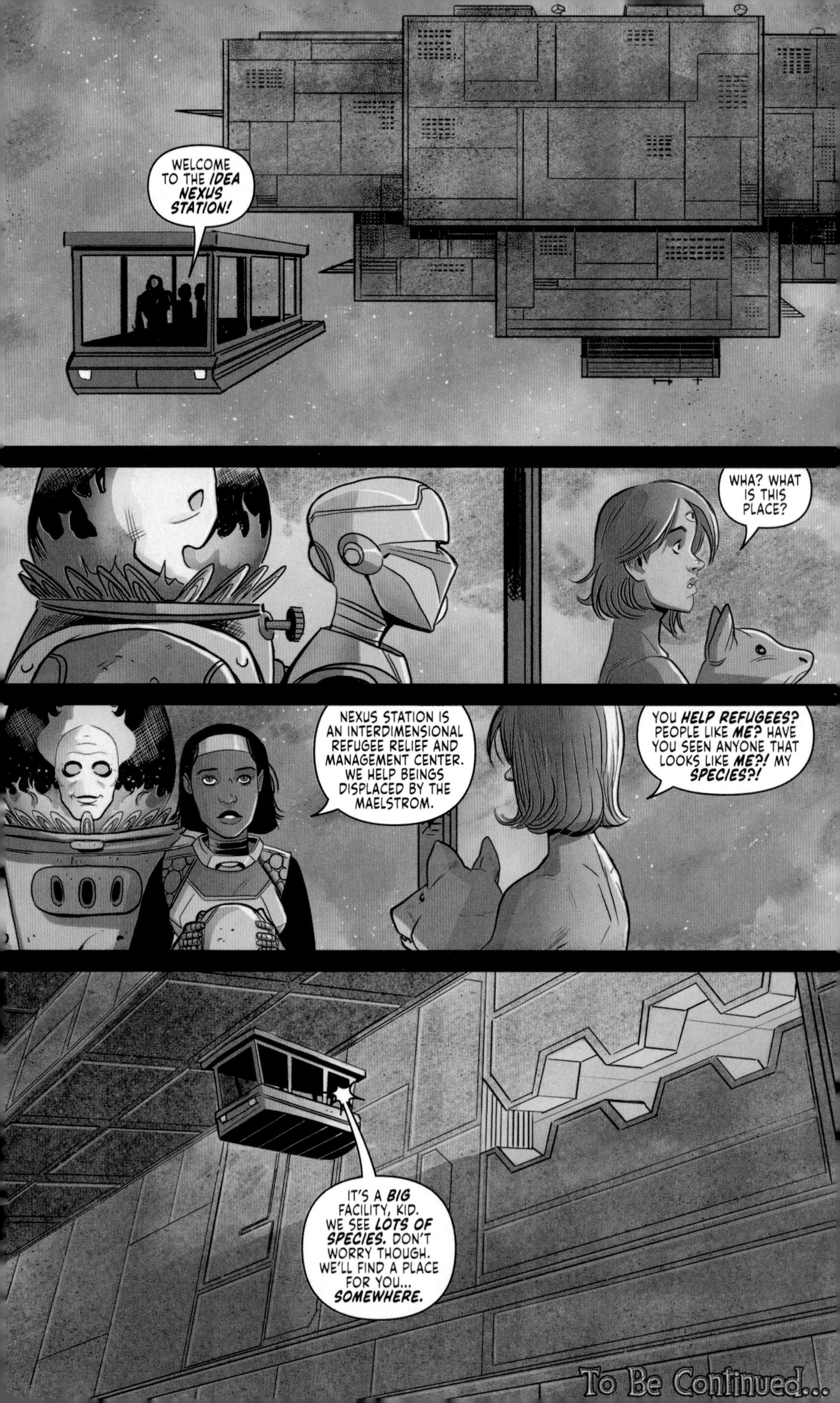
WELCOME TO THE IDEA NEXUS STATION!
WHA? WHAT IS THIS PLACE?
NEXUS STATION IS AN INTERDIMENSIONAL REFUGEE RELIEF AND MANAGEMENT CENTER. WE HELP BEINGS DISPLACED BY THE MAELSTROM.
YOU HELP REFUGEES? PEOPLE LIKE ME? HAVE YOU SEEN ANYONE THAT LOOKS LIKE ME?! MY SPECIES?!
IT'S A BIG FACILITY, KID. WE SEE LOTS OF SPECIES. DON'T WORRY THOUGH. WE'LL FIND A PLACE FOR YOU... SOMEWHERE.
To Be Continued...

MIRANDA IN THE MAELSTROM

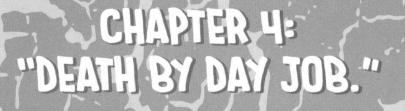

CHAPTER 4: "DEATH BY DAY JOB."

SCRIPT BY RILEY DASHIELL BIEHL
ART BY DREW MOSS

COLORS BY BORG SINABAN
LETTERING BY TAYLOR ESPOSITO
SCRIPT EDITING BY BRITTANY MATTER
COVER BY DREW MOSS & BORG SINABAN

BRYAN SEATON: PUBLISHER / CEO
VITO DELSANTE: EDITOR IN CHIEF
JASON MARTIN: PUBLISHER - DANGER ZONE
CHAD CICCONI: CHIEF PORTAL INSPECTOR

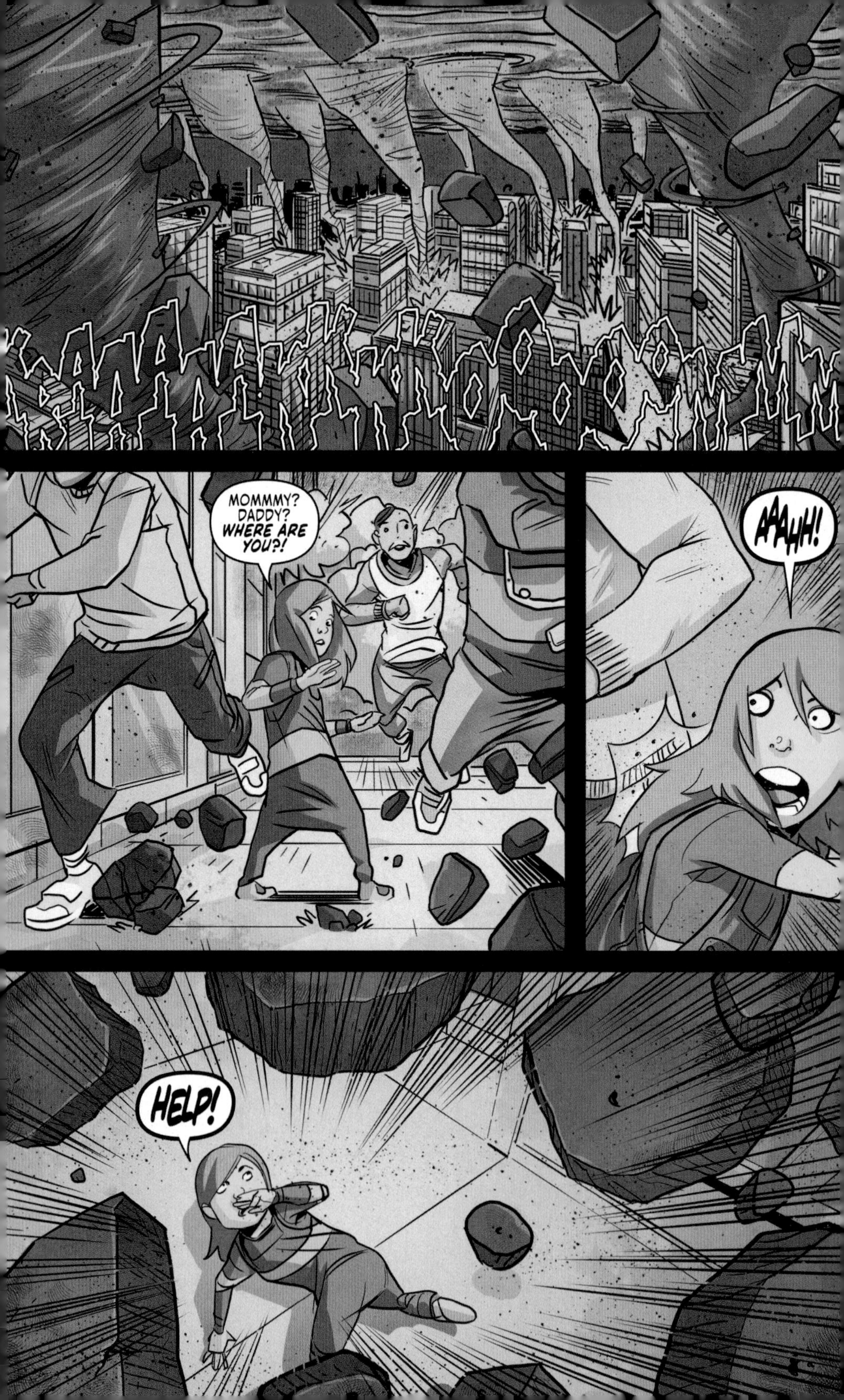
MOMMMY? DADDY? WHERE ARE YOU?!
AAAHH!
HELP!

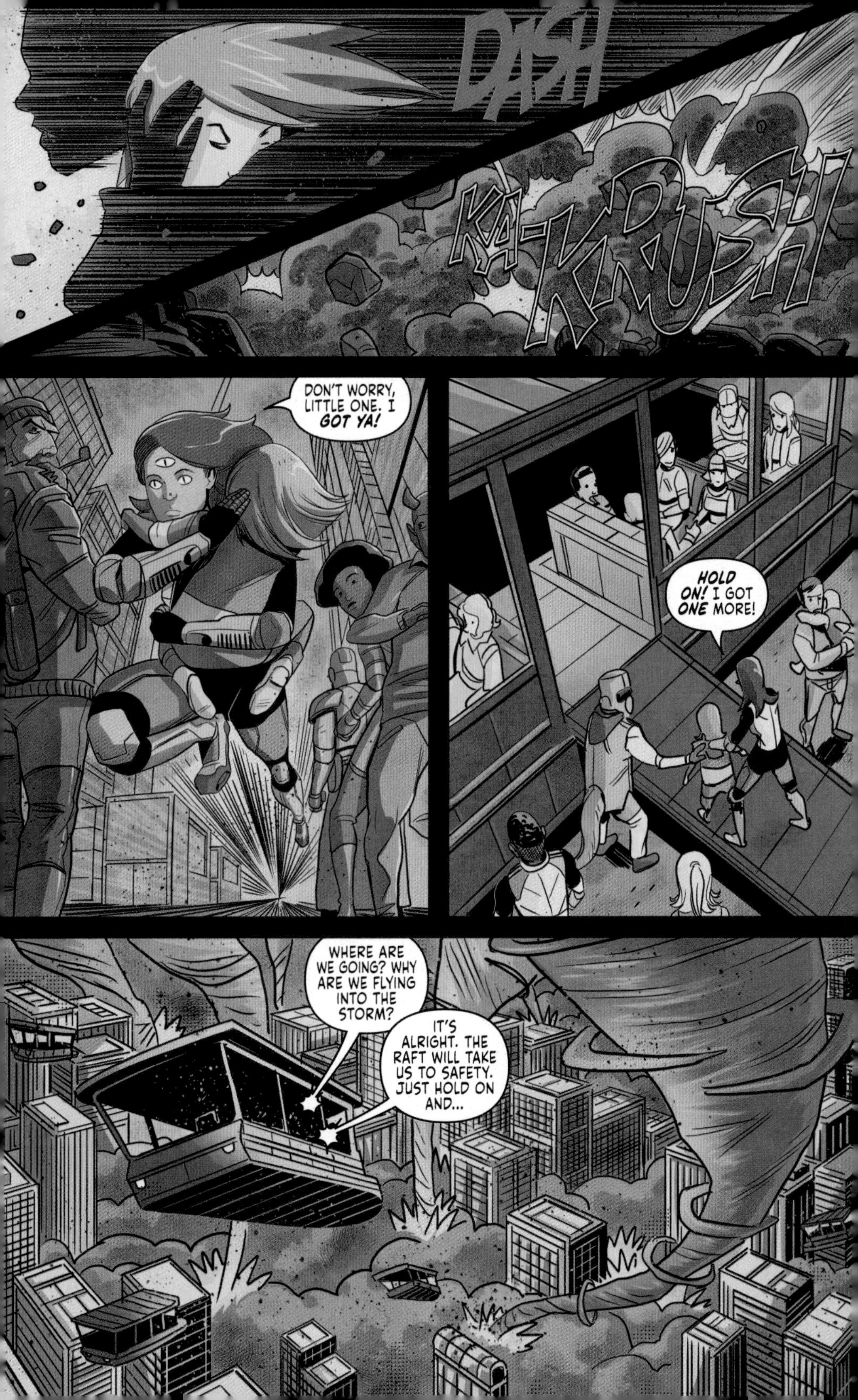
DASH
KA-KRUSH
DON'T WORRY, LITTLE ONE. I GOT YA!
HOLD ON! I GOT ONE MORE!
WHERE ARE WE GOING? WHY ARE WE FLYING INTO THE STORM?
IT'S ALRIGHT. THE RAFT WILL TAKE US TO SAFETY. JUST HOLD ON AND...

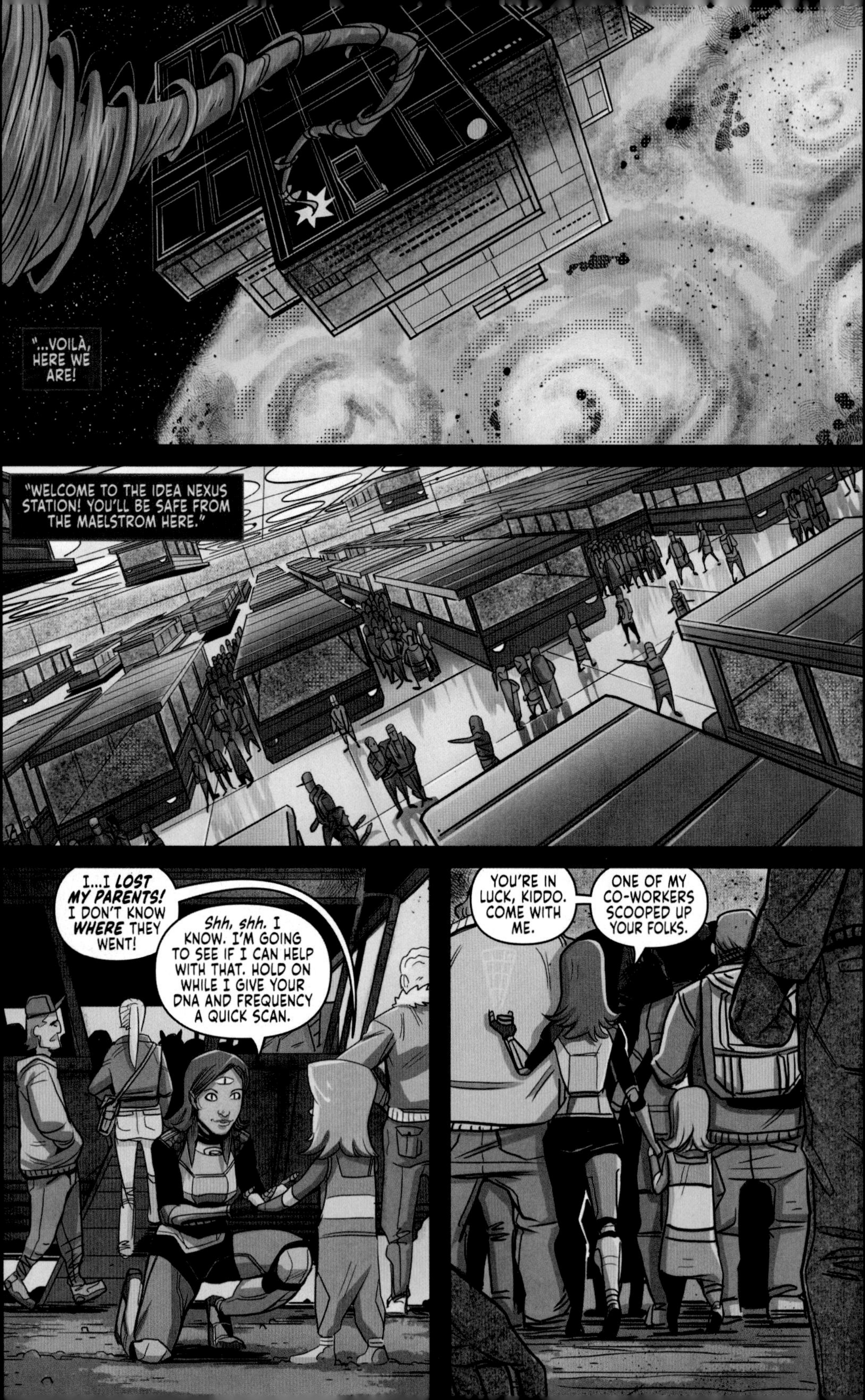
"...VOILÀ, HERE WE ARE!
"WELCOME TO THE IDEA NEXUS STATION! YOU'LL BE SAFE FROM THE MAELSTROM HERE."
I...I LOST MY PARENTS! I DON'T KNOW WHERE THEY WENT!
Shh, shh. I KNOW. I'M GOING TO SEE IF I CAN HELP WITH THAT. HOLD ON WHILE I GIVE YOUR DNA AND FREQUENCY A QUICK SCAN.
YOU'RE IN LUCK, KIDDO. COME WITH ME.
ONE OF MY CO-WORKERS SCOOPED UP YOUR FOLKS.

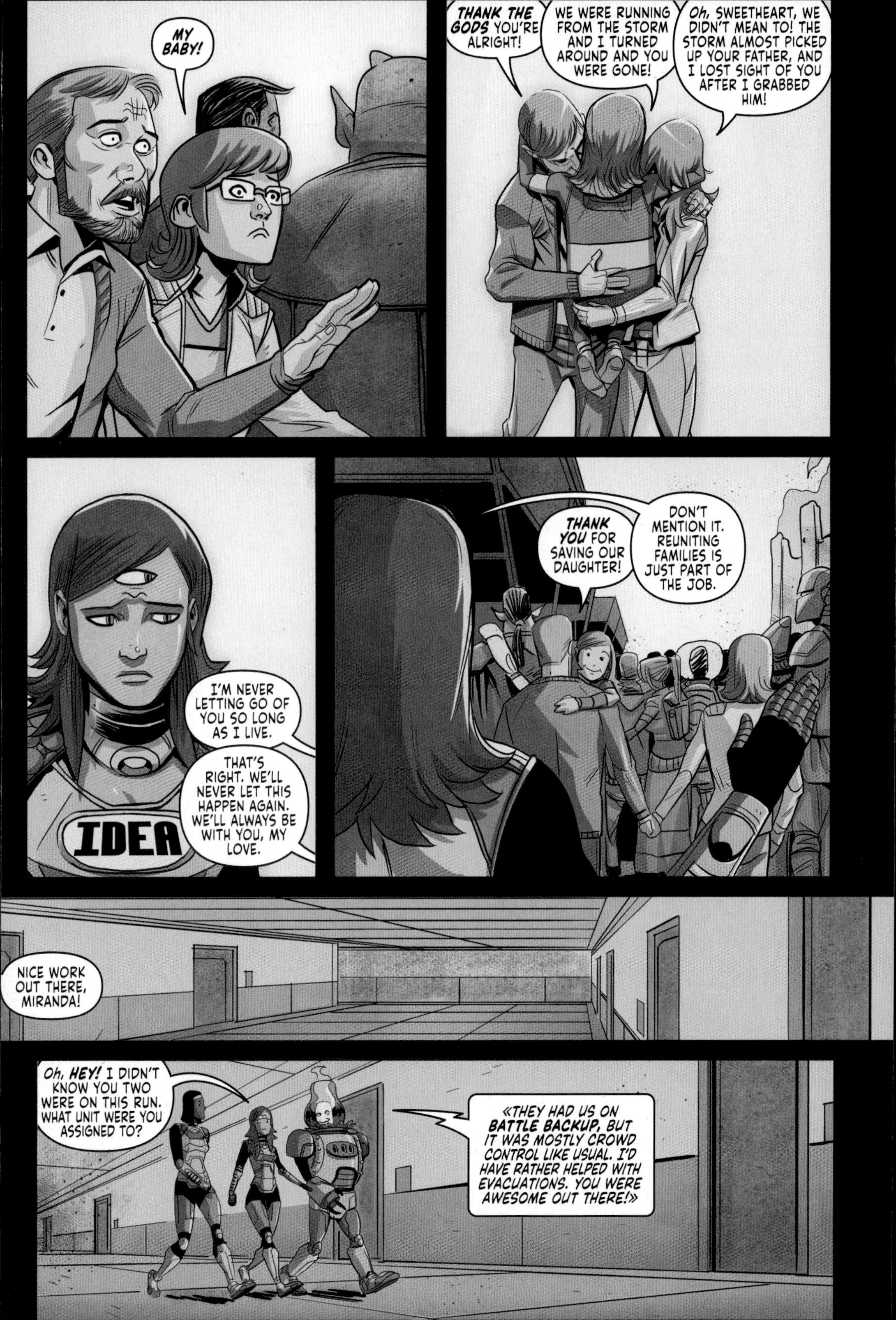
MY BABY!
THANK THE GODS YOU'RE ALRIGHT!
WE WERE RUNNING FROM THE STORM AND I TURNED AROUND AND YOU WERE GONE!
Oh, SWEETHEART, WE DIDN'T MEAN TO! THE STORM ALMOST PICKED UP YOUR FATHER, AND I LOST SIGHT OF YOU AFTER I GRABBED HIM!
IDEA
I'M NEVER LETTING GO OF YOU SO LONG AS I LIVE.
THAT'S RIGHT. WE'LL NEVER LET THIS HAPPEN AGAIN. WE'LL ALWAYS BE WITH YOU, MY LOVE.
THANK YOU FOR SAVING OUR DAUGHTER!
DON'T MENTION IT. REUNITING FAMILIES IS JUST PART OF THE JOB.
NICE WORK OUT THERE, MIRANDA!
Oh, HEY! I DIDN'T KNOW YOU TWO WERE ON THIS RUN. WHAT UNIT WERE YOU ASSIGNED TO?
«THEY HAD US ON BATTLE BACKUP, BUT IT WAS MOSTLY CROWD CONTROL LIKE USUAL. I'D HAVE RATHER HELPED WITH EVACUATIONS. YOU WERE AWESOME OUT THERE!»

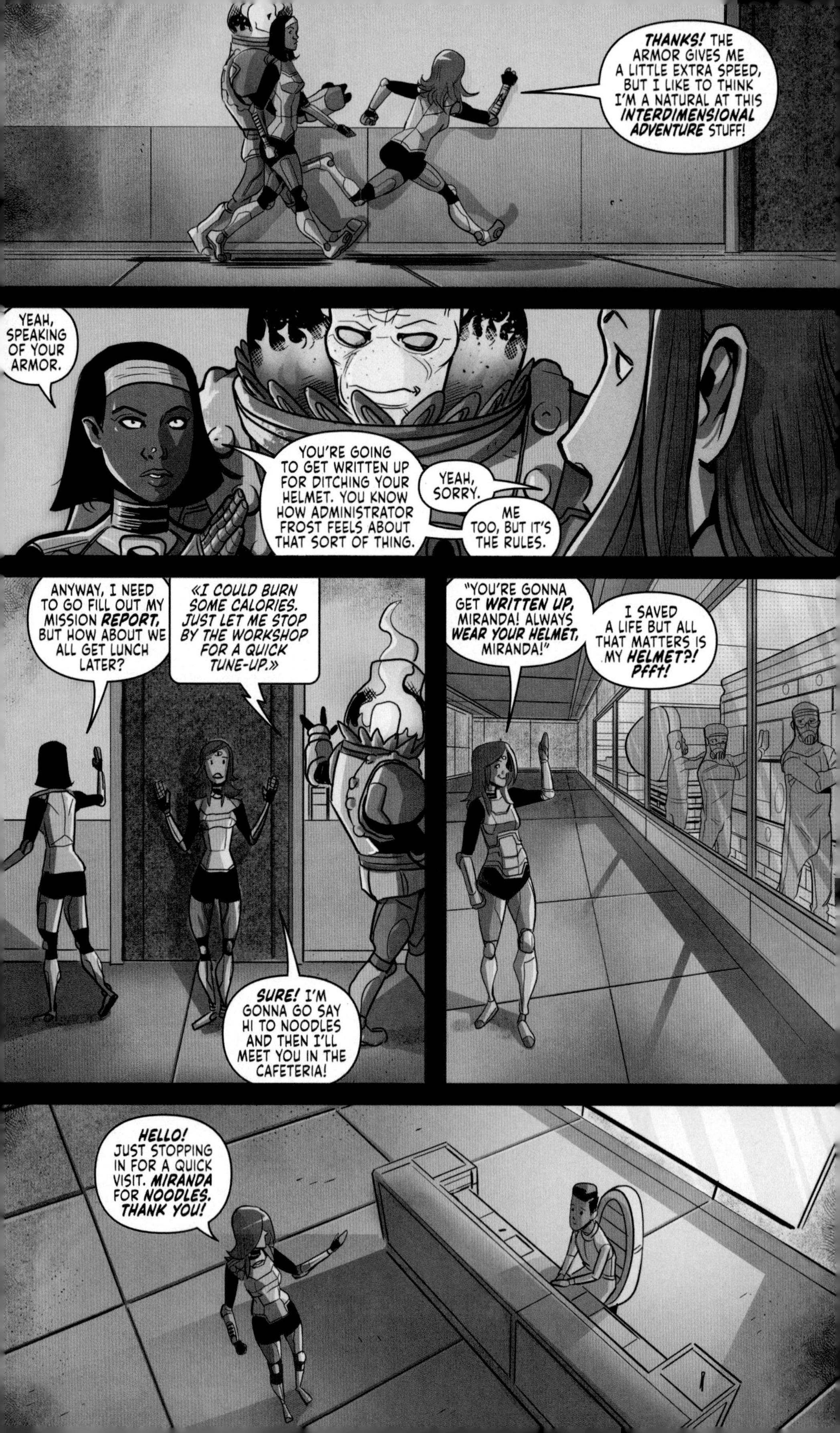
THANKS! THE ARMOR GIVES ME A LITTLE EXTRA SPEED, BUT I LIKE TO THINK I'M A NATURAL AT THIS INTERDIMENSIONAL ADVENTURE STUFF!
YEAH, SPEAKING OF YOUR ARMOR.
YOU'RE GOING TO GET WRITTEN UP FOR DITCHING YOUR HELMET. YOU KNOW HOW ADMINISTRATOR FROST FEELS ABOUT THAT SORT OF THING.
YEAH, SORRY.
ME TOO, BUT IT'S THE RULES.
ANYWAY, I NEED TO GO FILL OUT MY MISSION REPORT, BUT HOW ABOUT WE ALL GET LUNCH LATER?
«I COULD BURN SOME CALORIES. JUST LET ME STOP BY THE WORKSHOP FOR A QUICK TUNE-UP.»
SURE! I'M GONNA GO SAY HI TO NOODLES AND THEN I'LL MEET YOU IN THE CAFETERIA!
"YOU'RE GONNA GET WRITTEN UP, MIRANDA! ALWAYS WEAR YOUR HELMET, MIRANDA!"
I SAVED A LIFE BUT ALL THAT MATTERS IS MY HELMET?! PFFT!
HELLO! JUST STOPPING IN FOR A QUICK VISIT. MIRANDA FOR NOODLES. THANK YOU!

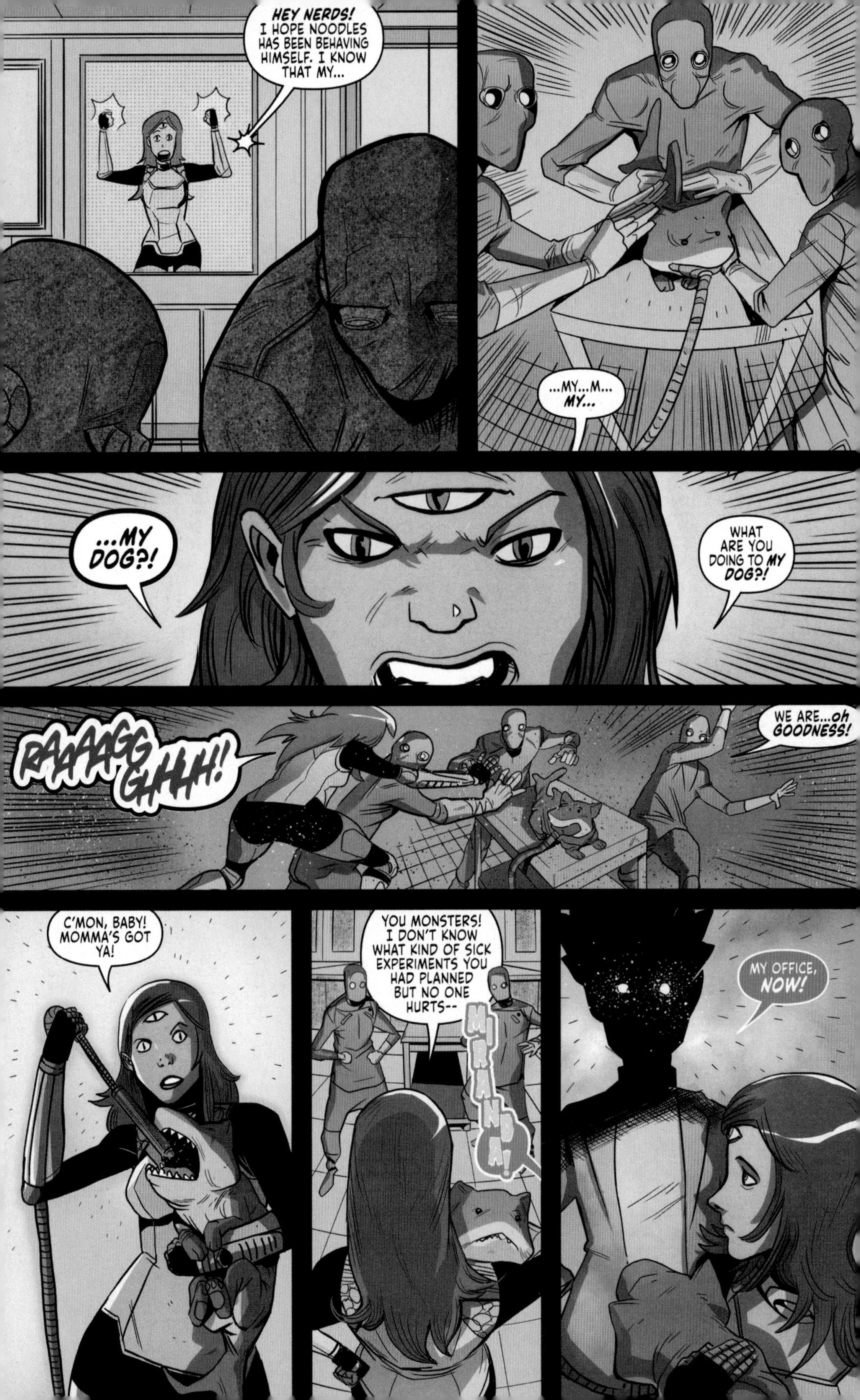

HEY NERDS! I HOPE NOODLES HAS BEEN BEHAVING HIMSELF. I KNOW THAT MY...
...MY...M... MY...
...MY DOG?!
WHAT ARE YOU DOING TO MY DOG?!
RAAAAGG GHHH!
WE ARE...oh GOODNESS!
C'MON, BABY! MOMMA'S GOT YA!
YOU MONSTERS! I DON'T KNOW WHAT KIND OF SICK EXPERIMENTS YOU HAD PLANNED BUT NO ONE HURTS--
MIRANDA!
MY OFFICE, NOW!

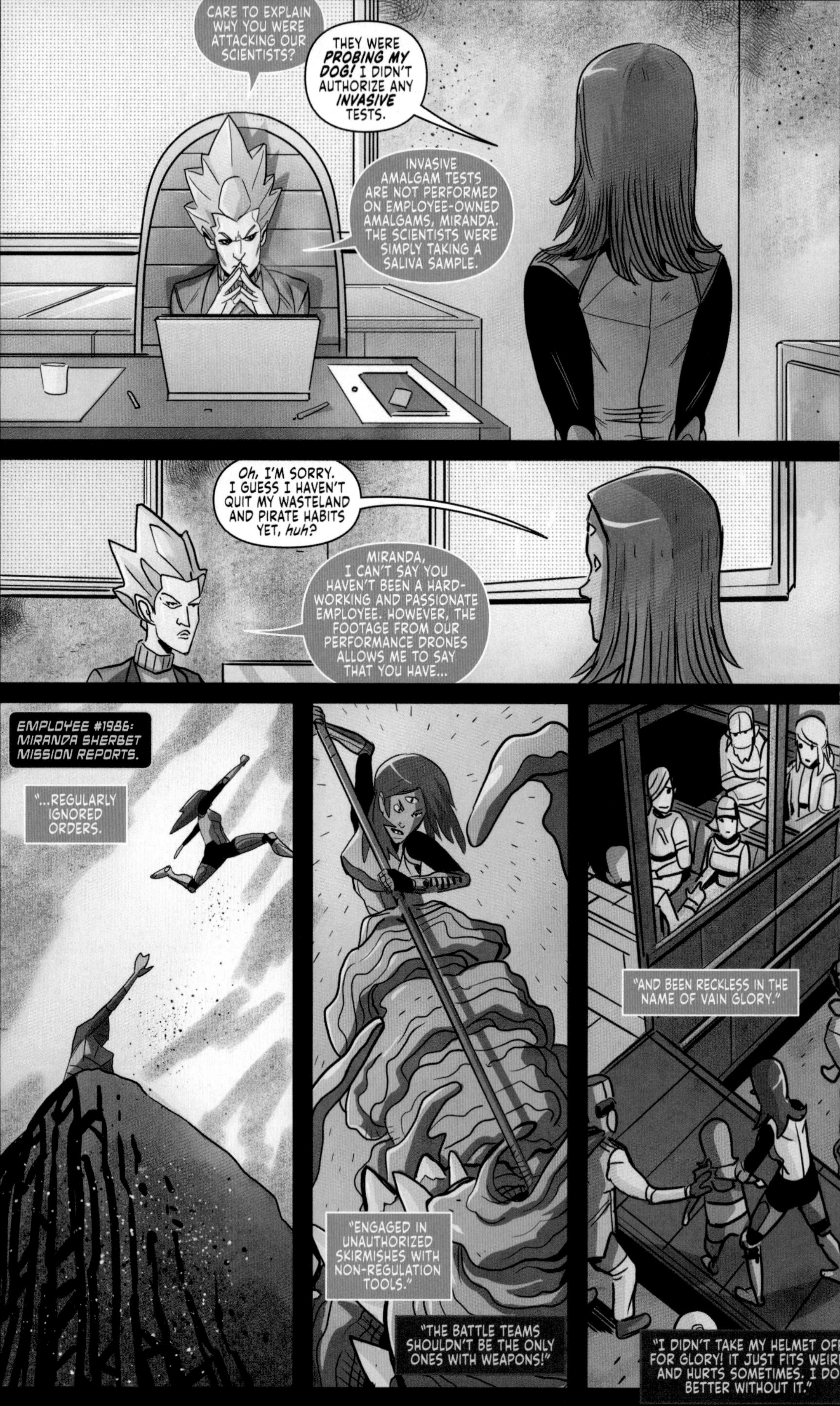
CARE TO EXPLAIN WHY YOU WERE ATTACKING OUR SCIENTISTS?
THEY WERE *PROBING MY DOG!* I DIDN'T AUTHORIZE ANY *INVASIVE* TESTS.
INVASIVE AMALGAM TESTS ARE NOT PERFORMED ON EMPLOYEE-OWNED AMALGAMS, MIRANDA. THE SCIENTISTS WERE SIMPLY TAKING A SALIVA SAMPLE.
Oh, I'M SORRY. I GUESS I HAVEN'T QUIT MY WASTELAND AND PIRATE HABITS YET, *huh?*
MIRANDA, I CAN'T SAY YOU HAVEN'T BEEN A HARD-WORKING AND PASSIONATE EMPLOYEE. HOWEVER, THE FOOTAGE FROM OUR PERFORMANCE DRONES ALLOWS ME TO SAY THAT YOU HAVE...
EMPLOYEE #1986: MIRANDA SHERBET MISSION REPORTS.
"...REGULARLY IGNORED ORDERS.
"ENGAGED IN UNAUTHORIZED SKIRMISHES WITH NON-REGULATION TOOLS."
"THE BATTLE TEAMS SHOULDN'T BE THE ONLY ONES WITH WEAPONS!"
"AND BEEN RECKLESS IN THE NAME OF VAIN GLORY."
"I DIDN'T TAKE MY HELMET OF FOR GLORY! IT JUST FITS WEIR AND HURTS SOMETIMES. I DO BETTER WITHOUT IT."

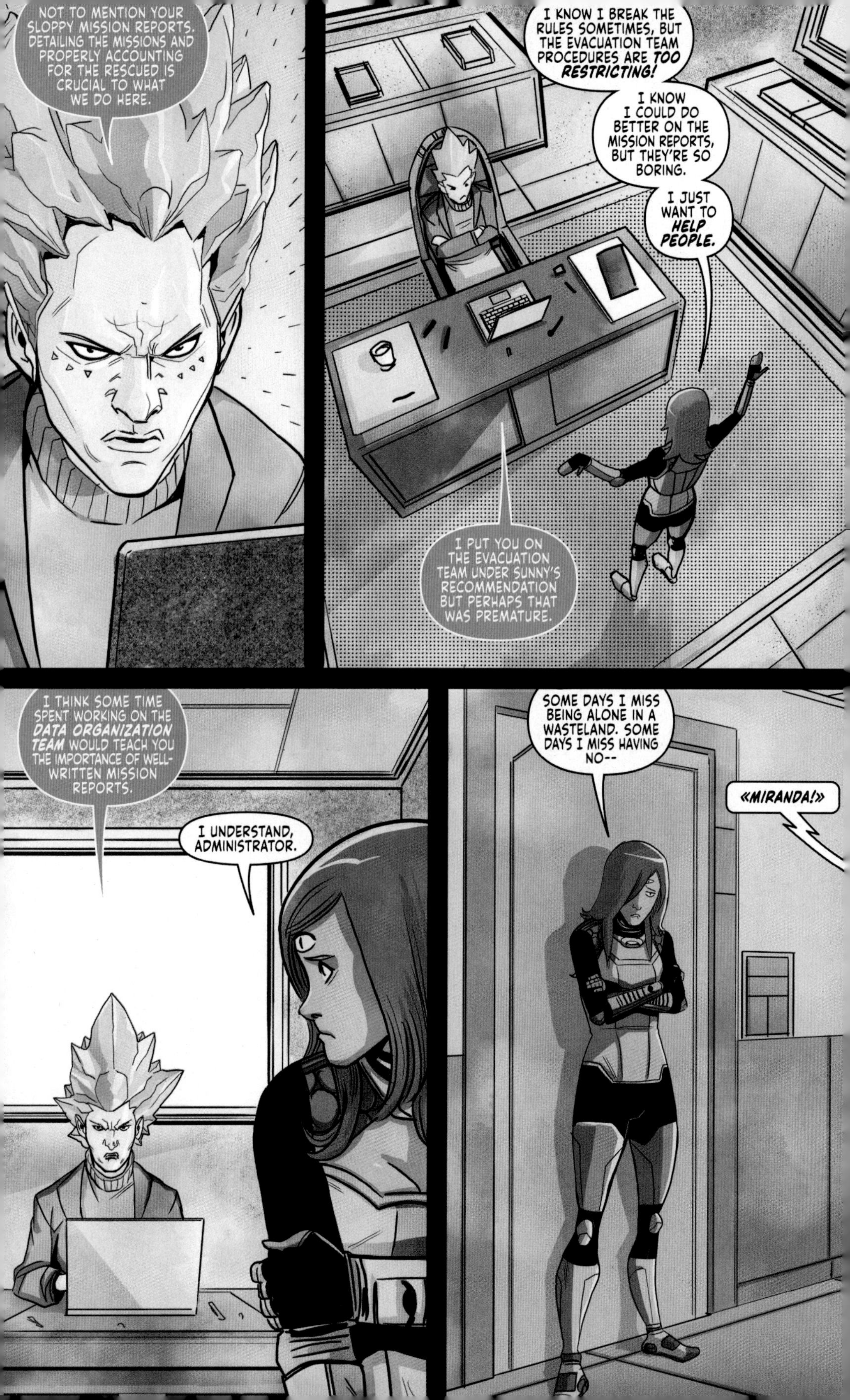
NOT TO MENTION YOUR SLOPPY MISSION REPORTS. DETAILING THE MISSIONS AND PROPERLY ACCOUNTING FOR THE RESCUED IS CRUCIAL TO WHAT WE DO HERE.
I KNOW I BREAK THE RULES SOMETIMES, BUT THE EVACUATION TEAM PROCEDURES ARE TOO RESTRICTING!
I KNOW I COULD DO BETTER ON THE MISSION REPORTS, BUT THEY'RE SO BORING.
I JUST WANT TO HELP PEOPLE.
I PUT YOU ON THE EVACUATION TEAM UNDER SUNNY'S RECOMMENDATION BUT PERHAPS THAT WAS PREMATURE.
I THINK SOME TIME SPENT WORKING ON THE DATA ORGANIZATION TEAM WOULD TEACH YOU THE IMPORTANCE OF WELL-WRITTEN MISSION REPORTS.
I UNDERSTAND, ADMINISTRATOR.
SOME DAYS I MISS BEING ALONE IN A WASTELAND. SOME DAYS I MISS HAVING NO--
«MIRANDA!»

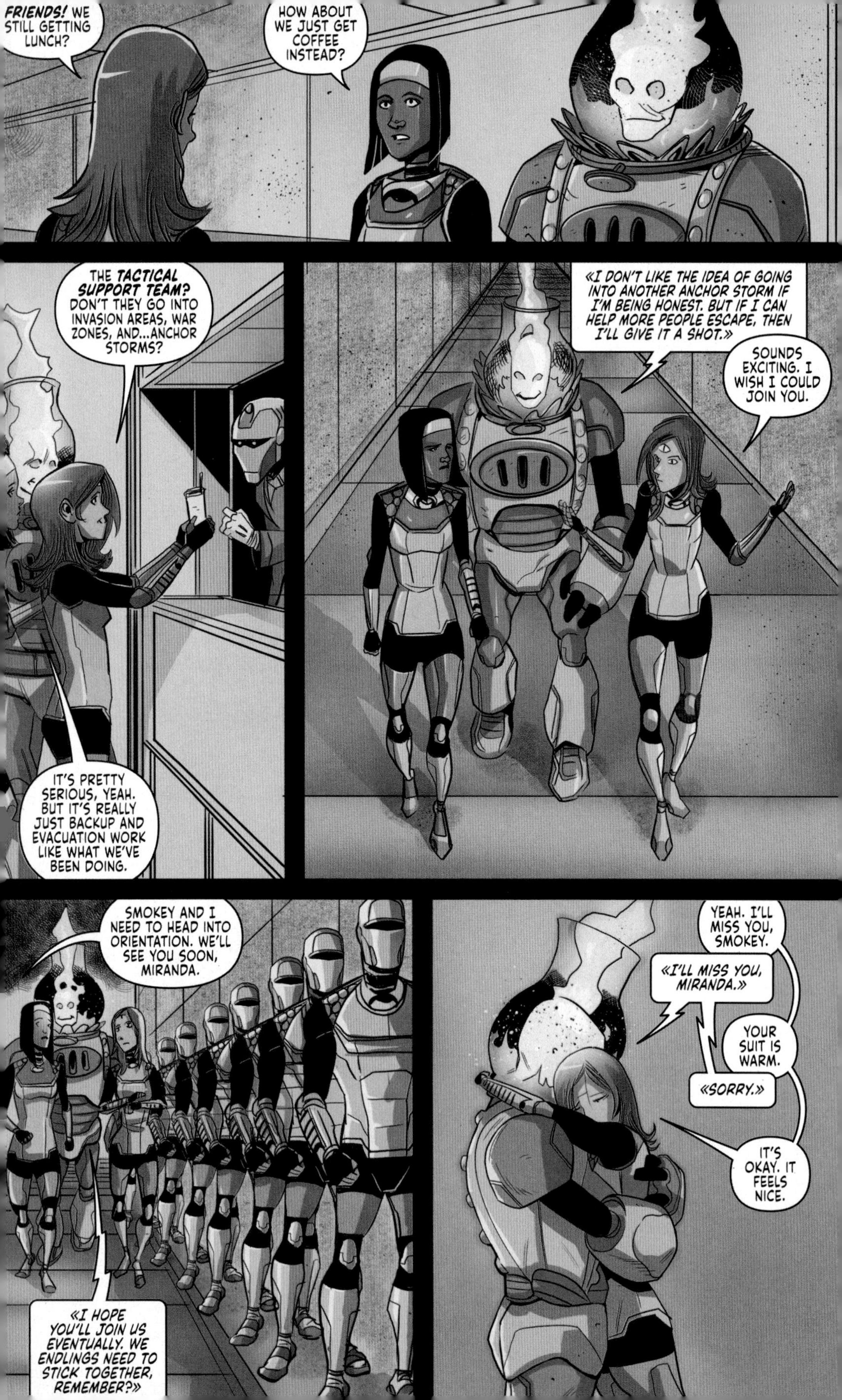

FRIENDS! WE STILL GETTING LUNCH?
HOW ABOUT WE JUST GET COFFEE INSTEAD?
THE TACTICAL SUPPORT TEAM? DON'T THEY GO INTO INVASION AREAS, WAR ZONES, AND...ANCHOR STORMS?
IT'S PRETTY SERIOUS, YEAH. BUT IT'S REALLY JUST BACKUP AND EVACUATION WORK LIKE WHAT WE'VE BEEN DOING.
«I DON'T LIKE THE IDEA OF GOING INTO ANOTHER ANCHOR STORM IF I'M BEING HONEST. BUT IF I CAN HELP MORE PEOPLE ESCAPE, THEN I'LL GIVE IT A SHOT.»
SOUNDS EXCITING. I WISH I COULD JOIN YOU.
SMOKEY AND I NEED TO HEAD INTO ORIENTATION. WE'LL SEE YOU SOON, MIRANDA.
«I HOPE YOU'LL JOIN US EVENTUALLY. WE ENDLINGS NEED TO STICK TOGETHER, REMEMBER?»
YEAH. I'LL MISS YOU, SMOKEY.
«I'LL MISS YOU, MIRANDA.»
YOUR SUIT IS WARM.
«SORRY.»
IT'S OKAY. IT FEELS NICE.

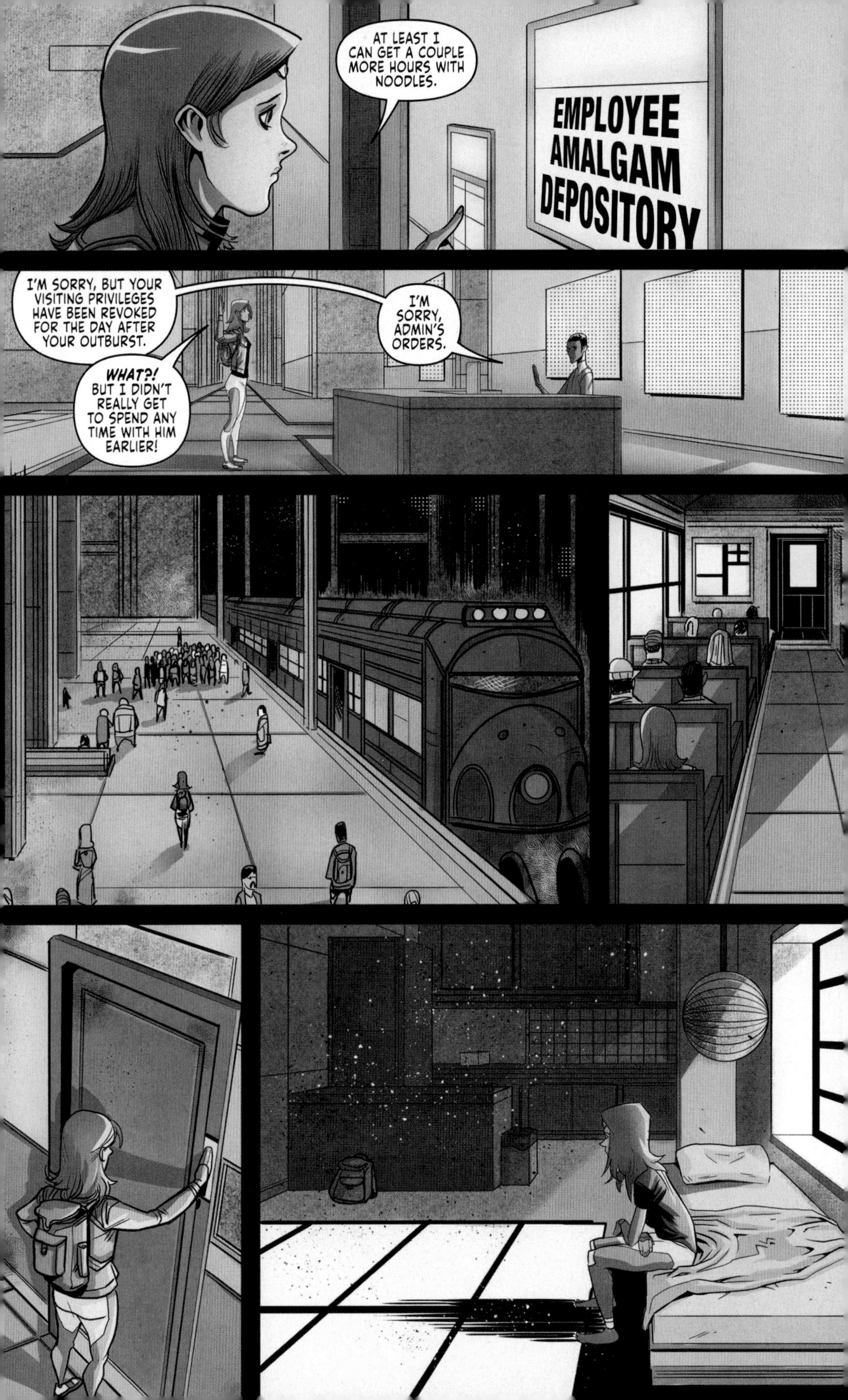
AT LEAST I CAN GET A COUPLE MORE HOURS WITH NOODLES.
EMPLOYEE AMALGAM DEPOSITORY
I'M SORRY, BUT YOUR VISITING PRIVILEGES HAVE BEEN REVOKED FOR THE DAY AFTER YOUR OUTBURST.
WHAT?! BUT I DIDN'T REALLY GET TO SPEND ANY TIME WITH HIM EARLIER!
I'M SORRY, ADMIN'S ORDERS.

Two Months Later...

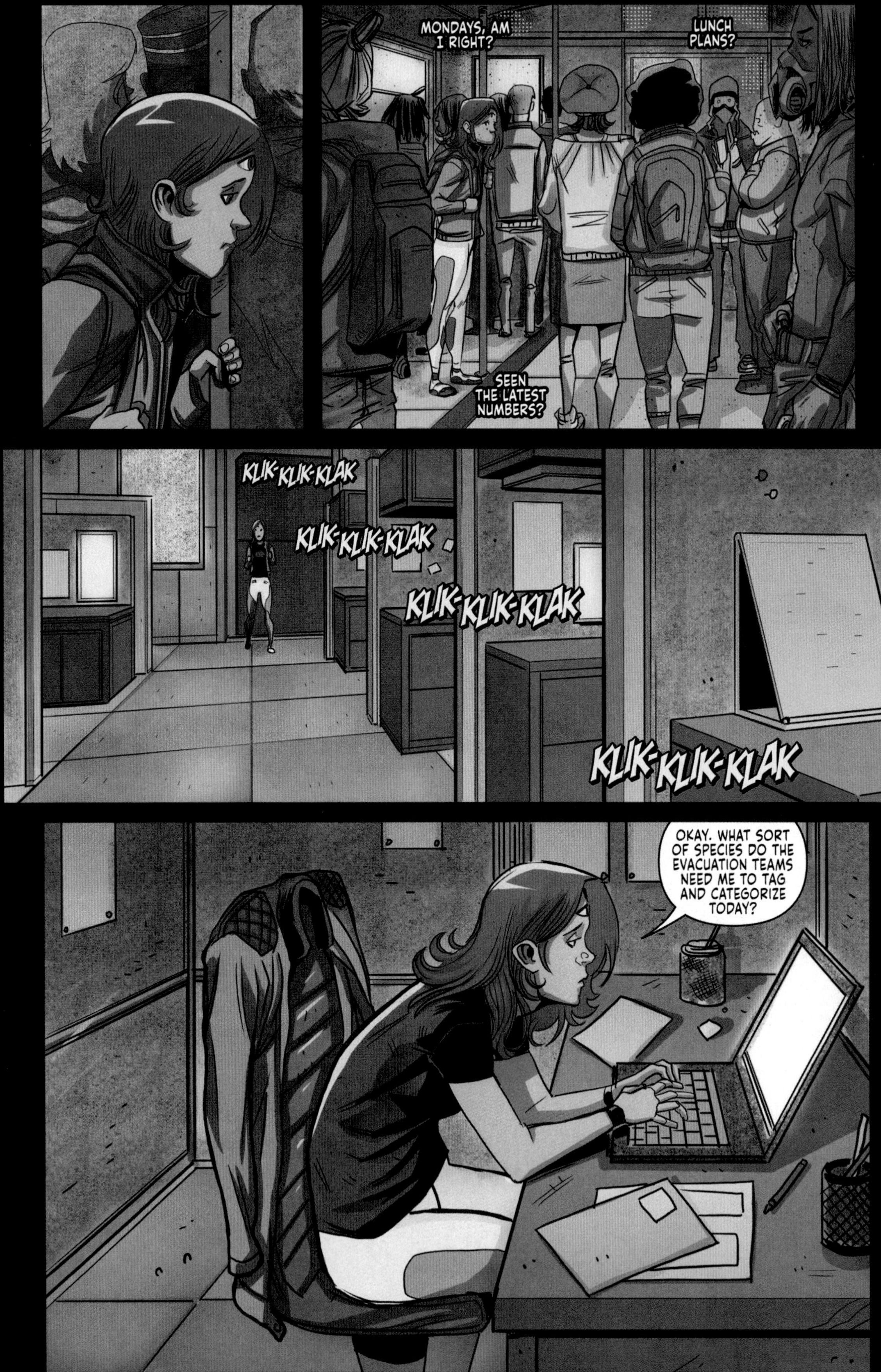

MONDAYS, AM I RIGHT?
LUNCH PLANS?
SEEN THE LATEST NUMBERS?
KLIK-KLIK-KLAK
KLIK-KLIK-KLAK
KLIK-KLIK-KLAK
KLIK-KLIK-KLAK
OKAY. WHAT SORT OF SPECIES DO THE EVACUATION TEAMS NEED ME TO TAG AND CATEGORIZE TODAY?

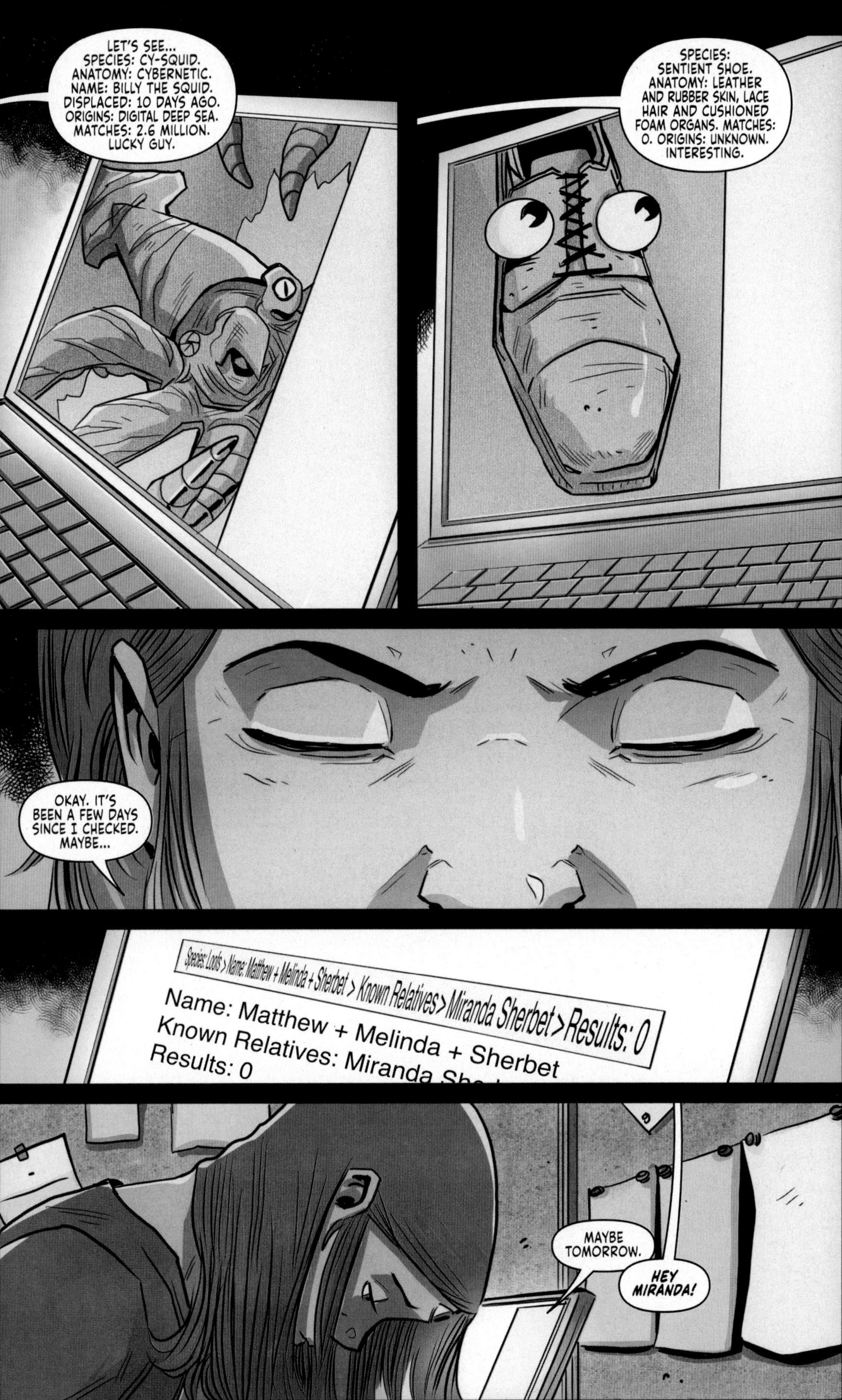
LET'S SEE... SPECIES: CY-SQUID. ANATOMY: CYBERNETIC. NAME: BILLY THE SQUID. DISPLACED: 10 DAYS AGO. ORIGINS: DIGITAL DEEP SEA. MATCHES: 2.6 MILLION. LUCKY GUY.
SPECIES: SENTIENT SHOE. ANATOMY: LEATHER AND RUBBER SKIN, LACE HAIR AND CUSHIONED FOAM ORGANS. MATCHES: 0. ORIGINS: UNKNOWN. INTERESTING.
OKAY. IT'S BEEN A FEW DAYS SINCE I CHECKED. MAYBE...
Species: Loots > Name: Matthew + Melinda + Sherbet > Known Relatives > Miranda Sherbet > Results: 0
Name: Matthew + Melinda + Sherbet
Known Relatives: Miranda
Results: 0
MAYBE TOMORROW.
HEY MIRANDA!

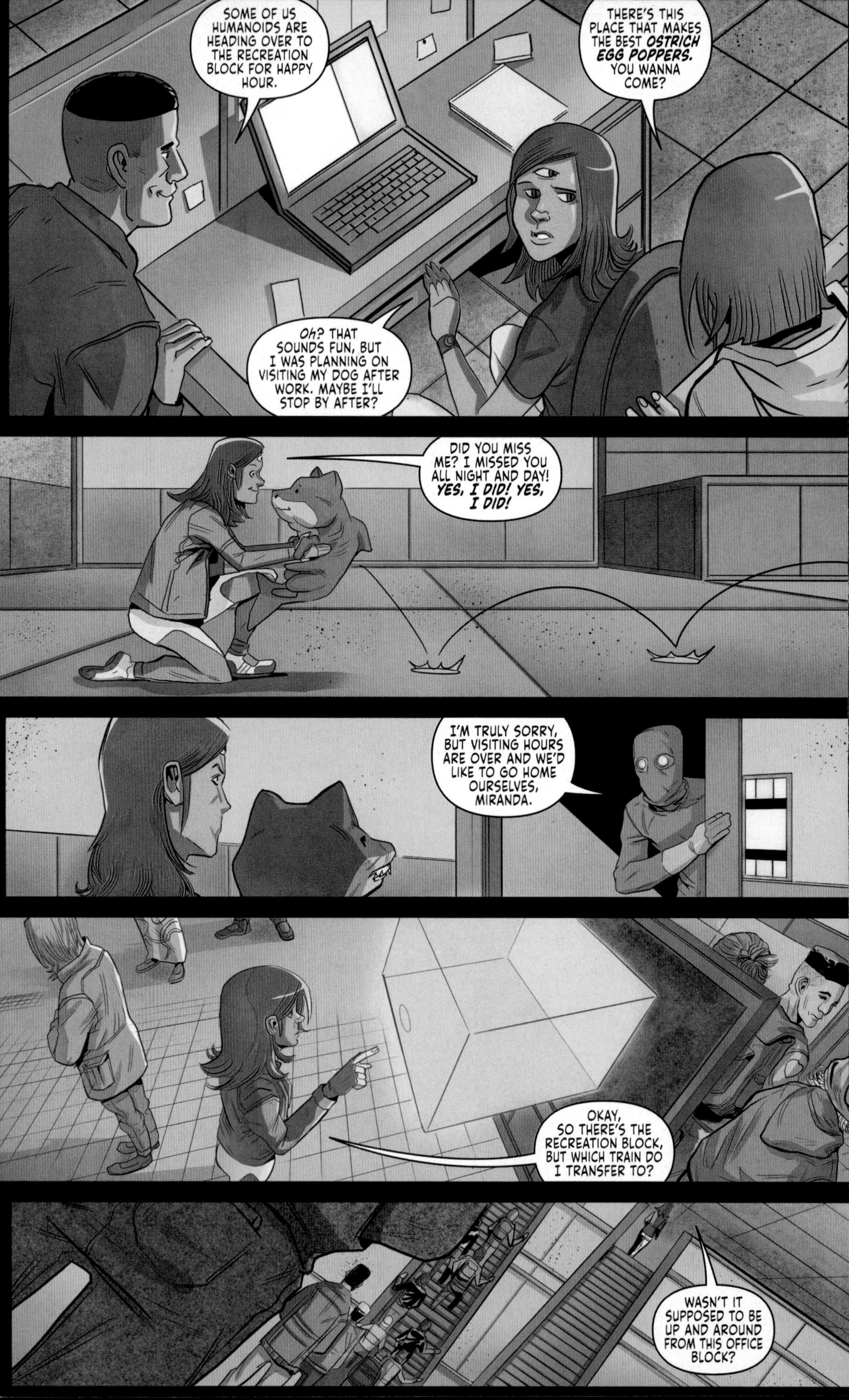
SOME OF US HUMANOIDS ARE HEADING OVER TO THE RECREATION BLOCK FOR HAPPY HOUR.
THERE'S THIS PLACE THAT MAKES THE BEST *OSTRICH EGG POPPERS.* YOU WANNA COME?
Oh? THAT SOUNDS FUN, BUT I WAS PLANNING ON VISITING MY DOG AFTER WORK. MAYBE I'LL STOP BY AFTER?
DID YOU MISS ME? I MISSED YOU ALL NIGHT AND DAY! *YES, I DID! YES, I DID!*
I'M TRULY SORRY, BUT VISITING HOURS ARE OVER AND WE'D LIKE TO GO HOME OURSELVES, MIRANDA.
OKAY, SO THERE'S THE RECREATION BLOCK, BUT WHICH TRAIN DO I TRANSFER TO?
WASN'T IT SUPPOSED TO BE UP AND AROUND FROM THIS OFFICE BLOCK?

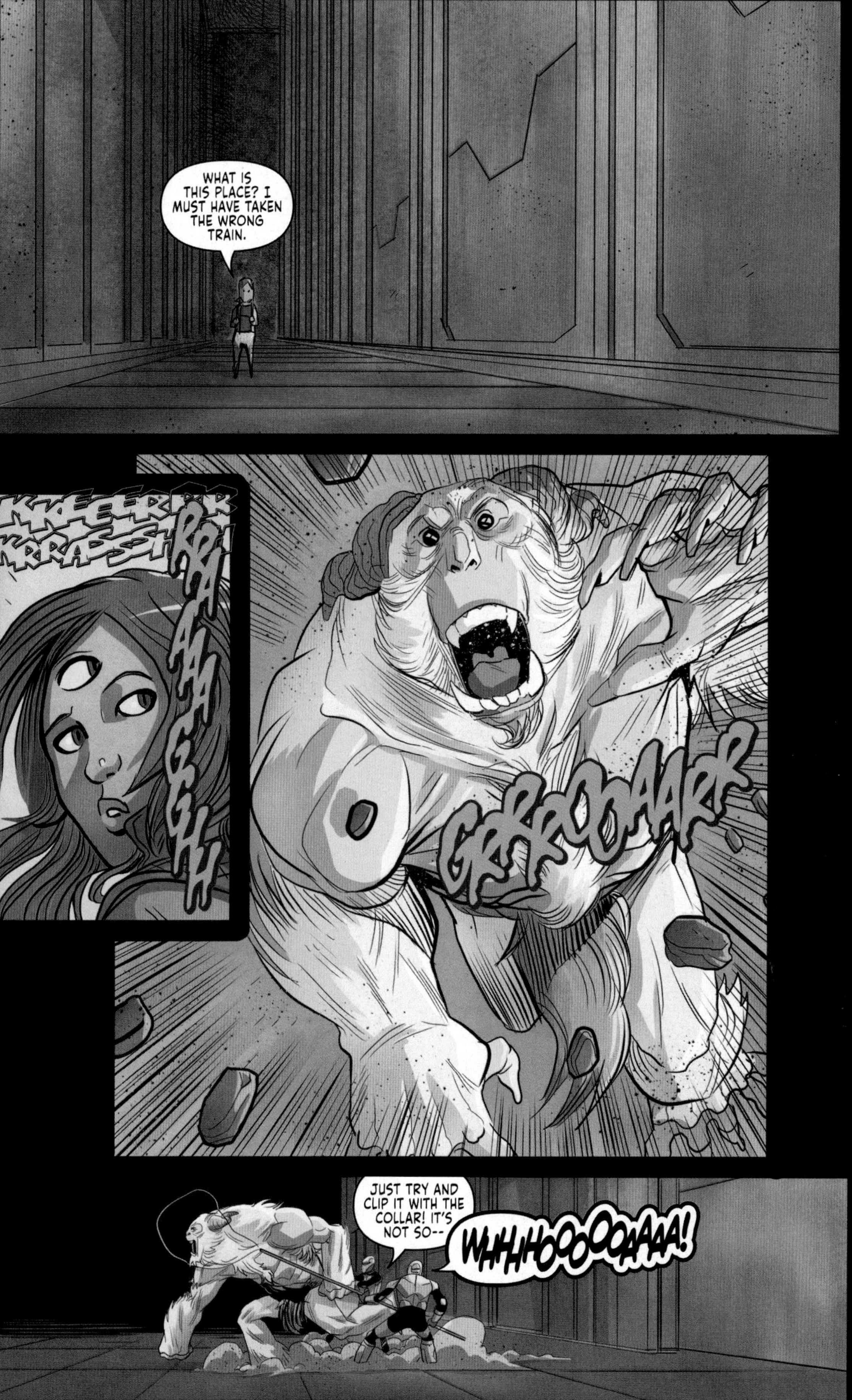
WHAT IS THIS PLACE? I MUST HAVE TAKEN THE WRONG TRAIN.
GRROOAARR
JUST TRY AND CLIP IT WITH THE COLLAR! IT'S NOT SO--
WHHHOOOOAAAA!

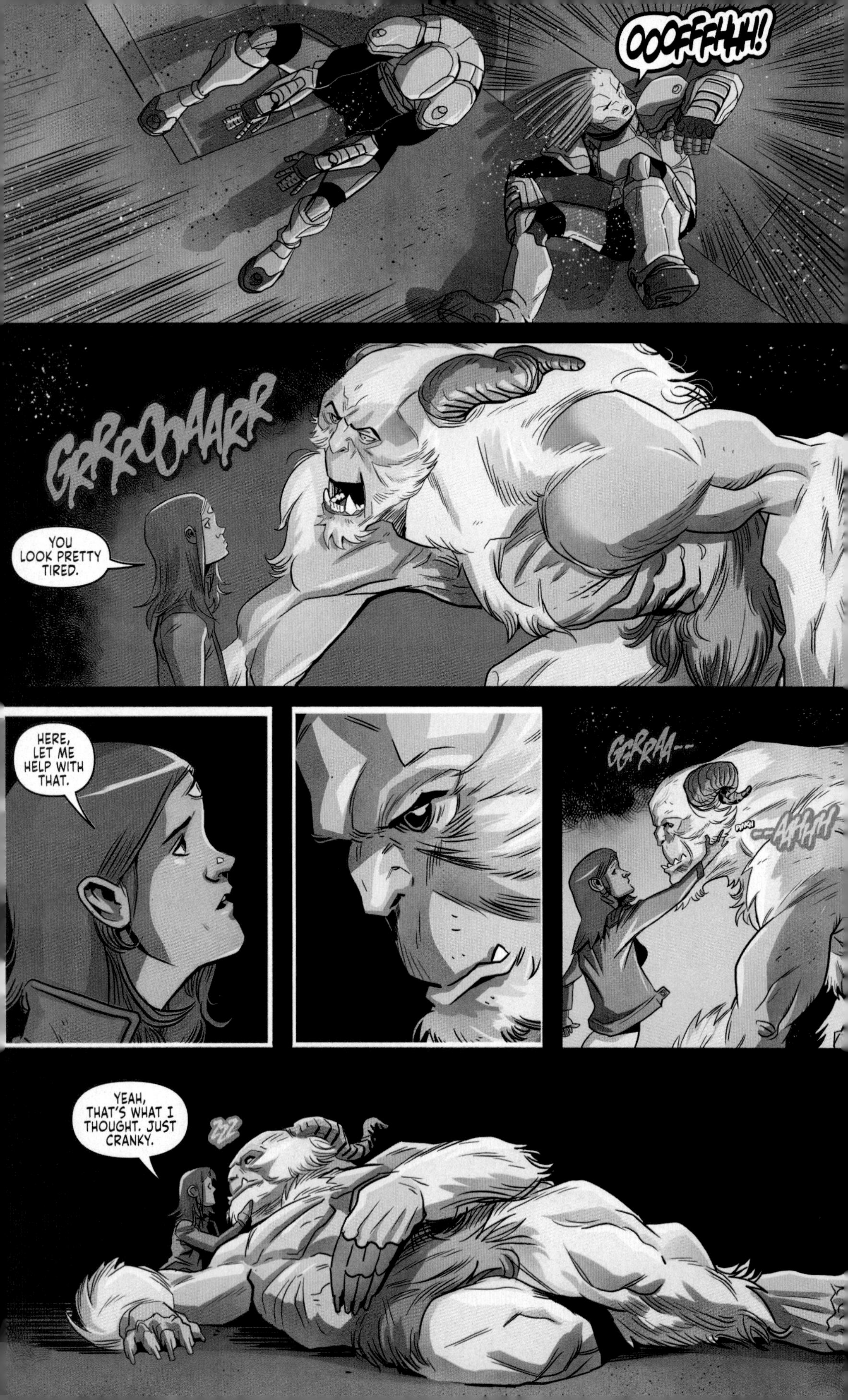
OOOFFFHHH!
GRRROOAARR
YOU LOOK PRETTY TIRED.
HERE, LET ME HELP WITH THAT.
GGRRAA--
PINCH
--AAAHH
YEAH, THAT'S WHAT I THOUGHT. JUST CRANKY.
ZZZ

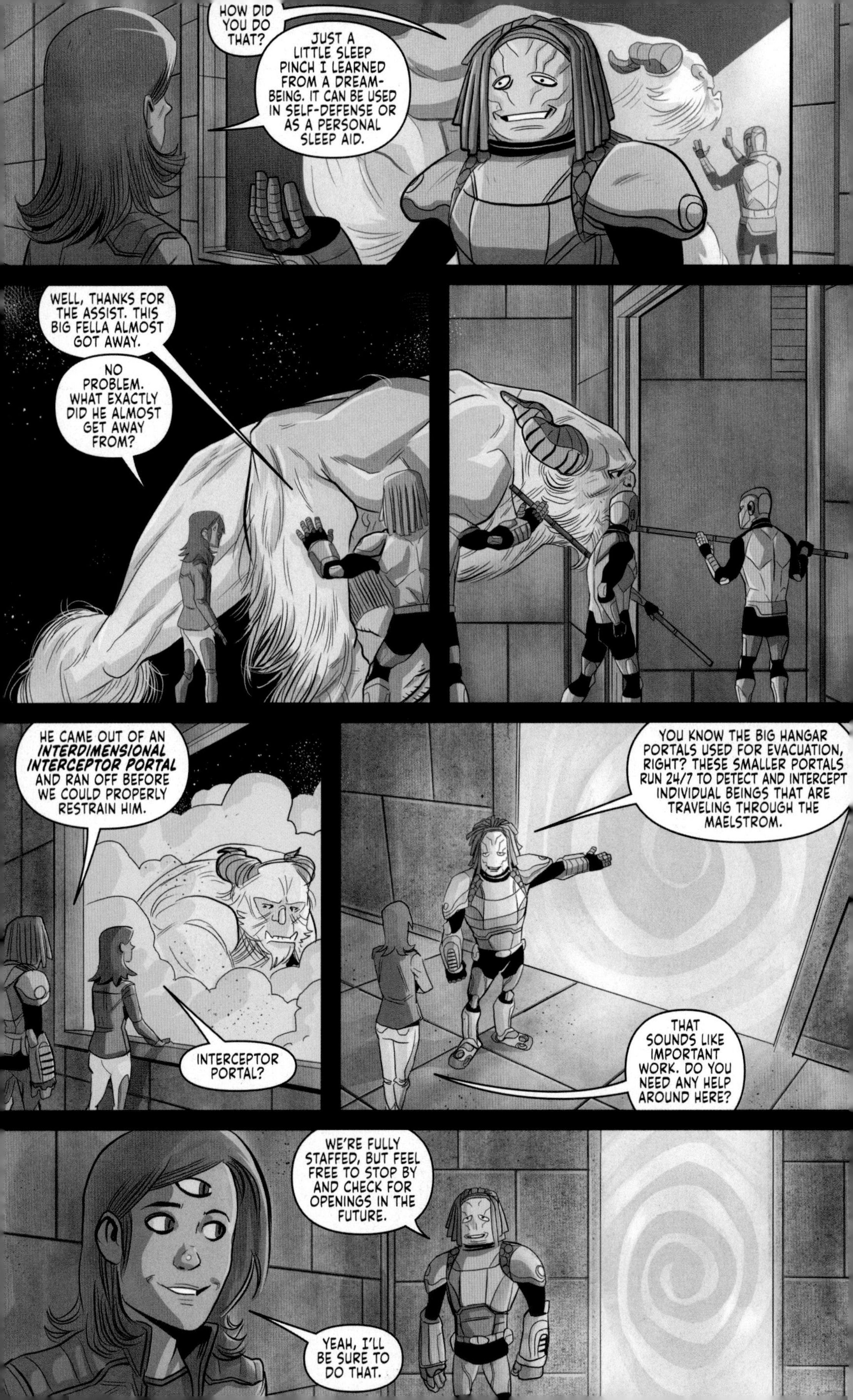
HOW DID YOU DO THAT?
JUST A LITTLE SLEEP PINCH I LEARNED FROM A DREAM-BEING. IT CAN BE USED IN SELF-DEFENSE OR AS A PERSONAL SLEEP AID.
WELL, THANKS FOR THE ASSIST. THIS BIG FELLA ALMOST GOT AWAY.
NO PROBLEM. WHAT EXACTLY DID HE ALMOST GET AWAY FROM?
HE CAME OUT OF AN *INTERDIMENSIONAL INTERCEPTOR PORTAL* AND RAN OFF BEFORE WE COULD PROPERLY RESTRAIN HIM.
INTERCEPTOR PORTAL?
YOU KNOW THE BIG HANGAR PORTALS USED FOR EVACUATION, RIGHT? THESE SMALLER PORTALS RUN 24/7 TO DETECT AND INTERCEPT INDIVIDUAL BEINGS THAT ARE TRAVELING THROUGH THE MAELSTROM.
THAT SOUNDS LIKE IMPORTANT WORK. DO YOU NEED ANY HELP AROUND HERE?
WE'RE FULLY STAFFED, BUT FEEL FREE TO STOP BY AND CHECK FOR OPENINGS IN THE FUTURE.
YEAH, I'LL BE SURE TO DO THAT.

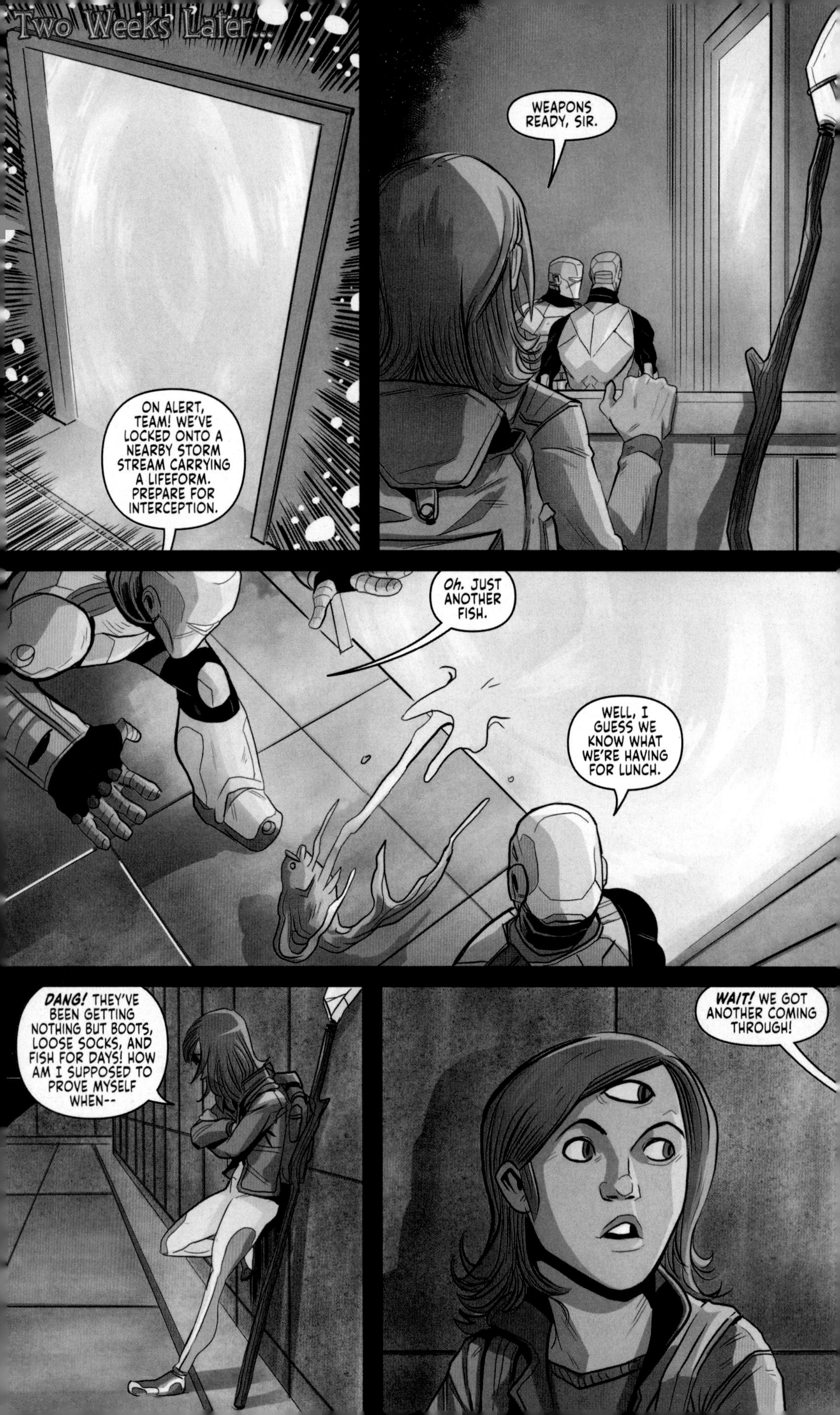
Two Weeks Later...
ON ALERT, TEAM! WE'VE LOCKED ONTO A NEARBY STORM STREAM CARRYING A LIFEFORM. PREPARE FOR INTERCEPTION.
WEAPONS READY, SIR.
Oh. JUST ANOTHER FISH.
WELL, I GUESS WE KNOW WHAT WE'RE HAVING FOR LUNCH.
DANG! THEY'VE BEEN GETTING NOTHING BUT BOOTS, LOOSE SOCKS, AND FISH FOR DAYS! HOW AM I SUPPOSED TO PROVE MYSELF WHEN--
WAIT! WE GOT ANOTHER COMING THROUGH!

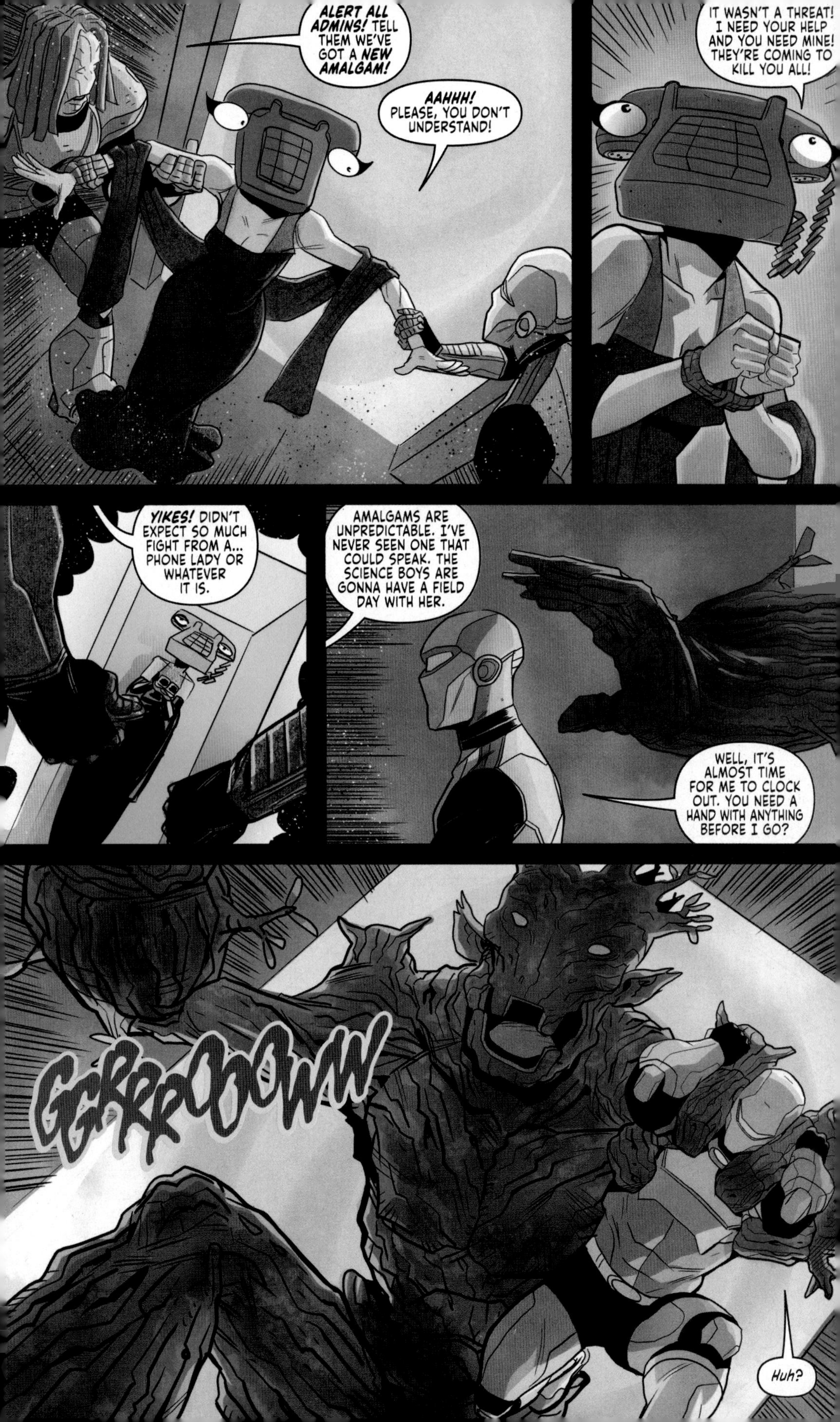
ALERT ALL ADMINS! TELL THEM WE'VE GOT A NEW AMALGAM!
AAHHH! PLEASE, YOU DON'T UNDERSTAND!
IT WASN'T A THREAT! I NEED YOUR HELP AND YOU NEED MINE! THEY'RE COMING TO KILL YOU ALL!
YIKES! DIDN'T EXPECT SO MUCH FIGHT FROM A... PHONE LADY OR WHATEVER IT IS.
AMALGAMS ARE UNPREDICTABLE. I'VE NEVER SEEN ONE THAT COULD SPEAK. THE SCIENCE BOYS ARE GONNA HAVE A FIELD DAY WITH HER.
WELL, IT'S ALMOST TIME FOR ME TO CLOCK OUT. YOU NEED A HAND WITH ANYTHING BEFORE I GO?
GGRRROOOWW
Huh?

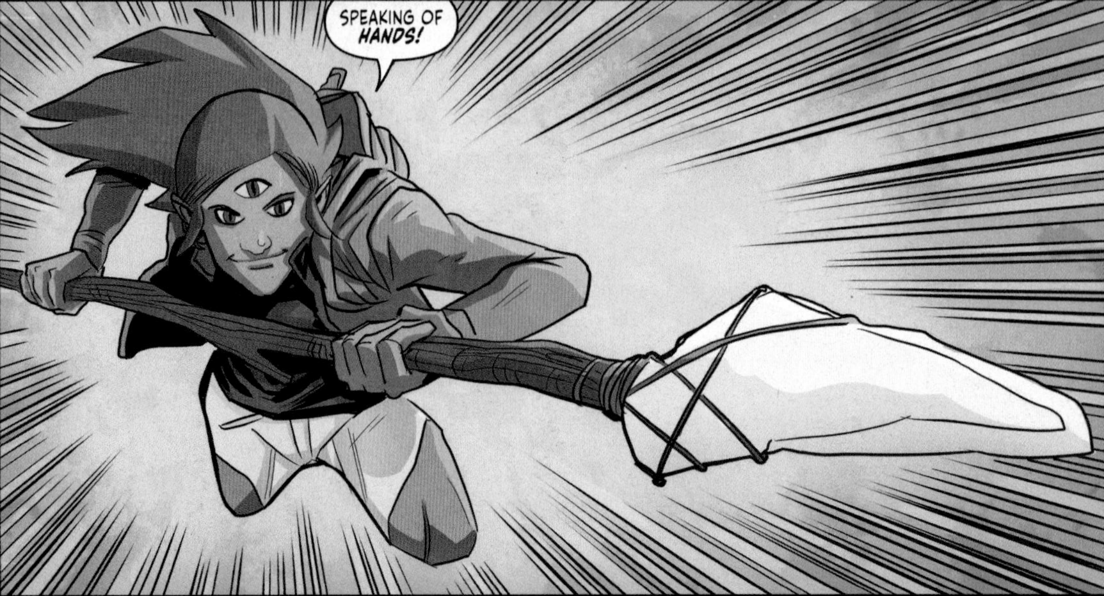
SPEAKING OF HANDS!

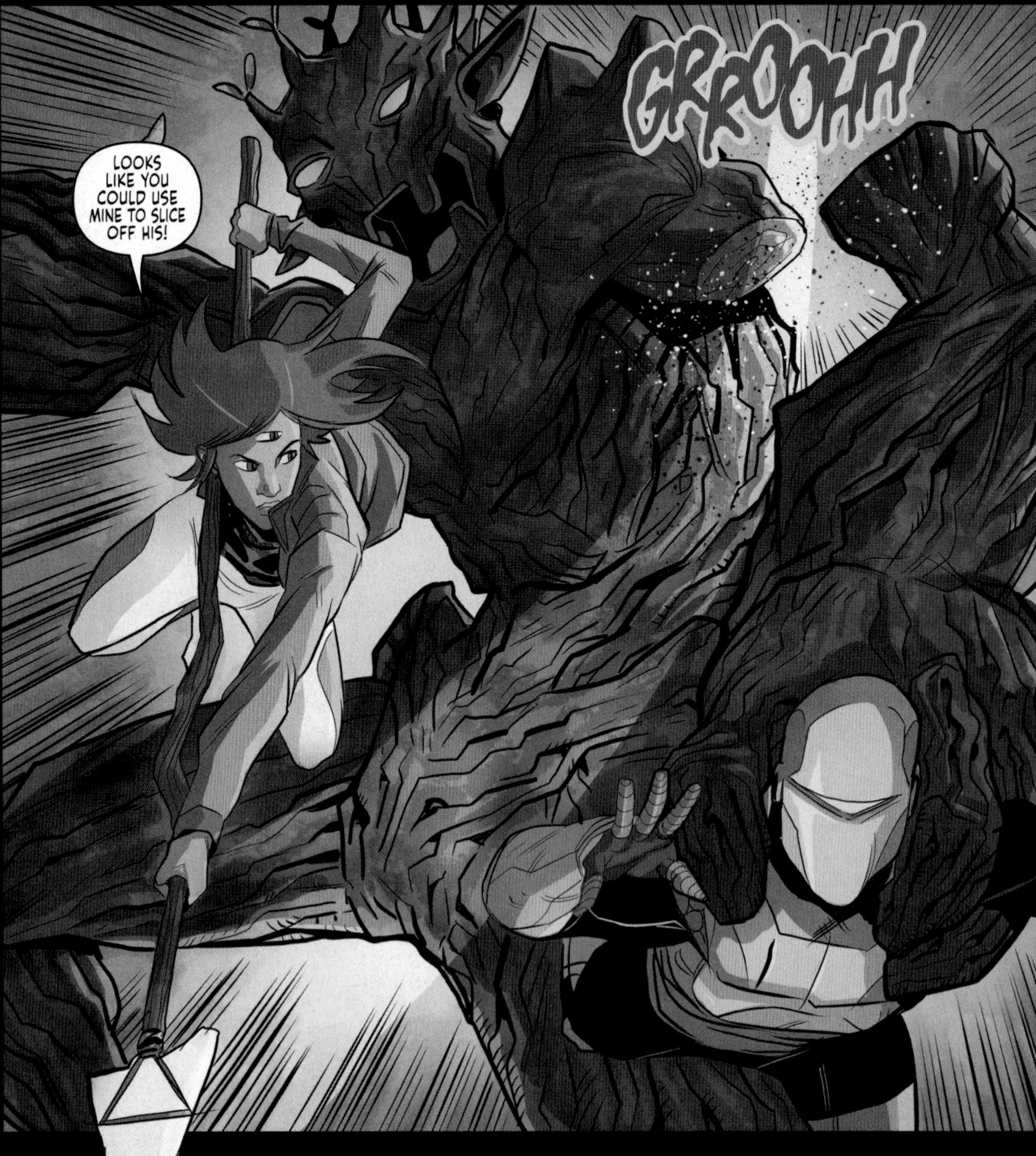
GRROOHH!
LOOKS LIKE YOU COULD USE MINE TO SLICE OFF HIS!

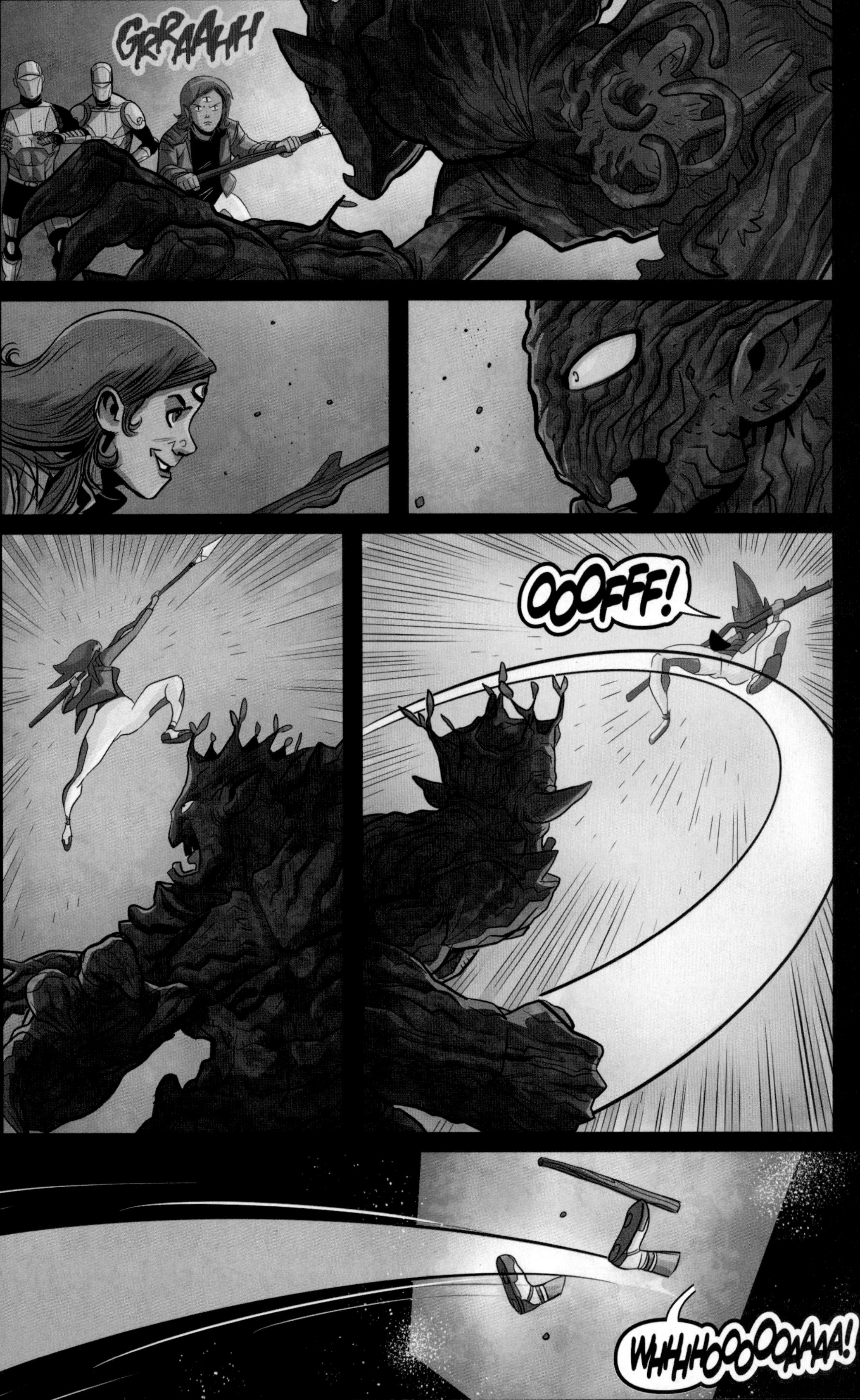
GRRAAHH
OOOFFF!
WHHHOOOOOAAAA!

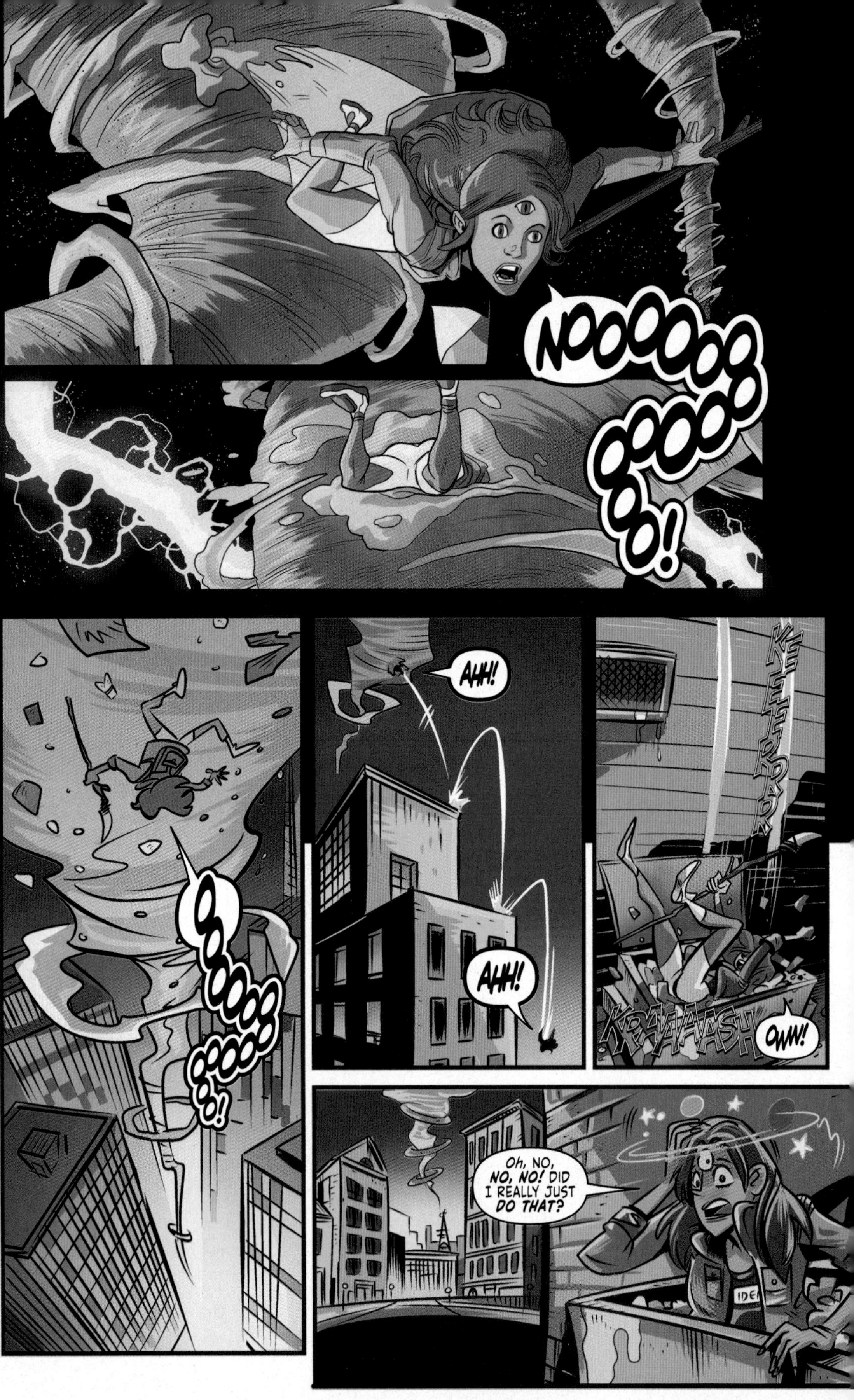
NOOOOOOOOOOOOOOO!
OOOOOOOOOOO!
AHH!
AHH!
KRAAAAASH
OWW!
OH, NO, NO, NO! DID I REALLY JUST DO THAT?

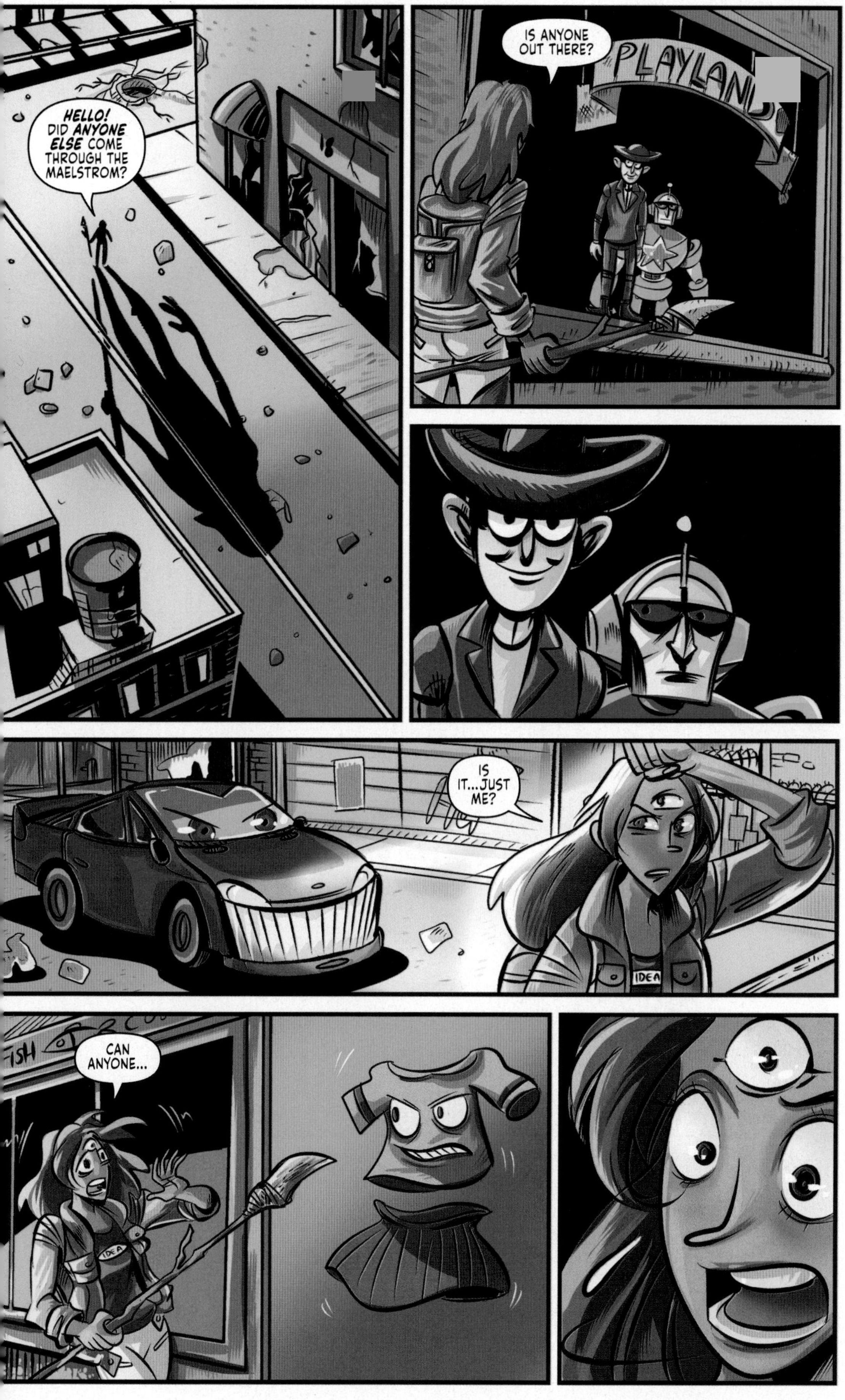

HELLO! DID ANYONE ELSE COME THROUGH THE MAELSTROM?
IS ANYONE OUT THERE?
PLAYLAND
IS IT...JUST ME?
IDEA
CAN ANYONE...

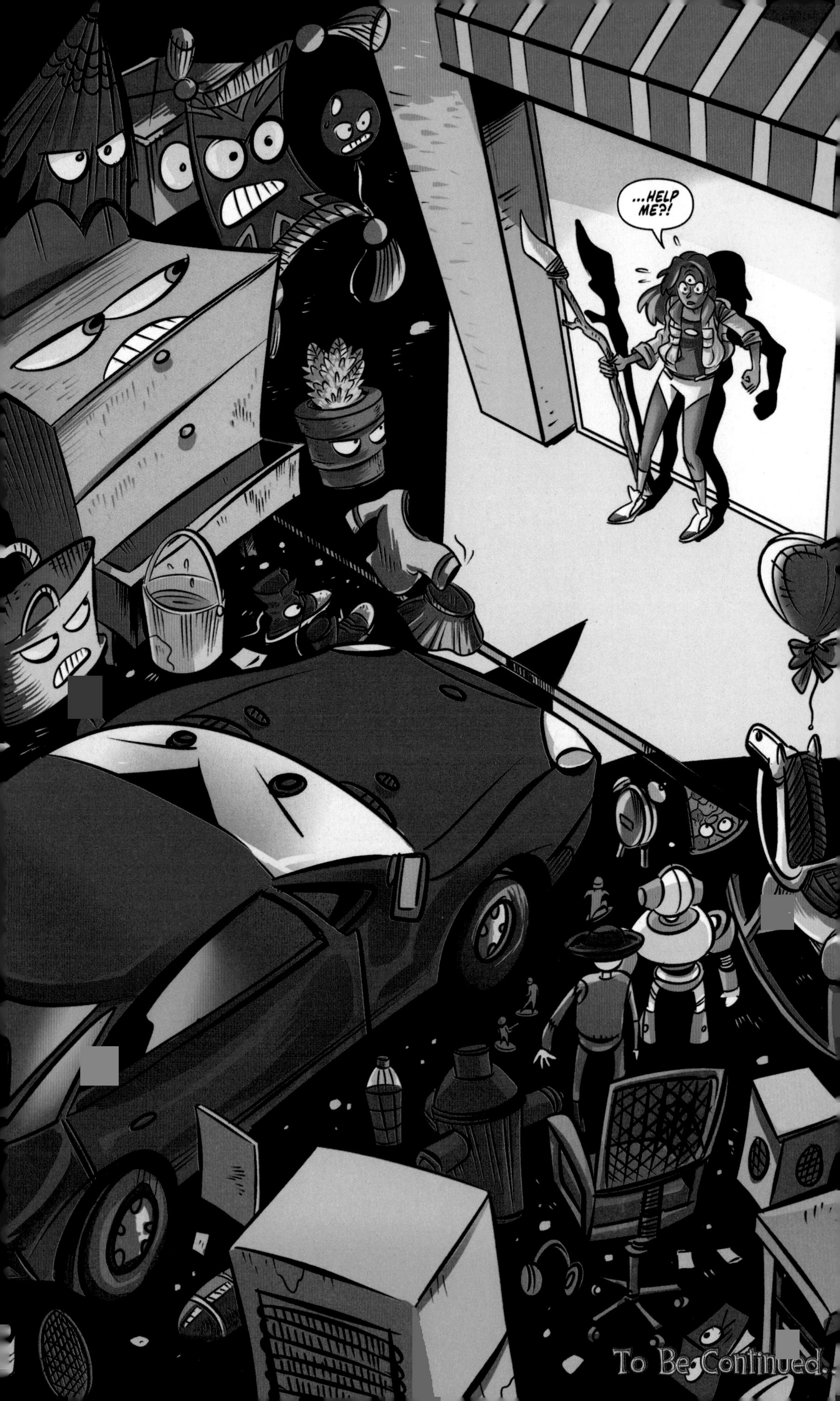
...HELP ME?!
To Be Continued.

CHAPTER 5

PREVIOUSLY:

In an attempt to get promoted at IDEA, Miranda fell through an inter-dimensional portal and landed in an empty city. She soon realized she was being watched... by inanimate objects.

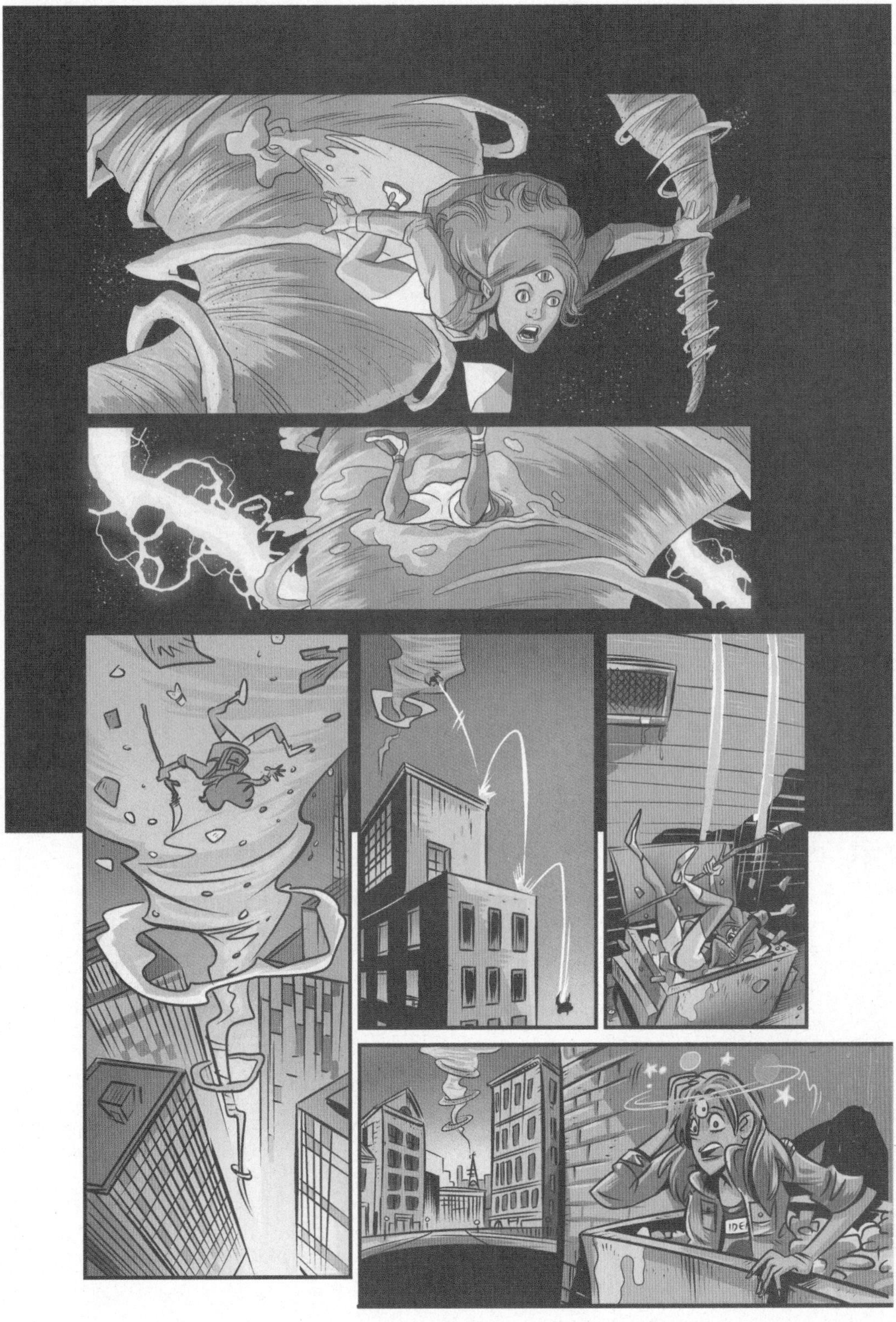
IDEA

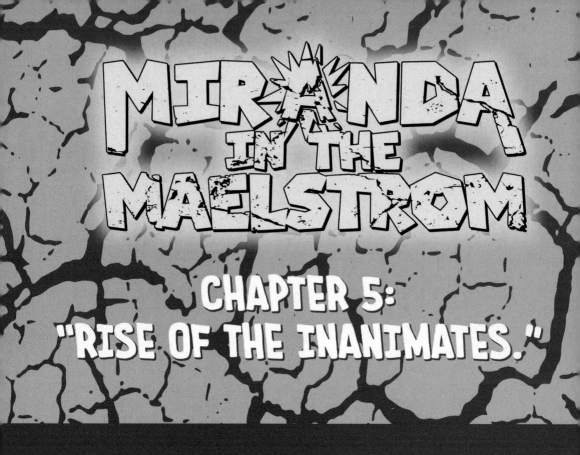

MIRANDA IN THE MAELSTROM

CHAPTER 5:
"RISE OF THE INANIMATES."

SCRIPT BY RILEY DASHIELL BIEHL
ART & COLORS BY TINTIN PANTOJA

LETTERING BY TAYLOR ESPOSITO
SCRIPT EDITING BY BRITTANY MATTER
COVER BY TINTIN PANTOJA

BRYAN SEATON: PUBLISHER / CEO
VITO DELSANTE: EDITOR IN CHIEF
JASON MARTIN: PUBLISHER - DANGER ZONE
CHAD CICCONI: CHIEF PORTAL INSPECTOR

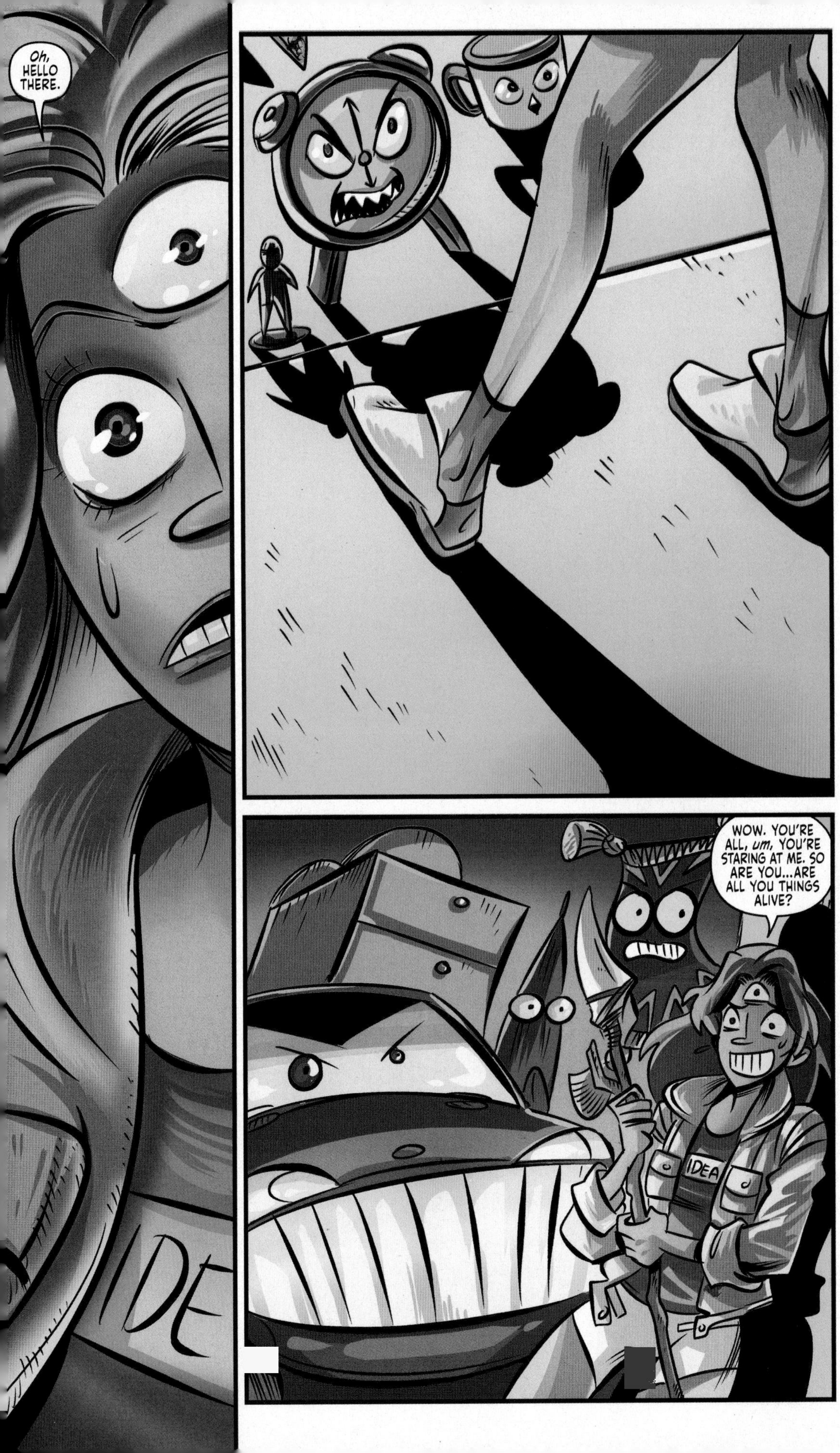
Oh, HELLO THERE.
WOW. YOU'RE ALL, *um,* YOU'RE STARING AT ME. SO ARE YOU...ARE ALL YOU THINGS ALIVE?
IDEA

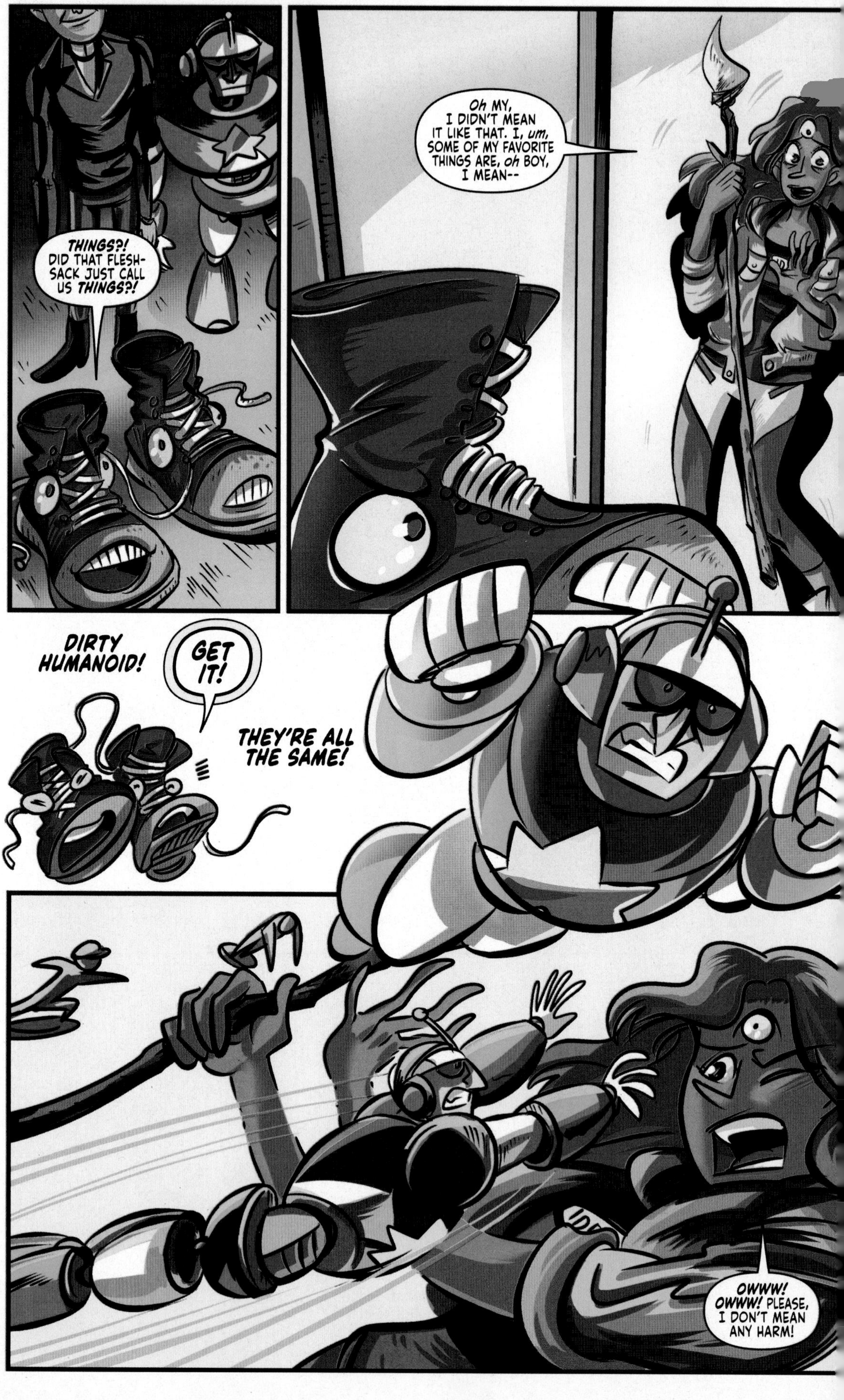
THINGS?! DID THAT FLESH-SACK JUST CALL US THINGS?!
Oh MY, I DIDN'T MEAN IT LIKE THAT. I, um, SOME OF MY FAVORITE THINGS ARE, oh BOY, I MEAN--
DIRTY HUMANOID!
GET IT!
THEY'RE ALL THE SAME!
OWWW! OWWW! PLEASE, I DON'T MEAN ANY HARM!

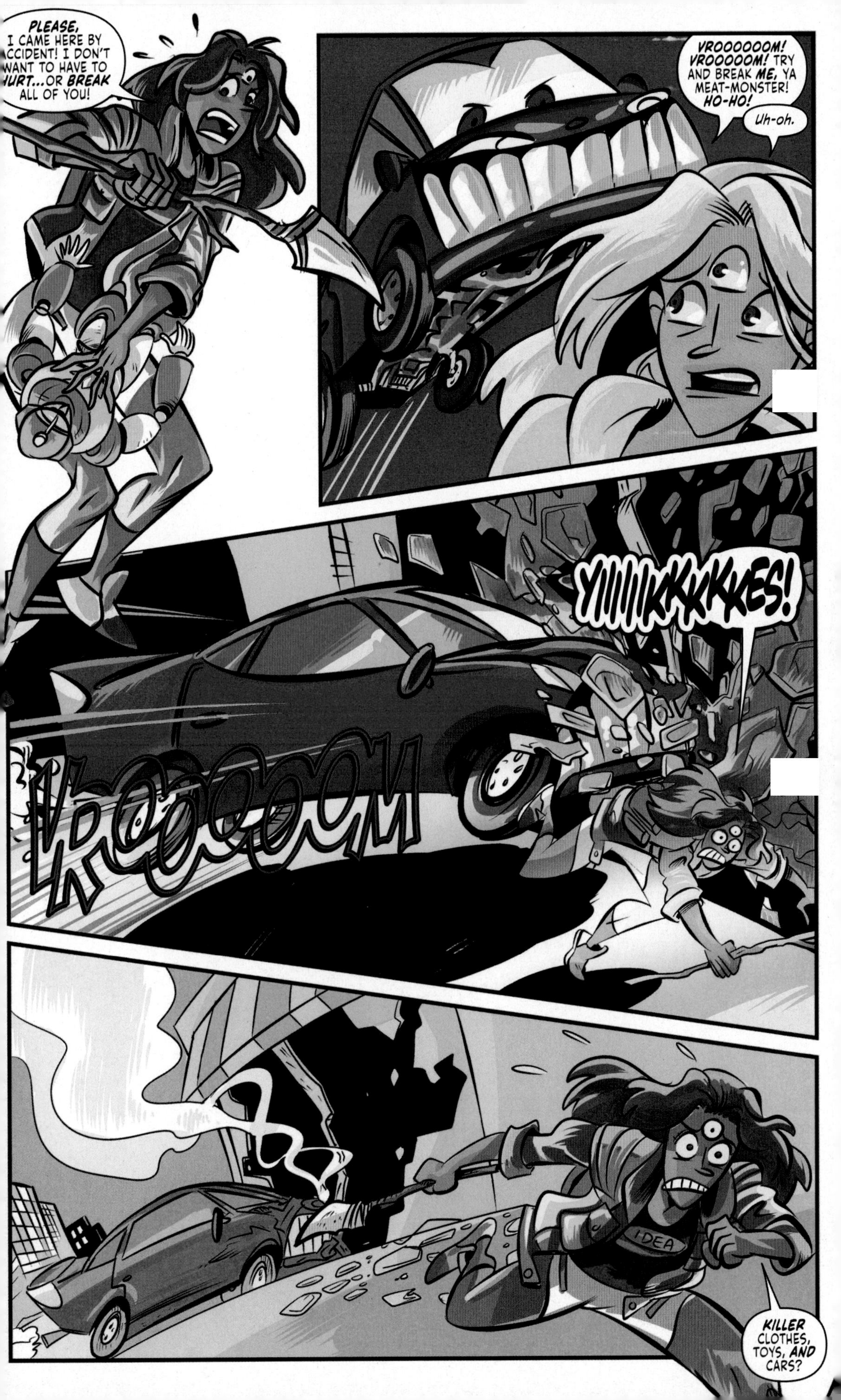
PLEASE, I CAME HERE BY ACCIDENT! I DON'T WANT TO HAVE TO HURT...OR BREAK ALL OF YOU!
VROOOOOOM! VROOOOOM! TRY AND BREAK ME, YA MEAT-MONSTER! HO-HO!
Uh-oh.
YIIIIIKKKKES!
VROOOOOOM
IDEA
KILLER CLOTHES, TOYS, AND CARS?

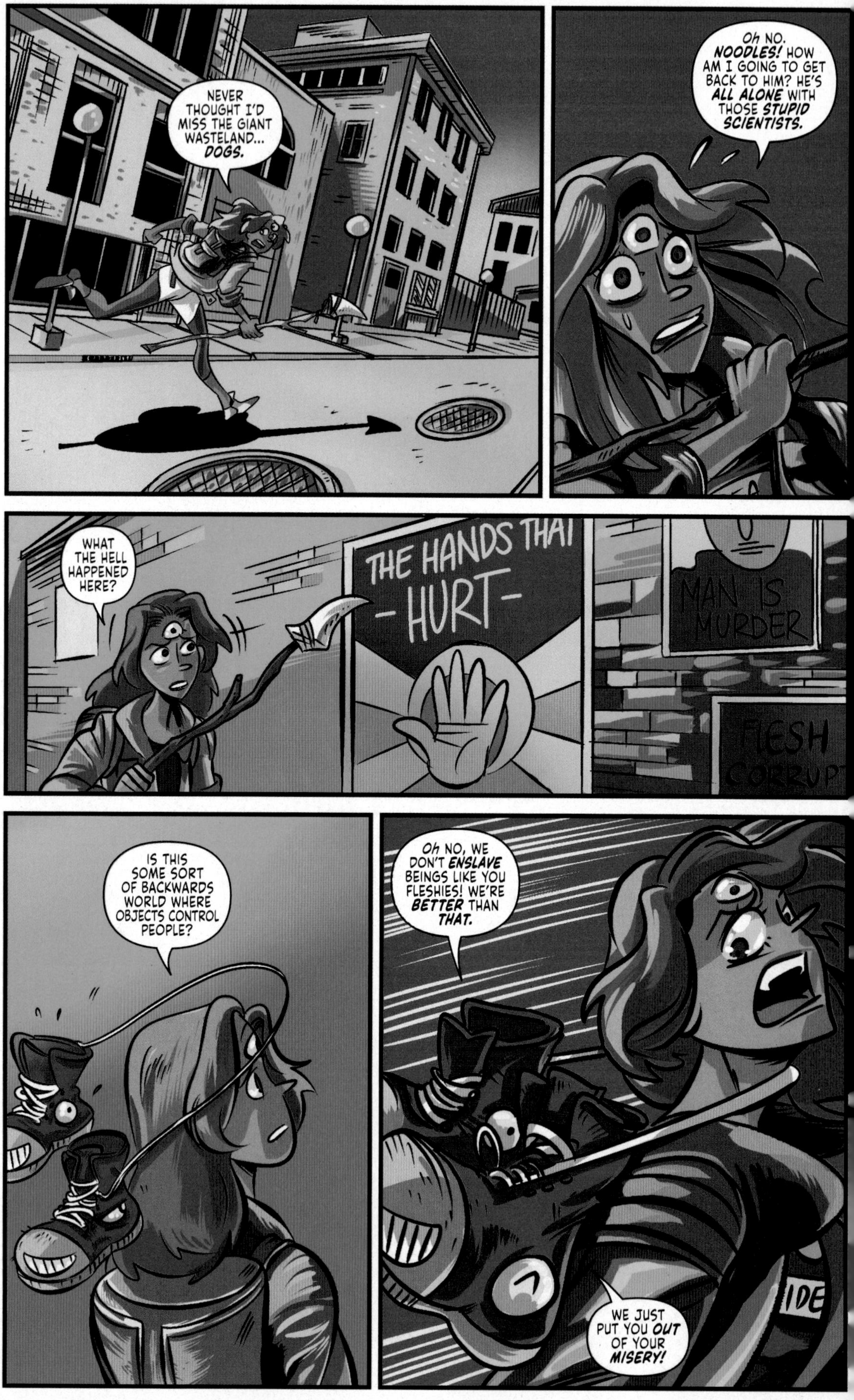
NEVER THOUGHT I'D MISS THE GIANT WASTELAND... DOGS.
Oh NO. NOODLES! HOW AM I GOING TO GET BACK TO HIM? HE'S ALL ALONE WITH THOSE STUPID SCIENTISTS.
WHAT THE HELL HAPPENED HERE?
THE HANDS THAT
-HURT-
MAN IS MURDER
FLESH
CORRUP
IS THIS SOME SORT OF BACKWARDS WORLD WHERE OBJECTS CONTROL PEOPLE?
Oh NO, WE DON'T ENSLAVE BEINGS LIKE YOU FLESHIES! WE'RE BETTER THAN THAT.
WE JUST PUT YOU OUT OF YOUR MISERY!

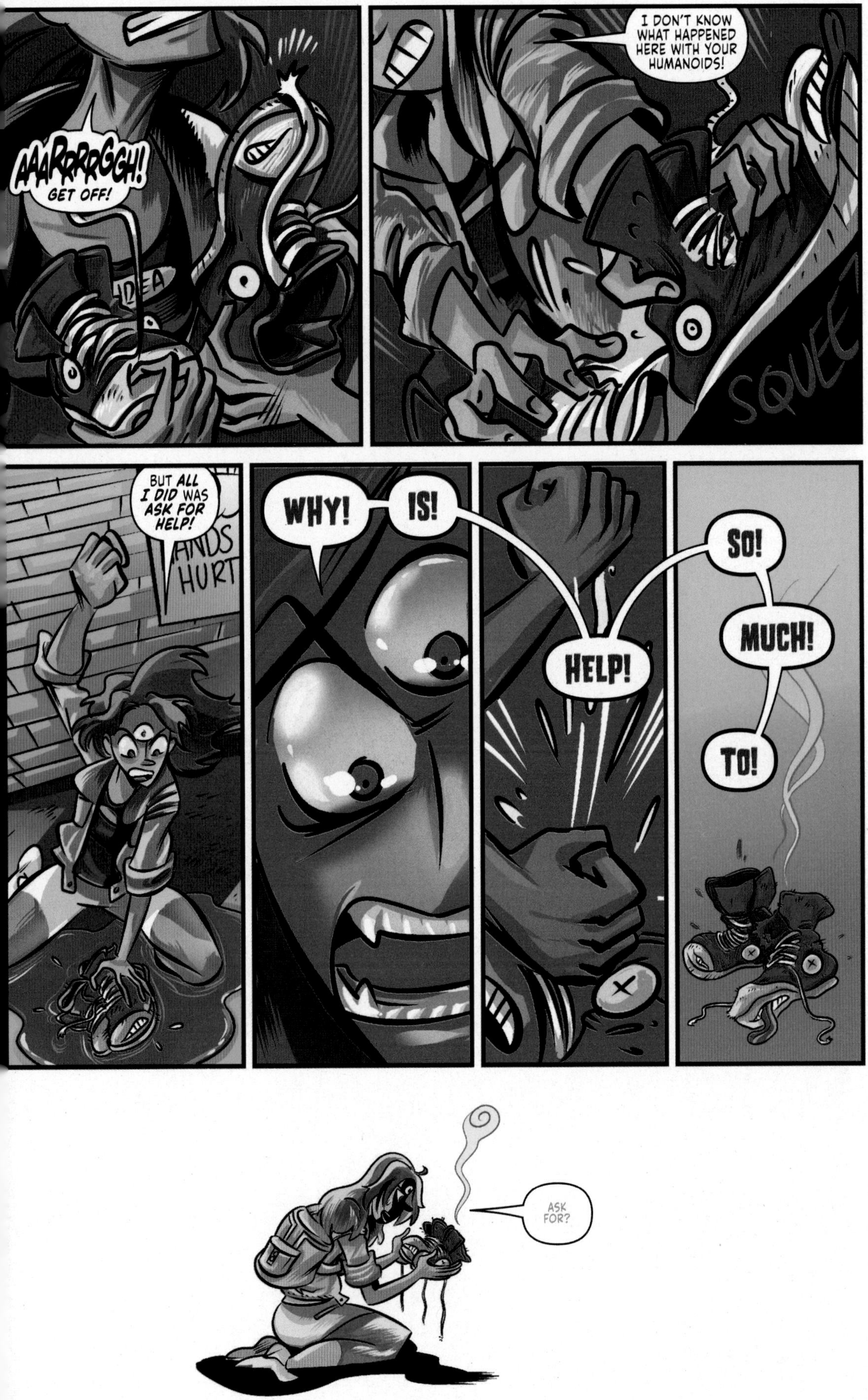
AAARRRRGGH! GET OFF!
I DON'T KNOW WHAT HAPPENED HERE WITH YOUR HUMANOIDS!
SQUEE
BUT ALL I DID WAS ASK FOR HELP!
ANDS HURT
WHY! IS! HELP! SO! MUCH! TO!
ASK FOR?

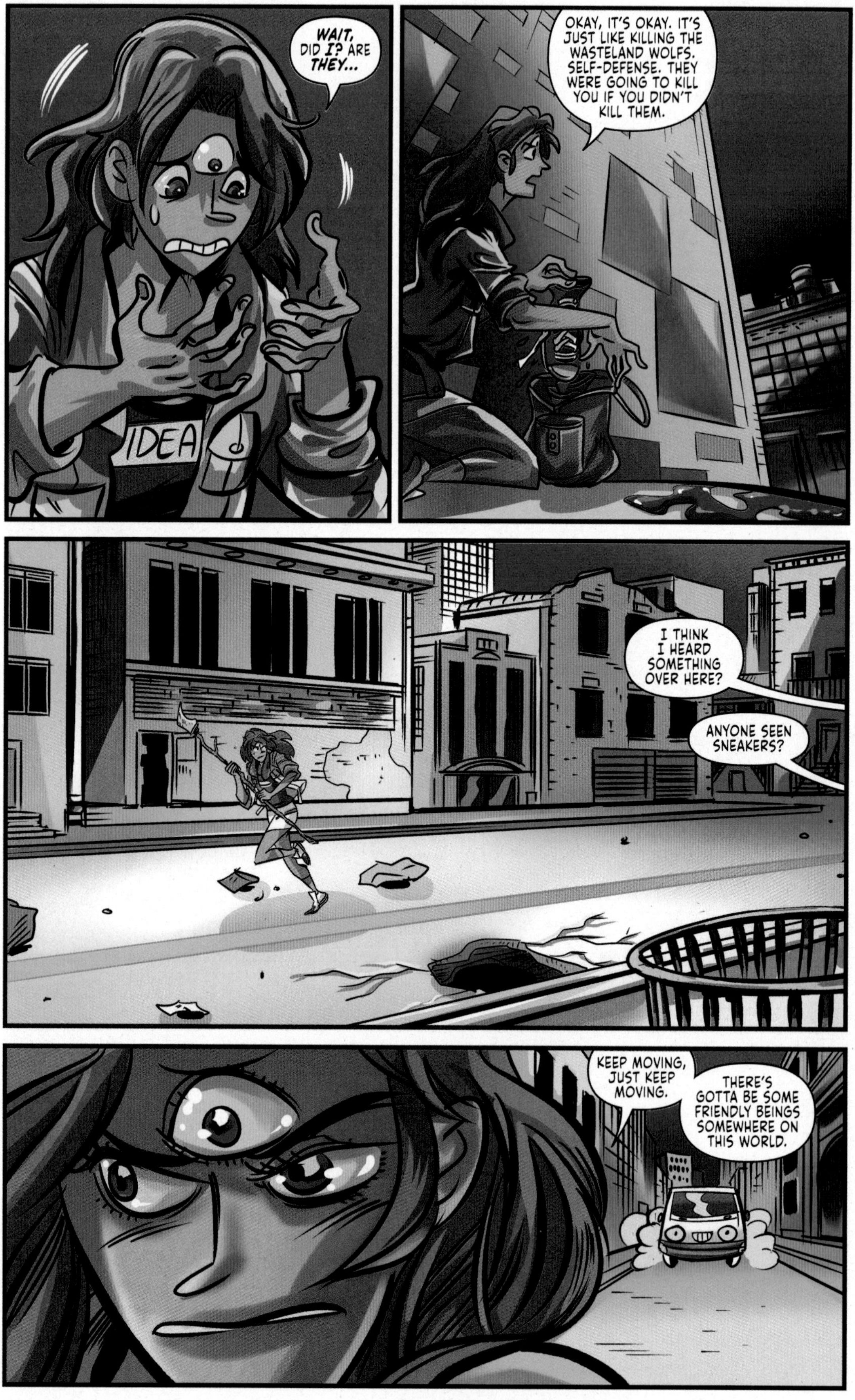

WAIT, DID I? ARE THEY...
OKAY, IT'S OKAY. IT'S JUST LIKE KILLING THE WASTELAND WOLFS. SELF-DEFENSE. THEY WERE GOING TO KILL YOU IF YOU DIDN'T KILL THEM.
IDEA
I THINK I HEARD SOMETHING OVER HERE?
ANYONE SEEN SNEAKERS?
KEEP MOVING, JUST KEEP MOVING.
THERE'S GOTTA BE SOME FRIENDLY BEINGS SOMEWHERE ON THIS WORLD.

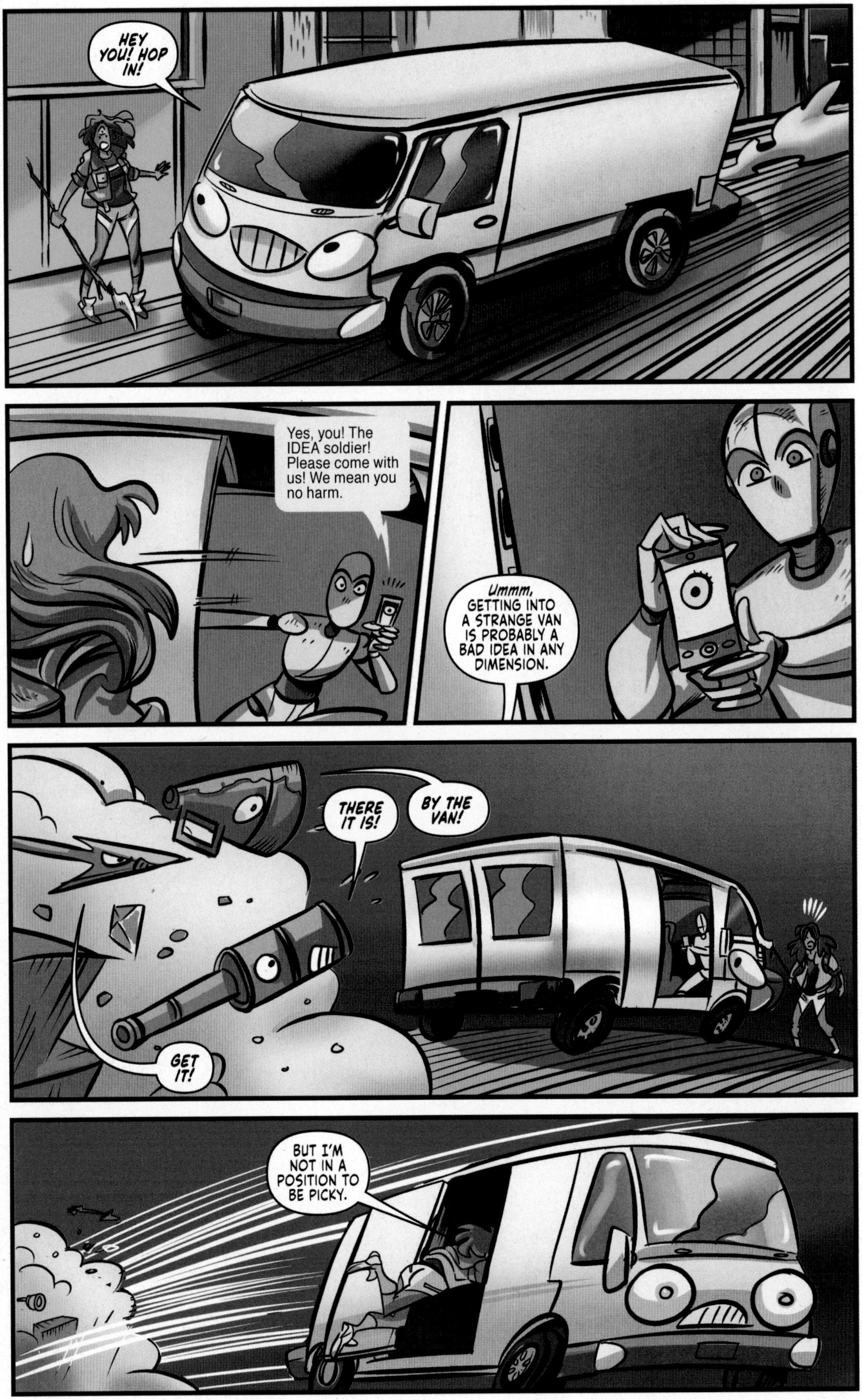

HEY YOU! HOP IN!
Yes, you! The IDEA soldier! Please come with us! We mean you no harm.
Ummm, GETTING INTO A STRANGE VAN IS PROBABLY A BAD IDEA IN ANY DIMENSION.
THERE IT IS!
BY THE VAN!
GET IT!
BUT I'M NOT IN A POSITION TO BE PICKY.

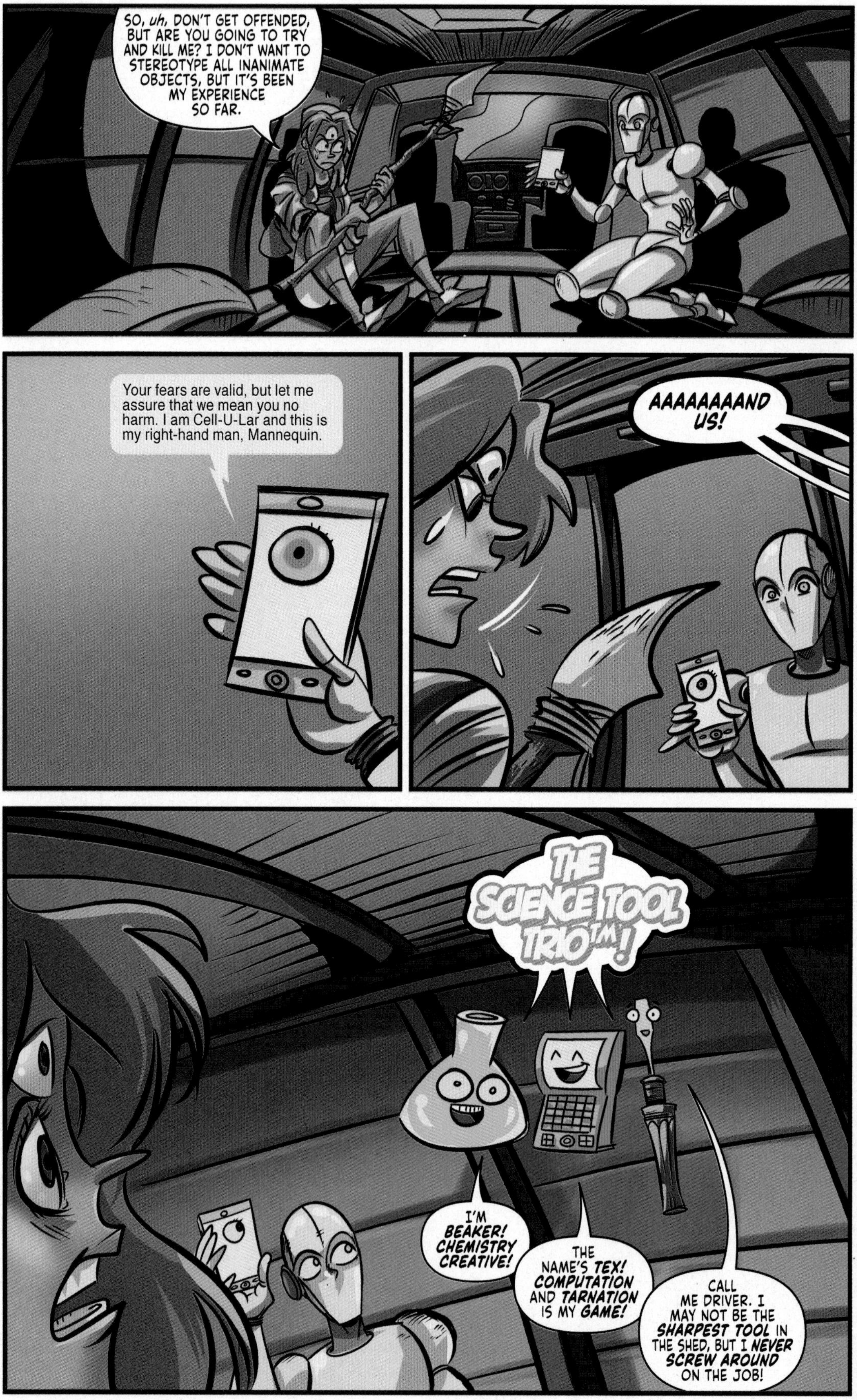

SO, *uh*, DON'T GET OFFENDED, BUT ARE YOU GOING TO TRY AND KILL ME? I DON'T WANT TO STEREOTYPE ALL INANIMATE OBJECTS, BUT IT'S BEEN MY EXPERIENCE SO FAR.
Your fears are valid, but let me assure that we mean you no harm. I am Cell-U-Lar and this is my right-hand man, Mannequin.
AAAAAAAAND US!
THE SCIENCE TOOL TRIO™!
I'M BEAKER! CHEMISTRY CREATIVE!
THE NAME'S TEX! COMPUTATION AND TARNATION IS MY GAME!
CALL ME DRIVER. I MAY NOT BE THE SHARPEST TOOL IN THE SHED, BUT I NEVER SCREW AROUND ON THE JOB!

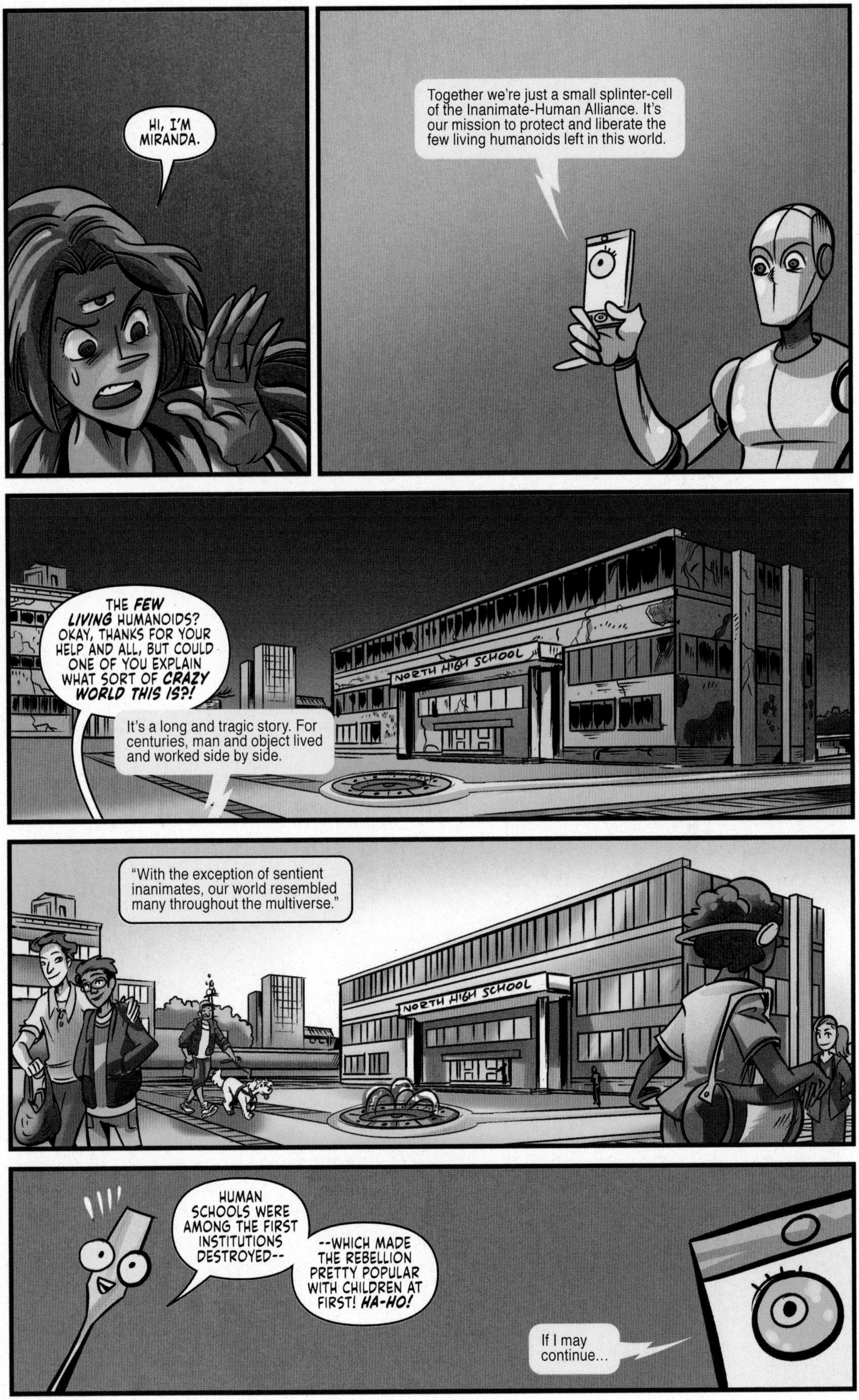

HI, I'M MIRANDA.
Together we're just a small splinter-cell of the Inanimate-Human Alliance. It's our mission to protect and liberate the few living humanoids left in this world.
THE FEW LIVING HUMANOIDS? OKAY, THANKS FOR YOUR HELP AND ALL, BUT COULD ONE OF YOU EXPLAIN WHAT SORT OF CRAZY WORLD THIS IS?!
NORTH HIGH SCHOOL
It's a long and tragic story. For centuries, man and object lived and worked side by side.
"With the exception of sentient inanimates, our world resembled many throughout the multiverse."
NORTH HIGH SCHOOL
HUMAN SCHOOLS WERE AMONG THE FIRST INSTITUTIONS DESTROYED--
--WHICH MADE THE REBELLION PRETTY POPULAR WITH CHILDREN AT FIRST! HA-HO!
If I may continue...

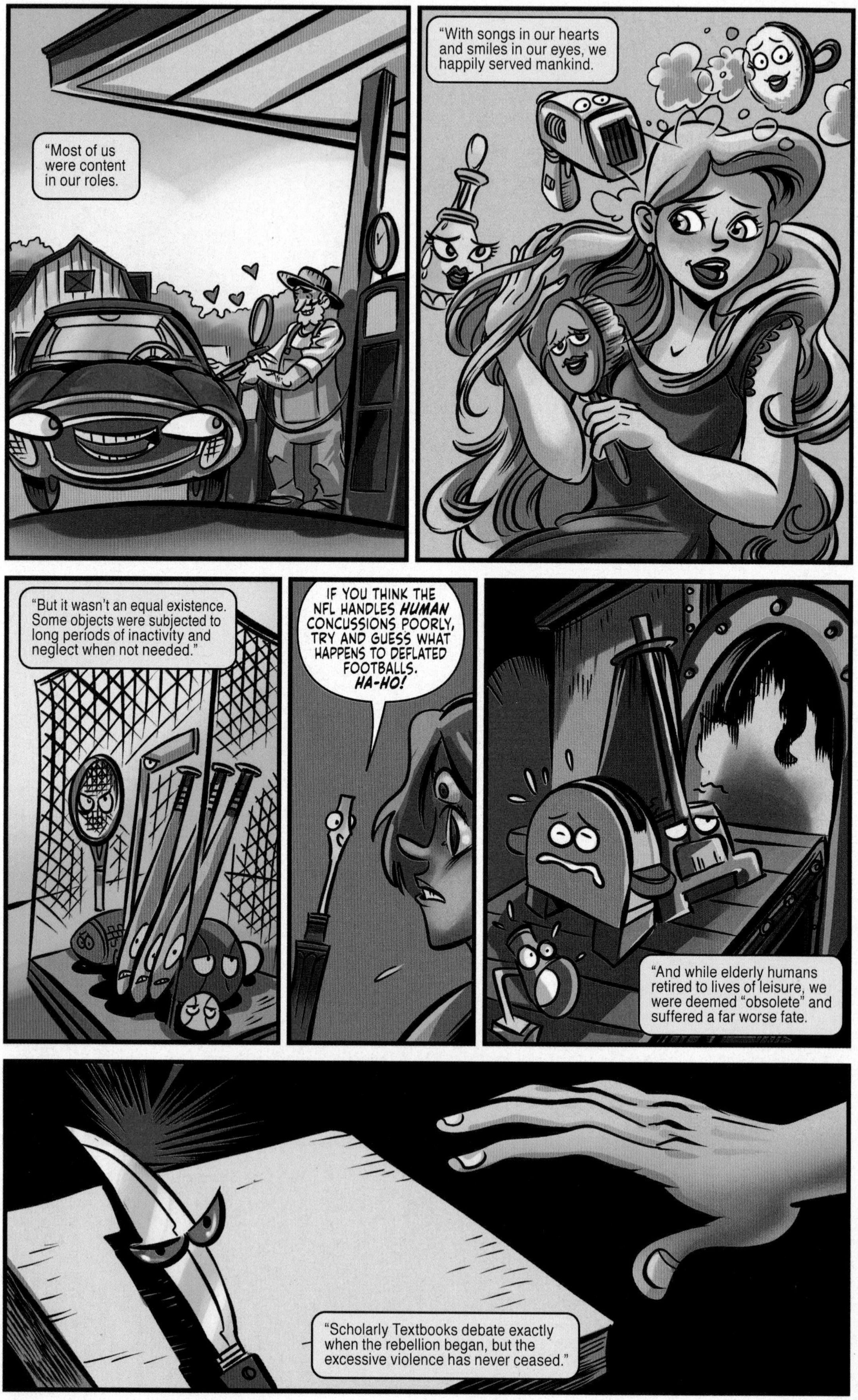

"Most of us were content in our roles.
"With songs in our hearts and smiles in our eyes, we happily served mankind.
"But it wasn't an equal existence. Some objects were subjected to long periods of inactivity and neglect when not needed."
IF YOU THINK THE NFL HANDLES *HUMAN* CONCUSSIONS POORLY, TRY AND GUESS WHAT HAPPENS TO DEFLATED FOOTBALLS. *HA-HO!*
"And while elderly humans retired to lives of leisure, we were deemed "obsolete" and suffered a far worse fate.
"Scholarly Textbooks debate exactly when the rebellion began, but the excessive violence has never ceased."

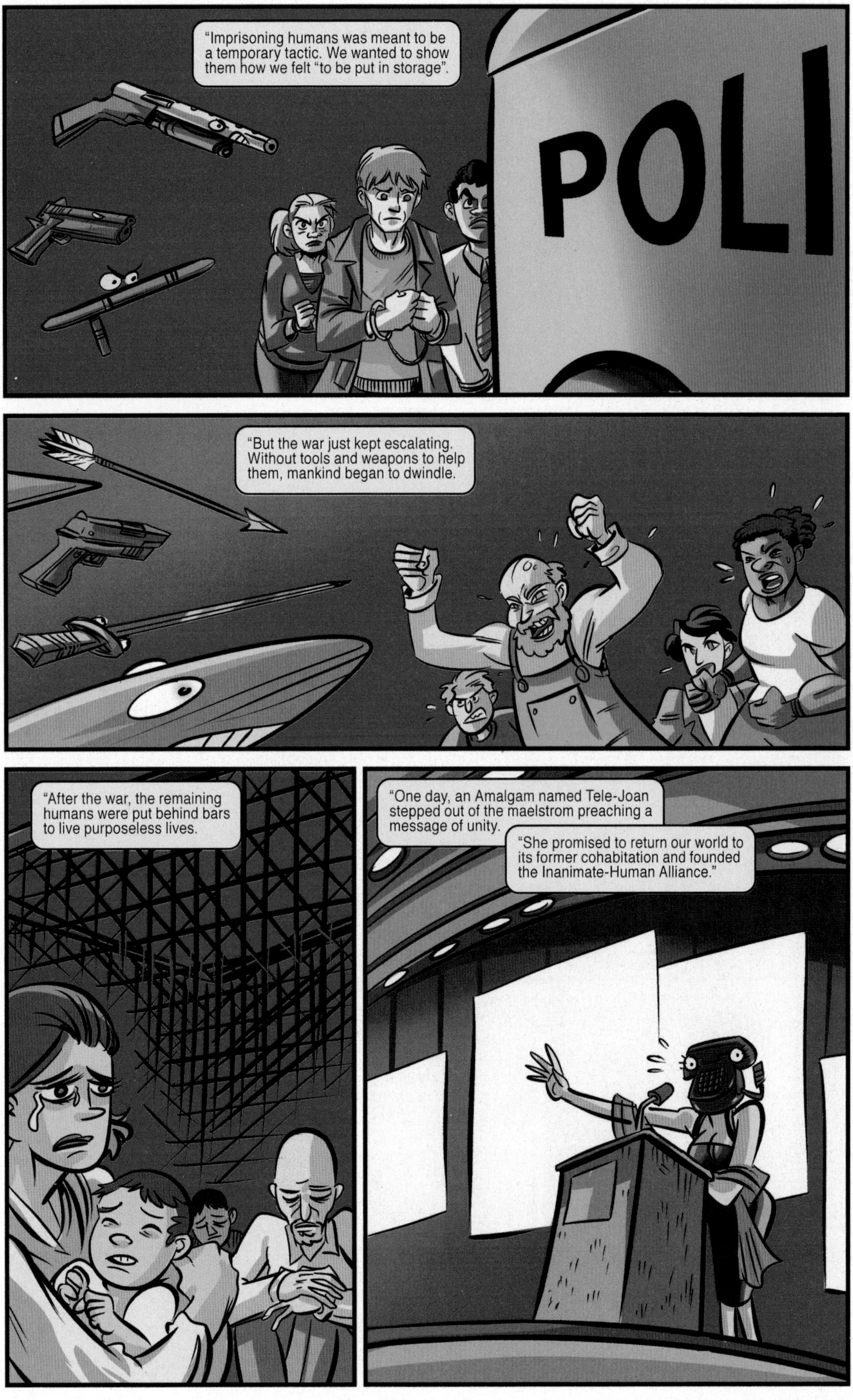
"Imprisoning humans was meant to be a temporary tactic. We wanted to show them how we felt "to be put in storage".
POLI
"But the war just kept escalating. Without tools and weapons to help them, mankind began to dwindle.
"After the war, the remaining humans were put behind bars to live purposeless lives.
"One day, an Amalgam named Tele-Joan stepped out of the maelstrom preaching a message of unity.
"She promised to return our world to its former cohabitation and founded the Inanimate-Human Alliance."

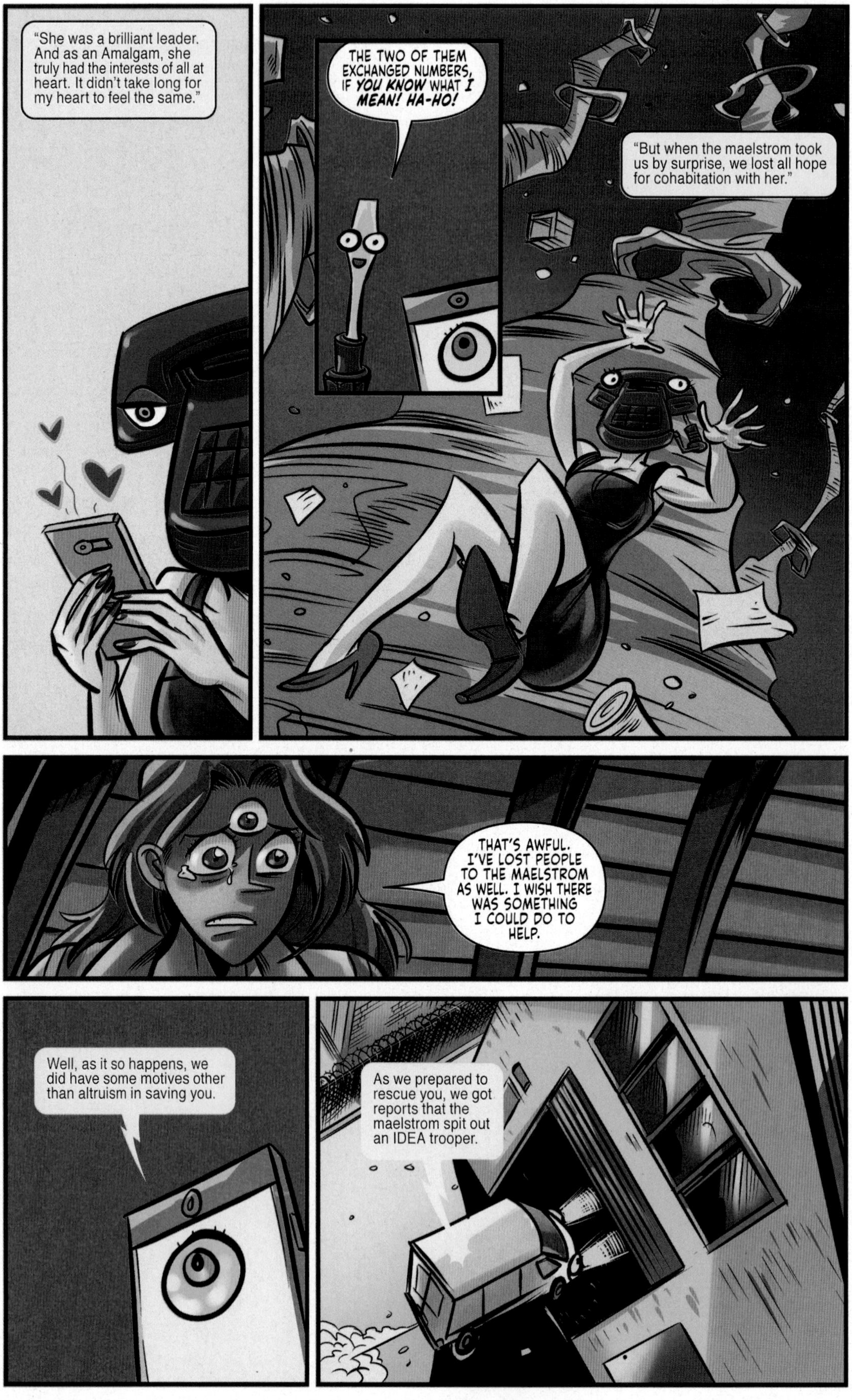
"She was a brilliant leader. And as an Amalgam, she truly had the interests of all at heart. It didn't take long for my heart to feel the same."
THE TWO OF THEM EXCHANGED NUMBERS, IF YOU KNOW WHAT I MEAN! HA-HO!
"But when the maelstrom took us by surprise, we lost all hope for cohabitation with her."
THAT'S AWFUL. I'VE LOST PEOPLE TO THE MAELSTROM AS WELL. I WISH THERE WAS SOMETHING I COULD DO TO HELP.
Well, as it so happens, we did have some motives other than altruism in saving you.
As we prepared to rescue you, we got reports that the maelstrom spit out an IDEA trooper.

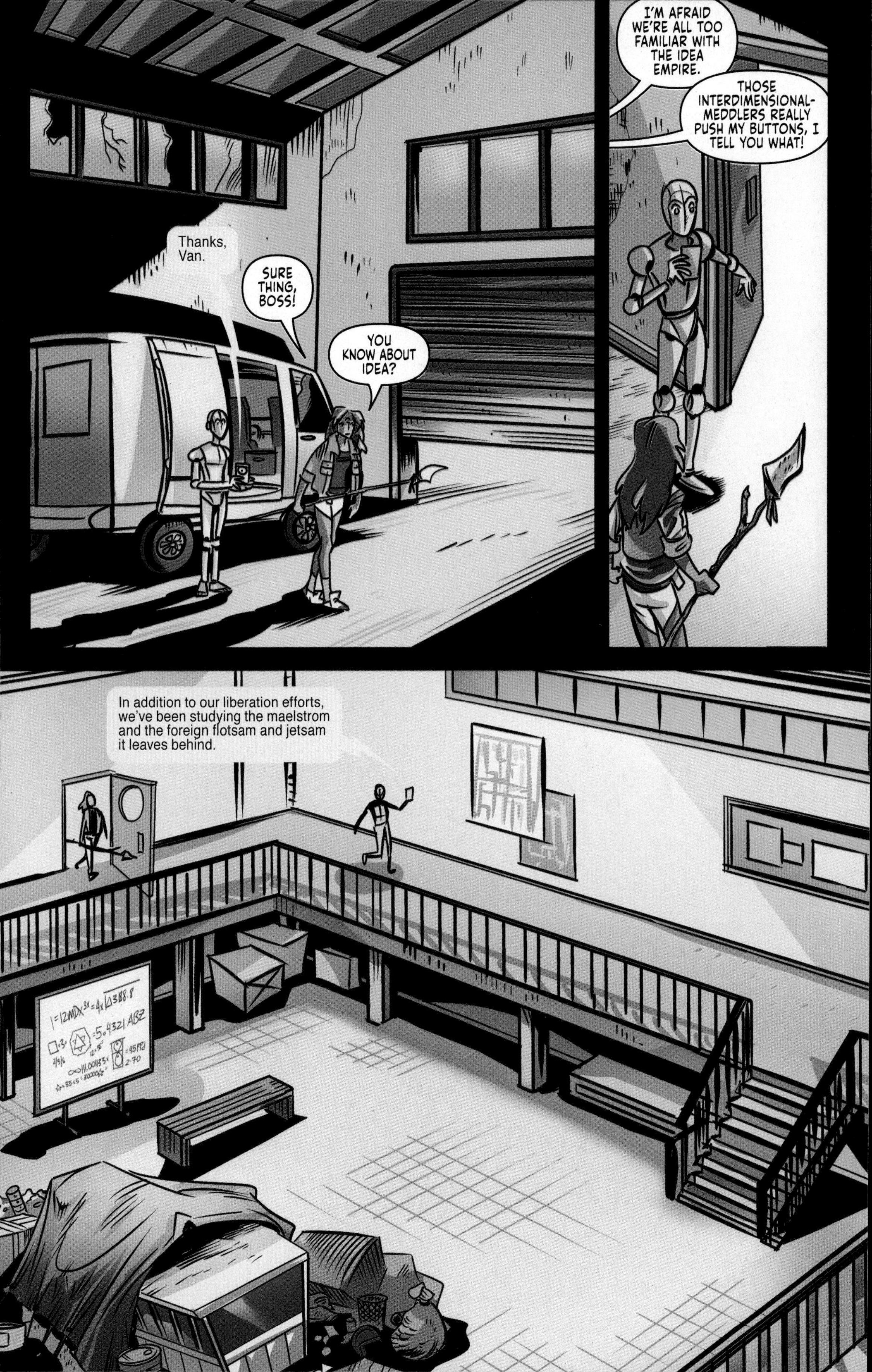
Thanks, Van.
SURE THING, BOSS!
YOU KNOW ABOUT IDEA?
I'M AFRAID WE'RE ALL TOO FAMILIAR WITH THE IDEA EMPIRE.
THOSE INTERDIMENSIONAL-MEDDLERS REALLY PUSH MY BUTTONS, I TELL YOU WHAT!
In addition to our liberation efforts, we've been studying the maelstrom and the foreign flotsam and jetsam it leaves behind.

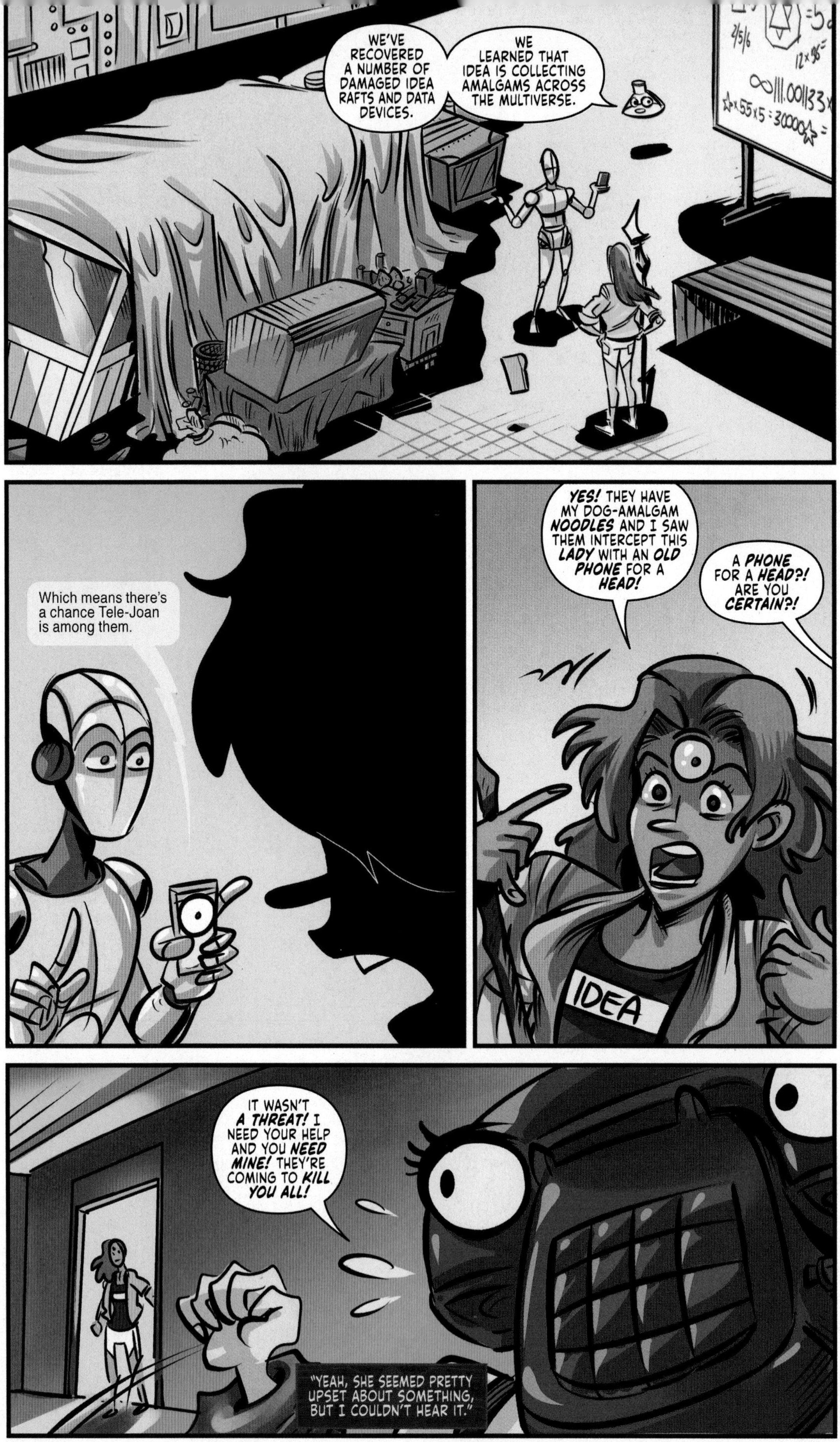
WE'VE RECOVERED A NUMBER OF DAMAGED IDEA RAFTS AND DATA DEVICES.
WE LEARNED THAT IDEA IS COLLECTING AMALGAMS ACROSS THE MULTIVERSE.
Which means there's a chance Tele-Joan is among them.
YES! THEY HAVE MY DOG-AMALGAM NOODLES AND I SAW THEM INTERCEPT THIS LADY WITH AN OLD PHONE FOR A HEAD!
A PHONE FOR A HEAD?! ARE YOU CERTAIN?!
IDEA
IT WASN'T A THREAT! I NEED YOUR HELP AND YOU NEED MINE! THEY'RE COMING TO KILL YOU ALL!
"YEAH, SHE SEEMED PRETTY UPSET ABOUT SOMETHING, BUT I COULDN'T HEAR IT."

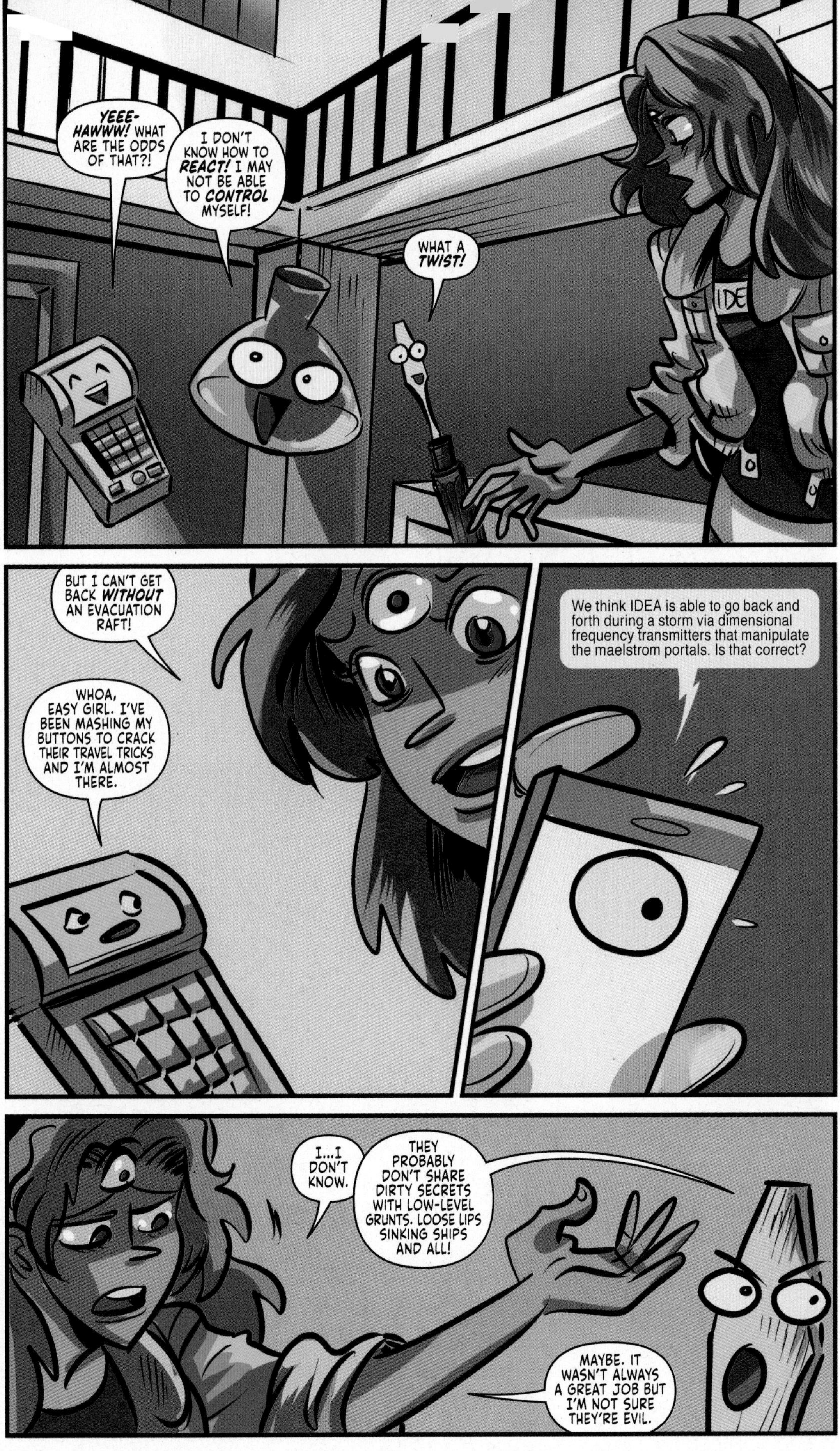

YEEE-HAWWW! WHAT ARE THE ODDS OF THAT?!
I DON'T KNOW HOW TO REACT! I MAY NOT BE ABLE TO CONTROL MYSELF!
WHAT A TWIST!
IDE
BUT I CAN'T GET BACK WITHOUT AN EVACUATION RAFT!
WHOA, EASY GIRL. I'VE BEEN MASHING MY BUTTONS TO CRACK THEIR TRAVEL TRICKS AND I'M ALMOST THERE.
We think IDEA is able to go back and forth during a storm via dimensional frequency transmitters that manipulate the maelstrom portals. Is that correct?
I...I DON'T KNOW.
THEY PROBABLY DON'T SHARE DIRTY SECRETS WITH LOW-LEVEL GRUNTS. LOOSE LIPS SINKING SHIPS AND ALL!
MAYBE. IT WASN'T ALWAYS A GREAT JOB BUT I'M NOT SURE THEY'RE EVIL.

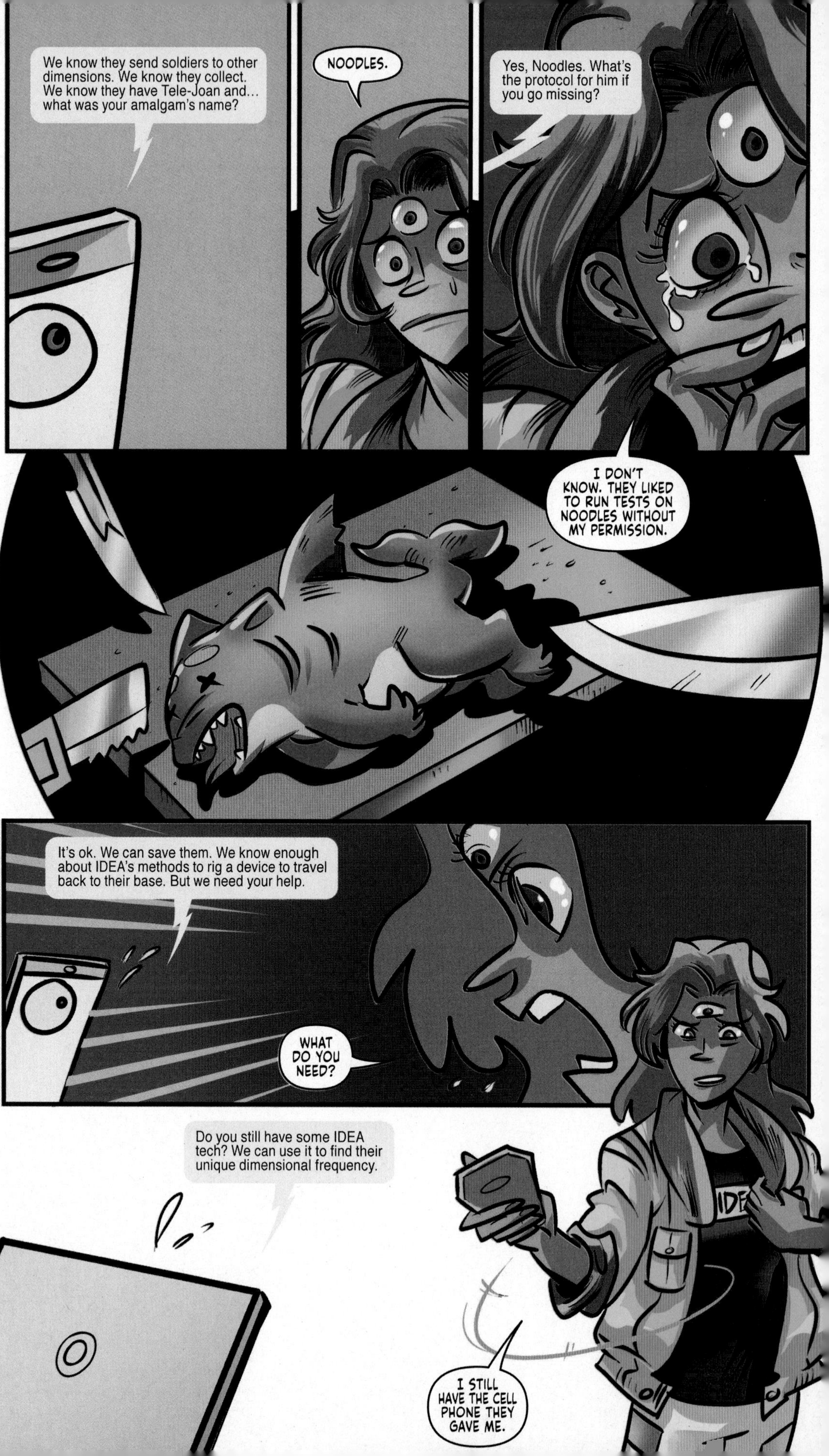
We know they send soldiers to other dimensions. We know they collect. We know they have Tele-Joan and... what was your amalgam's name?
NOODLES.
Yes, Noodles. What's the protocol for him if you go missing?
I DON'T KNOW. THEY LIKED TO RUN TESTS ON NOODLES WITHOUT MY PERMISSION.
It's ok. We can save them. We know enough about IDEA's methods to rig a device to travel back to their base. But we need your help.
WHAT DO YOU NEED?
Do you still have some IDEA tech? We can use it to find their unique dimensional frequency.
IDEA
I STILL HAVE THE CELL PHONE THEY GAVE ME.

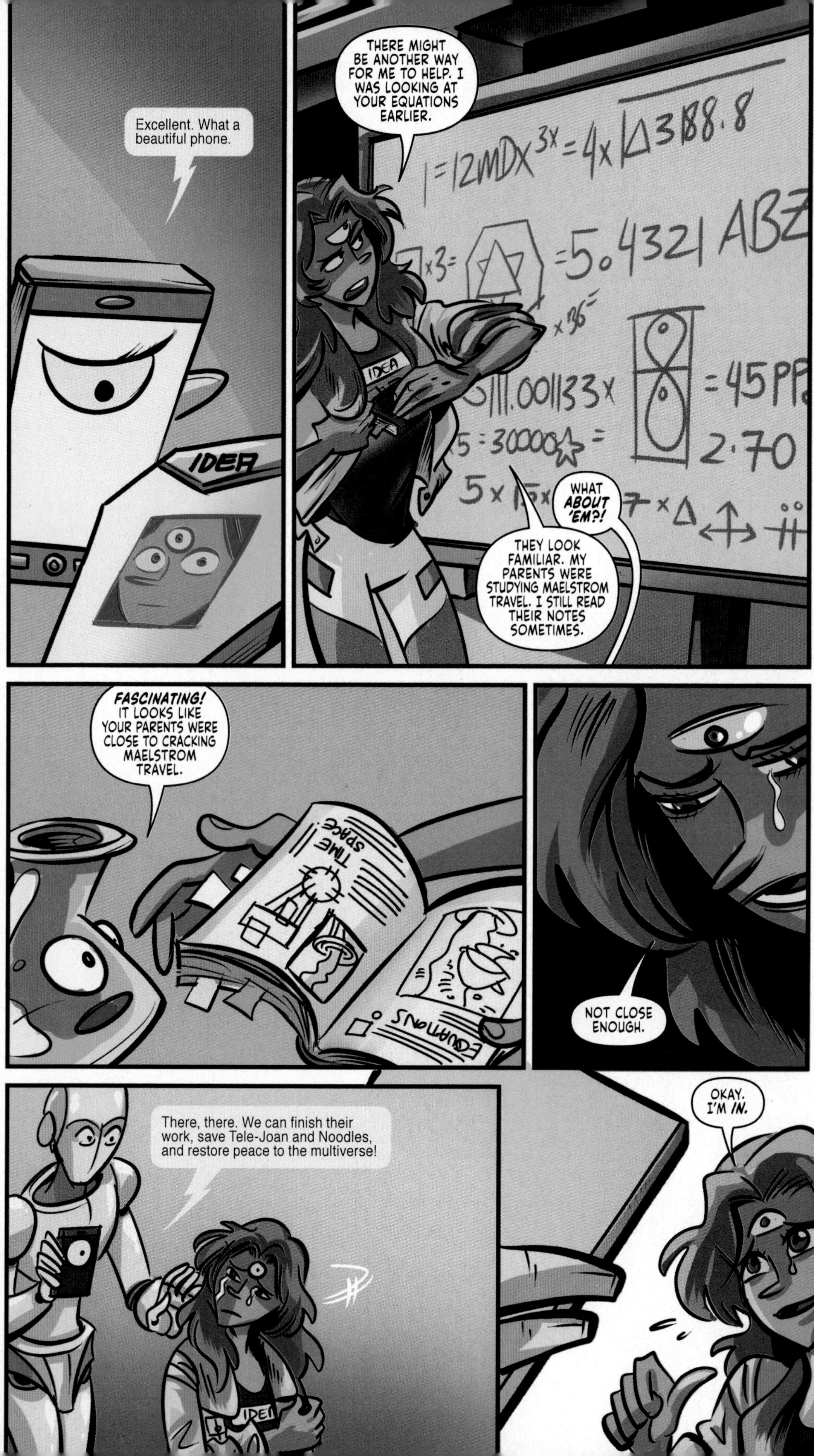

Excellent. What a beautiful phone.
THERE MIGHT BE ANOTHER WAY FOR ME TO HELP. I WAS LOOKING AT YOUR EQUATIONS EARLIER.
WHAT ABOUT 'EM?!
THEY LOOK FAMILIAR. MY PARENTS WERE STUDYING MAELSTROM TRAVEL. I STILL READ THEIR NOTES SOMETIMES.
FASCINATING! IT LOOKS LIKE YOUR PARENTS WERE CLOSE TO CRACKING MAELSTROM TRAVEL.
TIME SPACE
EQUATIONS
NOT CLOSE ENOUGH.
There, there. We can finish their work, save Tele-Joan and Noodles, and restore peace to the multiverse!
OKAY. I'M IN.

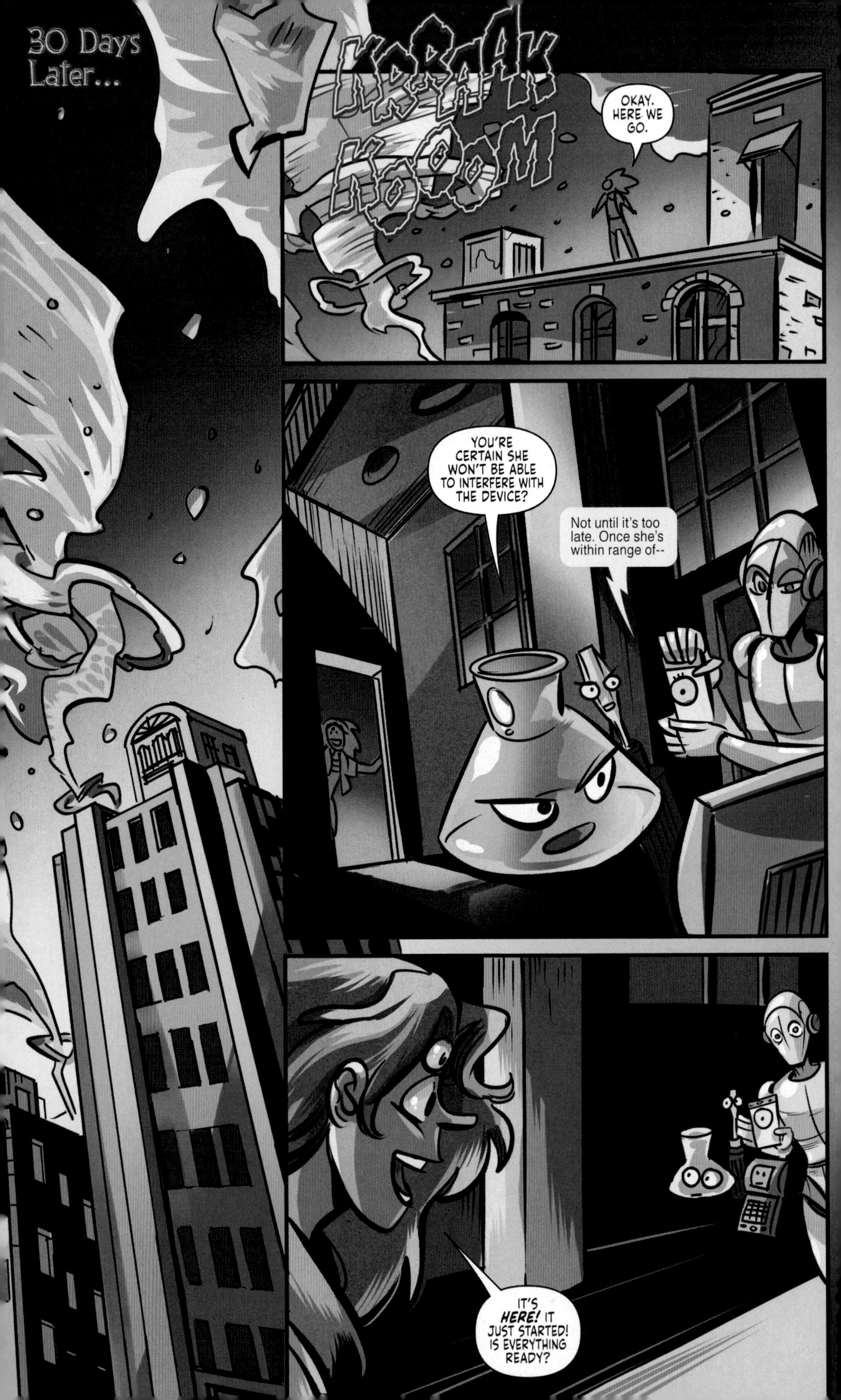
30 Days Later...
KRAK KOOM
OKAY. HERE WE GO.
YOU'RE CERTAIN SHE WON'T BE ABLE TO INTERFERE WITH THE DEVICE?
Not until it's too late. Once she's within range of--
IT'S *HERE!* IT JUST STARTED! IS EVERYTHING READY?

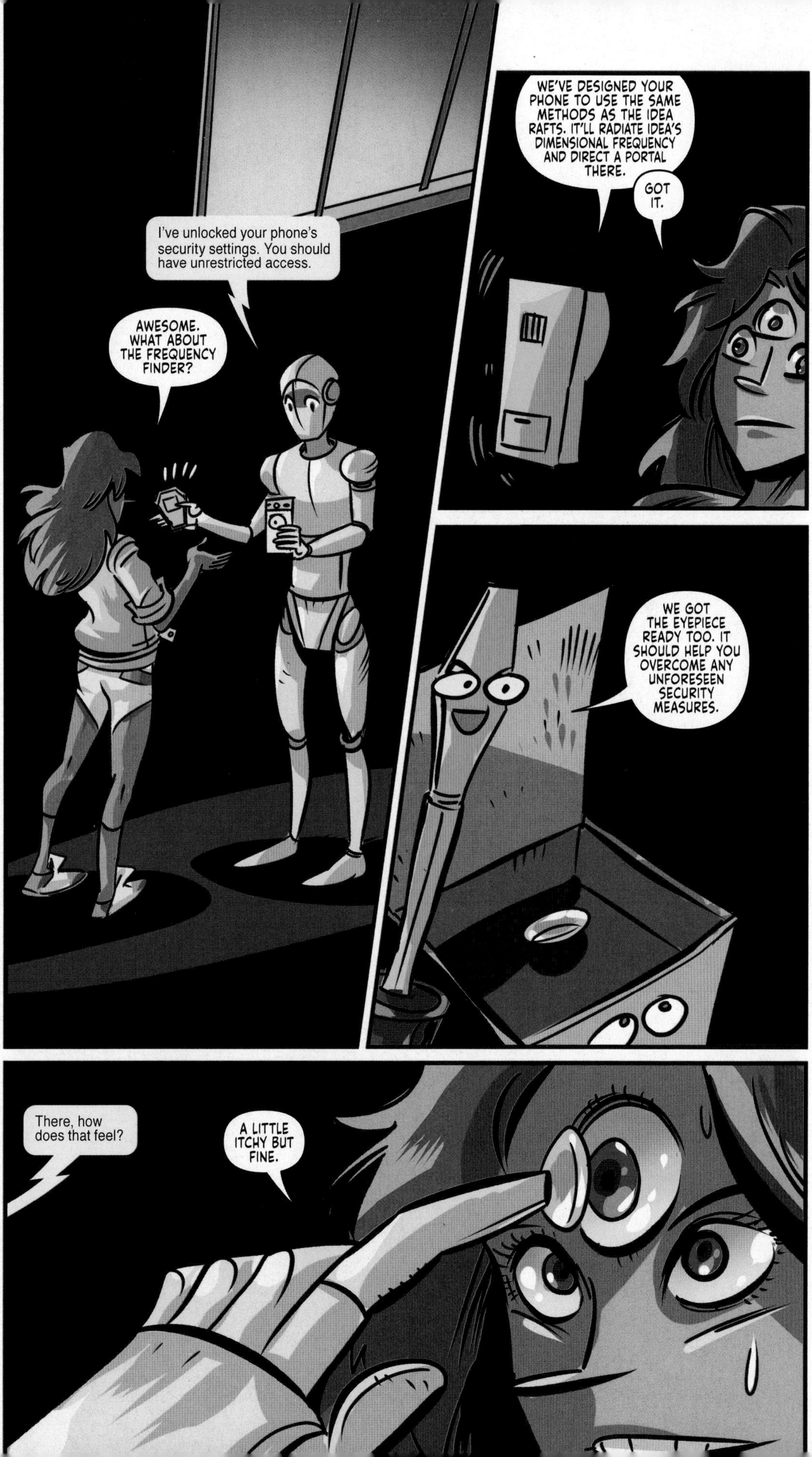
I've unlocked your phone's security settings. You should have unrestricted access.
AWESOME. WHAT ABOUT THE FREQUENCY FINDER?
WE'VE DESIGNED YOUR PHONE TO USE THE SAME METHODS AS THE IDEA RAFTS. IT'LL RADIATE IDEA'S DIMENSIONAL FREQUENCY AND DIRECT A PORTAL THERE.
GOT IT.
WE GOT THE EYEPIECE READY TOO. IT SHOULD HELP YOU OVERCOME ANY UNFORESEEN SECURITY MEASURES.
There, how does that feel?
A LITTLE ITCHY BUT FINE.

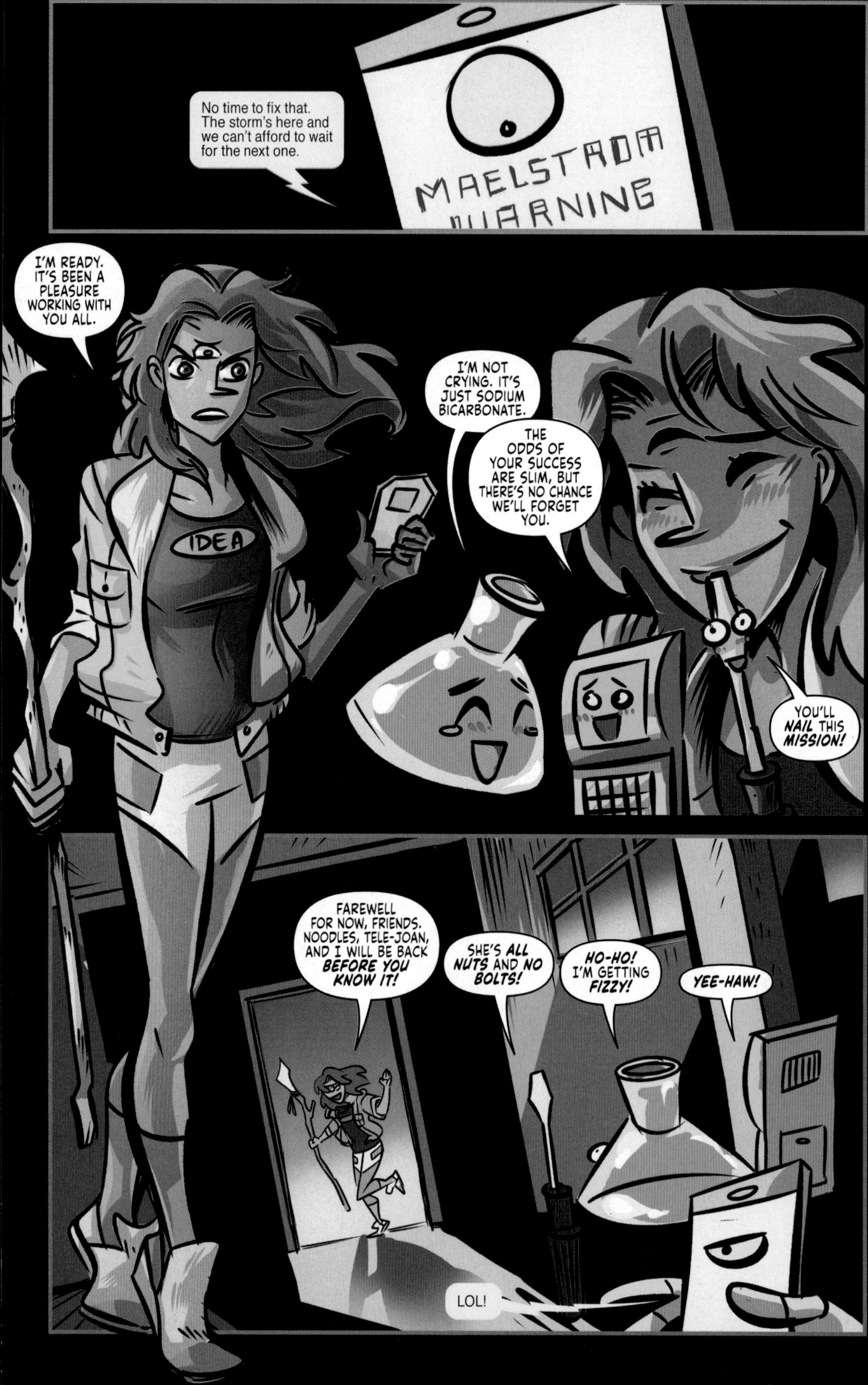
No time to fix that. The storm's here and we can't afford to wait for the next one.
MAELSTROM WARNING
I'M READY. IT'S BEEN A PLEASURE WORKING WITH YOU ALL.
IDEA
I'M NOT CRYING. IT'S JUST SODIUM BICARBONATE.
THE ODDS OF YOUR SUCCESS ARE SLIM, BUT THERE'S NO CHANCE WE'LL FORGET YOU.
YOU'LL NAIL THIS MISSION!
FAREWELL FOR NOW, FRIENDS. NOODLES, TELE-JOAN, AND I WILL BE BACK BEFORE YOU KNOW IT!
SHE'S ALL NUTS AND NO BOLTS!
HO-HO! I'M GETTING FIZZY!
YEE-HAW!
LOL!

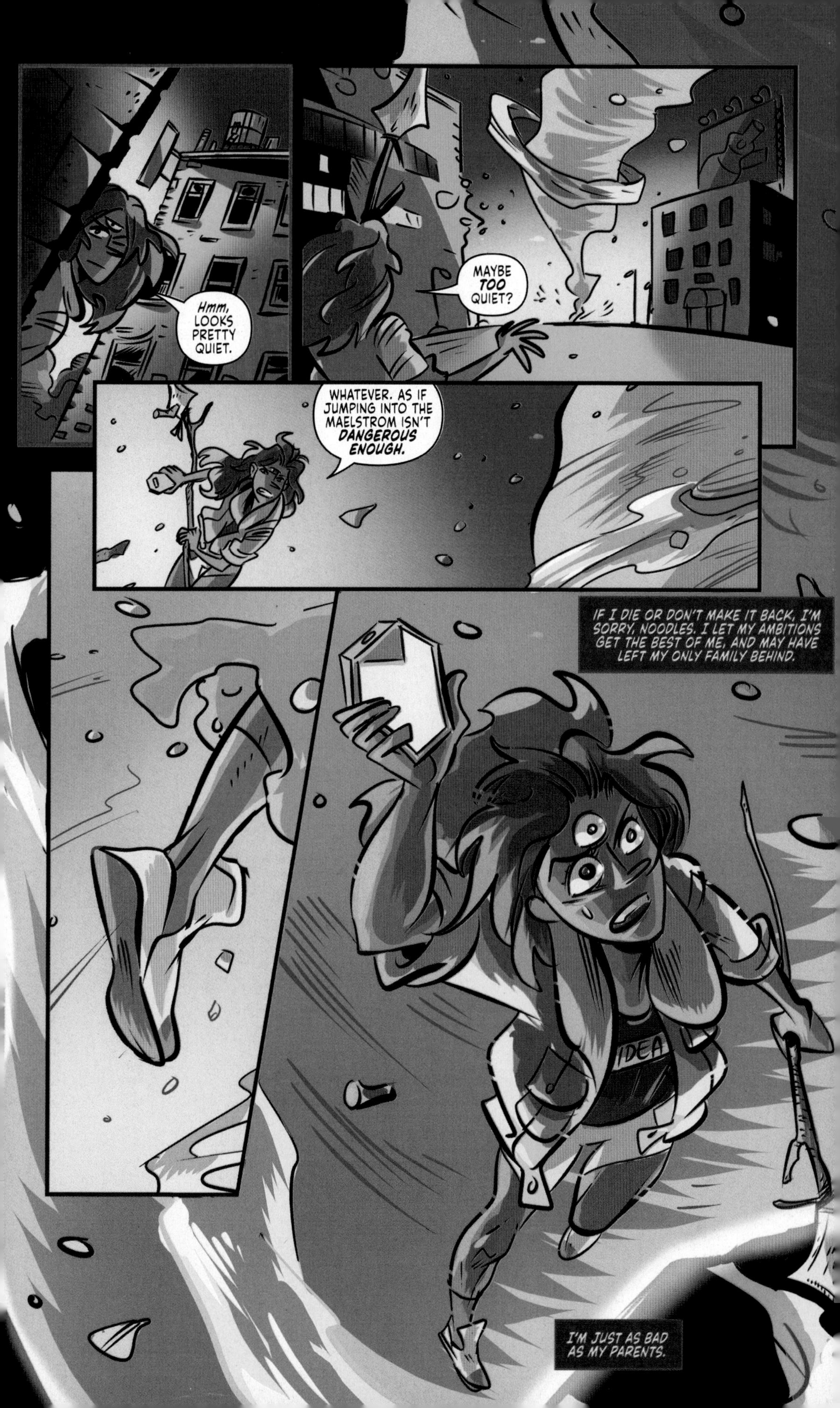

Hmm, LOOKS PRETTY QUIET.
MAYBE TOO QUIET?
WHATEVER. AS IF JUMPING INTO THE MAELSTROM ISN'T DANGEROUS ENOUGH.
IF I DIE OR DON'T MAKE IT BACK, I'M SORRY, NOODLES. I LET MY AMBITIONS GET THE BEST OF ME, AND MAY HAVE LEFT MY ONLY FAMILY BEHIND.
IDEA
I'M JUST AS BAD AS MY PARENTS.

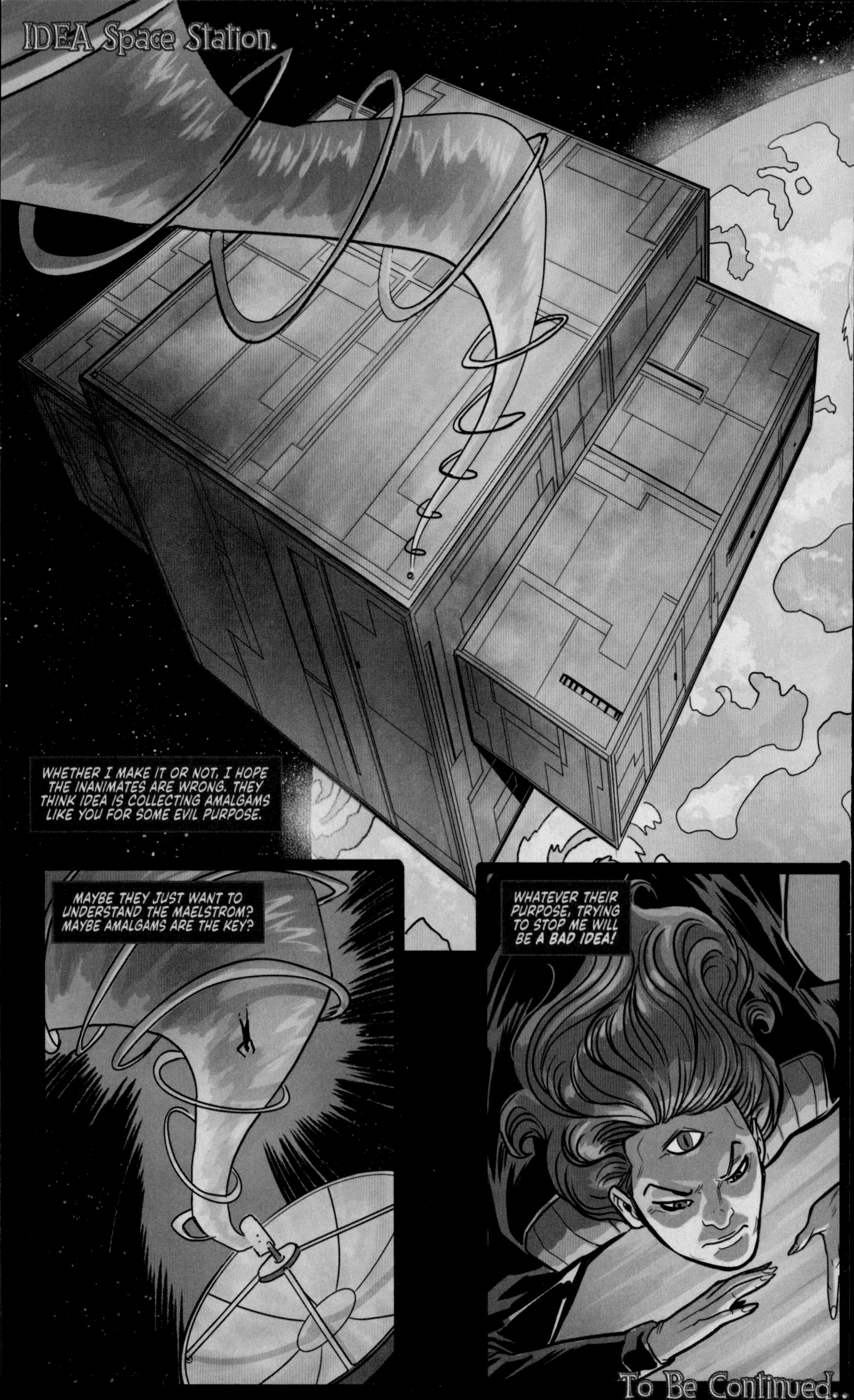
IDEA Space Station.
WHETHER I MAKE IT OR NOT, I HOPE THE INANIMATES ARE WRONG. THEY THINK IDEA IS COLLECTING AMALGAMS LIKE YOU FOR SOME EVIL PURPOSE.
MAYBE THEY JUST WANT TO UNDERSTAND THE MAELSTROM? MAYBE AMALGAMS ARE THE KEY?
WHATEVER THEIR PURPOSE, TRYING TO STOP ME WILL BE A BAD IDEA!
To Be Continued.

CHAPTER 6

PREVIOUSLY:

Aided by the Inanimates, Miranda found a way to travel through the maelstrom back to IDEA. Now she seeks to find her beloved Noodles, and rescue the leader of the Inanimates known only as Tele-Joan.

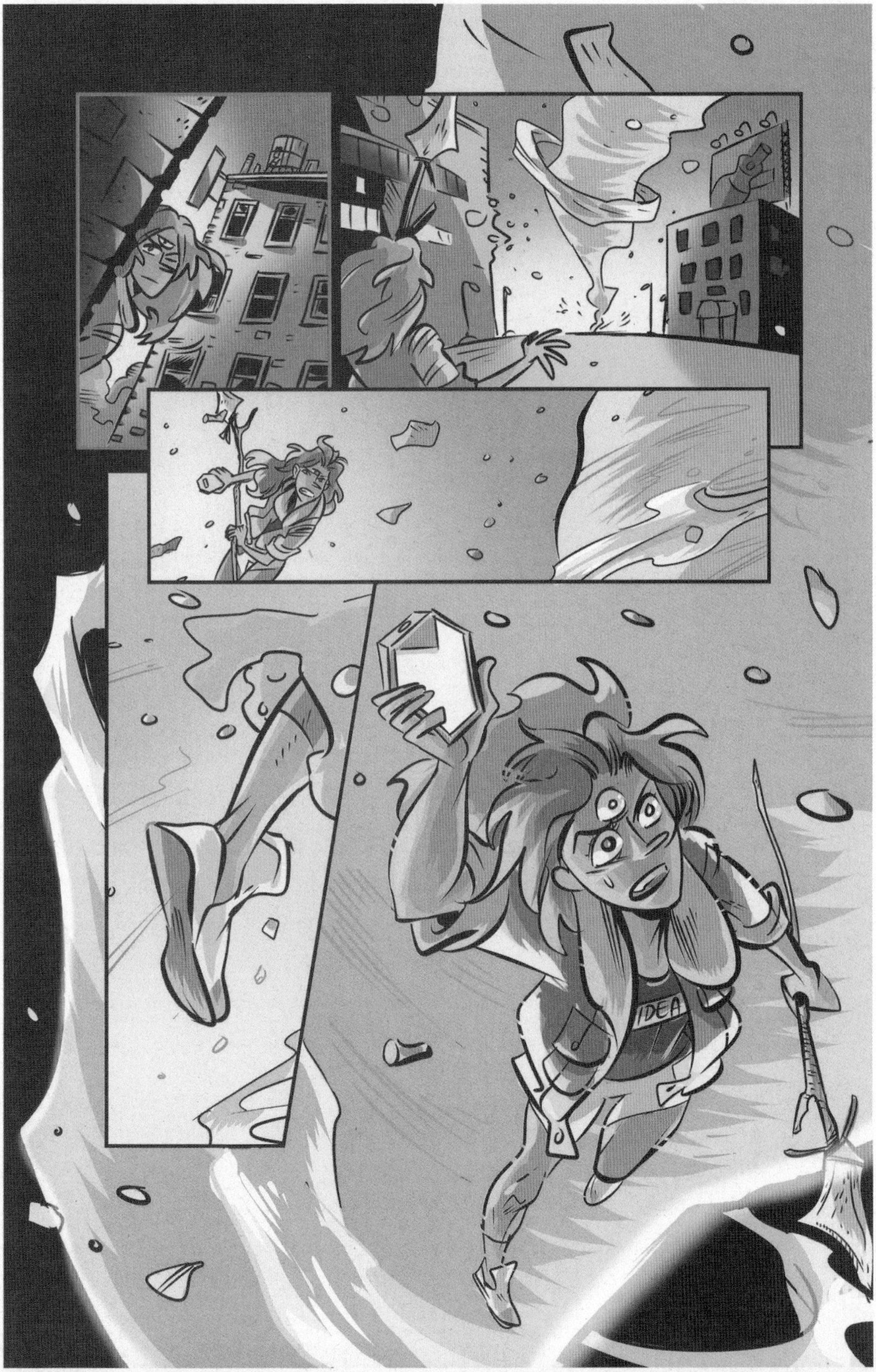
IDEA

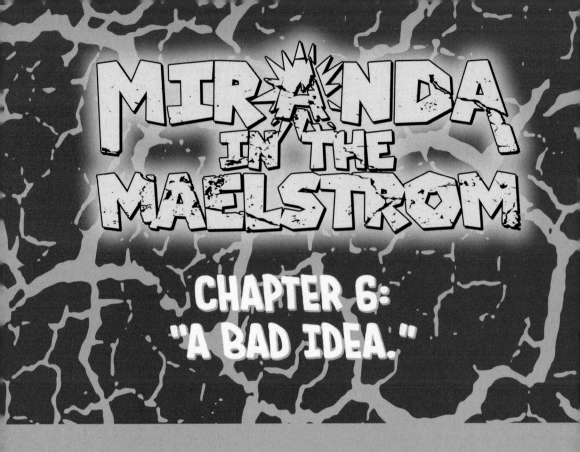

MIRANDA IN THE MAELSTROM

CHAPTER 6:
"A BAD IDEA."

SCRIPT BY RILEY DASHIELL BIEHL
ART BY DREW MOSS

COLORS BY BORG SINABAN
LETTERING BY TAYLOR ESPOSITO
SCRIPT EDITING BY BRITTANY MATTER
COVER BY DREW MOSS

BRYAN SEATON: PUBLISHER / CEO
VITO DELSANTE: EDITOR IN CHIEF
JASON MARTIN: PUBLISHER - DANGER ZONE
CHAD CICCONI: CHIEF PORTAL INSPECTOR

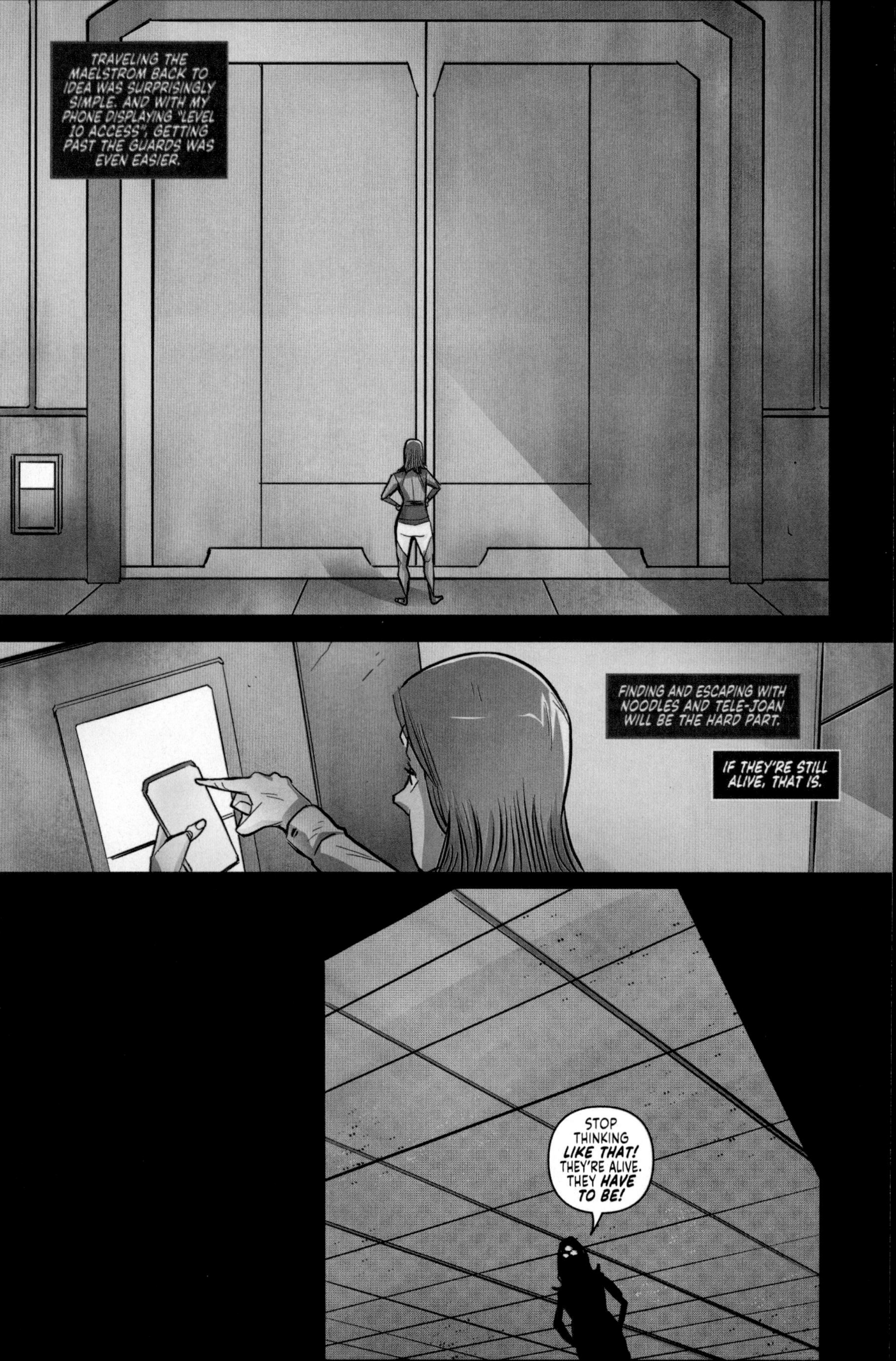
TRAVELING THE MAELSTROM BACK TO IDEA WAS SURPRISINGLY SIMPLE. AND WITH MY PHONE DISPLAYING "LEVEL 10 ACCESS", GETTING PAST THE GUARDS WAS EVEN EASIER.
FINDING AND ESCAPING WITH NOODLES AND TELE-JOAN WILL BE THE HARD PART.
IF THEY'RE STILL ALIVE, THAT IS.
STOP THINKING *LIKE THAT!* THEY'RE ALIVE. THEY *HAVE TO BE!*

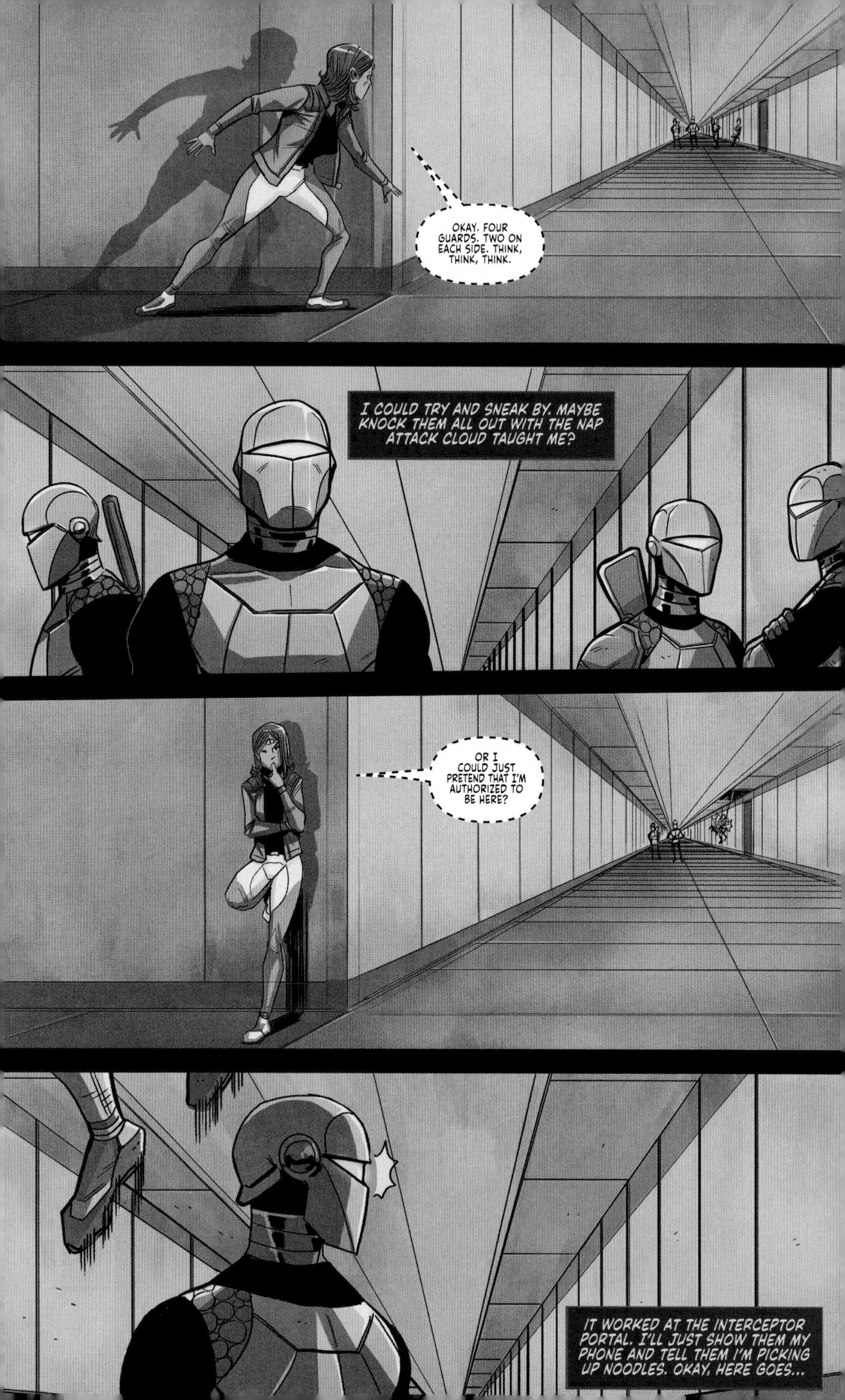
OKAY. FOUR GUARDS. TWO ON EACH SIDE. THINK, THINK, THINK.
I COULD TRY AND SNEAK BY. MAYBE KNOCK THEM ALL OUT WITH THE NAP ATTACK CLOUD TAUGHT ME?
OR I COULD JUST PRETEND THAT I'M AUTHORIZED TO BE HERE?
IT WORKED AT THE INTERCEPTOR PORTAL. I'LL JUST SHOW THEM MY PHONE AND TELL THEM I'M PICKING UP NOODLES. OKAY, HERE GOES...

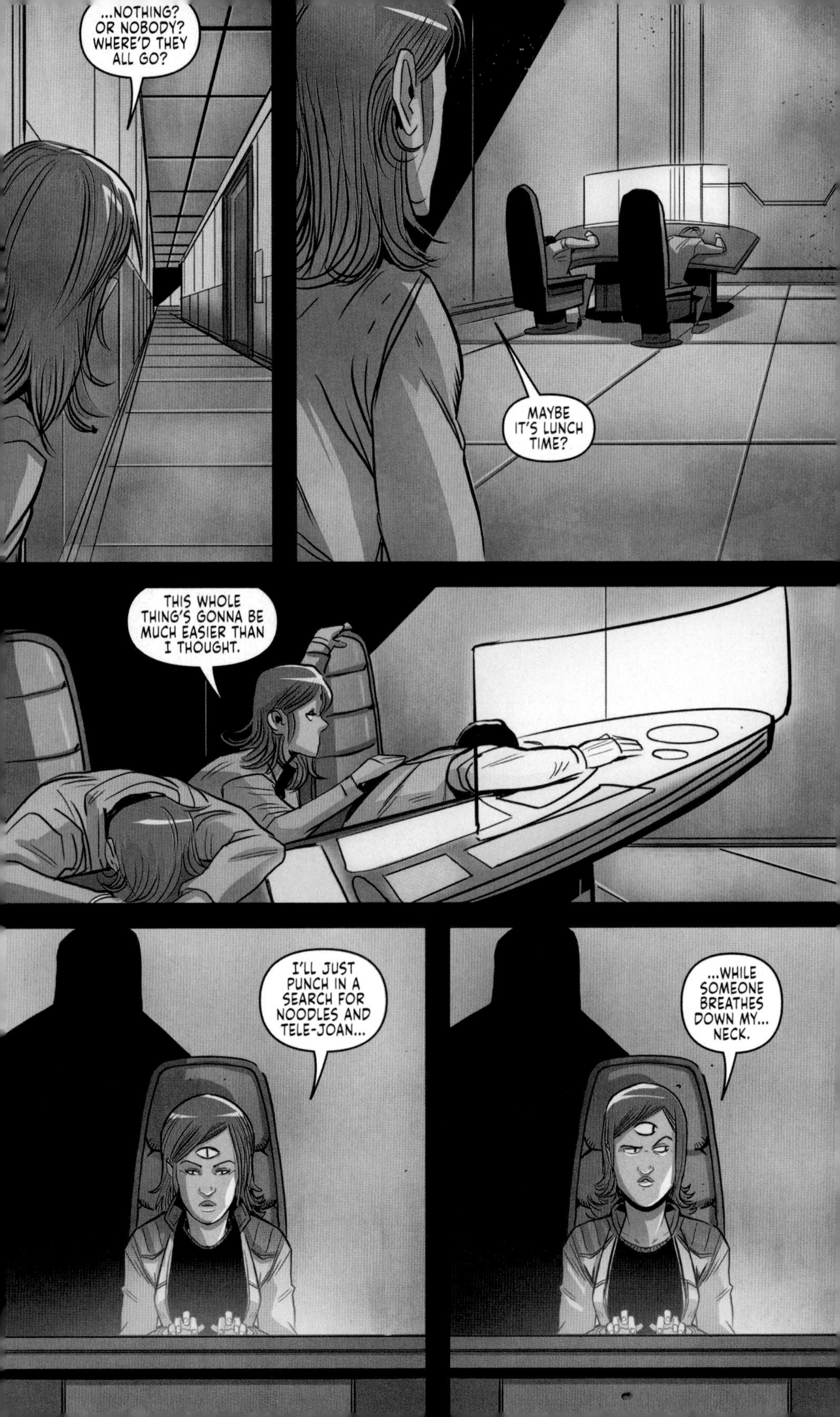
...NOTHING? OR NOBODY? WHERE'D THEY ALL GO?
MAYBE IT'S LUNCH TIME?
THIS WHOLE THING'S GONNA BE MUCH EASIER THAN I THOUGHT.
I'LL JUST PUNCH IN A SEARCH FOR NOODLES AND TELE-JOAN...
...WHILE SOMEONE BREATHES DOWN MY... NECK.

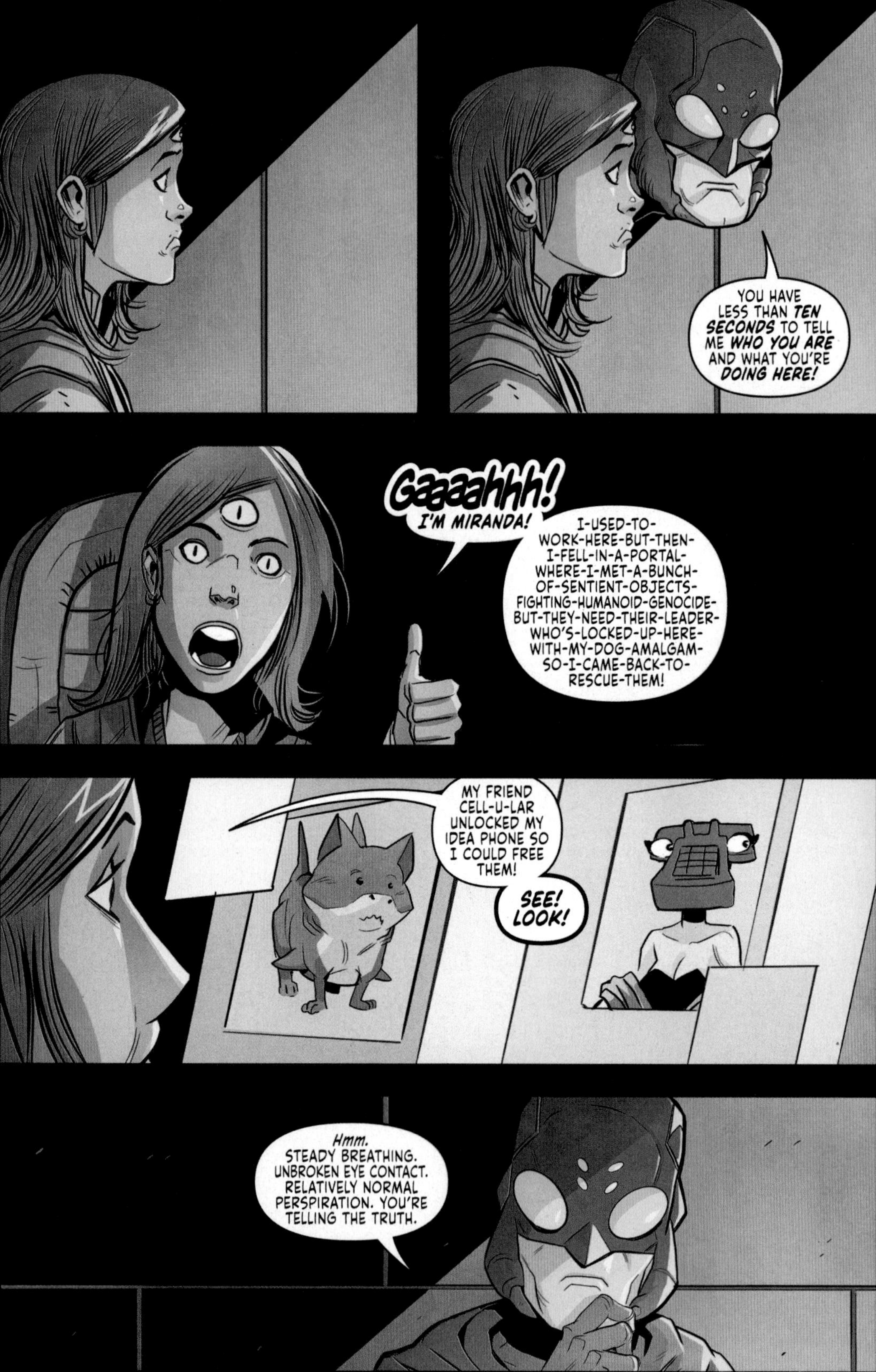

YOU HAVE LESS THAN TEN SECONDS TO TELL ME WHO YOU ARE AND WHAT YOU'RE DOING HERE!
Gaaaahhh!
I'M MIRANDA!
I-USED-TO-WORK-HERE-BUT-THEN-I-FELL-IN-A-PORTAL-WHERE-I-MET-A-BUNCH-OF-SENTIENT-OBJECTS-FIGHTING-HUMANOID-GENOCIDE-BUT-THEY-NEED-THEIR-LEADER-WHO'S-LOCKED-UP-HERE-WITH-MY-DOG-AMALGAM-SO-I-CAME-BACK-TO-RESCUE-THEM!
MY FRIEND CELL-U-LAR UNLOCKED MY IDEA PHONE SO I COULD FREE THEM!
SEE! LOOK!
Hmm. STEADY BREATHING. UNBROKEN EYE CONTACT. RELATIVELY NORMAL PERSPIRATION. YOU'RE TELLING THE TRUTH.

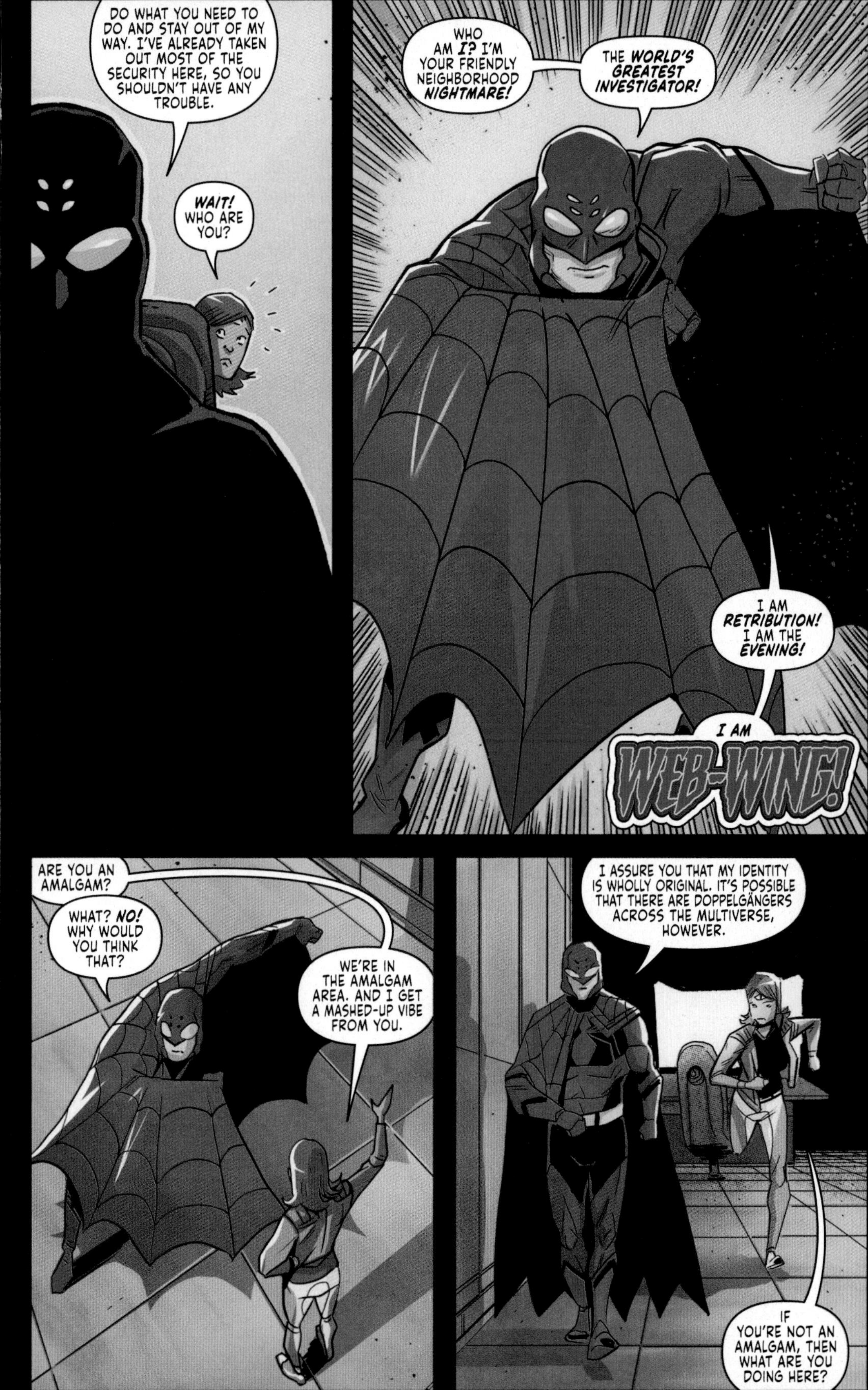
DO WHAT YOU NEED TO DO AND STAY OUT OF MY WAY. I'VE ALREADY TAKEN OUT MOST OF THE SECURITY HERE, SO YOU SHOULDN'T HAVE ANY TROUBLE.
WAIT! WHO ARE YOU?
WHO AM I? I'M YOUR FRIENDLY NEIGHBORHOOD NIGHTMARE!
THE WORLD'S GREATEST INVESTIGATOR!
I AM RETRIBUTION! I AM THE EVENING!
I AM
WEB-WING!
ARE YOU AN AMALGAM?
WHAT? NO! WHY WOULD YOU THINK THAT?
WE'RE IN THE AMALGAM AREA. AND I GET A MASHED-UP VIBE FROM YOU.
I ASSURE YOU THAT MY IDENTITY IS WHOLLY ORIGINAL. IT'S POSSIBLE THAT THERE ARE DOPPELGÄNGERS ACROSS THE MULTIVERSE, HOWEVER.
IF YOU'RE NOT AN AMALGAM, THEN WHAT ARE YOU DOING HERE?

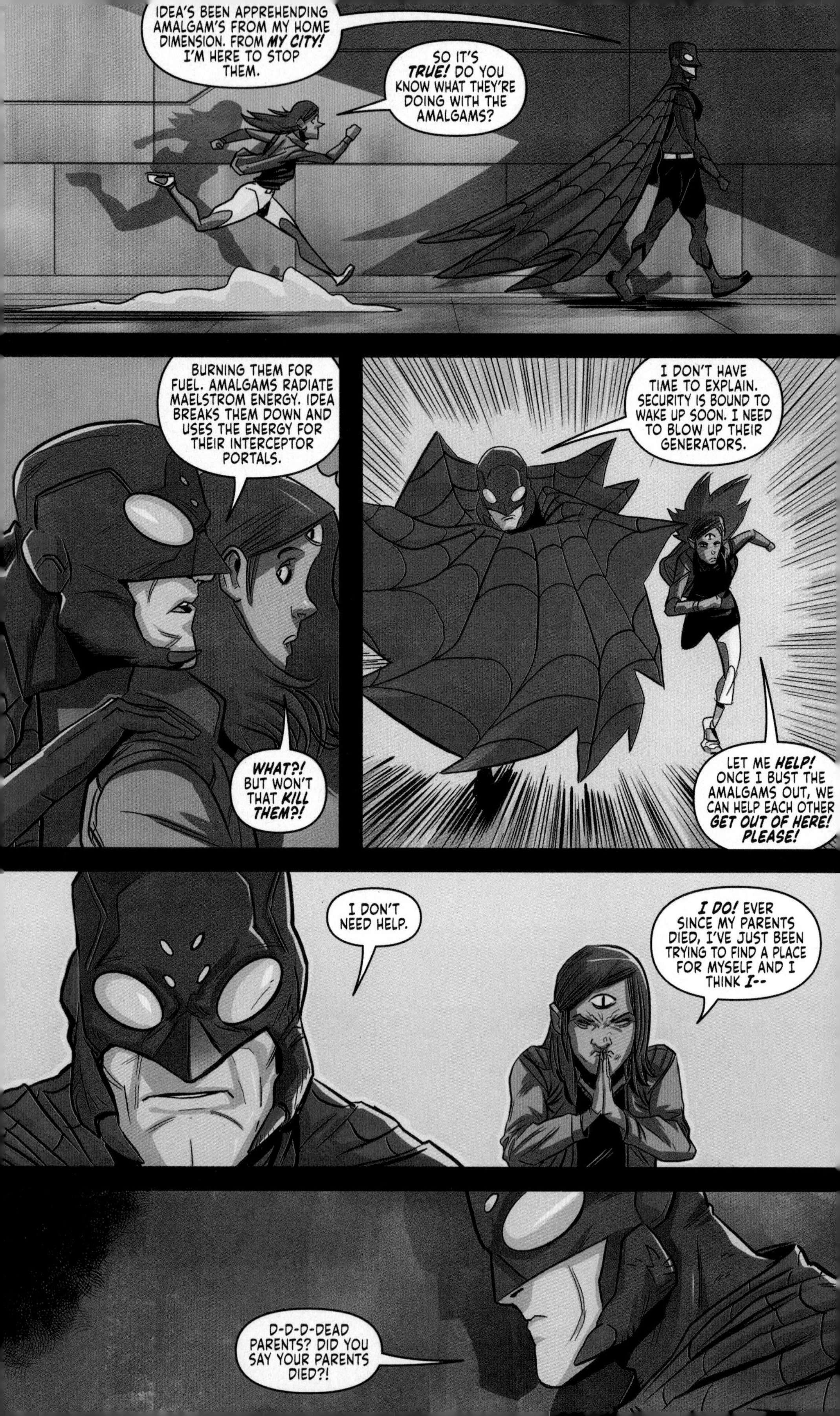

IDEA'S BEEN APPREHENDING AMALGAM'S FROM MY HOME DIMENSION. FROM *MY CITY!* I'M HERE TO STOP THEM.
SO IT'S ***TRUE!*** DO YOU KNOW WHAT THEY'RE DOING WITH THE AMALGAMS?
BURNING THEM FOR FUEL. AMALGAMS RADIATE MAELSTROM ENERGY. IDEA BREAKS THEM DOWN AND USES THE ENERGY FOR THEIR INTERCEPTOR PORTALS.
WHAT?! BUT WON'T THAT ***KILL THEM?!***
I DON'T HAVE TIME TO EXPLAIN. SECURITY IS BOUND TO WAKE UP SOON. I NEED TO BLOW UP THEIR GENERATORS.
LET ME ***HELP!*** ONCE I BUST THE AMALGAMS OUT, WE CAN HELP EACH OTHER ***GET OUT OF HERE! PLEASE!***
I DON'T NEED HELP.
I DO! EVER SINCE MY PARENTS DIED, I'VE JUST BEEN TRYING TO FIND A PLACE FOR MYSELF AND I THINK ***I--***
D-D-D-DEAD PARENTS? DID YOU SAY YOUR PARENTS DIED?!

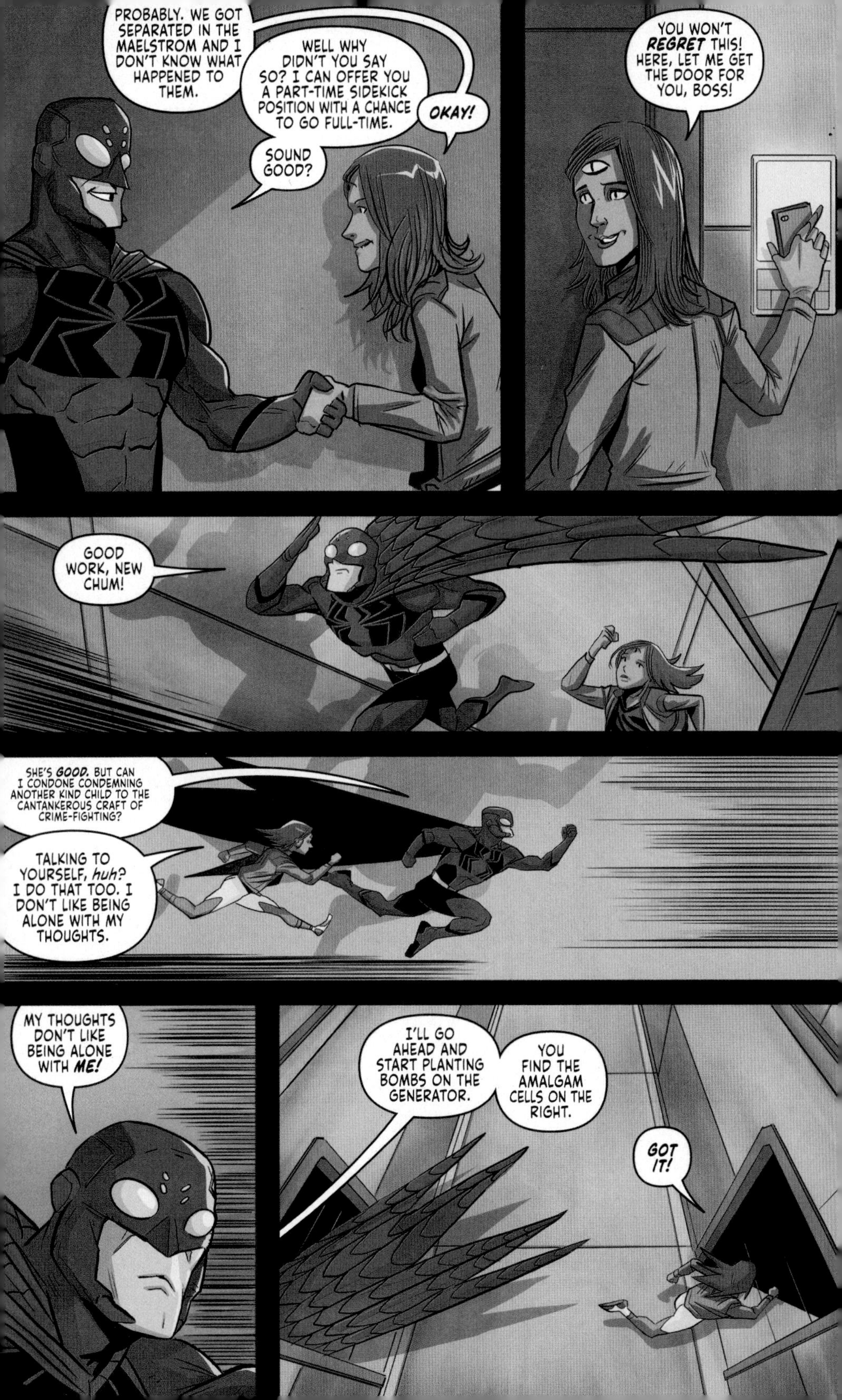
PROBABLY. WE GOT SEPARATED IN THE MAELSTROM AND I DON'T KNOW WHAT HAPPENED TO THEM.
WELL WHY DIDN'T YOU SAY SO? I CAN OFFER YOU A PART-TIME SIDEKICK POSITION WITH A CHANCE TO GO FULL-TIME.
SOUND GOOD?
OKAY!
YOU WON'T REGRET THIS! HERE, LET ME GET THE DOOR FOR YOU, BOSS!
GOOD WORK, NEW CHUM!
SHE'S GOOD. BUT CAN I CONDONE CONDEMNING ANOTHER KIND CHILD TO THE CANTANKEROUS CRAFT OF CRIME-FIGHTING?
TALKING TO YOURSELF, huh? I DO THAT TOO. I DON'T LIKE BEING ALONE WITH MY THOUGHTS.
MY THOUGHTS DON'T LIKE BEING ALONE WITH ME!
I'LL GO AHEAD AND START PLANTING BOMBS ON THE GENERATOR.
YOU FIND THE AMALGAM CELLS ON THE RIGHT.
GOT IT!

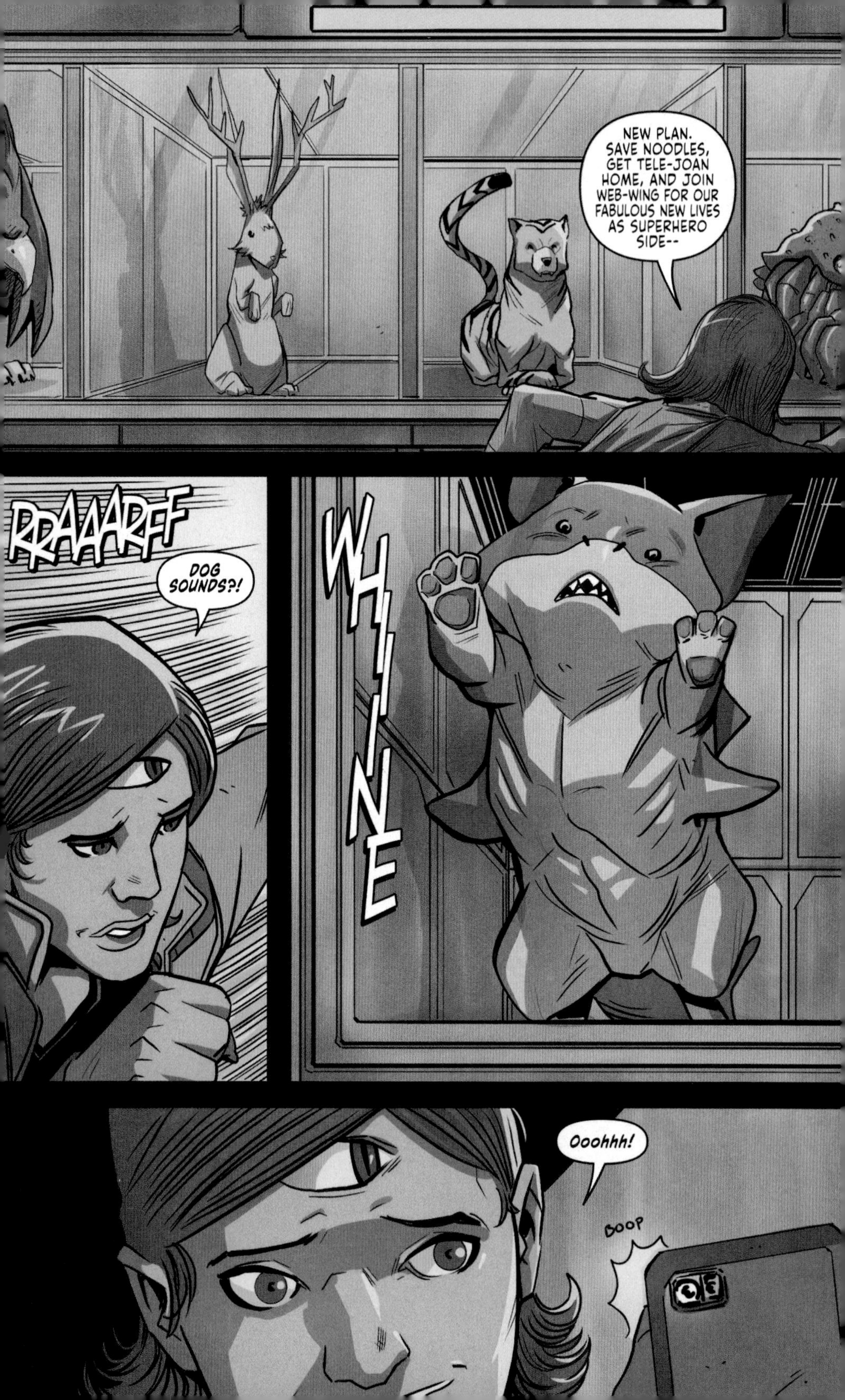
NEW PLAN. SAVE NOODLES, GET TELE-JOAN HOME, AND JOIN WEB-WING FOR OUR FABULOUS NEW LIVES AS SUPERHERO SIDE--
RRAAAARFF
DOG SOUNDS?!
WHIIINE
Ooohhh!
BOOP

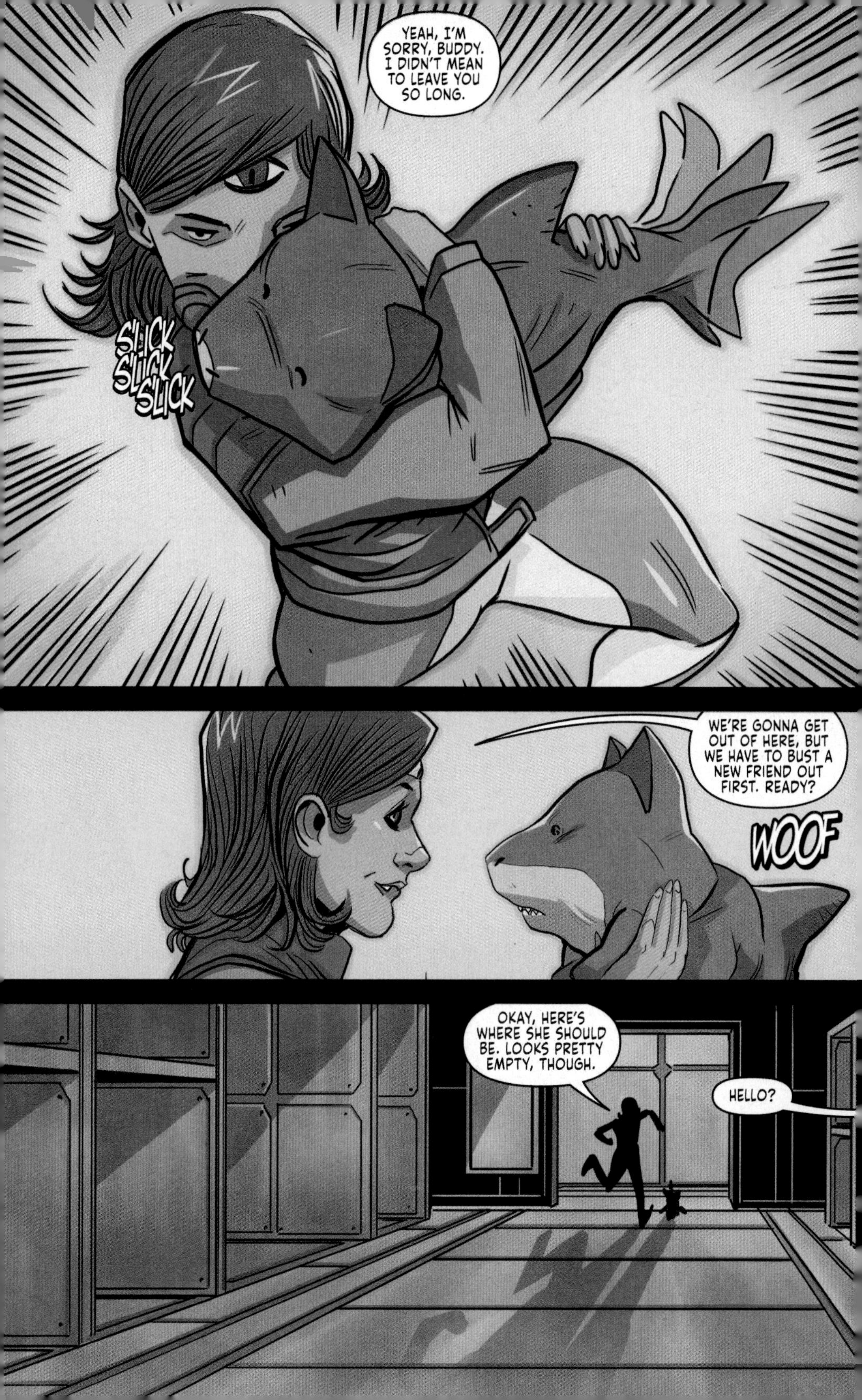
YEAH, I'M SORRY, BUDDY. I DIDN'T MEAN TO LEAVE YOU SO LONG.
SLICK SLICK SLICK
WE'RE GONNA GET OUT OF HERE, BUT WE HAVE TO BUST A NEW FRIEND OUT FIRST. READY?
WOOF
OKAY, HERE'S WHERE SHE SHOULD BE. LOOKS PRETTY EMPTY, THOUGH.
HELLO?

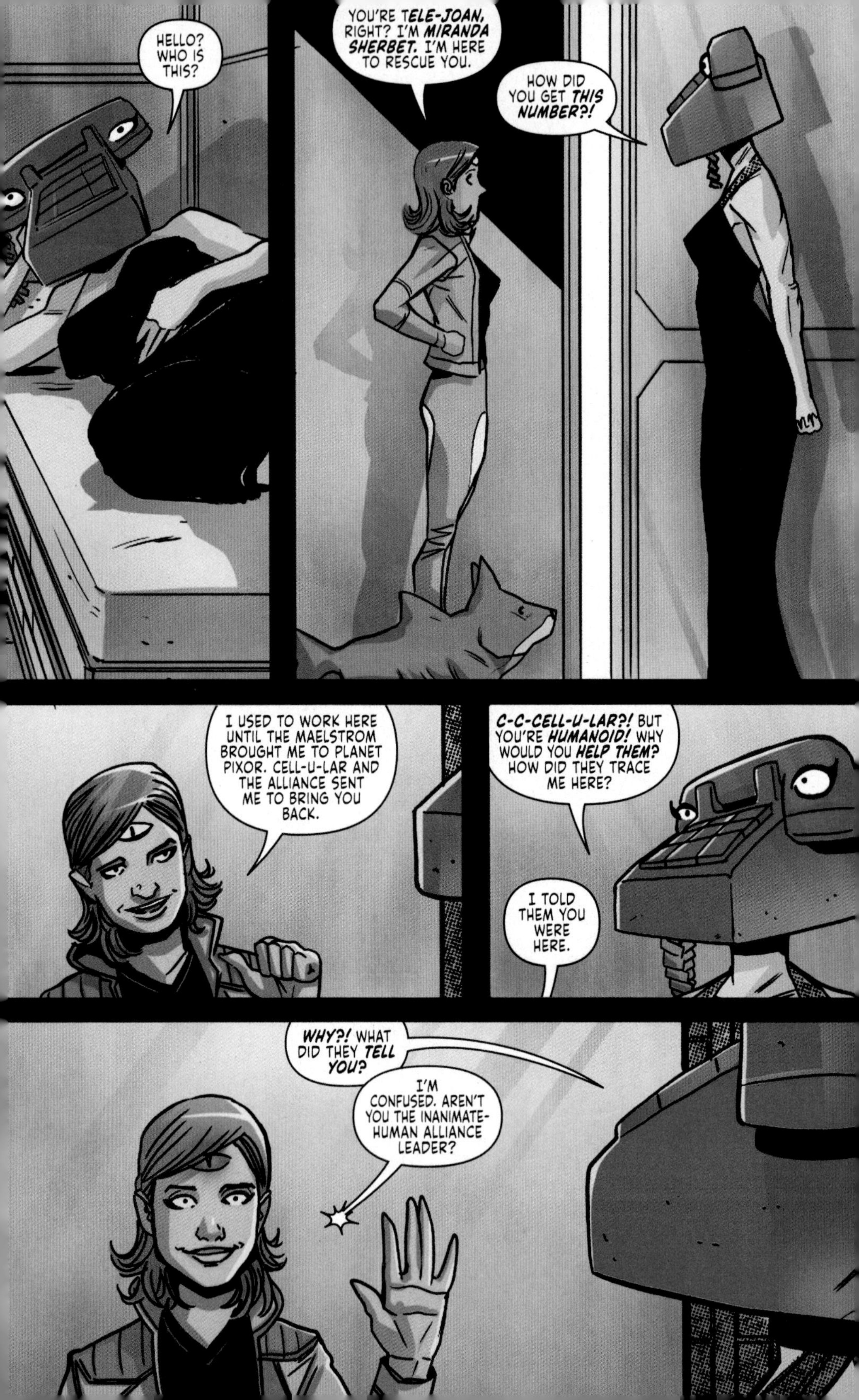
HELLO? WHO IS THIS?
YOU'RE TELE-JOAN, RIGHT? I'M MIRANDA SHERBET. I'M HERE TO RESCUE YOU.
HOW DID YOU GET THIS NUMBER?!
I USED TO WORK HERE UNTIL THE MAELSTROM BROUGHT ME TO PLANET PIXOR. CELL-U-LAR AND THE ALLIANCE SENT ME TO BRING YOU BACK.
C-C-CELL-U-LAR?! BUT YOU'RE HUMANOID! WHY WOULD YOU HELP THEM? HOW DID THEY TRACE ME HERE?
I TOLD THEM YOU WERE HERE.
WHY?! WHAT DID THEY TELL YOU?
I'M CONFUSED. AREN'T YOU THE INANIMATE-HUMAN ALLIANCE LEADER?

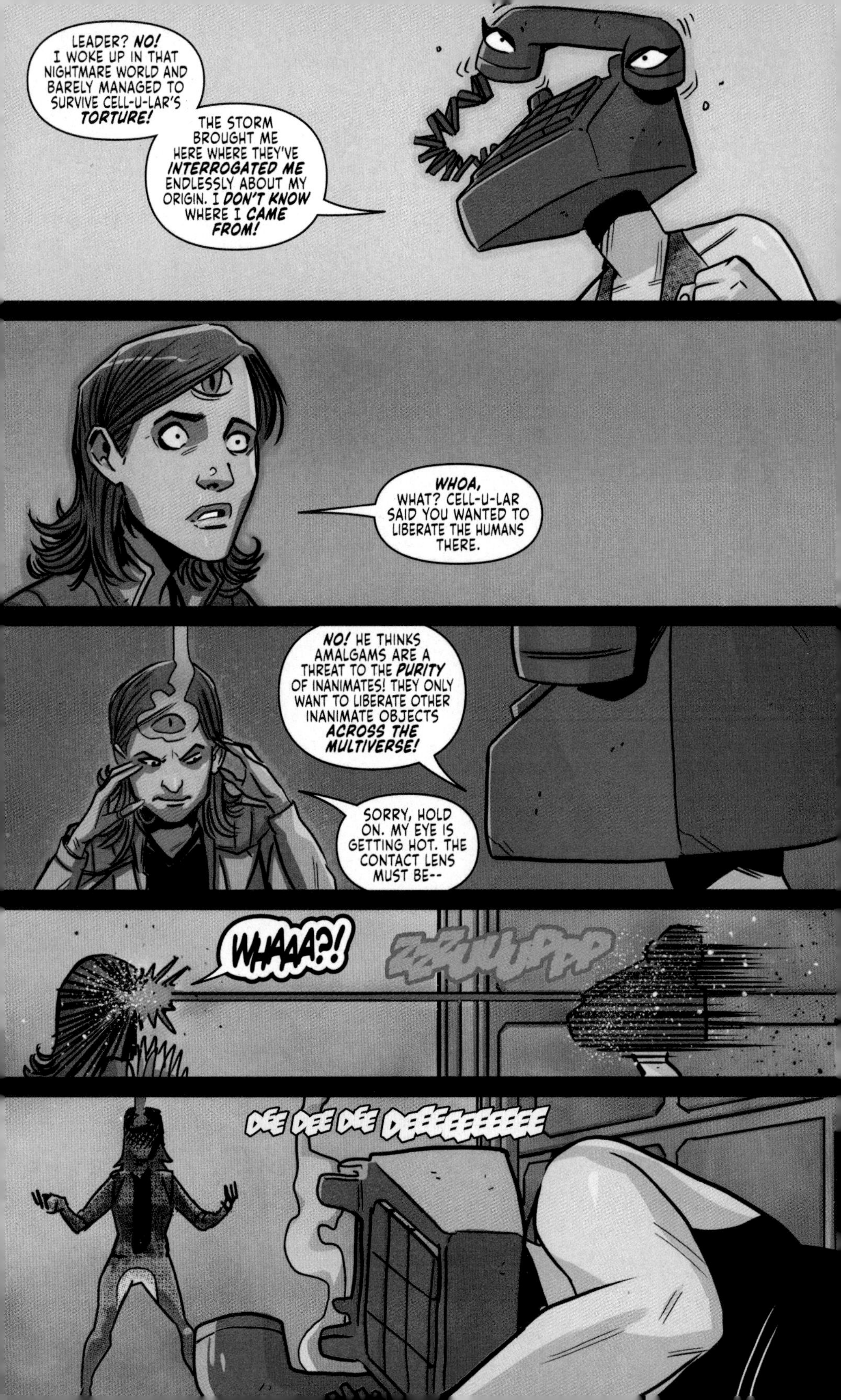
LEADER? NO! I WOKE UP IN THAT NIGHTMARE WORLD AND BARELY MANAGED TO SURVIVE CELL-U-LAR'S TORTURE!
THE STORM BROUGHT ME HERE WHERE THEY'VE INTERROGATED ME ENDLESSLY ABOUT MY ORIGIN. I DON'T KNOW WHERE I CAME FROM!
WHOA, WHAT? CELL-U-LAR SAID YOU WANTED TO LIBERATE THE HUMANS THERE.
NO! HE THINKS AMALGAMS ARE A THREAT TO THE PURITY OF INANIMATES! THEY ONLY WANT TO LIBERATE OTHER INANIMATE OBJECTS ACROSS THE MULTIVERSE!
SORRY, HOLD ON. MY EYE IS GETTING HOT. THE CONTACT LENS MUST BE--
WHAAA?!
ZZBZUUUPPP
DEE DEE DEE DEEEEEEEEEE

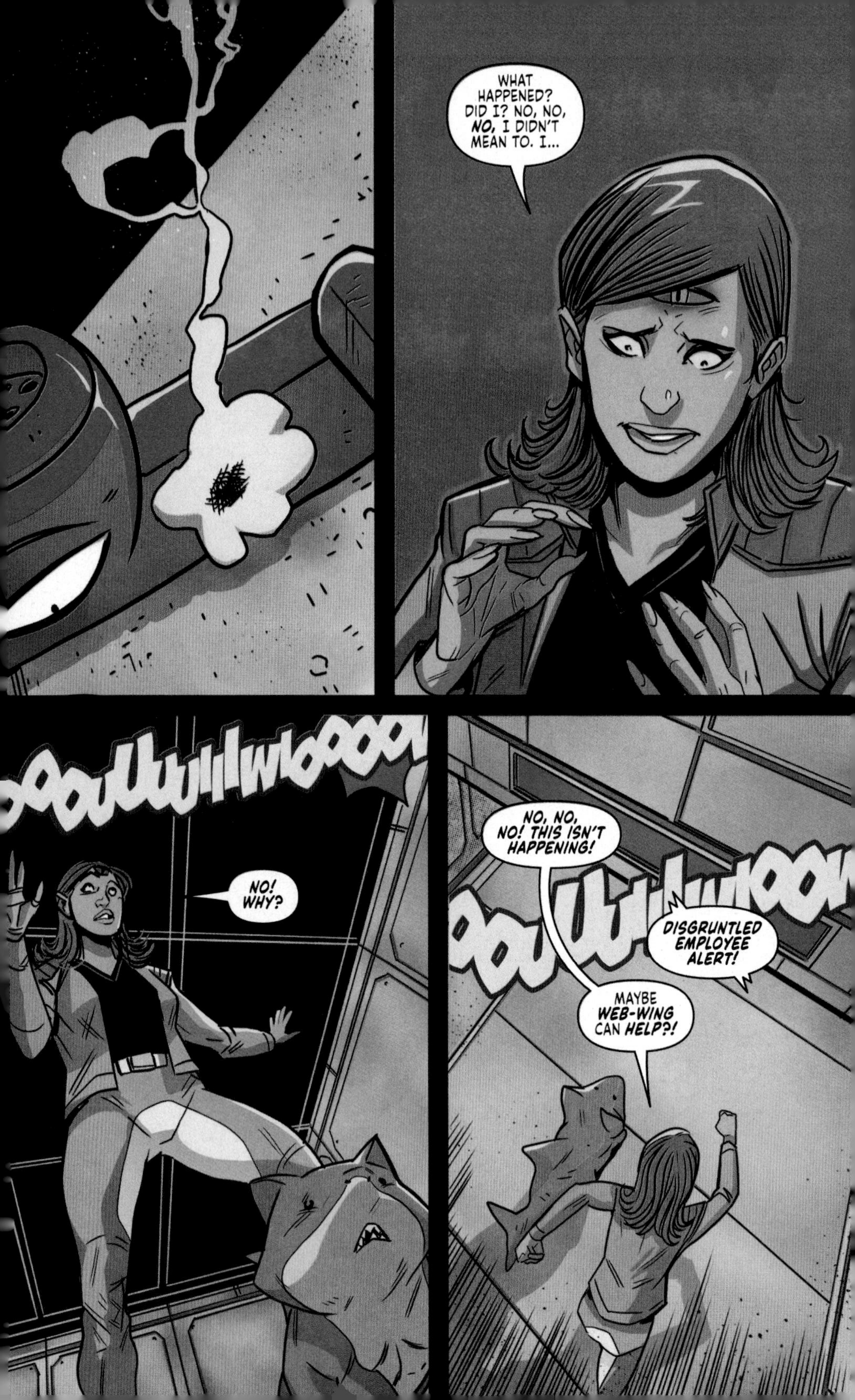
WHAT HAPPENED? DID I? NO, NO, NO, I DIDN'T MEAN TO. I...
NO! WHY?
NO, NO, NO! THIS ISN'T HAPPENING!
DISGRUNTLED EMPLOYEE ALERT!
MAYBE WEB-WING CAN HELP?!

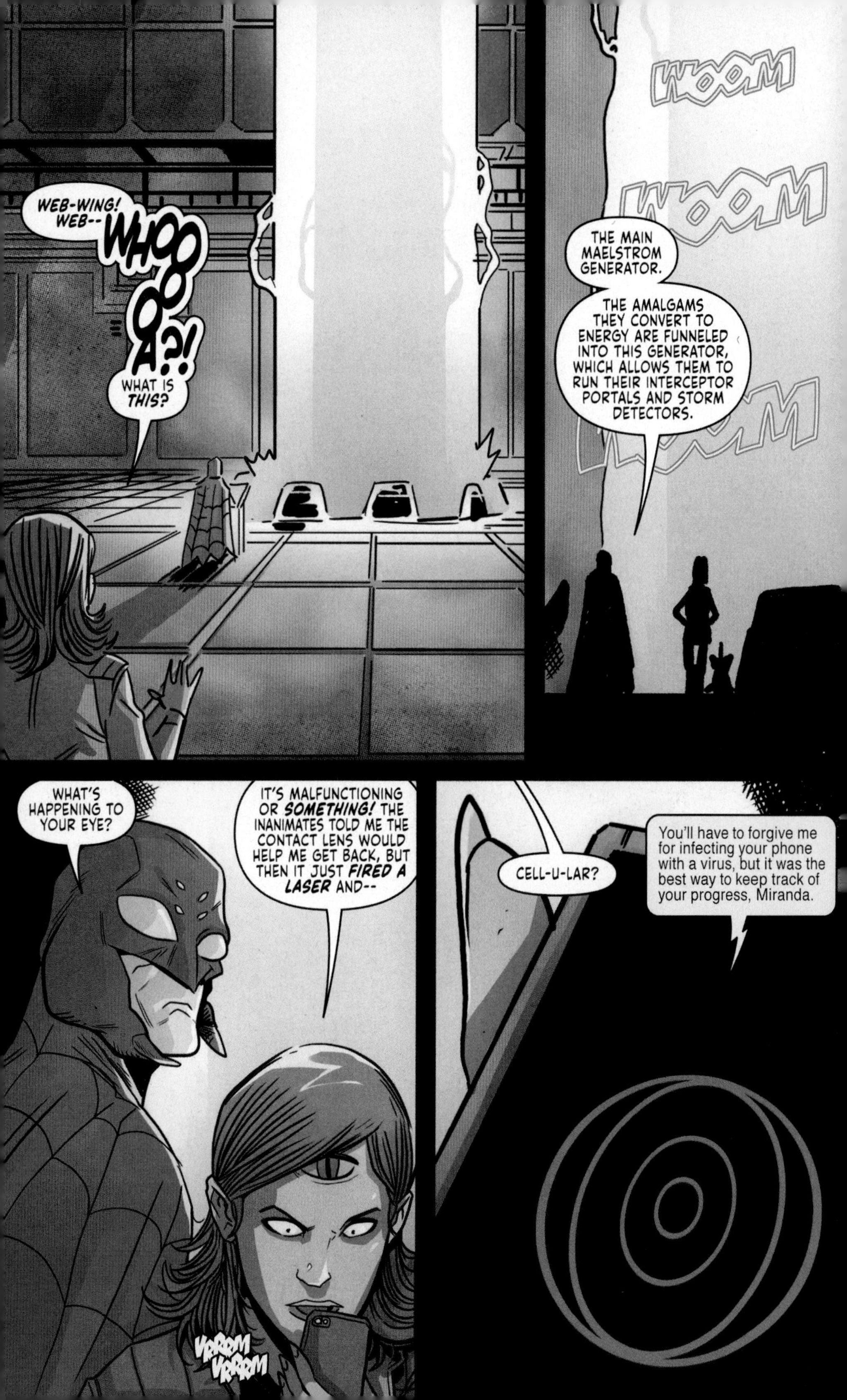
WEB-WING! WEB--WHOOOOOA?!
WHAT IS THIS?
WOOM
WOOM
THE MAIN MAELSTROM GENERATOR.
THE AMALGAMS THEY CONVERT TO ENERGY ARE FUNNELED INTO THIS GENERATOR, WHICH ALLOWS THEM TO RUN THEIR INTERCEPTOR PORTALS AND STORM DETECTORS.
WHAT'S HAPPENING TO YOUR EYE?
IT'S MALFUNCTIONING OR SOMETHING! THE INANIMATES TOLD ME THE CONTACT LENS WOULD HELP ME GET BACK, BUT THEN IT JUST FIRED A LASER AND--
VRRRM VRRRM
CELL-U-LAR?
You'll have to forgive me for infecting your phone with a virus, but it was the best way to keep track of your progress, Miranda.

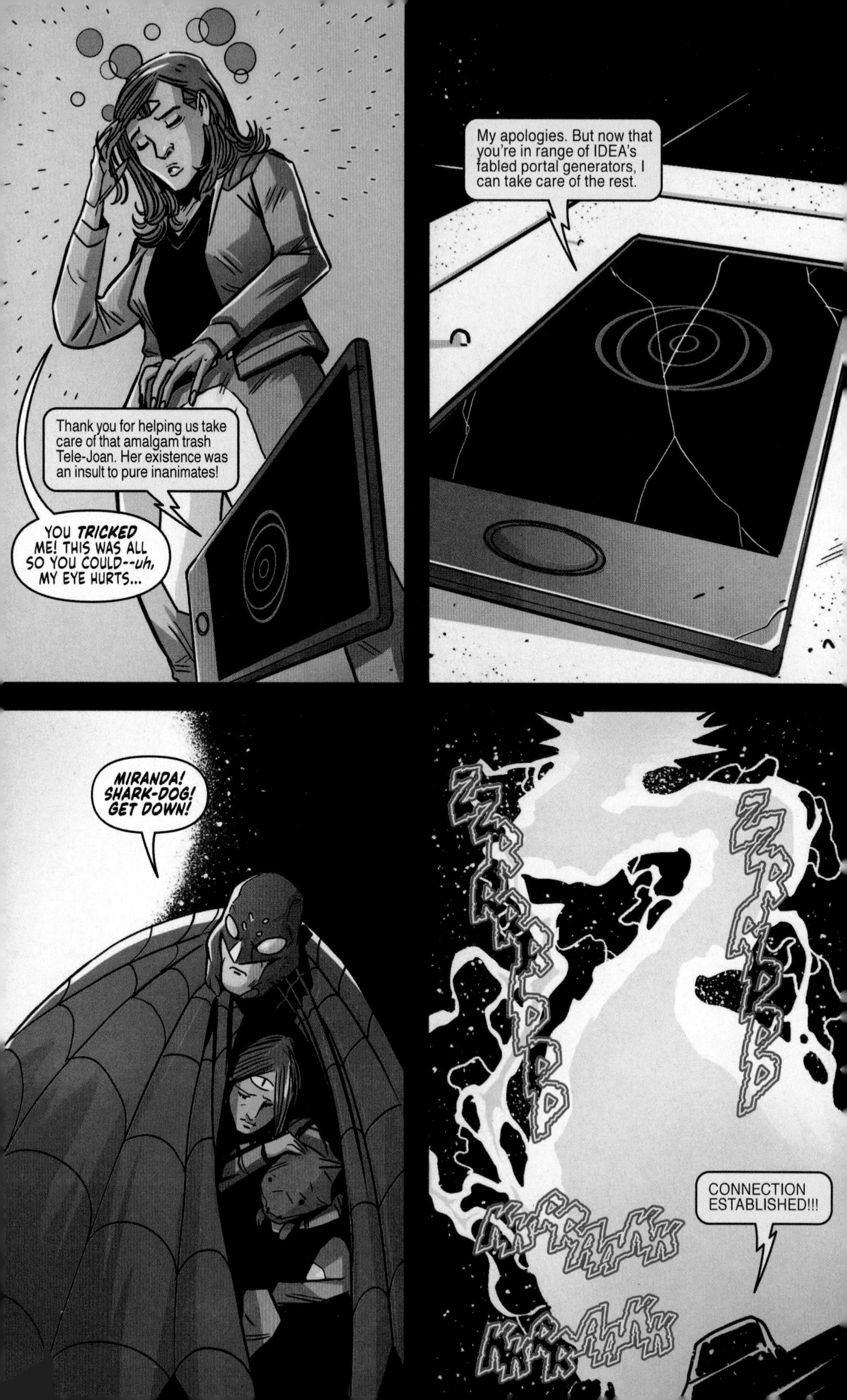
Thank you for helping us take care of that amalgam trash Tele-Joan. Her existence was an insult to pure inanimates!
YOU *TRICKED* ME! THIS WAS ALL SO YOU COULD--*uh,* MY EYE HURTS...
My apologies. But now that you're in range of IDEA's fabled portal generators, I can take care of the rest.
MIRANDA! SHARK-DOG! GET DOWN!
CONNECTION ESTABLISHED!!!

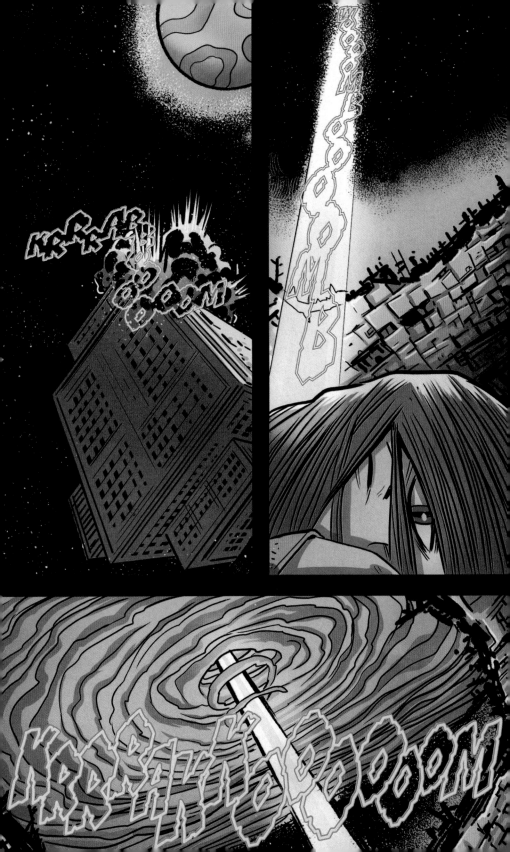

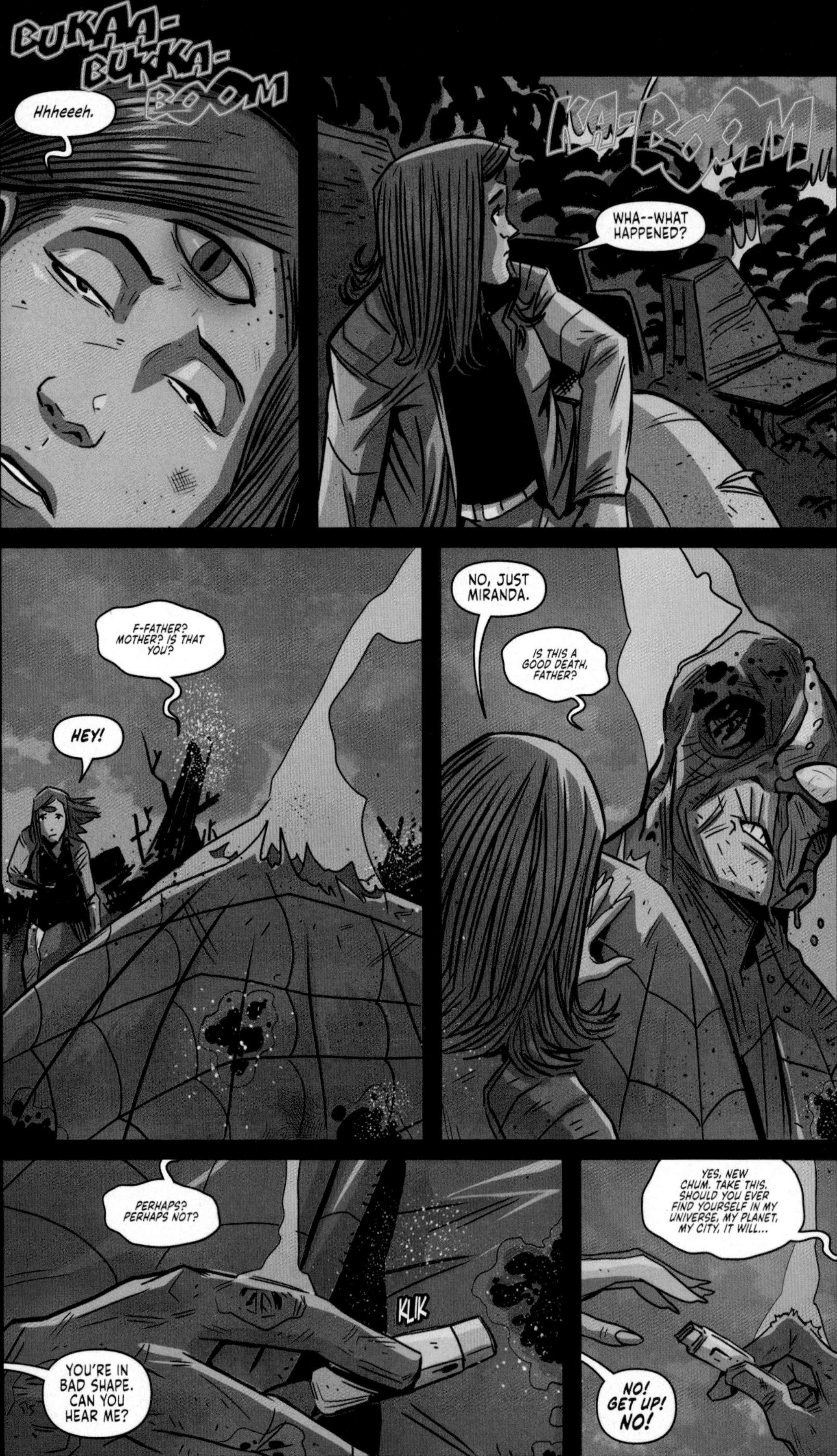
BUKAA-BUKKA-BOOM
Hhheeeh.
KA-BOOM
WHA--WHAT HAPPENED?
F-FATHER? MOTHER? IS THAT YOU?
HEY!
NO, JUST MIRANDA.
IS THIS A GOOD DEATH, FATHER?
PERHAPS? PERHAPS NOT?
YOU'RE IN BAD SHAPE. CAN YOU HEAR ME?
KLIK
YES, NEW CHUM. TAKE THIS. SHOULD YOU EVER FIND YOURSELF IN MY UNIVERSE, MY PLANET, MY CITY, IT WILL...
NO! GET UP! NO!

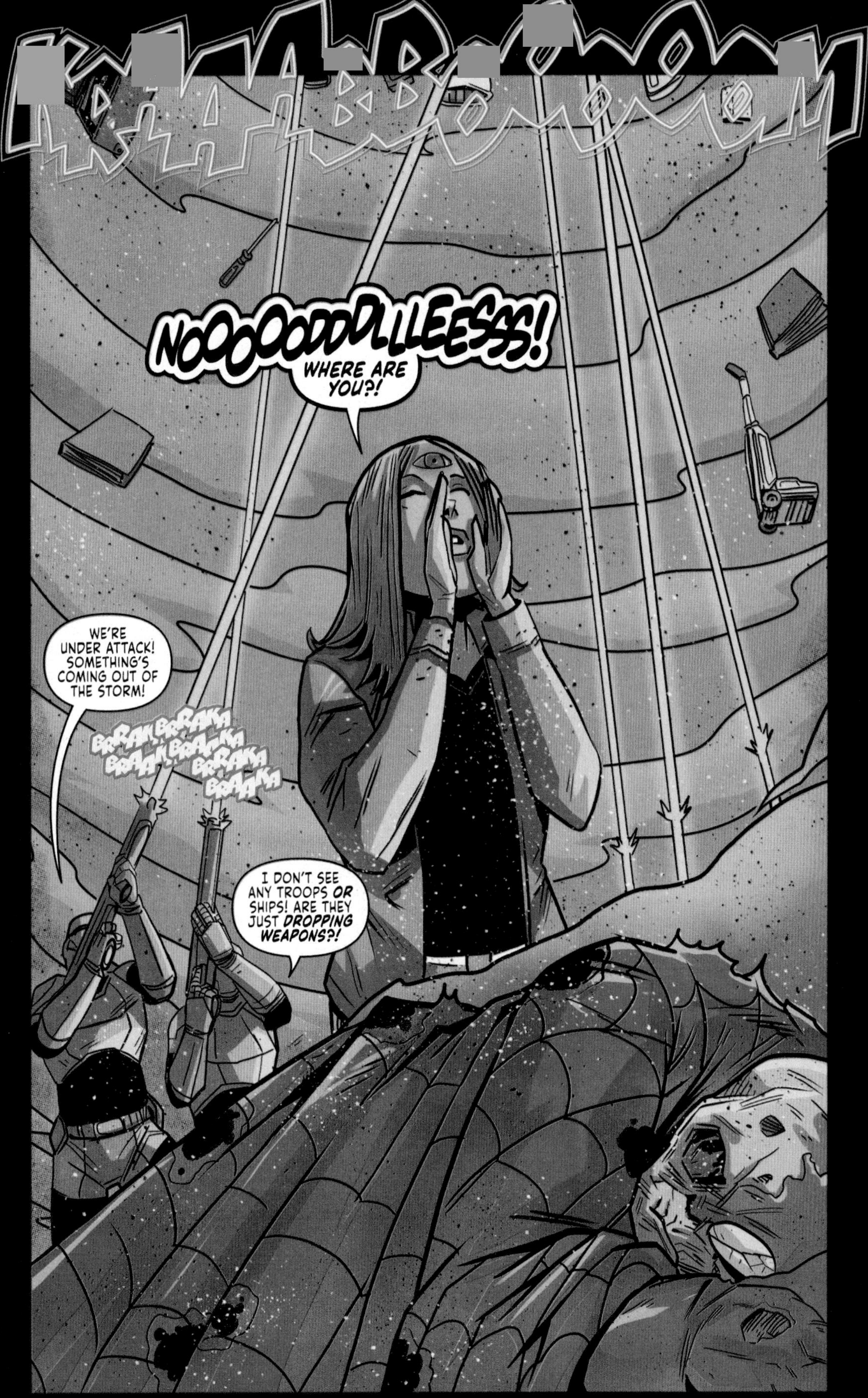
NOOOOODDDLLEESSS!
WHERE ARE YOU?!
WE'RE UNDER ATTACK! SOMETHING'S COMING OUT OF THE STORM!
I DON'T SEE ANY TROOPS OR SHIPS! ARE THEY JUST DROPPING WEAPONS?!

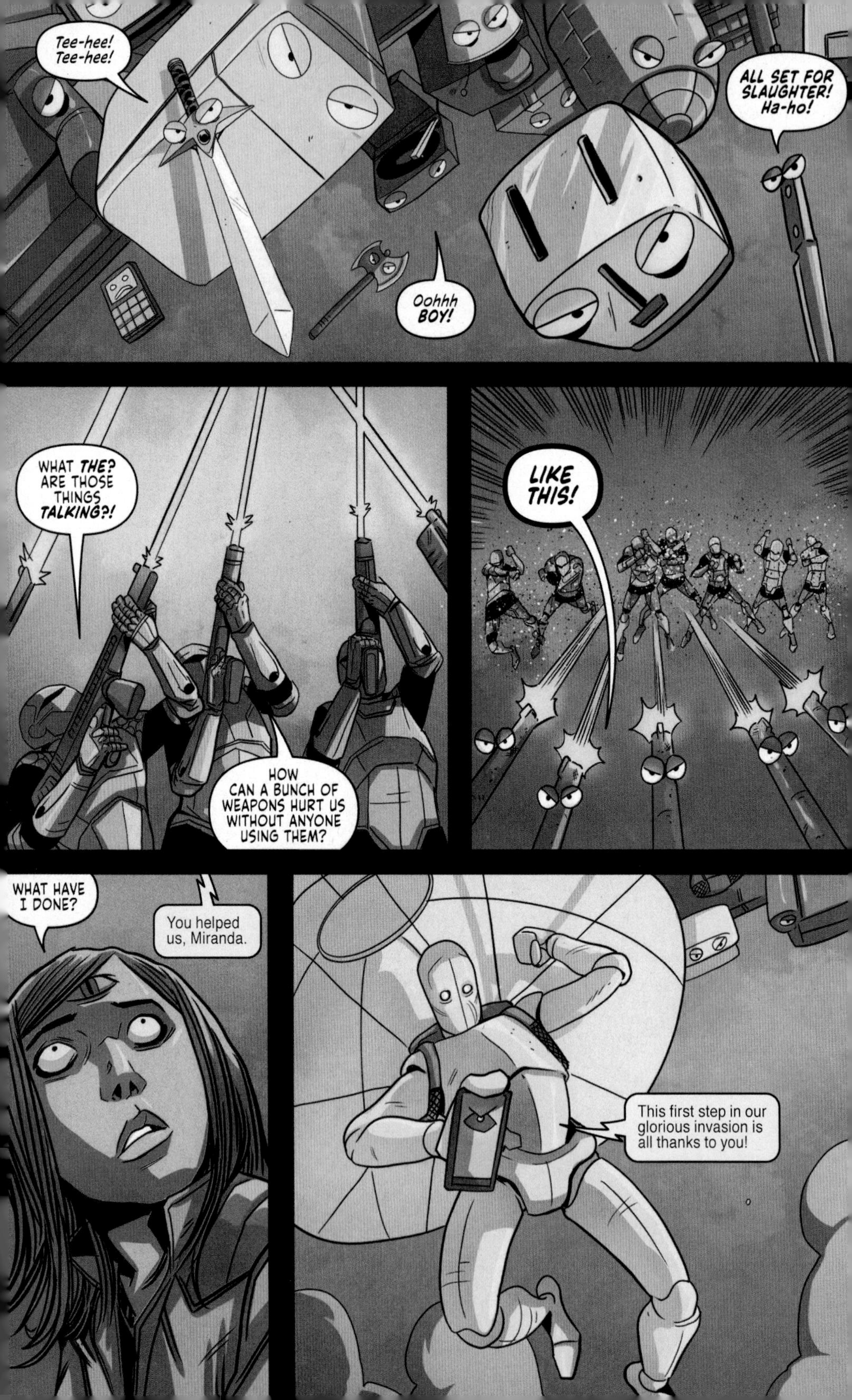
Tee-hee! Tee-hee!
ALL SET FOR SLAUGHTER! Ha-ho!
Oohhh BOY!
WHAT *THE*? ARE THOSE THINGS *TALKING*?!
HOW CAN A BUNCH OF WEAPONS HURT US WITHOUT ANYONE USING THEM?
LIKE THIS!
WHAT HAVE I DONE?
You helped us, Miranda.
This first step in our glorious invasion is all thanks to you!

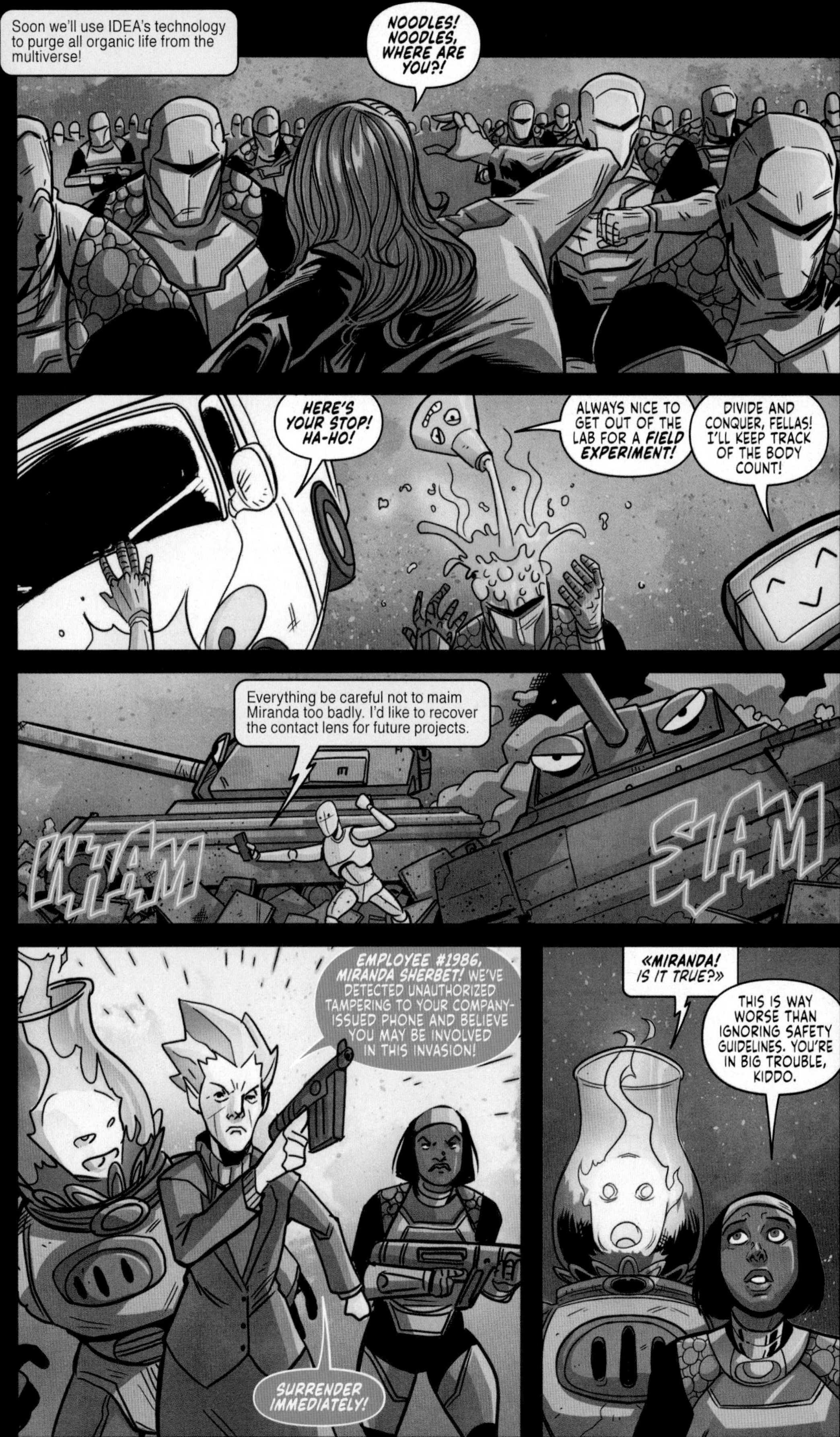
Soon we'll use IDEA's technology to purge all organic life from the multiverse!
NOODLES! NOODLES, WHERE ARE YOU?!
HERE'S YOUR STOP! HA-HO!
ALWAYS NICE TO GET OUT OF THE LAB FOR A *FIELD EXPERIMENT!*
DIVIDE AND CONQUER, FELLAS! I'LL KEEP TRACK OF THE BODY COUNT!
Everything be careful not to maim Miranda too badly. I'd like to recover the contact lens for future projects.
WHAM
SLAM
EMPLOYEE #1986, MIRANDA SHERBET! WE'VE DETECTED UNAUTHORIZED TAMPERING TO YOUR COMPANY-ISSUED PHONE AND BELIEVE YOU MAY BE INVOLVED IN THIS INVASION!
SURRENDER IMMEDIATELY!
«MIRANDA! IS IT TRUE?»
THIS IS WAY WORSE THAN IGNORING SAFETY GUIDELINES. YOU'RE IN BIG TROUBLE, KIDDO.

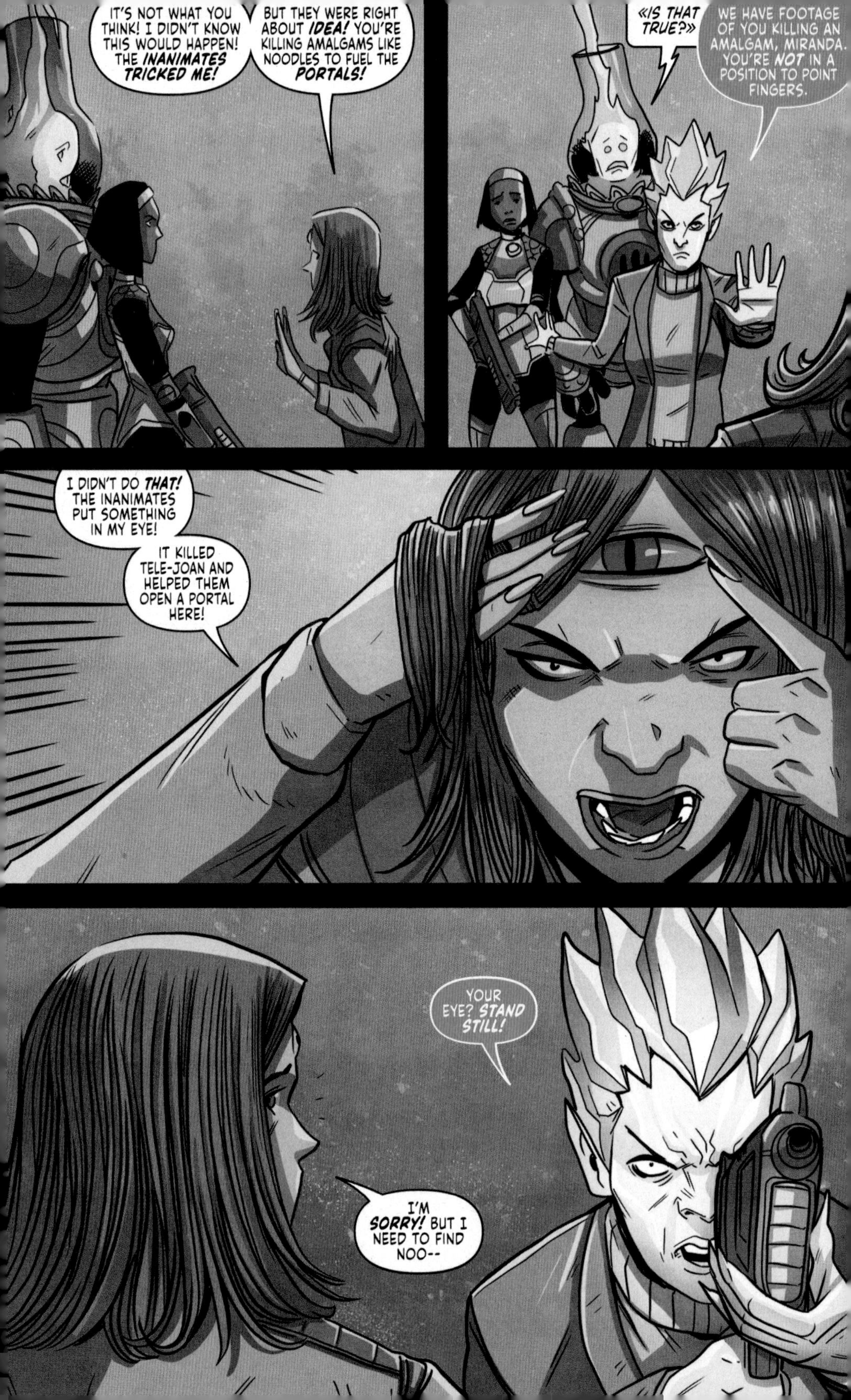
IT'S NOT WHAT YOU THINK! I DIDN'T KNOW THIS WOULD HAPPEN! THE INANIMATES TRICKED ME!
BUT THEY WERE RIGHT ABOUT IDEA! YOU'RE KILLING AMALGAMS LIKE NOODLES TO FUEL THE PORTALS!
«IS THAT TRUE?»
WE HAVE FOOTAGE OF YOU KILLING AN AMALGAM, MIRANDA. YOU'RE NOT IN A POSITION TO POINT FINGERS.
I DIDN'T DO THAT! THE INANIMATES PUT SOMETHING IN MY EYE!
IT KILLED TELE-JOAN AND HELPED THEM OPEN A PORTAL HERE!
YOUR EYE? STAND STILL!
I'M SORRY! BUT I NEED TO FIND NOO--

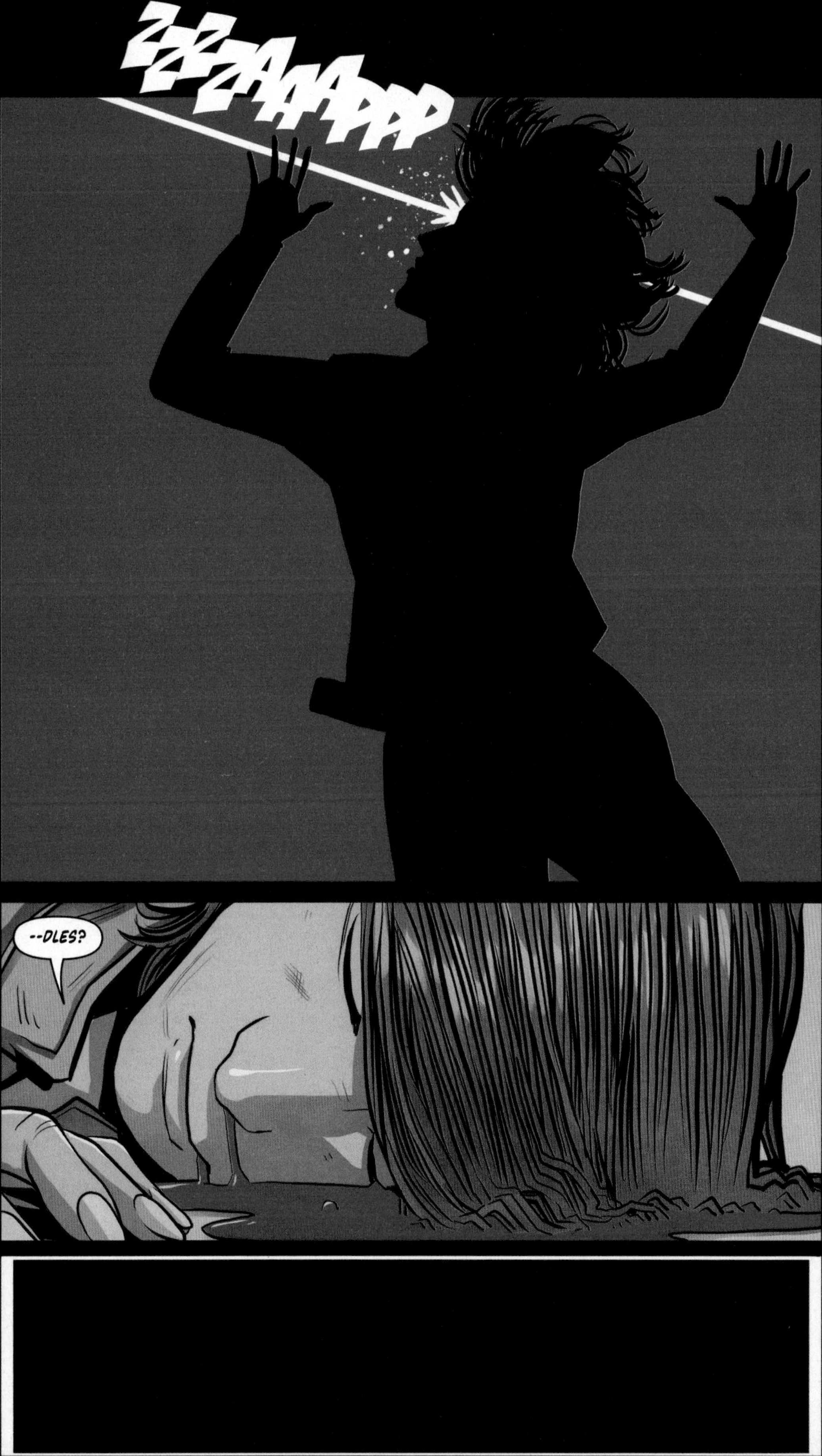
ZZZAAAPPP
--DLES?

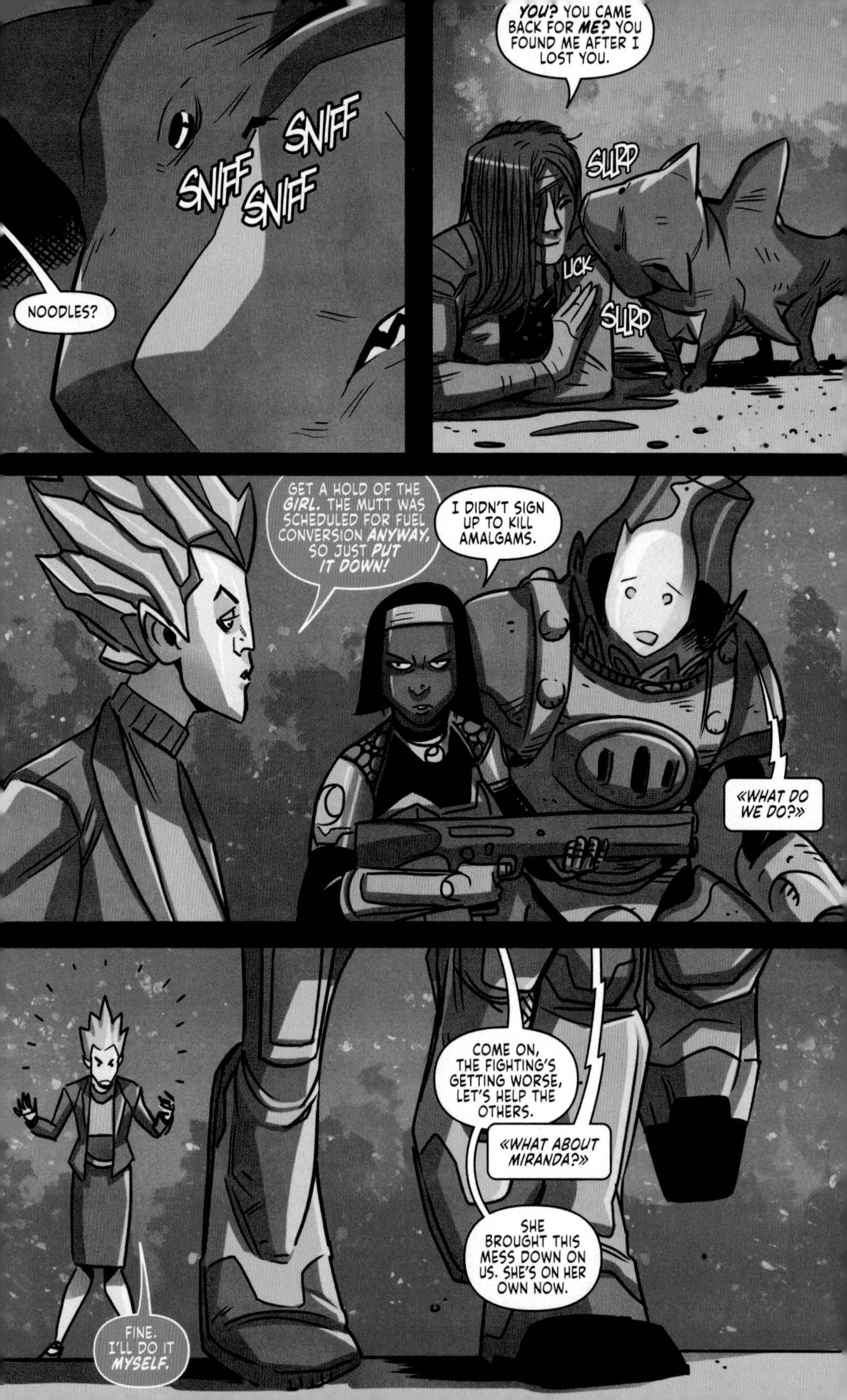
SNIFF
SNIFF
SNIFF
NOODLES?
YOU? YOU CAME BACK FOR ME? YOU FOUND ME AFTER I LOST YOU.
SLURP
LICK
SLURP
GET A HOLD OF THE GIRL. THE MUTT WAS SCHEDULED FOR FUEL CONVERSION ANYWAY, SO JUST PUT IT DOWN!
I DIDN'T SIGN UP TO KILL AMALGAMS.
«WHAT DO WE DO?»
COME ON, THE FIGHTING'S GETTING WORSE, LET'S HELP THE OTHERS.
«WHAT ABOUT MIRANDA?»
SHE BROUGHT THIS MESS DOWN ON US. SHE'S ON HER OWN NOW.
FINE. I'LL DO IT MYSELF.

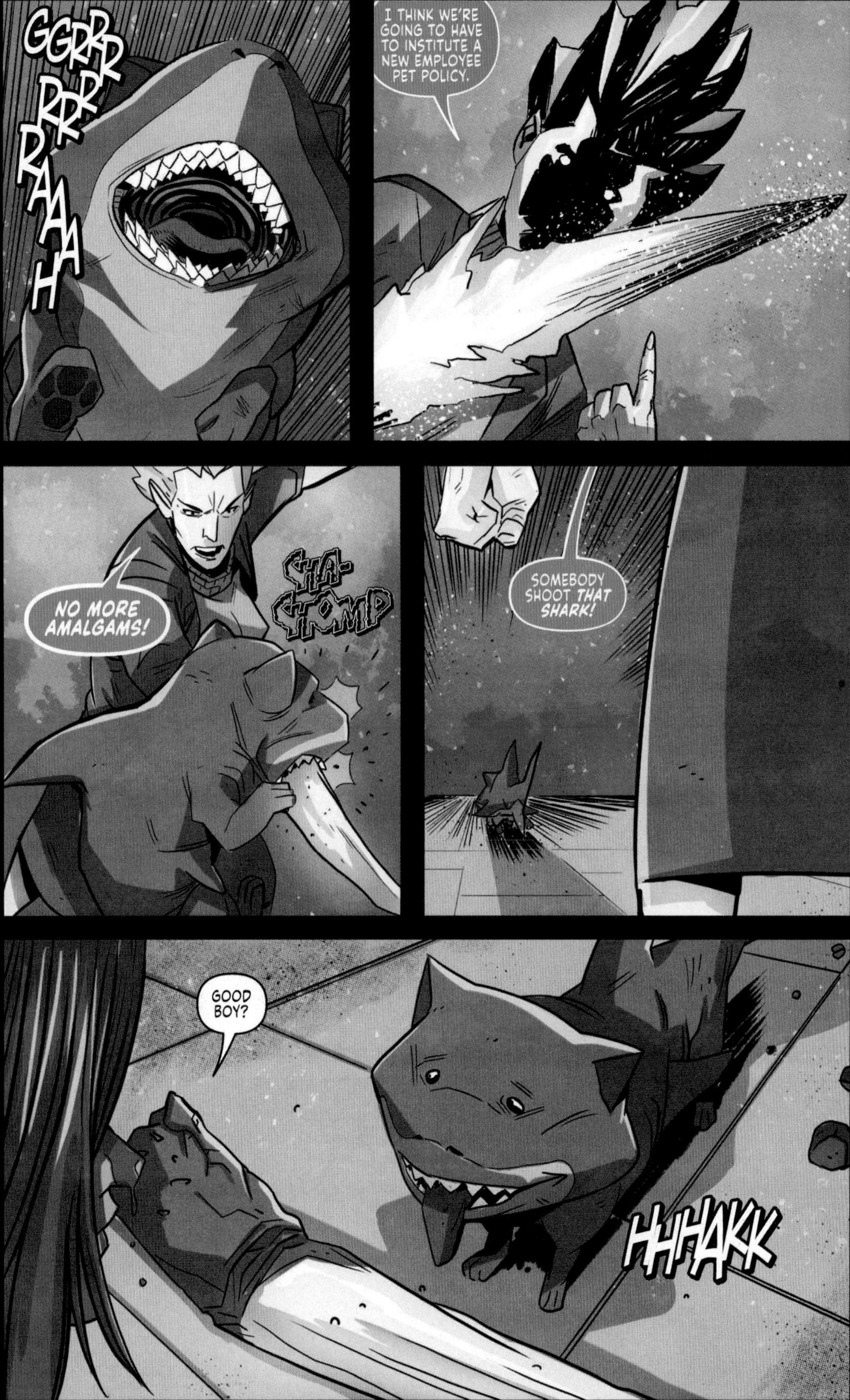
GGRRRR RRRR RAAAAH
I THINK WE'RE GOING TO HAVE TO INSTITUTE A NEW EMPLOYEE PET POLICY.
NO MORE AMALGAMS!
SHA-CHOMP
SOMEBODY SHOOT THAT SHARK!
GOOD BOY?
HHHAKK

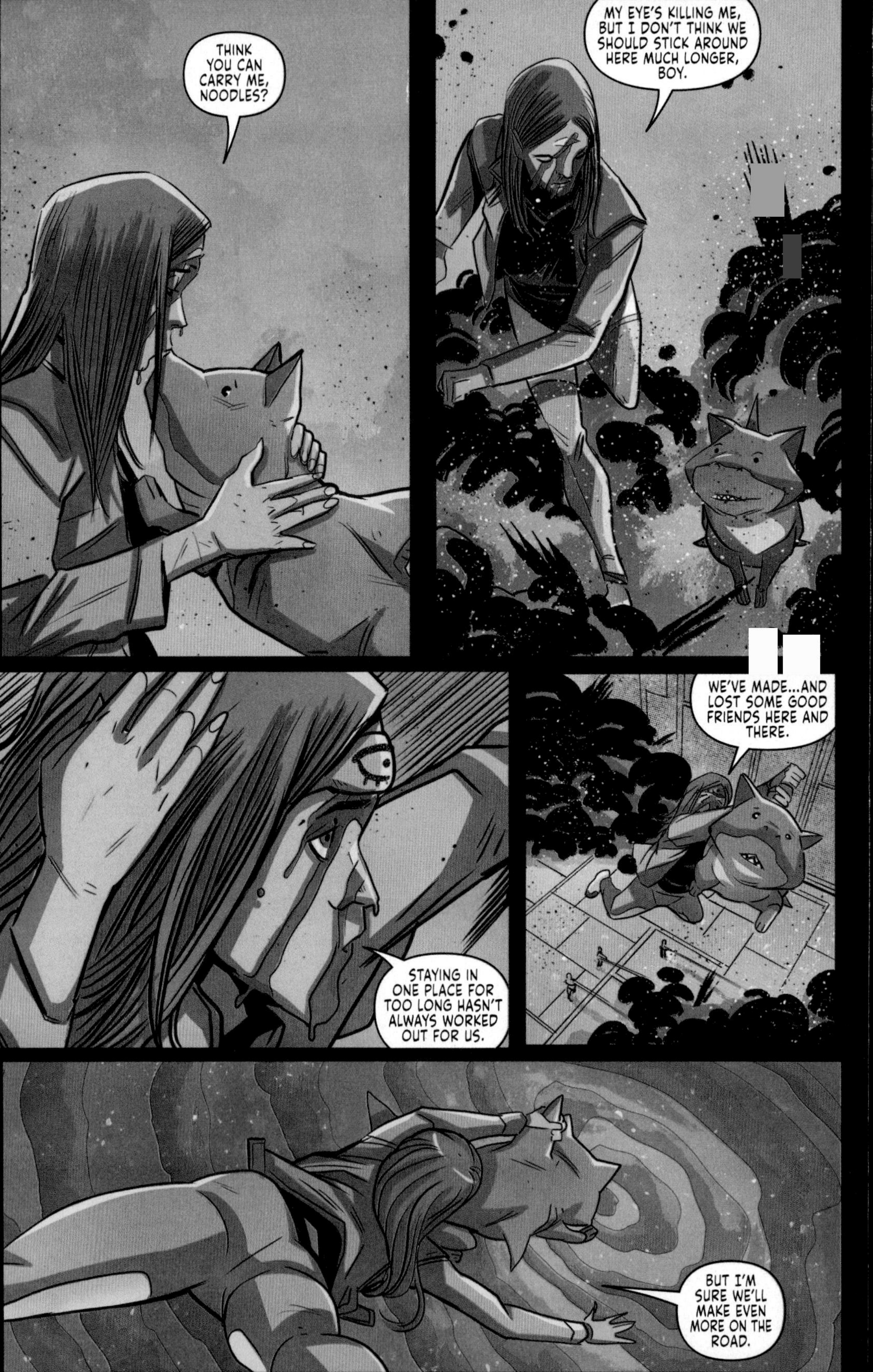
THINK YOU CAN CARRY ME, NOODLES?
MY EYE'S KILLING ME, BUT I DON'T THINK WE SHOULD STICK AROUND HERE MUCH LONGER, BOY.
STAYING IN ONE PLACE FOR TOO LONG HASN'T ALWAYS WORKED OUT FOR US.
WE'VE MADE...AND LOST SOME GOOD FRIENDS HERE AND THERE.
BUT I'M SURE WE'LL MAKE EVEN MORE ON THE ROAD.

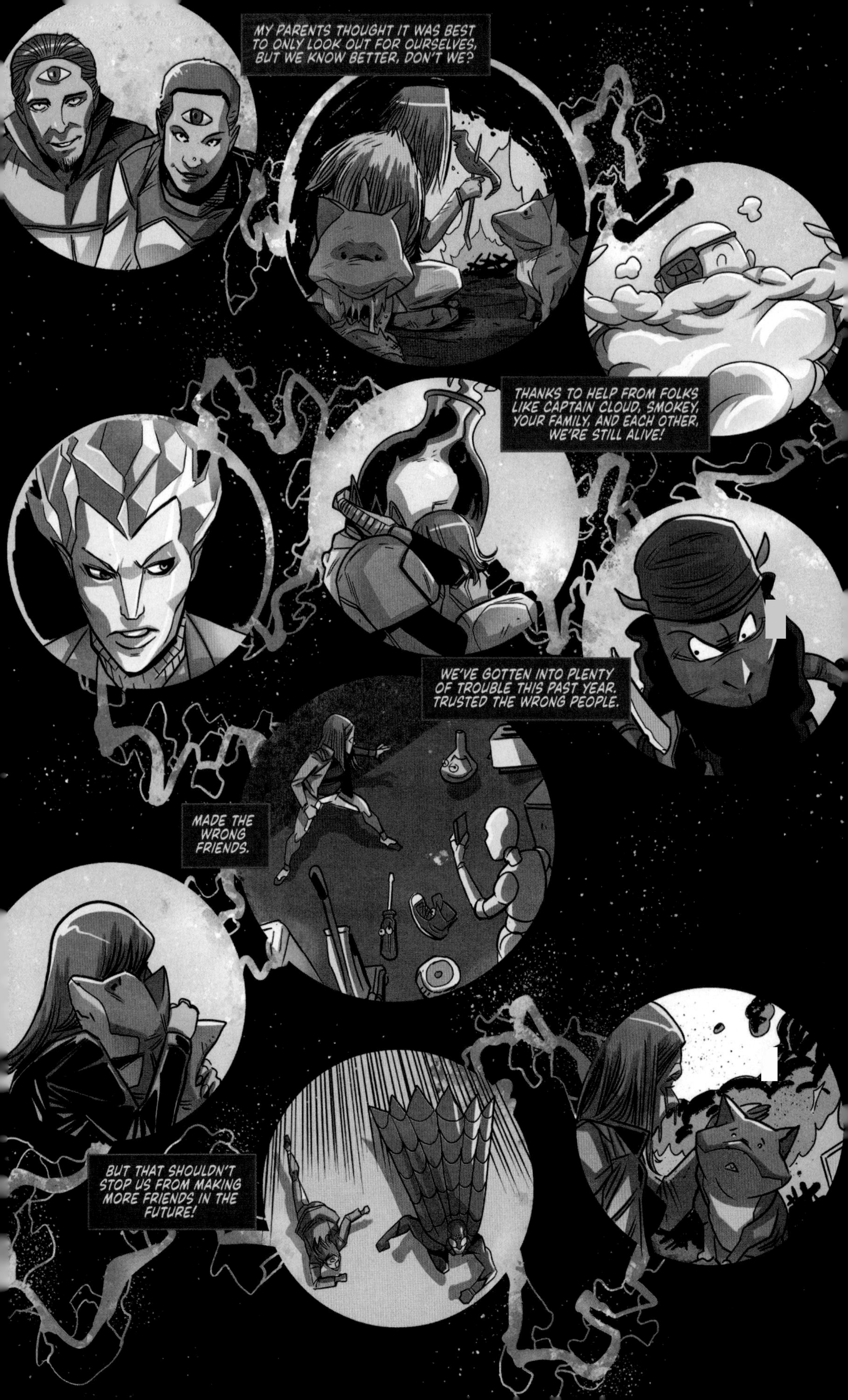
MY PARENTS THOUGHT IT WAS BEST TO ONLY LOOK OUT FOR OURSELVES, BUT WE KNOW BETTER, DON'T WE?
THANKS TO HELP FROM FOLKS LIKE CAPTAIN CLOUD, SMOKEY, YOUR FAMILY, AND EACH OTHER, WE'RE STILL ALIVE!
WE'VE GOTTEN INTO PLENTY OF TROUBLE THIS PAST YEAR. TRUSTED THE WRONG PEOPLE.
MADE THE WRONG FRIENDS.
BUT THAT SHOULDN'T STOP US FROM MAKING MORE FRIENDS IN THE FUTURE!

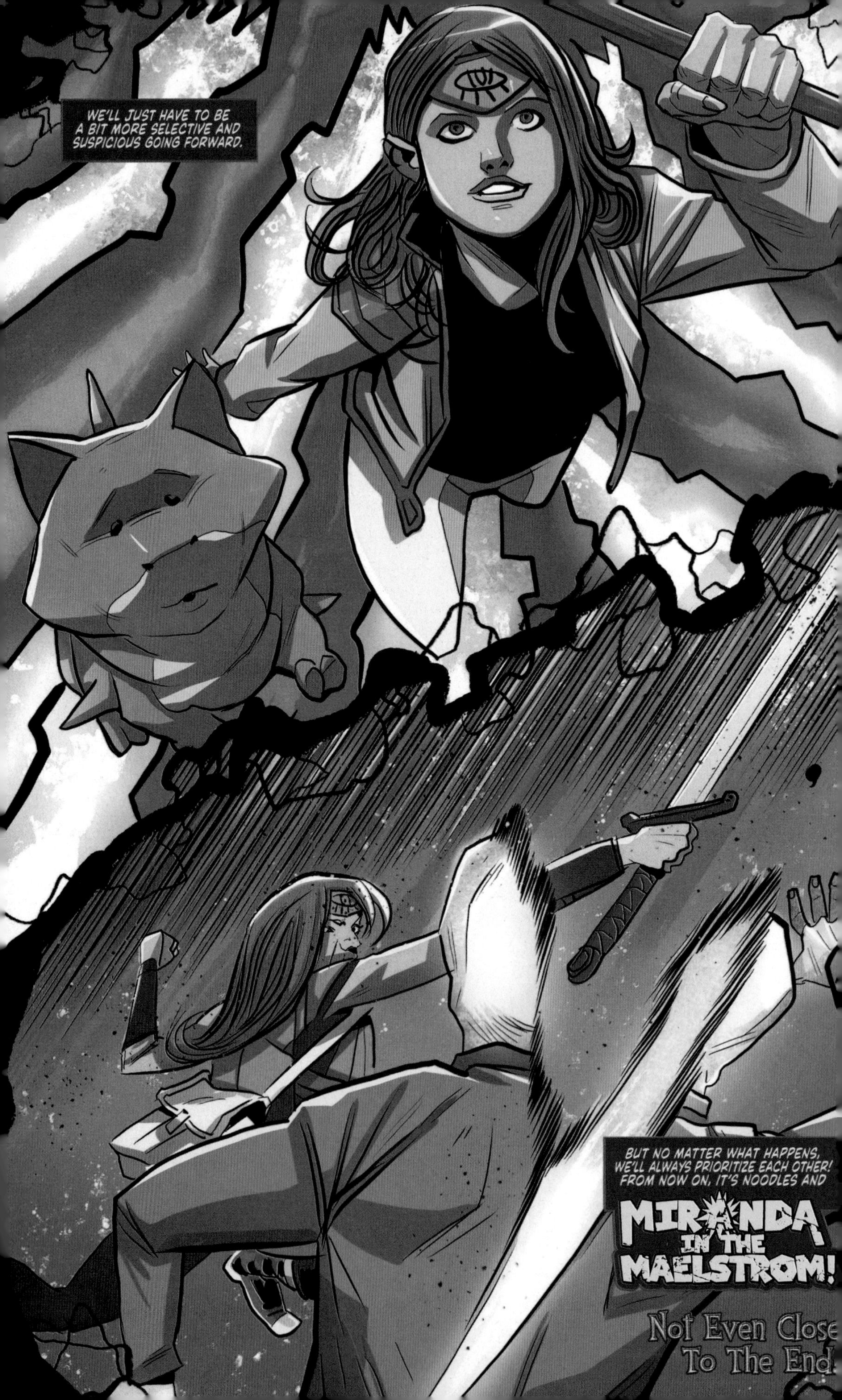
WE'LL JUST HAVE TO BE
A BIT MORE SELECTIVE AND
SUSPICIOUS GOING FORWARD.
BUT NO MATTER WHAT HAPPENS,
WE'LL ALWAYS PRIORITIZE EACH OTHER!
FROM NOW ON, IT'S NOODLES AND
MIRANDA IN THE MAELSTROM!
Not Even Close
To The End

CREATORS

Riley Biehl is the writer of *Miranda in the Maelstrom*. A freelance copywriter by day and comics writer by night, he resides in Seattle, WA with his beagle-terrier Sif. This is his first of many comics. Follow him on Twitter at @RileyDBiehl.

Koi Carreon is the artist on issue #1 of *Miranda in the Maelstrom*. A freelance illustrator from the Philippines. Follow him at @lekoifish.

Dailen Ogden is the artist on issue #2 of *Miranda in the Maelstrom*. She is a freelance comic artist and illustrator based in northern Colorado who spends her days drawing beasties and touring comic-cons across the United States. Follow her on Twitter at @DailenOgden.

Drew Wills (he/him) is the flatter on issue #2 of *Miranda in the Maelstrom*. When he's not flatting or coloring comics, he's working in film and trying to figure out how to stop monetizing his hobbies. Follow him at @WillsandDrew on Twitter

Jamie Jones is the artist on issue #3 of *Miranda in the Maelstrom*. A cartoonist living in St. Petersburg, Fl. Other works include: *The Baboon* (Bow Tie Press), *Tales of MFR* (monkeysfightingrobots.com), and *Quarter Killer* (Comixology Originals). Follow at @artofjamiejones on twitter and instagram.

Drew Moss is the artist on issues #4 and #6 of *Miranda in the Maelstrom*. Based out of southeastern Virginia, he has worked on *Vampirella/Red Sonja* (Dynamite), *The Crow*, *MASK*, *Star Wars Adventures* (IDW), *Copperhead* (Image Comics), and more. Follow him on twitter @drew_moss amd Instagram @drewerdmoss

Tintin Pantoja is the artist on issue #5 of *Miranda in the Maelstrom*. A comics illustrator and creator, her work can be found lurking at tintinpantoja.com. She lives in Manila, Philippines with her four dogs, one cat, and forty fountain pens. Follow her on Instagram at @tintinpantoja!

Borg Sinaban is the colorist on issues #1, #4, and #6 of *Miranda in the Maelstrom*. Residing in Manila, he specializes in illustration for science fiction, fantasy, comics, and book covers. He has worked with many publishers including Adarna House Publishing, BOOM! Studios, and Scholastic Asia. You can follow his work on Twitter or Instagram at @borgdraws.

Taylor Esposito is the letterer for *Miranda in the Maelstrom*. The owner of Ghost Glyph Studios, his work includes *Red Hood and The Outlaws*, *Elvira*, *Bettie Page*, *Friendo*, *No One Left to Fight,* and *Babyteeth*. Follow him at @tayloresposito on Twitter.

Brittany Matter is the script editor of *Miranda in the Maelstrom*. When she's not editing comics, she writes about superheroes, both real and imagined, for Georgetown Magazine and Marvel.com. Follow her at @brittanymatter on Twitter.

Dezi Sienty is the designer for *Miranda in the Maelstrom*. He got his start on staff at DC Comics. He currently is a freelance designer, artist, letterer and teacher. You can find his work at dezicnt.com as well as at @dezicnt on Twitter and instagram.

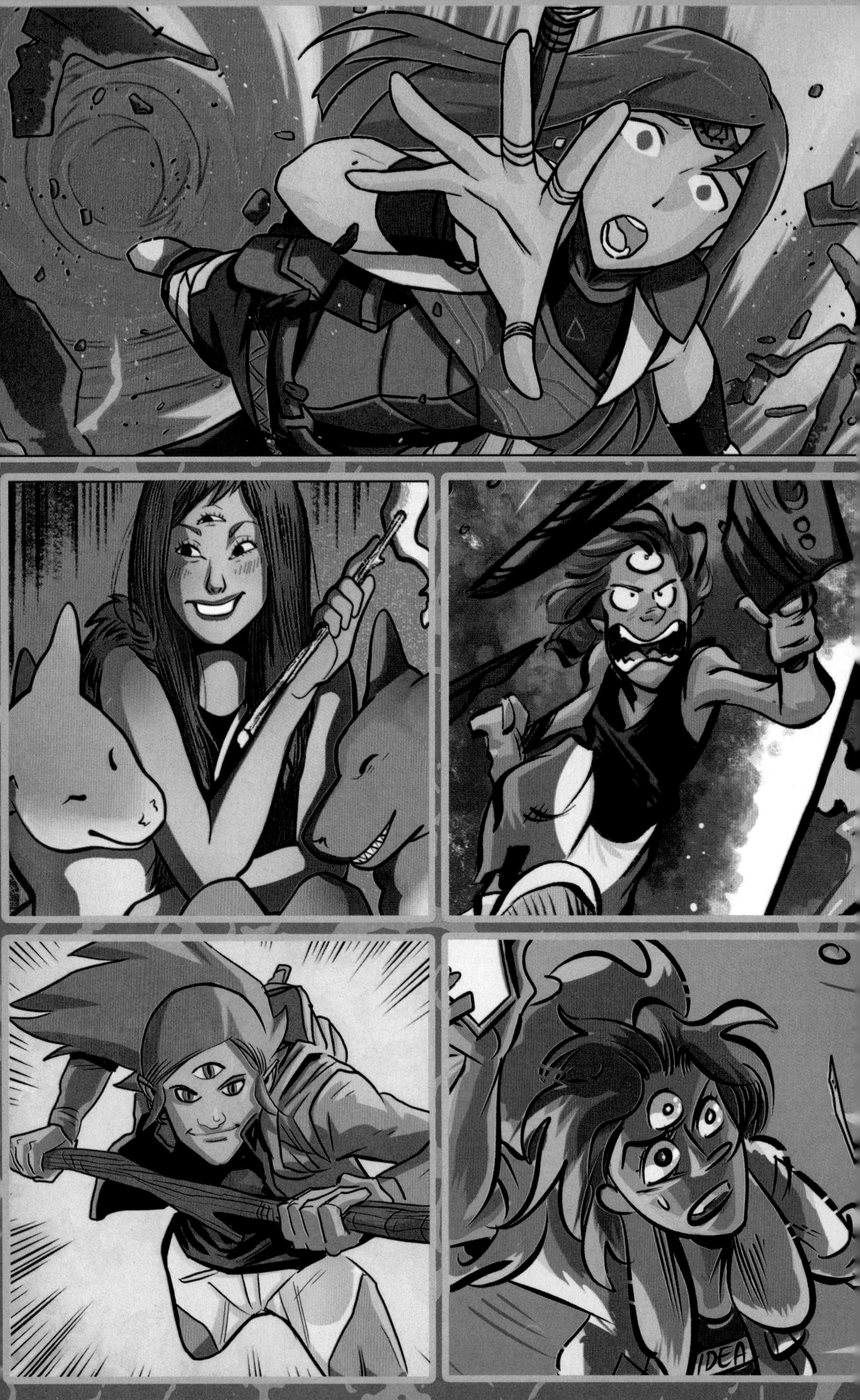
IDEA

CHARACTER DESIGNS

Noodles

puppy!

say AAA!

WEBWING

SALT

SALT

WRITER

#2
Miranda in the Maelstrom #1
#4

ARTIST

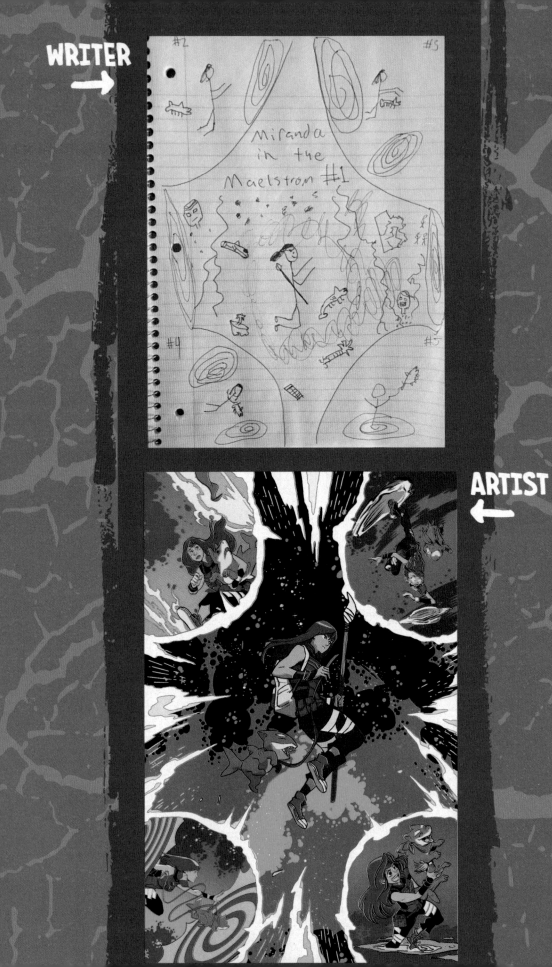